Sterling Books

Also by Cheryl Robinson

Memories of Yesterday (August 2002)

When I Get Free

a novel

Cheryl Robinson

Published by Sterling Books
PO Box 855
Roanoke, TX 76262

Copyright 2003 by Cheryl Robinson

You are invited to visit the author's website at:
www.cherylrobinson.com

Editor: Chandra Sparks Taylor
www.chandrasparkstaylor.com

Cover photography: James Robert, Jr.

Book and cover design: Stacy Luecker
www.essexgraphix.com

Library of Congress Control Number: 2003103989
ISBN: 0-9720867-1-4

Printed in the United States of America.
First Printing

For information regarding special discounts for bulk purchases of this book, please contact Sterling Books at:

PO Box 855
Roanoke, Texas 76262
Fax: 817-741-0820
sterlingbooks@msn.com

The sale of this book without its cover is unauthorized. If you purchased this book without a cover, you should be aware that it was reported to the publisher as "unsold and destroyed." Neither the author nor the publisher has received payment for the sale of this stripped book.

All rights reserved. No part of this book may be reproduced or transmitted in any form or by any means, electronic or mechanical, including photocopying, recording, or by any information storage or retrieval system, without the written permission of the publisher, except where permitted by law.

This novel is a work of fiction inspired by true events of an anonymous ex-con. Names, characters, places, and incidents are the product of the author's imagination or used fictitiously. Any resemblance to actual persons, living or dead; events; or locales is entirely coincidental.

*This book is dedicated to Anonymous
and all those serving unnecessary time in and out of prison.*

ACKNOWLEDGEMENTS

I must say that 2002 was a wonderful year, and I have many to thank.

To God for giving me another year and another story to share, for showing me the beauty of patience, and for everything that You continue to do in my life. I feel truly blessed for the opportunity to live out my dream.

My family has always been and continues to be a constant support. Thank you, Mom and Dad; my big sister, Janice Hunter, who is my marketing director/manager/promoter/business partner/publicist and best friend. To my nephew Sterling after whom my company is named, congratulations for completing high school, and welcome to the real world. Always follow your dreams. The best is yet to come! I love you. To my nephew Brandon, who is approaching his senior year in high school, you're almost there. Study hard and stay focused. I love you. To my angels in heaven: my brother Benjamin, my aunt Billy and my uncle Sherman, I always feel your presence…keep whispering in my ear. I love your guidance.

To all of those who read my first novel, thank you so much for your support.

To the many people, businesses, and organizations who assisted me in spreading the word about my first novel: Pia Wilson-Body, Anthony Body, K-104 and Skip Murphy's morning team, Nanette Lee, Sam Putney, Chris Arnold, The Wig, Cleatus, and June Bug. To

Desiree at Me Chel Lay's Salon in Fort Worth. The best hairdresser I've had who not only keeps my hair healthy but also promotes my books to her clients. What more can a writer ask for? Thank you so much for your support. Lisa Cross and The Sistah Circle Book Club of Dallas, Texas; Black Images Book Bazaar in Dallas; The Black Bookworm in Fort Worth, Texas; Jokae's Books in Dallas; Diane Simowski of Barnes & Noble Small Press Department; A&B Book Distributors in New York; Cydney Rax and Book-Remarks.com; Shunda Blocker and *Booking Matters* Magazine; The Black Library.com; Cushcity.com; Amazon.com; San Antonio Black; Tia Shabazz and Black Writers Alliance; Sisterfriends.net; Tee C. Royal and Rawsistaz.com; Yasmin Coleman and APOOO.org; Dawn Reeves; Jeanette Frommi; author Vanessa Morman; Pamela Walker Williams of Pageturner.net; Shannon Scott; Sherry Fields; Leah Evans; Gregory Chastang; Lucinda McNuckles; Jackie Theriot-Merchant; Raynette Owens; Dwayne and Charrise Walker; Carbette Miller; James Lisbon of AMAG, Inc.; Roshel Roberson with Sister Circle Book Group II; Anita Mazyck; Chiffon Myricks; Dorianne Johnson; Christine Levos; Stephanie Anderson; Karen Calloway; Michelle Bailey; Anthony Chester; and James Robert, Jr., for allowing me to use your prison photos.

I apologize in advance for any names I may have missed.

To Deirdre Southall, Lynn Nash, Chandra Dozier, Vera Giddings, Gloria Dixon, Cassandra Wilson, and all of the other members of Delta Sigma Theta Sorority, Dallas Alumnae. Thank you for inviting me to your author reception in April 2003 to introduce my first novel. It was a very fun and exciting event of which I felt blessed to be a part. To Delores Wilson, for inviting me to participate in Delta Sigma Theta's 2003 Southwest Regional Conference, Author's Pavilion. I was honored to participate.

To all of my colleagues at Daimler Chrysler Services: Janet Marzet, Wade Lewis, Bob Gay, Randy Gibbon, Valissa Armstrong, Lena Marshall. Regina Smith, Emma Stuckey, Brian Dunagan, Jeff Brown, Keisha Borders, Agatha Clark, Dewhana Jones, Cynthia Taylor, Jeanene Macias, Valerie Carter, Judy Britton, Robbie Waters, Juan Orellana, David Mancilla, Sandra Barclay, Naomi Muzquiz, Veronica Benson, Dominique Brown, Gerald Lemmons, Tamyra Anderson, Laverio Richardson, Jill McGraw, Vivi Congress, Carlene

Brown, Brian Gines, Donna Pack, Rene Bias, Lamar Cook, Princess Davis, Eddie Brooks, Yvonne Moore, Shayla Shannon, Arnold "Zeke" Mazyck, Gerald Leigh, Trina Mott, Ruby Hildreth, Sauna Witherspoon, Nekosher Dillard, Nicholas Robinson, Joseph Rechtiene, Timothy Denomie, Karen Green, Mary Jordan, Kalesha Turner, Brandi Freeman, Mychelle Turner, Billy Bolin, Kevin McKeever, Courtney Daniels, Carrie Massey, Felicia Starks, Narissa Waller, Moses Fagbeyiro, Jennifer Means, Jason Hughes, Dymond Williams, Jarred Howard Renda Johnson, Carmen Moore, Wayne Carter, Martez Young, Antoinette Elam, Lanita McGriff, Lester Winters, Ralph Williams, Erica Smith, Joe Williams, Maurice "Stylz" Broady, Kenny Edwards, Jeff Brown, Eric Paterson, Belinda Bynum, Andrea Jones, Frank Rhodes, Terri Lewis, Linda Thompson, Rodney Gilyard, Kenyea Dudley, Sara Karingatti, Glenda Howard, Diana Jordan, Lisa Thorn, Nick Miaoulis, Diana Howard, Cornelius Vance, Robert Lyles.

To Donnell Clark and Nelvin Hudgens who are currently serving time in federal prison in Louisiana and Texarkana. Thank you for your letters sharing your prison experiences. You provided me with an added source of inspiration that I needed during a few difficult scenes.

To Anonymous, for inspiring me to fill in the many blanks you left by urging me to use my imagination to come up with a story readers will enjoy and learn from. I hope all is well. Thank you.

To everyone who picks up my book and decides to purchase it, for allowing me to walk one step closer to my dream of writing full time.

Thank you and God bless,
Cheryl Robinson

"At the start of the 1990s, the United States had more black men (between the ages of twenty and twenty-nine) under the control of the nation's criminal justice system than the total number in college. This and other factors have led some scholars to conclude that crime control policies are a major contributor to the disruption of the family, the prevalence of single-parent families, and children raised without a father in the ghetto, and the inability of people to get jobs still available."

Source: Craig Haney, Ph.D., and Philip Zimbardo, Ph.D., "The Past and Future of U.S. Prison Policy: Twenty-five Years after the Stanford Prison Experiment," *American Psychologist,* Vol. 53, No. 7 (July 1998), p. 716.

CHAPTER 1

I've sat in my cell contemplating the night of my arrest many times.

"Are you carrying any drugs?" the Oklahoma highway patrolman asked as he leaned down and gave a long, searching look through my driver's window.

"No, sir," I said politely because I could tell that white man didn't take no mess. He was chewing on tobacco, and then he turned his face away from me and spit it out on to the road. His trooper hat and boots intimidated me more than the gun he was gripping in his side holster. I was staring down the throat of a sho'nuff redneck from the backwoods of Oklahoma—not Oklahoma City. Not Tulsa. Not even Muskogee. Nowhere I'd ever heard of—some small hick town whose name never made it on an exit sign.

"You sure ain't no drugs in here, boy?" he asked with a Southern drawl, even though Oklahoma wasn't quite the south. His eyes canvassed the inside of my rental car. "Don't have me call the dogs out."

"No, sir. We don't have drugs."

"Just hold on," he said, patting my car door once. "We got to finish talking to your partner. The one you said you don't know who knows you. Somebody needs to tell that boy that the horse races ended long time ago."

"Excuse me, sir?"

"The horse races. He said y'all were on your way to the horse races but those been over. Just hold on." The trooper had Stanley Holmes in the patrol car and had been talking to him for a while. Stanley came along just for the ride. He went to high school with Arturo Watts, Quentin Harris, and me, but he was tight with Arturo, who was one of the guys from my drug crew. Arturo was on the passenger side of the car behind mine. I could only imagine what he was thinking, knowing he had a trunkload of high-powered machine guns and rifles. Quentin Harris, my boy from as far back as I could remember, who grew up on my block—our birthdays were two days apart—was sitting in the rental car with me and a trunkful of drugs, not a small quantity either. Of all the places to get stopped, why this hick town?

"Fuck, we going to prison," Quentin said angrily. He sank down in the passenger seat. "Shit, if we even make it out these sticks alive. They might end up hanging our black asses from one of these trees."

"Man, calm down. We were stopped for speeding. We can't go to prison for that," I said.

Well, that's what I thought, but now I no longer trust what I'm thinking, which is why I've let a few voices live inside of my head, so I can listen to them instead. Prison was exactly where I ended up, when all I was doing—at least, all they knew for sure I was doing—was speeding down I-35. And, I was fined for it, too, if that's what you want to call a forty-year sentence. I never got a speeding ticket or an opportunity to take a defensive driving course because there is no defense for racists cops.

Prison wasn't what I thought. In some ways it wasn't as bad, but in most ways it was worse—a lot worse. The steel door played tricks on my mind. If I had to stay behind one for forty years, I would have been sixty-nine when I was released. I was thirty-nine. Ten years of my life had been taken away and thirty given back. Now they want to let me out. *Right now.* It's about damn time. I guess I'm supposed to walk out of this community center and go back to Fort Worth a changed man. *Shit.* Yeah, I'm changed all right, just not for the better. I'm what you call mad at the world.

While I was on the inside, I thought all about what I was going to do when I finally got free, who I was going to see first, how each of them would suffer. Only E.J. and Punisher, a couple of my boys from the inside, had known of my plans for revenge. The thought of getting even was the only thing that kept me alive for all of those years—the only thing that prevented me from hanging myself, slitting my wrist with a shank, or overdosing on the pills Medical gave out that I hid under my tongue and accumulated until I had enough to end my life, although I never did because at that time I was too afraid to die, but not too afraid to kill. Soon I feared neither. Eventually, my feelings of revenge left me, and I didn't care so much if Quentin and Arturo ratted. Instead, I started thinking about one thing and one thing only—freedom.

I did things on the inside that I'd regret for the rest of my life. I became a different person, and if Spivey the law clerk, hadn't showed me how to go about getting one of my sentences dropped due to double jeopardy, since I was charged twice for the same crime spree—unlawful possession of narcotics with intent to distribute and illegal trafficking in drugs—I would still be in that hell hole.

I took out the folded paper from the back pocket of my state-issued jeans and read Spivey's pencil writing:

First hour after release

Ex-offenders' bureau of prisons

Benefits available to former inmates

Note: You must first recognize that you are emotionally and mentally unprepared to hold a job because you are an ex-offender and trying to re-enter society.

SSI: First go to the social security office and ask to see a counselor and ask to apply for social security insurance emergency supplement benefits—$1,500. Show them your parole or release paper to prove you just got out of prison. Note: you should receive a check within 72 hours. While you are there, also fill out the forms for a $310 monthly disabilty benefit good for three months. Total of $930. Supplement social income U.S. law 42 u.s.c. 1383 (e); 20 cfb 416.305. Go to the closest welfare office and apply for general relief. Show parole or release papers. Tell them you need financial assistance immediately. A check for $150 should be issued to you in an hour. File for food stamps of $110. File also for medical benefits. Thirty hours to complete this.

That's the shit I got to look forward to when I get free—if I ever truly get free because my mind is still on lockdown.

It was Monday, the sixth day of March 2000, which was the day of my official release. I stood outside of the community center in Oklahoma waiting for my sister, Bernice, to pick me up. The time seemed longer than all the years I spent locked up so I reminded myself of something I did on the inside to prevent my mind from going idle. I counted. Counted every like object inside of my cell that took me past the number two—the bricks on the wall, 456; the tile on the floor, fifty-two pieces; everything that was behind the steel door that kept me caged in for eight years like an animal before my sentence was finally paroled and remanded to the Monroe Community Center to serve out my last two years in the work program.

I had been under the supervision of the Oklahoma prison system for a little more than ten years. I should have been out in December of the previous year, or at the latest by February, but the people at the Department of Corrections were dragging their feet getting my interstate compact approved, which was an agreement allowing me to transfer from Oklahoma back to my hometown of Fort Worth, Texas.

I couldn't sleep the night before because I was going home the next day. Knowing I'd be a free man by the next afternoon was nearly impossible to comprehend so I sat up in my cot with the pillow propped behind my back, thinking. I guess, in some ways, I thought that my nightmare had finally ended, even though I knew my head wasn't right. I still wanted a chance. We all make mistakes, so why should one take away my entire life? I had a woman I almost loved before I went in. I never almost loved any woman before, and I doubt if I'll ever almost love another, but I almost loved Lisa Alvarado. I almost loved her because I thought she had my back. I almost loved her because she was the mother of my child, the one born while I was in prison who I'd never seen and didn't even know the sex of. I almost loved her because I thought we were going to be a family. I'm sure if I hadn't gone in, I probably would've married her.

After ten years I'm sure I would've. But instead, I got caught up in the drug game and lost it all.

When I first went in, I was a hundred and eighty pounds and stood six-feet-one. I had a boyish look, but I was still every bit a man. My body wasn't as strong as my mind, but now it's the reverse. In order to mentally survive in the pen, I had to keep a routine, which entailed working out every day without fail. I took my anger out on the metal weights, pumped iron until I could hardly breathe. Now, I had a body that put Mr. Universe's to shame, but bodybuilding wasn't my thing, and I didn't know what was. Even though I look much younger than I am, my face has hardened. That's what prison does to you—takes away your hope. I gained close to ninety pounds from lifting, and most people would probably find me intimidating, which is exactly what I want.

I was a free man. I was going home. I wasn't like Jose Ramirez, an inmate who was released from the community center two days before me. He was dropped off at the bus station with a one-way ticket to San Antonio, Texas; a fifty-dollar check from the State of Oklahoma; his boxes; and a good-luck farewell. Ironically, Bernice was the one who volunteered to come get me even though she never once came to visit while I was in. Never even wrote. Only other person who wrote regularly besides my parents and Granny Pearl was Mrs. Johnson, the court's clerk. Every holiday I received a card from her and about once a month I received a letter. I kept them all, even though I wondered why this white woman who was in her late fifties, married with children, wrote me at all. The same white woman who read off my verdict in the courtroom, who I considered to be as much of an enemy as the white highway patrol officers who arrested me, the white attorney who prosecuted me, the all-white jury who found me guilty, and the white judge who sentenced me to forty consecutive years.

I was guilty of more than the court system will ever know. Guilty of being a black man growing up in the hood and lured by the temptation of fast money, fancy cars, and fine women. I think Mrs. Johnson felt guilty because she knew the things she heard in that courtroom weren't right. Those troopers weren't right. The verdict wasn't right, and neither was the sentence, and that's why she wrote so much, trying to encourage me by telling me to stay strong.

I did a lot of reading while I was locked up. I'm not claiming to be a scholar, but I know a few things. I read a study in a psychology journal called, "The Past and Future of U.S. Prison Policy: Twenty-five Years After the Stanford Prison Experiment." It said, "Due to harsh new sentencing guidelines, such as 'three strikes, you're out,' a disproportionate number of young black and Hispanic men are likely to be imprisoned for life under scenarios in which they are guilty of little more than a history of untreated addiction and several prior drug-related offenses. States will absorb the staggering cost of not only constructing additional prisons to accommodate increasing numbers of prisoners who will never be released but also warehousing them into old age."

I know what a lot of other people don't or those who do know don't think about—that even though you're free, even though you're out—you can still be in prison and in some cases serving a life sentence.

While I waited for my sister, I continued counting—the cars that passed by, the specks of dirt on the concrete, anything I could to pass the time. I watched the seventeenth car as it came down the road toward me. It was dark, but I couldn't tell if it was Bernice's burgundy Taurus because I didn't know what a Taurus looked like these days. I hadn't seen one since 1989, and even though I'd worked the city roads and saw hundreds of cars pass me each day, I didn't pay attention to any of them. I tried not to because I knew I couldn't go where they were going—home, out to dinner, a bar, a movie. To me those were just people in cars who had no idea how good their life was even on their worst day.

As the dark car came closer, I saw the Ford symbol on the grill, and then I noticed a black woman with braids sitting behind the steering wheel with a man beside her. I didn't see a child—Bernice's son, Curtis—but I'm sure he was in the backseat. He was nine, but my mother said he was small for his age.

I walked inside of the community center to retrieve three boxes with my belongings—mostly books, magazines, and old letters. I didn't have much because when they lock you up, they take away everything, and when you're finally let out, you're left with even less. I had given away my sweats, state-issued shirts, and anything else that I felt would be better used by those still serving time.

"Can I get my boxes?" I asked one of the guards.

"This is it, right?" the guard asked. I nodded and then followed him as he walked into the utility closet with his keys in his hand. He never spoke. Not until somebody was getting ready to walk, leave that place. He was nice to those leaving because he didn't want an ex-con attacking him on the street, which has happened to some of the guards in the past. One guard was killed by an ex-con.

"Don't be like some of these fools in for the second and third time. You got something, something these other fools don't." He tapped his index finger against his temple. "Brains."

I sat in the backseat of Bernice's Taurus with my head glued to the window, nearly touching the glass, observing stretches of Oklahoma highway.

I was finally out, but my head still felt empty, my heart was still hollow, and my eyes functioned as lenses into my past, capturing permanent pictures that I've tried many times to erase, but too often they'd pop up, and all I could do was let them play like a bad movie that I wanted to walk out on. Only this was no movie—this was my life. *This time can be different,* the nice voice that lives inside of my head said. *This time you're going in the opposite direction of the prison and that community center.*

This time I was free.

You ain't free yet, my mean voice said. *You gonna find the exact same thing that was in that prison out in the world. It's still gonna be a bunch of fools you can't trust who are trying to get over on you.*

I looked up toward the sky, focusing on the grayness of the clouds. The voices coming from Bernice and my brother, George, were placed on mute in my mind. I blocked out the ones occupying my head, and at that moment I had no other thoughts until I began to wonder how I would turn on the switch and start my life over.

How many years would it take for me to recharge myself, and could I do it alone or even at all?

I despised the Monroe Community Center and all it represented, but in some ways I knew that it probably saved my life. After spending eight years in prison, my mind finally snapped. It was a gradual decay that eventually dwindled to almost nothing. The hope I held on to for an early release had all but left—more papers to file, more cases to review. I began to speak with my tongue, words my heart could no longer fight—"I ain't never gettin' out of here." Finally I was paroled and sent to the community center. It served as a halfway house and was supposed to provide a smooth transition for us prisoners as we migrated back into society. We were allowed to work for the city during the day and earn up to fifteen dollars a month in what the Department of Corrections referred to as "gang pay." In the evening, we were transported back to the barrack-style community center to sleep on our bunk beds in the large open room with forty-seven others.

I participated in a special educational program, which allowed inmates with high school diplomas to earn an associate's degree. The college program opened up an even brighter world for me. I got started with that my first year at the community center. One of the judges in Oklahoma decided that prisoners needed to have the opportunity to go to college. The community college wanted our labor, so we traded that for classes. Only a few of us were selected for the program. The supervisor over the maintenance department at the college was sold on me anyway, after noticing how hard I worked for him. On my second day on the job, we were on top of the four-story administration building, trying to lift a heavy generator up with a hoist. The hoist broke and while four other workers, including my supervisor, huddled around its motor, trying to figure out what shorted it, I grabbed hold to the wire and used my strength to pull the generator on top of the building and carried it over to them. Their eyes got big as saucers as they looked at me in disbelief. "We better keep him around," I remember the supervisor saying. So I guess you can say I earned my brownie points after that. In fact, I could have stayed on at the college working maintenance but I wanted to go home and be with my family. If I stayed in Oklahoma, I would feel like I was still in prison. Having that degree allowed me to take a test for Allied Manufacturing, a major automotive parts supplier headquartered in Dallas, when they came to the college to recruit.

My nephew, Curtis, sat scrunched up against the back car door with his arms crossed, trying to avoid looking in my direction. He was afraid of me. Curtis didn't know me outside of what I'm sure he'd heard—that I couldn't be trusted and that I had led a double life for several years before the law finally caught up with me. And now my whole family probably thought I was crazy since I'd been locked up for years. All I really had was myself—a person hanging on by a thread. I learned quickly that I had no friends outside of the few I made in prison, had a family who wouldn't understand me, and a woman and child whom I'd have to find.

"Slow down," I mumbled after I saw my friends working the roads with the gun gang watching over them. I had been there, too, with my pitchfork in hand, repairing the roads, which I vowed never to do again.

"Did you say something?" Bernice asked, turning down the volume on the radio.

"Slow down and blow the horn," I said. Bernice blew her horn twice and reduced her speed.

A few of my friends looked up from their pitchforks and waved. I could read the mixed looks on their frustrated faces, that of elation and envy, because I knew the look well since my face had held on to it too many times to count. But now was my time to be chauffeured home. I raised my hand slowly and waved good-bye to men I planned to never see again, at least not on the inside. I'd kill myself or have court in the street before I went back in. I'd suffer the consequences of my actions, but prison and I would never be one again.

I turned away from the glass and rested my head against the backseat, taking the long ride home in utter silence, which would seem strange for most, but had become normal for me. I cracked the window some so I could smell the air of freedom. Occasionally, I'd turn to look out the window, watching the highway gradually change from Oklahoma to Texas. When we passed Granite Prison, I closed my eyes so I wouldn't be reminded of the time I spent there—a year with almost two months in extreme solitary confinement for assaulting another inmate while I was serving time at Murray State.

When I opened my eyes, I saw Bernice looking at me through her rearview mirror, focusing on my solemn face. She'd changed. Put on some extra weight. She wasn't fat, but she didn't have the body that had grown men following her home when she was only fourteen. She looked angry now. Her lips were curled in disgust. The dark circles under her glassy eyes told me she spent many nights worrying, and I'm sure not about me. George looked almost the same as he did ten years ago. He was still muscular. Only difference is he cut his S-curl out and was wearing a low-cut fade.

"You know you staying with me, right?" Bernice asked. "Mama doesn't have room, and you don't need to be over there no way because some of your same crew is over there, still selling them drugs. Tower, I swear, please do right this time."

"Thank you," I said in a lifeless monotone.

CHAPTER 2

No one was talking inside of the car. No voices were heard, only the radio tuned to an urban station playing a lot of oldies like Earth, Wind, and Fire, which brought me back to a day when my life wasn't so crazy.

As we drove south on I-35 toward Fort Worth, I looked out at the highway that had caused me so much trouble and robbed me of so many years. Hard to believe I rode that highway twice a week back and forth for several years, hustling, even while I worked at UPS for some of that time. I made decent money at UPS, but not good enough for the things I wanted. I had a new Camaro, but I wanted a Benz. I was able to buy a small two-bedroom house off East Berry Street in Fort Worth, but I wanted out of the hood altogether, and into one of those nice gated subdivisions. Eventually, I was fired from UPS for a freak accident. The gearshift in my truck slipped, and the UPS truck rolled into a light post while I was out delivering a package. I had to go to a union trial to see about keeping my job, and I lost that case too. That's when I started selling drugs full time, and it didn't take me long to rise. In my mind, I had come a long way from somebody who my high school principal said wouldn't amount to anything. Mr. Notary was a black man himself, if you wanted to call him that. He hated his own, especially those who grew up without much. He was dark. Real dark. Dark as a black man could get. He had a white wife, and whenever the two of them were together, his wife seemed to glow in his darkness. A lot of the black female teachers hated Mr. Notary. We'd hear them talking about the fact that he was a Republican who didn't believe in affirmative action. I didn't know anything about that then, but I knew that we all should have hated him because he could have helped. Been our role model instead of leaving that up to the drug man. Instead, he held his head up in the air like he was better because he was a doctor of education and his wife was a judge. They didn't have any kids, which was good, because people like him didn't need any. Whenever I sat in his office with the glass door closed, he always had something negative to say.

"I see you're back again, huh? Doesn't surprise me. Well, your mother is on her way. She had to leave work—again. I didn't have the heart to tell her over the phone what you did this time. She probably thinks it's another fight, but wait until she finds out that you've been smoking marijuana in the bathroom and skipping classes."

"Nobody saw me smokin' it," I said loudly.

"Mr. Winston found it in the stall you had just walked out of. The whole bathroom reeked from the smell."

"I ain't saying somebody wasn't in there smoking weed, but that somebody wasn't me."

"I know your mother tried her best, and I know it was hard on her with just a domestic job and very little education, especially trying to raise four children on her own with three no-good knucklehead black boys, but this is your second suspension, and we're not going to stand for it. Besides, you're always fighting."

"I'm not always fighting. I had one fight because that boy pushed me and called me special so I hit him."

"I don't care about the circumstances. All I know is the two of you were fighting."

"He said I was retarded. My mama said I don't belong in no special-ed class no way. She said they always put the black boys in there."

"Your *mama* said that, did she?" Mr. Notary asked with an attitude. "Your mother, who was probably in special ed herself. What makes her think she's an authority?"

"My mama graduated from high school with honors."

"High school?" He shook his head and laughed. "But she didn't go to college? Instead she's some white woman's maid."

"She ain't no maid. She's a cook. What you care anyway? You married to a white woman."

"Oh, I'm sorry. I guess there's a difference between being a maid and being a cook." He shook his head. "Some niggas ain't never gonna have."

"Who you calling a nigga? You black too."

"There's a difference between being black and being a nigga. You're a waste of my time, and your mother is too. Mark my words. As sure as today is Friday, March 4, 1977, you're going to be a statistic. You're going to end up in prison or dead and so are the rest of your hoodlum friends. My wife's a judge in the juvenile court system. Every night she comes home and talks about all the black boys getting into trouble and being sent to a juvenile center or to prison. I've tried to be sympathetic, but I'm tired of it." He wrinkled his nose. "I don't feel sorry for your mother or any of these single mothers who have three and four kids by different men and expect the schools to raise them. You're wasting everybody's time here because I already know you're not going to amount to shit."

I told my mama I wasn't going back to that school. Told her, not if she wanted me to graduate. She knew how Mr. Notary was. He'd told her some things about herself that made her unsure of whether she should cry or cuss him out instead. I used an aunt's address and went to O.D. Wyatt the next year.

The traffic started slowing down when Bernice passed a lake. The sign said roadwork was for the next eight miles. I looked out the window and saw The Fireworks Warehouse building with big painted letters—WORLD'S LARGEST MANUFACTURER. I saw a sign, REAL BEEF JERKY, which is what I had a taste for, either that or Robertson's Ham sandwiches, which was at the next exit, even though I gave up pork in prison. I was starving for some real food—something other than powdered eggs, bad meat, spoiled milk, and the bland food that tasted like stiff hot water that was served in the chow hall.

I saw a sign and realized that we were twenty miles from Gainesville and eighty-eight miles from Dallas, which was close enough to Fort Worth for me to close my eyes and dream about how the new chapter in my life would read.

I didn't expect a welcome home banner or a house filled with my closest relatives and distant friends so I wasn't disappointed when Bernice unlocked the front door, turned on the light switch, and the only one who came out to greet me was Bernice's white cat, Cotton, who hissed and hunched her back as she crossed my path. Bernice had already told me about three times in the car that I wouldn't see Mama and my stepdad until the next day, but she hadn't mentioned where her husband, Edwin, was, and I didn't ask.

"Tower, you were real quiet on the ride in. Three hours with no conversation," Bernice said as she tossed her car keys on the end table in the living room and plopped down on the sofa, kicking off her sandals. "I'd think you'd be on cloud nine to finally get out that damn place. Is the air on? Shit, it's hot in here, hotter in here than it is outside. Somebody check the thermostat."

I heard the toilet flush.

"Who the hell is that?" Bernice asked, standing.

"The air is on, Bernice," Edwin said as he walked out of the bathroom.

"What are you doing here?" she shouted.

"I'm here to see Tower on his first day back."

"Nah, like I said, what in the hell are you doing up in my house! How come your car isn't in the driveway?"

"It's in the shop."

"So how'd you get here?" Bernice asked.

"Mr. Joseph picked me up."

"I'm tired of you putting my business out to those gossiping neighbors. How would you like it if I went around telling them about you and your little habits?"

"What little habits you talkin' 'bout?"

"You know damn well what I'm talking about."

Edwin shook his head and looked over at George and me. When

I went in, Edwin and Bernice were newlyweds in love. Now they seemed to hate each other—at least Bernice was acting like she couldn't stand Edwin.

"What's wrong with your sister?" Edwin asked George.

"Don't even put me in that," George said. "I'm outta here. Tower, I'll swing by later in the week and show you around so we can catch up with old times, little brother, okay? Bernice, let me out your driveway."

Bernice shoved her sandals back on her feet. "Make sure this nigga don't take nothin' out my house," she said to me.

"What?" Edwin said to her as she was walking outside. "Why would I take something out my own house, Bernice? What's wrong with your sister?" he asked me.

I didn't respond. Instead I surveyed the living room, noticing what looked like Mama's sofa. I saw Bernice's daughter, my niece, Tanisha, in her cap and gown picture, which was hanging on the wall. "I can't believe that's Nisha looking all grown," I said to Edwin.

"She thinks she's grown too. Up at Grambling call herself engaged to some boy on the basketball team."

"Isn't that Mama's sofa?" I asked.

"She don't need it. She's been having pretty good luck at the casino in Shreveport. She hit for 'bout fifty thousand not too long ago and bought all new furniture. Didn't they tell you?"

I shook my head. "Nah. But that's good Mama hit," I said, smiling.

"Mmm-hmm, but your stepdad was mad 'cause your mama went out and bought a new car—a Dodge Intrepid, I think—and all new furniture even though he wanted a house. He said he's tired of living in the ghetto."

"They don't live in the ghetto," I said.

"Shit, you ain't been around for a while. It may not have been the ghetto before you went in, but it sure is now."

"I miss them."

Bernice walked back in the house and resumed her position on the sofa. She looked over at me. I could tell she wanted to say something but most likely she was trying to control her tongue since she figured I wasn't working with all of my faculties. Every time she saw my face and looked into my eyes, it seemed like she got angry. "You know Mama almost lost her mind when you went to prison. I still can't believe it." Bernice shook her head. I looked over at her in silence. "You had that good job at UPS and all the while you were selling dope. You're one sneaky muthafucka, I know that much. I would hate for your ass to be my man. You've always been a liar—always, long as I can remember. Lie about stupid shit too. Shit that don't even matter."

"Look," I snapped, but took a deep breath to calm myself, "it's my first day back, and I don't want to talk about my past or what I've always been."

"That's right, Bernice. It's the man's first day back," Edwin said as he stood in the center of the living room with his hand in his pants pocket, jingling change. "Let him relax."

"Yeah, you would say that because I know you believe in letting a man relax, don't you? Because that's all your ass ever does. You ever see a grown-ass, healthy man who can't keep a damn job to save his life?" Bernice pointed at Edwin, but I knew that wasn't true because Edwin had worked at Bell Helicopter for years. "What's your excuse? You've never been to prison so you can't use that."

"The economy, Bernice," Edwin said.

"The economy? Ain't shit wrong with the economy. Everybody else I know is working, except for Wallace. Maybe you got the same problem he does," Bernice said.

"What's wrong with Wallace?" I asked. "He don't work at GM no more?"

"Hell no. GM been over. He on that stuff is what's wrong with him," Bernice said.

"Wallace is on that stuff? What stuff you talking about? I know you don't mean no crack or no shit like that," I said.

"That's exactly what I mean. He's over Mama's house every day, worrying them to death, just like this fool right here is worrying me."

"Bernice, I got laid off. It's not like I'm not trying to work, damn! Anyway, do we have to talk about this right now on Tower's first day back?"

"*Tower's* first day back," Bernice said. "Not yours. Don't think you're slick and try to stay because my man is on his way over."

"What, y'all not together no more?" I asked.

"It's your sister. She wants me out. I'm trying to be here, be a husband and a father."

"You ain't trying to be shit. If you were trying, you'd get your ass out there and try to find a job. What kind of husband and father can you be without an income?" Bernice asked as she flicked her lighter and lit her cigarette.

"Bernice, I'm getting unemployment, and they're going to call me back real soon. Damn, you sure know how to ruin things. Your brother comes back after ten years and you try to ruin his thing too. You got a problem, Bernice."

"I sure do. Do you want to know what it is? It's you! Get the fuck out my house!" Bernice threw one of her sandals at Edwin, just missing the side of his leg as he jumped out of the way.

"It's my house too!"

"Well then get the fuck out *our* house."

"Bernice, can I talk to you in private please?" Edwin asked.

"Hell no! Didn't I tell you to leave? Leave!"

Edwin stood frozen, looking over at Curtis and me and then back toward Bernice. "I'm not leaving."

"Oh yes, you are," she said calmly. "I got my man coming over here tonight, and you will be leaving shortly."

"I'm going to tell you now, I don't want another man 'round my son."

"Don't try to dictate my fuckin' life. I do what the fuck I want to do when the fuck I want to do it."

"Why you got to cuss so much, Bernice?" Edwin asked. "Are you sure you're not the one who just got out of prison?"

"I didn't just get out but I might get put in for killing your sorry ass if you don't get the fuck out my house."

Curtis ran into his bedroom.

"See? See what you did, Bernice? You affecting my boy with your foolishness."

My mind was twisted in knots. I could already tell that my sister's home was going to be one filled with constant confusion, which was the last thing I needed after being locked up. "I've had enough of hearing about you and your damn boyfriend, especially right in front of my son. Let me tell you something, Bernice—"

"Ah, nah, you ain't tellin' me shit."

"We're still married. I'm telling you that."

"All I'm doing is waiting for your sorry ass to file. I know you don't think I'm going to pay for it."

Edwin turned away from Bernice and looked toward me. "Tell your sister something."

"I'm tired. I need to go to bed," I said to Bernice "Which room is mine?"

"The last door to your left." I started walking down the hallway. "Mama and Daddy are coming by here to see you tomorrow. They couldn't today because Mama had to take Daddy to the hospital. He had a stroke last year so he's back and forth seeing the doctor."

"Nobody told me Dad had a stroke," I said as I turned toward them.

"Nobody wanted to tell you 'cause we knew you had enough to worry about. We couldn't tell you everything. Damn," Bernice said.

"What else haven't you told me?" I asked.

"I don't know. Do you expect me to remember ten years worth of shit just like that?" she asked, snapping her fingers.

"Bernice," Edwin said.

"Don't you see I'm trying to talk to my brother? What do you want?" she asked as she bounced on the sofa like she was in the middle of having a fit.

"I don't want no other man around my son."

"What about Lisa?" I asked loudly.

"Who?" Bernice asked me.

"Did you hear me, Bernice?" Edwin asked.

"Edwin, I don't care what you want! Just like you didn't care what I wanted when you were out fuckin' around three years ago with prostitutes. I was through with your ass then. So what you do or don't want is the least of my concerns."

"How many times do I have to tell you that I wasn't soliciting no damn prostitute?"

"My girlfriend, Lisa. How can you forget about Lisa?" I asked.

"I don't care how many times you tell me," Bernice said to Edwin, ignoring me. "All I know is how low I felt when the Fort Worth police department called me to come bail your ass out. I get down there and ask what the charges are, and I have to hear a female officer tell me that my husband was on Rosedale Street soliciting a damn prostitute. How do you think that made me feel?"

"That woman waved me over there. I thought she needed help."

"I'm sure you did, and I bet you were willing to help her too. Get out!"

"How could you forget about Lisa? She had my baby," I said.

"Oh, that girl who was mixed with Mexican, white, and everything except black? Is that who you talking about? The one you had living with Mama and them? Nobody has heard from her since you went in."

"Since I went in, Bernice?" I asked. "I talked to her since I went in so that can't be true."

"Well, you know what I'm saying, in a long time. You said you were tired so go to sleep."

"I will but I want to know about Lisa."

"I don't know nothin' about her," Bernice said loudly. "That was ten years ago, Tower. Time to move on. Shit."

"But she has my baby."

"Okay, but I don't know where she is, and you need to take a nap because you getting on my damn nerves."

"Everything gets on your damn nerves," Edwin mumbled.

"You talking to me?" Bernice asked Edwin as she bucked her eyes at him.

I shook my head and walked to my room. I was tired of hearing the two of them fuss.

I couldn't even enjoy the feel of a real mattress for hearing Edwin and Bernice yelling from the living room. I had the door closed, even though it made me feel anxious; loud noises made me feel worse. It took a while but eventually I fell asleep. The last thing I remembered was leaning my head against the headboard and thinking about Lisa.

I woke up after Bernice nudged me to let me know dinner was ready, but not before she warned me that her man was over and told me if I couldn't sit at the dining room table quietly I should politely take my plate to my room and eat. I lay there for a minute longer, thinking more about Lisa and how jealous she was and how many times she pulled a gun on me. That was the type of woman I thought would stay by my side since she seemed to be so into me. Now, that's the kind of woman I'm going to stay clear of, because that type is probably like that with every man, and it probably didn't have shit to do with me.

I walked into the kitchen, watching Bernice as she was stirring a pot of what smelled like black beans on the stove.

"How can you do that?" I asked.

"What? Stir beans?"

"Nah, have another man around your son when you're still married?" It made me think about Lisa and the fact that she probably had my child calling some other man Daddy.

"Why don't you get married and have a child and then stay married for ten years to a no-good loser? Maybe then you can answer that question. Besides, if I didn't think this was serious, I wouldn't have him around my son."

I didn't say anything. I reminded myself that this was her house and I needed somewhere to stay, so what Bernice did behind closed doors was her business.

"Maybe you should eat in your room," she said as she handed me a plate of food.

I took the plate and walked into the dining room where Bernice's boyfriend, Marshall Phelps, was. The way Bernice talked about him, I thought he was going to be a big man, but he wasn't.

"You must be Tower," Marshall said, standing with his hand extended. I looked down at his sparkling fro. He couldn't have been any more than five-four, and he was skinny too. His voice was so loud I heard a ringing in my ear. I looked at Marshall's hand and decided to sit down and pick up my Texas toast instead. Marshall sat back down. "Bernice told me about your little situation, and I told her that anyone can make a mistake. I was almost there. I grew up in

Como." Como was on the west side of Fort Worth, and some people considered it to be the hood, but not me. It was one of my stomping grounds. "So, see, I know all about the street game. It's not what you did then, but it's what you do now. Let me ask you, do you have a church home yet?"

"I just got back today," I said.

"I understand that, but I want to invite you to the Potter's House. I'm not a member myself, but I do attend occasionally, and Bishop T.D. Jakes and the First Lady have a wonderful prison program."

"In case you didn't know, I'm no longer in prison."

"I understand that, but I'm sure they have something for people just getting out. I want to invite you to go one Sunday with Bernice and me."

"You and Bernice go to church together?"

"Yes, we do. Your sister is a powerful worshiper."

"What you in here saying to my brother?" Bernice asked as she walked in with a king-sized plate, placing it in front of Marshall before sitting in his lap. I'm sure he was uncomfortable because that was too much weight for that little man to handle.

"We're just talking," he said as he kissed Bernice's neck.

I focused on my steak, ripping the meat apart with my knife and fork.

"Tower, you need to listen to Marshall. He's a high school counselor."

"Last time I checked, I had already graduated from high school." I looked over at the two of them. Bernice was still sitting in Marshall's lap. When she started to feed him, I slid out of my seat.

"Where are you going?" Bernice asked.

"To my room. Do you mind?"

"Okay. We'll talk," Marshall said loudly.

Bernice puckered her lips and brushed me off with her hand. "Go on, Tower."

"We'll talk? No, we won't talk," I mumbled as I walked away, but not before I heard Bernice say, "I'm worried about my brother. Something is wrong with him. He ain't all there."

"If that man moves in, damn if I do stay here," I said to myself as I was walking down the hall. "I need to get a job and get my own place."

I walked into my room and slammed the door, then I sat on the edge of the bed with my head in the palm of my hands, rubbing my temples.

Tower, when you walk out that front door in the morning, you should be afraid. You should be afraid to go to sleep at night, afraid to open your eyes in the morning. Too bad you changed your mind when you were in prison and spared your life because you ain't gonna have much of one out here. You think you getting a job? Think again. Who's going to hire an ex-con convicted of selling drugs? What you gonna do if you can't find a job? You gonna go back to selling or maybe you can start stealing cars again. You used to be good at that, my mean voice said.

"Shut the fuck up!" I said, using my hands to cover my ears. "I don't want to hear it! I don't know what I'm going to do. Just leave me the fuck alone for now!" I stood slowly and walked to the dresser to look at myself in the mirror. "Maybe I am crazy," I said and laughed. "Bernice is right. I am crazy." I turned to focus on the crack in my door and my nephew's eyes peeping through it. "Boo," I shouted.

Curtis slammed the door, and I heard him running.

CHAPTER 3

"When are you supposed to go to the parole office to sign up?" Bernice asked. She was rushing around the kitchen, getting ready to leave for work.

"I got seventy-two hours to report," I said as I sat at the kitchen table with my cup of coffee.

"You mean forty-eight hours now. You been here a day."

"I don't think they count the first day."

"You don't think? Don't you think you should know, Tower? Curtis, come on so you won't be late for school," Bernice shouted.

"I got seventy-two hours," I repeated. "Only thing I got to do is get to the social security office today to file my benefits."

"And how are you going to get there?"

"Buses still run, don't they?"

"I'm just saying because I'll be at work, and Mama doesn't like to be gone too long from Daddy."

"I can take the bus."

"Next thing you need to start doing is looking for a job. I might be able to get you on at Miller Brewing, but, Tower, I'm telling you now, if I do and you fuck up—"

"I can get my own job, thanks."

"Well, let me go before I'm late. Curtis!" she yelled. "Call Mama today and let her know we made it in okay. They must've been at the hospital all night 'cause nobody answered when I tried to call yesterday evening. Not even Granny, but you know Granny don't like fooling with no phone."

Bernice kept talking as she and Curtis headed for the door, and I continued to tune her out as I looked out of the window at the backyard, thinking about my childhood. I was back in the same house I grew up in. Only it was Mama's house then and now it's Bernice's. We were poor but we were happy. Then out of nowhere I had a flashback—E.J, one of my friends from prison, behind the gym stabbing a dude in the throat with a shank. I hit my forehead a few times with the palm of my hand trying to knock the memory out of my consciousness, but it was still there.

You need help!

I called over Mama's house, and my dad answered the phone, carrying on two conversations. He was my stepdad really, but I never knew my real father and I got along with my stepdad so good that I considered him to be like my real one. He was fussing with my oldest brother, Wallace, about having his raggedy pickup parked in their driveway, leaking oil everywhere.

I could tell from the hesitation in my dad's voice that he was surprised to hear me on the other end before the operator came on asking if they'd accept the charges.

"Tower, is that you, son? So you made it in. We wanted to come see you yesterday, but I was feeling a little under the weather."

"Is anyone over there who can come pick me up and take me to the social security office?" I asked.

"Wallace can do it. I'm sending him right now."

Wallace came and took me to the social security office an hour and a half later, even though my parents lived only twenty minutes away. I think he paid the drug man a visit first. Bernice told me that Wallace got hooked on that stuff after his wife left him. Ended up losing his job at General Motors and working a bunch of odds and ends. He went from owning a nice home on Crowley, right down from my other brother George to renting a dump on Yuma. Before

I went in, Wallace was the one who was the most together. He'd been married for almost twelve years, but they didn't have any kids 'cause he never wanted any. Just wanted to work all those hours at the plant and buy Carla whatever she wanted. Now all Wallace had was his raggedy pickup, and he was trying to sell that to me.

"I'll give you a real good deal for it," Wallace said. "It's a 1995. I bought it new."

"Why it look so old?" I asked.

"I don't know. I guess they don't make these American cars to last."

"I don't even have my driver's license yet."

"Yeah, but you getting one, right? All I want is fifteen hundred dollars."

"Where you think I been? You know I don't have that kind of money. I don't even have a job yet."

"A job? Come on, Tower. I know you. You always kept a little something stashed. You've been like that your whole life. I know you got some money somewhere."

"Wrong. The little money I did have Lisa ran off with."

"How much can you come up with?"

"I'm not sure. I hear you hittin' that pipe now. Is that what you need the money for?"

"Pipe? Nah, man, it ain't even like that. I ain't on no crack. I'm just really trying to help you out. Get you started on the right foot is all."

One thing I could spot was a user. I'd been around enough of 'em. Yeah, Wallace was on that shit and that would explain why he was trying to sell a 1995 GM Sierra for so cheap. It may have had a little rust on it and a dent on the bumper, but even the salvage would be more than that.

"Wait a few days. I should have my SSI money then," I said.

"I ain't got a few days. I need that money now."

"Why do you need it now, Wallace? I thought this was all about helping me out."

"Yeah, it is, but—"

"But what, Wallace? Be honest, man. You on something, ain't you?"

"I smoke a few primos every now and then, just between you and me. Not enough to say I'm *on* it."

"You're high right now, ain't you?"

"No, I'm not high. Do you really think I would go over Mama's house high?"

"You acting like you are."

"Well, I'm not. It's been hard for me since Carla left."

"Bernice said that was six years ago."

"And it's been hard for six years. She just walked out. Never told me there was a problem or nothing. Why would she do that?"

I shrugged. "Y'all never had any problems at all?"

"Nah. I came home every night. I wasn't cheating. I was just working hard. But she sure didn't wait to get with some other muthafucka. And had a baby by him. Wouldn't give me no baby. I should tell her I want to take a blood test. That could be my baby."

"How old is the baby?"

"Two or three."

"If she been gone for six years, you know damn well that's not your baby."

"I guess you right. I guess it's not my baby."

"You never wanted a baby no way. Even I remember that."

"I would have done anything for that girl." He pulled up in my parents' driveway and put the truck in park, but kept the motor running.

"You not coming in?" I asked.

"Nah. I have some shit that I need to do."

"What, get high?"

"Damn! Nah, I ain't getting high. I ain't going in because this is your day, and I don't want to take from it. I'm already feeling a little down, and that shit can be contagious."

"Look, man, I ain't in no position to really give nobody no advice. Hell, this is my second day back, but if you need to talk, just holla. But I do know one thing," I said as I stared at Carla's picture. "You need to take her picture off your dashboard. That's why she's always on your mind."

He snickered and shook his head. "I got this under control," he said as he looked at the picture. "I still love her."

I looked over at him, but I couldn't comment because I knew

how he felt. I wanted Lisa, but I just hadn't let my mind concentrate on what I was going to do to find her. I called the last few numbers I had for her. Her mother's and sister's number. One was disconnected and the other belonged to someone else.

"You sure you ain't coming in?" I asked as I opened the door to the pickup.

"I'm sure, man."

A few minutes later, I turned the knob to see if my parents still left the door unlocked, and they did. I walked in and heard shouts of joy coming from Mama and Granny Pearl. They rushed to the door and surrounded me with hugs and kisses. I could smell southern cooking. I knew my granny had been up since that morning fixing the food. When it was time to throw down, like for Thanksgiving and Christmas, I remembered how Granny Pearl would do. She wouldn't sleep the night before, or if she did, she'd rest on the sofa in the living room and get up occasionally to check the kitchen, making sure she had all the seasonings she needed or checking on her chittlins that she usually let cook through the night at a low temperature.

My stepdad told me that Mama and Granny Pearl were cooking so much food that I was going to take one look and get full. But I knew better. After all those years in the pen, I was looking forward to this meal and many more like it. I headed straight for the kitchen.

"What you got?" I asked, trying to peek in the pots.

"Whatever I got, you gonna love it, like you always do," Granny Pearl said.

"I know that's right, Granny." I picked her off the floor in a bear hug. "I missed you, Granny."

"Boy, you better put me down fo' I get dizzy."

I put her on the floor.

"You miss me, Granny?"

"What you think? I prayed every day for God to keep you safe and bring you home, and that's what He did, praise the Lord, just like He promised. You know God ain't never gonna let us down."

"No, He won't, Granny. What's all this food you cooking?"

"Name something, and I'm sure we gonna have it. I remember

all your favorites," Granny Pearl said as she eyed Mama fixing the chicken.

"Hot-water corn bread?" I asked.

"You know I got that," she said to me. "You fryin' that chicken or you bakin' it?" Granny Pearl asked Mama.

"I'm baking it. Why?" Mama asked.

"Well if you baking it, you need to put more seasoning on it than that. Why don't you move out the way and let me do it?"

"No. You can't make all this food by yourself," Mama said.

"I don't see why not. I've been doing it for years," Granny Pearl said.

"I want to help," Mama said.

"I hope you made sweet potato pies," I said.

"They're in the dining room, but don't go in there messing with them, Tower," Mama said.

"The boy can go in there and do whatever he wants. This is his day," Granny said.

"But you know he can eat a whole pie by himself. Look how big he is."

"I can eat two," I said.

"Well then go ahead, baby, 'cause I baked four. Granny Pearl is cooking for you and only you today." Granny Pearl went and stood over my mama.

"Will you let me fix the chicken?" Mama asked.

"Tower, who's chicken you like the best, mine or your mama's?" Granny asked.

They were both staring me down with their arms folded. "Can I plead the fifth? I don't want to hurt nobody's feelings."

"Oops, you know what that mean, don't you?" Granny Pearl asked Mama. "Not yours, 'cause Tower know can't nobody hurt my feelings."

"Who's dressing you like better?" Mama asked.

"Don't fall for it," Dad said from the sofa in the living room. "Just tell them you been away too long to remember."

"I been away too long to remember," I said.

"You 'bout to cook that chicken in that pan?" Granny Pearl asked Mama.

"Yes. What's wrong with this pan?"

Granny Pearl frowned.

"Now I see why y'all have to start cooking so early. You need about four hours for the debate," I said.

Mama waved her hand in the air. "You cook the damn chicken then."

"I will. And who you cussin' at? Don't be cussin' at me. I don't care how grown your ass is. . .I'm still your mama."

"Just cook so Tower can eat."

"It's gonna take a while, Tower. Have a piece of pie. We're making all your favorites today. And just about every one of your relatives is coming over," Granny Pearl said.

"Where's Granddad?"

"Tower," Mama said, "don't get your granny started."

"You and Granddad still ain't back together after all these years? I thought I'd come back and you two would be living happily ever after."

"Ain't nothin' happy about me and your granddad being back together. That's a damn nightmare is what it is," Granny said.

"Stop talking about my daddy," Mama said.

"I hope Tommy's bringing my VCR back," Dad said as he walked into the kitchen. "I loaned it to him, not gave it to him." Tommy was my dad's youngest son. He was two years older than me, which would make him forty-one. He was also the one person I forgot all about while I was locked up. It was easy to throw him out of my mind. Most of our family couldn't stand him, including the side that was his own blood, like my stepsister, Constance.

"What we need with a VCR when we have a DVD player?" Mama asked.

"I'm sick of Tommy anyway," Dad said. "He only come around when he want to eat good. If y'all weren't cooking this big dinner today we wouldn't see his ass 'til Easter. I can't help if he married a woman who can't cook. And the thing that gets me is they come right when we serving and leave right after they ass eat."

"What about Aunt Cora? She comin'?" I asked.

"She can't make it today," Granny Pearl said.

Not today or ever probably, I thought. We were close. Aunt Cora was my mama's youngest sister. We were only eight years apart so we could relate to each other real well. I was her favorite nephew before I went to prison. I even tried to call her a few times from inside, but she never accepted my calls. I wrote her, too, but never heard nothing back. Mama said it would probably take Aunt Cora some time to come around, but she's had ten years, and like Granny Pearl said, she couldn't make it, and she probably won't ever be able to make it. Not for me.

Aunt Cora did well for herself. She was an educated woman with a master's degree, a member of one of those sororities, and a business owner. Mama kept me updated while I was in prison, about how Aunt Cora opened a temporary employment agency right after I went in, but it was her husband's company, Strickland Construction, that was really making money. She and her husband lived in Plano in a big house. I guess having a nephew who went to prison isn't good dinner conversation.

"We gonna have a good time, just the same though," Mama said.

"We gonna have a better time is what we gonna have," Dad said. "I'm glad Cora's bourghetto ass ain't coming. I still remember when she brought her bourgeois family over here and spent the night last year while they were getting their hardwood floors redone. She had the nerve to walk in our bedroom when me and your mama was just about to get busy asking your mama for the damn thread count on the bedsheets. 'These can't be 350. I can't sleep on anything lower than 350, and I normally sleep on 450.' I told her 'look a here, then you should have brought your own damn sheets because we bought these at Super Wal-Mart on sale for $29.99, complete with the comforter so whatever the thread we get for that, we glad for.' I can't stand nobody just step out the ghetto and think they all that."

"I'm proud of my sister. She did good for herself," Mama said.

"She married into money is what she did, and I'm proud of her, too, but I'd be prouder if she learned how to share some of it. I wish I would have a sister, brother, cousin—hell, a close damn friend—who's a millionaire and can't throw a little something my way. I wouldn't do nobody I was close to like that. Do you know Cora's sitting over in Plano with a damn four-car garage and a car up in every one of 'em? Their sixteen-year-old drives a Corvette to high school, but when our car broke down, before we got the new one, she said, 'well I wish I could help.' Woman, you can."

"I'm happy for them. It's no need to be jealous," Mama said.

"I'm not jealous. The Powerball is up to $135 million, and I'm driving to Louisiana to buy my ticket tomorrow. And let me tell you something, when I hit she better not bring her ass around here looking for a penny. Cora may have one or two million but not no $135 million."

"Ooh, that would be so sweet," I said, "to win all that money."

"Look, don't worry. If I hit, I won't be like your stingy aunt. You'll get a few million from me."

"That would be right on time," I said.

"Wouldn't it? You want to ride up there with me?" Dad asked.

"You don't need to drive to Louisiana," Mama said to Dad.

"It's only going to take a couple of hours."

"The doctor said to take it easy."

"I'm taking it easy, but I'm not dead. If I hit for $135 million, that's when I just might have a heart attack."

"I'll go with you," I said.

"Good. We can leave bright and early so you might as well spend the night."

"I ain't bring my stuff."

"It's stuff still here of yours," Mama said. "And we got packages of toothbrushes that aren't even open yet."

"I can't wear the same stuff I wore ten years ago, Mama."

"Yeah, I guess you can't. You are a lot bigger now. Look like one of them body builders. Well, I'll just wash what you got on."

"Okay," I said, grinning. I was happy to be around my parents. They made me feel at home. I'd love it if they could hit that Powerball and live out some of their dreams before they got too old to enjoy any of them.

I walked into the den and looked through Dad's videocassette holder. Dad was a movie buff. He had a lot of movies that I hadn't heard of, ones that must of come out while I was in prison, like *Jerry*

Maguire and *Sling Blade*. I read the jackets, trying to decide what I was in the mood for. *Jerry Maguire* had five Academy Award nominations and the box said it was "a deliciously smart romantic comedy." But more than twenty-five critics agreed that *Sling Blade* was one of the Year's Top 10. "Two Thumbs Up" from Siskell and Ebert. "Riveting," according to *Rolling Stone*. And the *L.A. Times* called it "Powerful." It was about a simple man and a difficult choice. I read the back of both boxes, and it wasn't hard to eliminate one. *Sling Blade* was about a mentally challenged man who at age nine was incarcerated in a state hospital for the criminally insane for killing his mother and her lover. That didn't seem like the kind of movie that my mind could escape in. Didn't seem like the kind of movie that would make me laugh either.

"Is this any good?" I asked as I walked into the kitchen holding up the *Jerry Maguire* video.

"Yeah, that was real good," Dad said. "That's the one that black man won an Oscar for. I can't think of his name right now."

"Cuba Gooding, Jr.," I said.

"Yeah. How you know?" Dad asked.

"It's on the box."

"I know you ain't planning on watching it today because like I told your mama, Tommy got our VCR."

"Call Tommy up and tell him to bring the VCR with him," I said, "or give me his number and I'll tell him."

"That's what I'm talking about," Dad said and then rattled off Tommy's number.

I sat at the table, gulping down my water after taking a break from eating. My stomach was cramping after my third trip to the kitchen for some more greens, macaroni and cheese, corn-bread dressing, cabbage, sweet potatoes, fried corn, turkey, chicken, and hot-water corn bread. I saw a few sets of eyes watching me. I guess they'd never seen somebody eat so much so fast, but I knew I'd pay for it later and probably be sitting on the toilet all night.

Everybody looked so different. I tried not to look too hard at my stepsister, Constance, but I glanced over at her because she had gained a lot of weight since the last time I saw her. She was way bigger than Bernice, and during dinner, all Constance talked about was getting some kind of operation to lose weight.

"I know this white woman at my job who did it."

"*White* woman," Dad said. "Blacks don't do that. It's out our nature to get an unnecessary operation. We don't half like going to the doctor for routine checkups."

"Only reason I'm not getting it is because my insurance won't cover it, but next year I'm changing carriers, because I think Blue Cross covers some of it."

"Some of it, which means you gonna have to pay the rest. That's a waste of money. Just don't eat," Dad said, looking down at Constance's full plate.

"It's not that easy, Daddy. I need somebody to make my stomach smaller. I didn't have a problem until after I had those kids."

"Don't blame them kids. You know damn well it's hereditary. Your mama's big."

"Ooh," Mama said, hitting Dad's arm. "That was not nice. Don't talk about that child's mother, 'cause I'm far from skinny myself."

"She knows I'm joking, but I'm just letting her know it's in her genes."

"I don't have to be big, Daddy. Genes or not."

Constance stopped talking and continued eating. She'd had a crush on me when we were teenagers. We kissed only once, which was the first year our parents married, but I drew the line there and refused to cross it.

"We're glad to have you back, Tower," Constance said with a seductive smile.

"It's good to be back," I said quickly.

"I can't get over how muscular you are," Constance said.

"Yeah, you look like you been in prison," Tommy said.

"What kind of shit is that to say?" Dad asked.

"What? He do," Tommy said. "When you see a dude all swole up with a stone face, that's the first thing you think is prison."

"What, they teach you that in security guard school? Your wanna-be-cop ass," Dad said, laughing.

"I am a cop."

"You a security guard is what you are," Dad said.

"For the city," Tommy said. "My paycheck is drawn off the same check theirs is."

"And what that mean, because it's for the city it makes you a cop? I retired from the federal government. My paycheck came from the same place the President's came from. Does that make me the damn President?"

"You know what I mean," Tommy said.

"Nah, I don't," Dad said, laughing.

"Well, I know a lot of cops," Tommy said.

"I know a millionaire, but does that make me one? Not yet, anyway, but I will be, once I hit the Powerball."

"Don't listen to Tommy," Constance said to me. "He just jealous of your fine ass."

"Watch it now," Dad said. "Fine ass? That's your brother you talking about. I don't like the way that sound."

"Stepbrother," Tommy mumbled.

"What you say?" Dad asked Tommy.

"Nothin'."

"That's what I thought," Dad said.

"Look," Tommy said. "If I had spent ten years in the pen, I'd be built just like that. I'm an overweight lover, and Sheila loves it. Don't you, Sheila?"

"You could stand to lose some weight," Sheila said, rolling her slanted eyes. "A whole lot of weight. Tower, you look good, just like Constance said. And you don't look like you just got out of prison either. Tommy, you never say the right thing."

Now, Sheila was somebody I had been with before Tommy had even met her. She used to be so fine, and she'd hang down at the clubs I'd frequented. She looked just like a black china doll with them slanted eyes and straight black hair with bangs. She willingly gave it up to Arturo, Quentin, and me all on the same night. Six months later, Tommy brought her home on Thanksgiving and introduced her to the whole family as his fiancée. When I walked into the dining room that day, her slanted eyes opened real wide.

Late that night, she called me, begging me not to say anything, and I never did. She said she'd changed. Didn't matter to me if she had or not, 'cause I couldn't stand Tommy so hopefully she hadn't.

"What you mean I never say the right thing?" Tommy asked Sheila.

"Just what I said, Tommy. I got my hair done yesterday. I was thinking I was looking cute until I walked in the house. This man didn't even let me take off my jacket before he says, 'I know you ain't just get your hair done. I know I didn't give you thirty-five dollars for that. You better go on back there and ask for my money back.' So Tower, don't feel bad because Tommy is real ignorant."

"Tommy don't faze me," I said. "Never has and really never will now."

"I guess not much can faze your ass after being locked up for ten years," Tommy said.

We stared each other down.

"What's this shit all about? You drunk? I know you didn't come over my house drunk. Is he drunk?" Dad asked Sheila.

"He's been drinking. I don't think he's drunk though. You know he can't hold his liquor."

"You better check your ass into somebody's AA program and don't come over my house acting no fool," Dad said.

"I'm not drunk! Sheila don't know what she's talking about. I had one beer before I came over here, and that's it."

"See, Tower. See what I'm talking about," Sheila said. "He talks to everybody like he's crazy, and that's because when a person got issues like he does, they love taking them out on everybody else because they can't stand to see anybody having a good time."

"You see what twelve years with the same woman has gotten me?" Tommy said. "Nothin' but disrespect."

"Nah, that's what twelve years with the same woman when you ain't nothing but a fool gonna get you," Dad said.

"He's just mad 'cause I called over there for the VCR," I said to Dad, but deep down Tommy was still jealous because I had a better relationship with his dad than he did.

"Mmm-hmm. That's all it is," Dad said.

"I could give less than a damn about a VCR. I stopped by Wal-Mart on the way here and bought one for $79, so I don't need your VCR. I brought it back, didn't I?"

"You didn't want to," Sheila said. "You were fussing the whole way, mad because you had to buy your own."

"That's so disrespectful, Sheila. Whose side are you on? I'm your husband."

"So!" Sheila said loudly.

"You married?" I asked Constance. I was trying to find one couple who got along and weren't fussing all the time.

"No, she's living in sin," Dad said.

"I'm engaged," Constance said.

"You've been engaged to that man for eight years and y'all have two kids. So like I said, y'all living together in sin. And how come you didn't bring your family with you?" Dad asked.

" 'Cause I wanted a break," Constance said.

Granny Pearl just sat back frowning, critiquing her meal. "I don't like the way these sweet potatoes turned out. They too sweet."

"No they're not, Granny. They're perfect," I said.

"My dressing is good. But I think I cleaned the taste off them chittlins."

"How the chicken taste?" Mama asked Granny Pearl sarcastically.

"Best I've ever made," Granny Pearl said as she rolled her eyes.

I walked away from the table and into the den to finally watch *Jerry Maguire*. About a half hour into the movie while my folks were putting away food and wrapping up what they were taking, Constance came in and sat next to me on the sofa. "You staying with Bernice, right?" she asked, speaking softly.

"Mmm-hmm," I said, focusing on the TV screen.

"You need me to take you home?"

I shook my head. "I'm staying over here tonight. Me and Dad going to Shreveport in the morning."

"Then let's go for a ride."

"Nah," I said, shaking my head. I walked away from her and into the kitchen to help Granny with the dishes.

"You don't have to do that, Tower," Granny said when I picked up a pot and started scrubbing with the Brillo pad.

"I don't mind. I'm so glad to be home, Granny. You just don't know."

"I can imagine. You got your week planned out? I know you're going with your dad tomorrow."

"Yeah, and I'm going to start looking for a job soon. I got a lot to do, Granny, but I'm so glad to be home." I kissed her on her cheek. "I love you, Granny."

"I love you too," she said as she looked into my eyes. "Let it go," she said as she grabbed hold to my arms and shook me.

I nodded. She could read me like a book. Let it go. I wish I could let it go.

Let it go? Tell her what all you got to let go. Tell her it's too much to let go. There's so much that there's nowhere to let it go to. Tell her about prison and how lonely you felt. Tell her about them damn guards and the goon squad who tore your cell apart night after night just because they could. Tell her about all those times you pretended you were eating her food instead of that shit they served in chow hall. Tell her about the times you were in the hole talking to yourself and answering back. Tell her about the times you wanted to die. Tell her about the people you helped kill. Go on and tell her. Tell her about who your friends were. Tell her about E.J. who was in for murder, Famous who was in for statutory rape, Punisher the hit man, and Slim Earl the pimp. Go on and tell her because you need to tell somebody all this shit. Ain't you getting tired of carrying it around? my mean voice asked.

CHAPTER 4

After Dad bought his Powerball tickets, he asked me if I wanted to go to Harrah's and try to strike it rich. I was so glad to be out and about, enjoying the ride that I told him whatever he wanted to do was fine with me. While Dad was playing blackjack, determined to win, I was walking around looking at everything. All of this was new to me—not casinos, but casinos in Shreveport. The last one I went to was in Reno before my trial started. Lisa and I drove there to visit her mama and while I was there, I tried my luck one last time, since it had failed me so badly up until that point. I wanted to hit big so I could leave the country and not worry about my parents losing their house, which they put up as collateral against my bond before the trial started. But when I didn't win more than fifty dollars, I was right back in Oklahoma appearing for my preliminary hearing.

I found a seat near the nickel slots and played a dollar's worth of nickels, won back about five dollars and once I lost that, I sat back, ready to go.

I felt a tap on my shoulder. "Are you playing this machine?" a young lady asked.

"Huh?" I asked as I looked up at her.

"The machine you're sitting at. You've been sitting there for a while, and I was wondering if you were playing the slots or just resting because there aren't any more available machines."

"I guess I was just resting," I said as I stood. She was a young black lady, probably in her late twenties. Her hair was in a short curly Afro. She wasn't the most attractive woman in the world, but she was the first woman who had spoken to me outside of one of my relatives since I'd been out in the world. "I guess now you want to try your luck on the machine I warmed up for you. It's all yours, but you do know if you hit, I expect half, right?"

"You may have warmed up the seat, but that's about it. I'm not much of a gambler, but I will play the nickel slots. I came with my sister and her husband." She sat down. "Are you from here?"

"Who, me?"

"Yeah, you. Who else would I be talking to?"

"I'm from Fort Worth."

"Really? So am I. Are you here by yourself?"

"I'm with my dad. He's over at the blackjack table, probably losing all his money. I guess I'll go over there and save him."

"Since we're both from Fort Worth, we should get together sometime." She took a business card and pen from her purse and handed it to me so we could exchange numbers.

"You're a loan officer?" I asked, looking down at her card.

"Yes. Why, do you need a house?"

"I will soon."

"We should have dinner one day and discuss it," she said, smiling. "The interest rates are coming down, and there are a lot of good programs that I can get you in where you won't have to put any money down."

I nodded. "Okay, that's cool."

I walked over to the blackjack table, and Dad was still there. "Did you win any money?"

"What I won, I lost back. I'm ready. You?" he asked. I nodded.

As we were driving on I-20, I took the lady's business card out and stared at her picture. Michelle Fines was her name. Fines, hmm, not that she was. If I decided to call her, I wouldn't exactly know what to say, but she seemed like she was easy to talk to.

"Whose card you got?" Dad asked.

I handed the business card to him.

"When you meet her?"

"Today, at the casino."

"She works in Arlington, huh?" he asked as he quickly studied the card. "You gonna call her?"

I shrugged. "I don't know. I ain't ready to start dating."

"Yeah, but you gonna need a friend. It's not like you gotta tell her right off where you been. That ain't nobody's business." I nodded. "When you meet a woman, let her get to know you first. That's what I would do. Because if you tell her first thing, the average woman probably won't deal with it, and then the ones who will deal with it, you're going to wonder why, so just tell her at the right time."

"When's the right time to tell a woman you're interested in that you've been locked up?"

"You'll know when the time is right. A friend is a friend regardless, so develop the friendship first, and if she can't accept where you've been, then guess what? She ain't your friend. Now, that's my advice for the day. I've just lost sixteen hundred dollars. I better hit that Powerball this Saturday, or I'll be testing your mama's friendship when she finds out."

CHAPTER 5

I entered the two-story building and took the stairs up to the second floor to Suite 211. The waiting area was full. Some people were sitting behind booths filling out paperwork while others sat in the chairs along the wall or stood waiting to be called to the back by a parole officer. I looked around the room for a few seconds and realized that I had to approach the receptionist and sign in before the process even got started.

"Is this your first time here?" the young woman at the receptionist's desk asked.

"Yes," I said.

She cleared her throat and handed me a clipboard with several sheets of paper and a pen attached. "You need to fill out those forms. We also need a forty-dollar cashier's check or money order made out to the Department of Corrections Restitution and Accounting. Do you have that?" I nodded. "Okay, you'll be assigned a parole officer shortly." After I completed the forms and took them back to the front along with my money order, I stood, leaning against the wall, waiting for my name to be called.

"You better hope you don't get Mary Davis—I mean Mrs. Davis. Don't call her by her first name. She's a bitch in heels," the white man who was standing next to me said. He was wearing a cowboy hat and boots. "She let her little authority go straight to her head." I didn't respond. "She makes up rules. And believe it or not, she's especially hard on blacks."

"Theodore Evans," a black woman said. She had her hair pulled back and gathered into a fat bun resting on top of her head. She put on her half glasses and looked down at the file she was carrying for a brief moment. She peered over the frames to look out at the crowd.

I looked down at her three-inch heels.

"That's her," the cowboy said. "Bitch in heels," he mumbled. "Good luck. You gonna need it."

"Theodore Evans," she repeated. I walked toward her. She turned quickly without acknowledging me. I guess I was just another number.

I walked casually through the door, closing it behind me, and followed her and the loud clicks from her shoes to a private office. She sat behind the desk and opened the file. I sat in the chair across from her desk, focusing on her nametag—Mary Davis, just like he said.

"Bitch in heels," I mumbled.

"What?"

I shook my head. "Nothing."

She flipped through several pages of the file. "Trafficking, huh? Figures." She sighed. "Do you understand the conditions of an interstate compact?" she asked without looking up from the papers.

I didn't answer immediately. My mind questioned what she meant when she said, figures. Figures because I'm a black man? Figures because she can tell that I grew up in a low-income area from the addresses I listed? Figures. Why it figures? I could only hope that she wasn't a female version of my high school principal, Mr. Notary.

"Do you?" she asked, frowning as she finally focused on me.

"Do I what?" I asked with attitude.

"Do you understand the conditions of an interstate compact?"

"I think I do."

"Well I guess I better go over them because it's very important that you *know* that you do. There are several rules and conditions of your parole." She handed me the interstate compact agreement.

"Please read over that form and sign below. The most important thing to understand is that you were released early. If you violate your parole, you can get sent back to prison to serve the remainder of your sentence, which means fifteen years, plus any new sentence that may be imposed. So take your time reading the agreement, and if you have any questions, let me know."

I read over all seventeen lines of the rules and conditions very carefully. "I have a question."

"What?" she snapped.

"Under special conditions it says electronic monitoring, attend NA, and intensive parole. Can you explain all that? How long do I have to wear an ankle monitor? And how often do I have—"

"Wait, don't be shooting questions at me left and right." She darted her eyes in my direction and shifted in her seat. "I can't tell you how long you're going to be wearing an ankle monitor. It all depends. NA is Narcotics Anonymous. Since you were convicted of a drug crime, it's mandatory that you go to NA meetings."

"I went to NA when I was in prison."

"And you're going to go again once a week now that you're out. You need to stay gainfully employed or go to school. You'll need to work on establishing yourself within the next thirty days. You can't leave the state or even the county without prior written permission." *I guess that means no more going to Shreveport or anywhere for that matter,* I thought. Tarrant County is large, but it ain't that big. "You will be on a curfew of 10:00 P.M. for a minimum of ninety days unless it's violated, and then it will be extended. I will do periodic visits to your home, and possibly even your job, when you get one. I'll need a complete list of all addresses you plan on visiting along with phone numbers of relatives and friends. Do you have any more questions?" I shook my head.

"Sign this form and you're free to go. One more thing." She walked over to a metal wall cabinet, unlocked it, and removed an ankle monitor. "Do you remember your curfew?"

"Didn't you say eleven?"

"I see you don't listen very well," she said as she kneeled down and strapped the monitor to my ankle. "You're going to need to listen to every damn word I say. I *said* ten o'clock. Can you remember that?"

"Yes, ma'am."

"Good. One last thing: Make sure you and your electronic monitor are together at all times. We know when they're being tampered with. Don't try me, okay?"

"No, ma'am, I won't."

Yes, ma'am. No, ma'am. Fuck you, ma'am.

CHAPTER 6

The phone was ringing. I'm not sure how many times, but I was thankful it was because I needed something to snap me out of my thoughts. I was sitting in Bernice's living room, using the remote to flip through the TV, but I wasn't paying much attention, because my mind was preoccupied with more thoughts of prison and survival.

"You haven't forgotten about our lunch date, have you?" a woman's voice asked.

"Michelle?"

"Yes. You forgot. Didn't you? We're supposed to be going to Sweet Georgia Brown's. Remember?"

"I remembered." Now that she was calling, it reminded me that I didn't want to go. Not with her. One week had passed since I met her, and in that time we had lunch once at Papadeux. She drove, after I lied about my car being in the shop. All the girl talked about were those damn home loan programs her company offered. I'm sure she was anxious to get her commission, especially after I lied and told her that I earned $65,000 a year as a foreman at GM, only I was on temporary disability after I hurt my back. She wanted me to fill out a loan application, but I wasn't about to put my social security number down. No telling what might come up.

"Well, I'm on my way."

"Okay, but, I got food over here we can eat." There was silence.

"Hello. Did you hear me?"

"Yes. Okay, that'll be fine. I'll see you in a few."

I hung up the phone and walked into the kitchen to look through the fridge. There was leftover fried chicken, fixings for a salad, and bread, all of which were good enough. I walked back into the living room and collapsed on the sofa, staring at the ceiling.

That bitch is stuck-up. I can tell by the way she talks. She says she's from Fort Worth but she don't sound like it. Talking through her nose like she need to blow it. You know she's not your type. She don't look nothin' like Lisa. But that don't mean you can't fuck her...bust a nut 'cause it's been so long you need to release it on somebody, and since all she's thinking about is her commission anyway, she'd probably give you some, my mean voice said.

The two plates were laying on the living room floor beside us with most of the food still on them. My face was buried between Michelle's legs. My hands were caressing her naked body, massaging her small breasts, and squeezing her fat nipples. All I could think about were the ten years I spent locked up without the taste of any, the smell of any, or the sensation of my dick inside of any. I pulled my jeans down to my ankles. I wanted to take them off and go buck wild, but couldn't because I didn't want Michelle to see my monitor. I got on top of her as her legs straddled my back, and I went deeper inside of her until she gasped.

"Am I hurting you?" I asked as I rose and looked down at her. She shook her head. "Are you sure?" She nodded. She felt so good. Too damn good. I wanted to cum but I wouldn't allow myself to because I didn't want that feeling to leave so I kept at it until she said, "Are you about to cum?"

"Do you want me to? What, you don't like it?" I asked.

"I like it, but we've been doing it for at least an hour," she said as she looked at her watch.

"I'll cum if you want me to. Do you?"

"Yes, please cum," she said.

I closed my eyes and started visualizing those naked ladies in the magazine, the faces and bodies I'd jacked off to while I was in prison.

I was faithful to those women, especially one in particular, whom I nicknamed, Lisa. The more I saw that lady named Lisa, the faster and deeper I went inside of Michelle. "Tell me you like it," I said to Michelle."

"I do. I like it."

"Talk dirty to me," I said.

"I like it, Tower. I really like it."

"Talk dirty," I insisted.

"I can't, but I like it."

"Okay, then don't say nothing," I said as I took my mind deeper until I came and quietly rolled off her.

"Did you cum?" she asked.

"Yes."

"Are you sure?"

"I'm positive. See," I said, showing my limp dick and the condom filled with my cum.

"You were so quiet when you came," she said, wrinkling her brows.

I shrugged. "Sorry, I'll try to be louder next time." I stood, removed the condom, and pulled my pants up. I walked to the bathroom, threw the condom in the toilet, and flushed.

The doorbell rang.

I stuck my head out the bathroom and looked in the direction of the door. It was Mrs. Davis. Luckily for me, she had her head turned sideways and didn't see me. I didn't answer. Eventually the rings stopped, and her face left from in front of the glass, but Michelle's thousand questions began.

"Was that your girlfriend?" she asked as she stood and dressed.

"I don't have a girlfriend. I thought I told you that. That was a friend of my sister's."

"You did, but I'm not stupid. Most men have someone in their life."

"Not this one. I'm too busy right now. I just want a friend is all."

"I'll be your friend. I'll be your best friend if you buy a house from me," she said with a smile. "Just kidding." I knew she wasn't, but it might as well have been a joke because I couldn't afford a house. Slim Earl, the pimp from the pen, said it was easy conning women, but I didn't know it was that easy. I didn't know they'd believe every damn word a man said.

CHAPTER 7

My head was turned looking out of the car window, paying attention to the things I hadn't seen for so long, but in other ways, thinking about when I should tell Michelle the truth so she could stop hassling me about that home loan. We were on our way to the mall to look for her mama a birthday gift. I'd been in the bed all morning so when she called and asked if I wanted to hang with her, I jumped at the opportunity to get out and see new things.

When she stopped for a red light on East Berry Street and the I-35 service drive, a black woman ran up to the passenger's side of the car, waving what looked like a long, thick straw.

"Can you help out our ministry, sir?" the woman pleaded. "One dollar. That's all I need." As she stuck the straw and a small sheet of paper through the opening in the window, Michelle sped off. "Muthafucka!" the woman yelled.

I looked in the passenger's side mirror and saw the woman jumping up and down, waving a handful of candy straws.

Michelle started laughing. "That's what she gets for running up to my car begging."

"You want this? It's candy inside." I asked as I put the straw on her lap."

"Hell no. No telling what's really in there as dirty as she looked." Michelle let her window down and threw the straw out as she was merging on to I-35.

I picked up the small piece of paper from my lap and read it: *Are you hooked on drugs or know someone who is? First call on the Lord Jesus Christ. Second. Call us.*

"Do you know someone on drugs?" Michelle asked.

"Nah," I said as I balled up the paper and tossed it out my window.

We'd been driving for about twenty minutes in silence, when she asked, "Is everything okay?"

"Yep. Everything is fine."

"Why are you being so quiet?"

"No reason. I just like to look around."

"Look around at what? Sometimes I feel like I need a change of atmosphere. Don't you ever feel like that? I get so tired of Fort Worth. Don't you?"

"Not really. I mean, I've been other places, but I'd rather be here than where I've been."

"Where else have you been?" she asked.

"Just other places."

"So, you must like to travel."

"Not really. I'm getting more settled now."

The Galleria Mall hadn't changed much, or maybe I couldn't remember much about it other than all the times Lisa and I used to shop there. The times I'd let her buy whatever she wanted because I could afford it, and it helped my guilty conscience because I was always up to no good. Always laying down with some woman I wasn't supposed to, but telling Lisa otherwise.

The part I missed most about ballin' was my ability to buy what I wanted whenever I wanted—to live the way the other side, the rich folks did. I wanted to shop without worrying about price. Have Nordstrom's and Dillard's as my regular stores instead of Target and Wal-Mart.

It felt strange to walk around the largest mall in Dallas. I was constantly looking around, wondering when something was going to break out. A place that big couldn't be completely safe. Some of everybody was there, and that made me nervous. And it seemed like everyone was staring at me. When I saw people laughing and looking in my direction, I thought they were saying, "Look at him. He must have just got out."

I followed Michelle in and out of several stores. I thought she was only there for one thing—a gift for her mother. I had no idea she was going to spend half a day looking for the perfect present.

"Are you hungry?" I asked.

"Yes, but I want to go in Saks first, okay? I'm sure I'll find something there."

"I guess," I said, dragging my voice.

I was walking a little behind her, when I heard a man say, "What's up, T? When you get out, man? Damn, I almost didn't recognize you." It was Steve, one of my boys from the hood. "Look how big you got. You must not have done nothin' in there but lift weights."

"I been out for a little while," I said.

"It's good to see you, man. I heard you got like twenty or thirty years. Look a here, let me give you my, um, number and things, and we need to get together one of these days. Man, it's good to see you." He patted my back. "This your woman right here?"

"Yeah. My friend," I said, looking at Michelle who was standing with her arms crossed, refusing to look back.

"Nice to meet you," Steve said, but Michelle didn't respond. "Well, I'm going to get on out of here, man, but like I said, take this number of mine and holla back at me. You looking good, man." He handed me a homemade card. The ink had run off the numbers, but instead of asking him for the missing ones, I put the card in my pocket because I had no plans to use it anyway

I walked over to Michelle. "I'm ready to go," she said coldly. I just nodded because I didn't know what to say.

It was 7:55 P.M when Michelle dropped me at Bernice's and sped off. We didn't say one word to each other in the car. She was driving so fast, I thought we were in the Indy 500. I'm sure she couldn't wait to drop me off so she could be done with me. There was no doubt in my mind that I'd never see or speak to her again, and that was cool. I wasn't going to cry over it.

Mrs. Davis' white state-issued car was in the driveway. "She was just over here yesterday. I guess that man didn't lie when he said she was a bitch in heels. I'm not going to be able to take this shit. This is harassment," I said to myself as I walked up the driveway and into the house, taking in several deep breaths.

"Here's Tower," Bernice said. "I was telling Mrs. Davis how you had just left to go to the store."

"No bags?" Mrs. Davis asked.

"No money. I just went looking," I said.

"I never heard of anybody window shopping at a grocery store."

"I forgot to give you money, didn't I, Tower?" Bernice asked. "I sent him to the store with a list and forgot to give him some money."

"I guess." I yawned. "I'm tired. I got to go to bed."

"Wait. I'm not done with you," Mrs. Davis said. "I have some questions to ask."

"Nothing has changed since yesterday."

"I need to give you a UA." She opened her metal briefcase, took out a pair of gold latex gloves, put them on, and then handed me a plastic cup.

"So I'm supposed to piss in this, I guess?"

"Tower, why you talking like that?" Bernice asked.

"I need to do a urine analysis to make sure you're not using drugs," Mrs. Davis said.

"Whatever you say," I said as I took the cup from her and headed to my room.

"Wait. Where do you think you're going?" Mrs. Davis asked. "You can't take that in your bedroom. I need you to go straight to the bathroom and don't let me hear any water running."

"So I can't even wash my hands?" I asked.

"After I get my sample you can."

"Yes, ma'am. Anything you say, ma'am." I walked into the bathroom that was in the hallway leading to the kitchen and closed the door.

"Oh no. I can't have that," Mrs. Davis said loudly as she knocked on the bathroom door. "You need to keep the door cracked so I can see the sink to make sure you're not running the water."

"If I keep the door cracked, the sink ain't the only thing you gonna see. Besides, if I were running water, you'd be able to hear it, don't you think?" I said sarcastically.

"I need the door cracked."

"Mrs. Davis, Tower is right," Bernice said. "If he cracks the door, you'll be able to see him using the bathroom. I don't think that's policy, is it?"

"If I happen to see his penis, it won't be the first and it won't be the last, but I'm not looking for that. I just need to see the sink."

"Well, I ain't never heard—"

"Skip it, shit," I said, cutting off Bernice. "I'll crack the door. Ain't no thing. I'm used to being treated like I ain't shit."

"I don't even like this," Bernice said "I'm like Tower now—bitch is crazy."

"Are you talking to me?" Mrs. Davis asked.

"No, I'm talking to my damn self. Don't come questioning me because I'm not the one on parole."

I flushed the toilet and walked out of the bathroom with a cup half full with urine and placed it in Mrs. Davis' gloved hand. "Is that all you need?"

Bernice took her pack of Kools from the kitchen counter, removed a cigarette, and turned on the stove to light it. She was standing with one hand on her hip and the other dangling her cigarette as she gawked at Mrs. Davis.

"Now, we need to talk. I need to get an update," Mrs. Davis said.

"What kind of update? I mean I haven't even been out a couple weeks. There's not much to update."

"How's your job search coming? Are you going out every day looking?"

"Look, ma'am, don't I get some time to regroup? I'm trying to go with your little program, but I don't understand it. The ink ain't even dried on my release papers, and you want to know if I'm working."

"No, I want to know if you're looking for a job."

"Yes, I'm looking for a job, and I'm also waiting to hear back from Allied, so what do you want from me?" I asked, raising my voice.

"Tower," Bernice snapped, "calm down. Don't let her get to you."

"I can't help it. She's coming by the house every day. Calling to check on me all times of the day and night. Ain't nothin' changed since yesterday. Shit, has it even been a full twenty-four hours since I seen you last? Do you need to ask me some more questions or can I go lay down?" I stood with my hands behind my back, stiff, as if handcuffed. My mind was racing. I was afraid of what I might say if I had to stand there another minute.

"Is this how you're going to act when you get a job and your supervisor asks you a question?" Mrs. Davis asked. "Are you going to puff all up like you're ready to fight? Part of my job is to help you assimilate back into society."

"Then help me by limiting your visits. At least until I get settled."

"Now is not the time to be lax. You need to find a job."

"Ma'am, correct me if I'm wrong, but nowadays it's hard for people who've never been to prison to find a job, so how do you expect me to go out and find one with a record? I don't see you supplying me with no leads."

"The papers are filled with them. I'll give you a few weeks, but I will be checking in on you occasionally."

I turned and walked away while Mrs. Davis was saying something that my mind refused to process. Something about NA classes and a schedule she was going to drop by. I nodded. I went to my bedroom, sat on the bed, and flipped through the channels of the thirteen-inch television that was sitting on the dresser in front of me.

Tower, listen up. This Mrs. Davis bitch in heels ain't no joke, but she is a woman, and like Slim Earl used to say, every woman can be broken down, so please break her down so we can all have a little room to breathe, my mean voice said.

CHAPTER 8

I was in my sister's garage in my gray sweats with no shirt, punching my Everlast speed bag that Dad bought me because he knew I was frustrated. Couldn't find a job—I hit the bag. Couldn't afford my own place—I hit the bag harder. Didn't know how to talk to a woman—I hit the bag so hard it flew off the mounting plate and landed on the other side of the garage.

"That's some real power," Mrs. Davis said. No, she had it all wrong. She had the real power—the power to send my ass back in. That's some real power.

I sighed and removed my boxing gloves. "Maybe I should become a heavyweight and get paid to do what I did for years in the pen just to survive—kick ass."

"I came to bring your schedule for your NA meeting. The first one is this Thursday night."

"This Thursday?"

"This Thursday from seven 'til eight."

"I hope I don't have to talk because I'm not sayin' nothing. That shit's a waste of my time."

"If you don't want to talk, no one's going to force you." She handed me the slip of paper. I snatched it. "I see you still haven't learned how to control your attitude. You don't need it out here."

"Then why you got one?" I asked.

"This is just one side of me."

"Same here, so you need anything else? I'm still not working. You need me to piss in another cup for you?"

"I just need you to go to the NA meeting. They take attendance so make sure you're there because if not, I'll hear all about it."

―――――

We were in a large meeting room at a community college in Fort Worth. There were about twelve of us sitting in chairs that had been placed in a circle. I sat slumped in my chair with my head resting in my hand, looking the way I felt—uninterested.

"Being high isn't something I can really explain," a young white girl said. She looked like she was still in her teens. I'd give her twenty at the most. "I loved getting high. In the beginning, it made me feel like a bird, like an eagle soaring above everyone. I hate to glorify drugs by making them sound so good when we're all in here struggling to stay off them—"

"But they are good," a black woman cut in. "Not the drugs themselves, but the feeling they give you, better than the feeling I had when I wasn't on them." I could tell she'd been through it. Her complexion was four different shades of black. When I looked into her glassy eyes, I saw her hard life. Those eyes would never be clear again. "I found ways to get drugs even when I didn't have money. I was tricking just to get high. Giving up my body for a hit."

"A strawberry," I mumbled.

"That's right, that's what they called me—a strawberry. But then I was so strung out and looking so bad that I couldn't even give my body up. So then I had to take my—" she paused, put her hand over her mouth, and started to cry—"thirteen-year-old daughter to the crack house and let the dope man do whatever he wanted with her so I could get high. Going to prison saved my life, if that's how you want to look at it, but I know I'll never have a relationship with my daughter again."

So what! my mean voice said. *Ain't you tired of hearing that same old sob story over and over? She wasn't thinking about her daughter when she was getting high. She right about one thing, her daughter ain't never gonna have a relationship with her, and why should she? She fucked up her daughter's life for good. Well, Tower, that's one thing you can't do. You can't blame your folks for the way you turned out. Can't use that sob story. I guess you could go with the 'didn't know your real daddy' line, but that's played out too.*

Played out! my nice voice shouted. *That's the truth. Tower not knowing his real father had a lot to do with the mistakes he's made in his past.*

Yeah, right, if you say so.

Tell him, Tower.

"Users are selfish," I said, ignoring my voices, and not focusing on any person in particular because each one was a user or ex-user so to me they were all selfish. I was the only one in the room who was an ex-dealer. All the people in the circle looked at me. When you had something to say, you had to sit in the chair that was in the middle of the circle and speak, so that's what I did.

"I want love!" the young white girl screamed as I sat in the chair.

I shook my head. "You might not have love, but at least you have money. A lot of us don't have either, and if you asked me to choose, I'd choose money over love any day."

"See, dealers are selfish too," the white man sitting directly across from me said. "All you all think about is money."

"It's a business. What else we supposed to think about? I never forced you to use drugs. I never put a gun to anybody's head and said, 'give me your money and take these drugs.' They came to me. When you're to the point where you could take your own child to a crack house and let a bunch of muthafuckas do whatever they want to her, you're dead. You don't have a soul. You don't have a spirit or a conscience either. You don't have shit. I've seen people go from having a whole lot of money to having none at all just because of drugs, and to someone like me who loves money, I don't understand it."

"You gave us drugs for free just to get us hooked," the white man said.

"I gave you drugs for free?" I said, pointing at myself and looking at him like he was crazy.

"Not you, but someone just like you."

"He wasn't just like me, because I ain't giving up shit for free."

"People like you sold to us. You didn't have to," the white man said.

"So, your drug habit is my fault? I don't think so. I was a drug dealer, but not for long. I stepped up my game and started trafficking, supplying to dealers so they could handle y'all fools so I wouldn't have to."

"Everyone I know gets high," the white teenage girl said. "When you go to parties and people are passing around weed and beer, that's one thing, but when they break out with the powdery shit, you have to decide real quick how bad do you want to fit in. I wanted to fit in real bad. Most of you are older than me, and I can't really express how it is these days. It's a lot of pressure to get good grades so you can go to the best college, pressure to dress the best and have a fly ride. Be the most popular. The prettiest. And still, even if you have all of that, you have to worry that some jealous bitch might shank you."

"Shank you? Little girl." I shook my head. "What you know about being shanked? Y'all kids love to play gangsta, but I wonder how many of y'all would make it in prison. I don't feel sorry for you. In fact, I don't feel sorry for none of y'all in here. I really don't."

"You don't know what it's like to be addicted," the black woman who let her daughter get raped said.

"My brother's on drugs. I know exactly what it's like," I said.

"That's different."

"No, it's not. And that goes right back to what I said in the beginning—a user is selfish. Y'all get so high you can't remember shit, so you not going through nothing. Your family is the one dealing with you running in the house, jumping out the second-story window because you think somebody's after you. You're stealing from us. You have your family worrying about you and afraid of you all at the same time. We—and I say we, as in drug dealers, because that's who I was—will always be out there waiting for you because you will always be out there looking for us."

I looked at several of the faces in the circle. Some had fallen into a daze. One woman was twisting her curly hair around her finger as she stared into space. The black lady was crying. I didn't want to be there, but since I was forced to come, I was going to tell the truth. Handle it if you can.

I noticed Mrs. Davis standing near the entrance door. I wasn't sure how long she'd been there, but just the fact that she was bothered me. I stared at her, wondering if I could put my plan into action. How did I really expect to get away with coming on to my parole officer? Why did I think she would risk her career to be with an ex-con? And besides, she's *Mrs.* Davis, which means she was married.

Don't get it twisted. This ain't gonna be no relationship, my mean voice said. *You're using her. You don't have feelings for her. You need to worry about Tower right now. You the one who got to get through this parole shit. And remember what Slim Earl said about women. All they really want is to be loved, to feel special, to feel needed. You can fake all that.*

I looked over at Mrs. Davis and forced my stern face to smile. She smiled back. Maybe I did have a chance. That's all life is anyway.

CHAPTER 9

While I was locked up, I couldn't worry about nobody. Nobody other than myself, but now that I was out, I was curious about some folks. I felt like catching up on the world. See how some of the people who I knew were doing—the ones whose obituaries weren't mailed to me by my mama while I was in prison. I saw Quentin Harris the other day, riding down East Berry in a black army-type vehicle. I was driving my brother's pickup. Wallace was in and out of rehab, and he wanted me to keep his truck while he tried to get himself together. I didn't think I'd see Quentin so soon. It brought back all those memories from the trial and how he and Arturo Watts got off while Stanley and I went to prison.

I stopped at the light and looked over to my right and there he was, talking on his cell phone with some rap music blasting. He didn't look over, but even if he had, he wouldn't have recognized me. I'm sure he thinks I'm still doing time. Quentin wasn't one of the people I wanted to see. Neither was Arturo. I wanted to see people like Gerald Moore, who grew up in the hood with me but wasn't a part of the street game. He didn't do any hustling. At least not drugs. Before I went in, he was bouncing around, in and out of jobs and relationships. Never had that much money in his pocket, but always had a good business idea in his head. He tried a handful of multilevel marketing businesses, Amway and others, but none of them materialized.

Mama said Gerald was married, had a couple kids, and was living in a two-story house in a new subdivision in Fort Worth complete with a media room. She knew because Gerald's Mama and mine belonged to the same church. Even though Mama stopped going to church when Dad did, a few years later she joined a new one. She still had Gerald's housewarming invitation from three years ago that Gerald's Mama had mailed her. It was stuffed in her letter drawer in the living room along with the letters I had written her over the years while I was in the pen. She handed me the invitation and I wrote down Gerald's address and phone number.

"Be sure to call him first. Let him know you're stopping by. It's not polite to go over unannounced." I understood what Mama was saying, but I was anxious to see Gerald again, and besides, I knew he'd be excited that I was finally out. My mama used to tell me in her letters that Gerald always asked about me. Even took down my information because he said he was going to write, but he never did. Not that I'm holding that against him. I know people get busy, and it gets hard to stop what they're doing to write a letter when they have work, family, bills, and all the other bullshit life throws at them to deal with. I was just happy he asked about me.

As I stood on Gerald's porch and rang the doorbell, I felt someone staring at me through the peephole. I could hear faint sounds, like people whispering, and then everything got quiet. No one came to the door, so I rung the bell one more time.

"Yes," a woman asked from behind the door.

"Is Gerald in?"

"Who are you?"

"Tower Evans. We grew up together."

There was silence for a few seconds then the woman said, "Wait a minute."

Gerald opened the door and came outside, closing the door behind him. He didn't bother inviting me in to see his new house. Instead, he stood on the porch with me.

"What's up, man?" Gerald asked. He seemed on edge.

"I can't complain. Just came by to see how you were doing."

"So when you get out? I'm surprised to see you. I heard you got a long sentence. Somebody said you got life."

I shook my head. "Stanley Holmes got life. I was in for ten, but it was supposed to be forty. I just got out less than a month ago."

"Hmm."

"So I hear you got married and had a couple kids. Congratulations," I said with a smile.

"Yep. I'm trying to do the family thing. I'm a lot different now than I was. I don't have time for no foolishness."

"Like those multilevel marketing schemes, huh?"

"Yeah, and other things," he said, eyeing me skeptically.

"They home?" I asked, hoping he'd introduce them.

"Who?"

"Your family."

"Nah, they're at the mall." I knew that was a lie because a woman asked me who I was from behind the door. Gerald started rubbing his arms. "I didn't realize it was this cold out. Hold on while I go in and get my jacket." He walked in the house and closed the door behind him. I heard the lock turn and that's when I knew I wasn't welcome.

When he returned, I said, "I just stopped by to say hey, but I didn't want nothing."

"Okay, well, it was good to see you. Take care of yourself."

"Yeah, you too." I turned and walked to the truck. In a way, I wasn't surprised. I guess if I wanted to feel more at home, I needed to visit some of my partners who were just like me—or the me I used to be.

It was Tuesday evening. I'd been home alone all day doing nothing except for loving the peace and quiet. No guard to wake me up. No worries about what was about to go down on the yard or in the chow hall. All I was doing was relaxing in my boxers and sweat socks, and then I heard tornado sirens wail through the air. Even with the heavy rain, high winds, and the sky's lightning show, I wasn't concerned about my own safety—just my family's. I remembered Bernice mentioning that she had something to do after work, but I couldn't remember what it was because as usual I wasn't listening to her. But I wished I had been.

I felt the windows rattle and the house shake, but that didn't bother me, not until all the electricity went off while I was warming up a steak Granny fixed the day before. I took it out of the microwave and ate it cold. It still tasted way better than what I'd been used to in the pen. I picked up the phone to dial my mama's number, but couldn't get a dial tone so I walked back to my bedroom and sat on the bed in total darkness. I heard a boom. It sounded like a cannonball exploding so I closed my eyes and went to sleep. I figured it would be all over whenever I decided to open my eyes again, which wasn't until the next morning around eight after the lights came back on.

"Bernice," I shouted as I walked into the hallway from my bedroom. "Bernice or Curtis, y'all here?" There was nothing but silence.

I turned on the TV and heard all the talk about the two twisters that hit downtown Fort Worth, killing at least three people with one missing and most likely dead, and another one hundred injured. Footage of uprooted trees, damaged homes, and dozens of abandon cars was shown. Fort Worth's mayor, Kenneth Barr, said that downtown was shut down until after the weekend for the cleanup of debris and falling glass coming from the tall buildings that were destroyed.

I walked into the kitchen and tried to use the phone again, but I still couldn't get a dial tone. That's why I needed a cell phone. I didn't like being stuck in the house with no way of calling out. Everybody had a cell phone, and that was what I was getting, even if I had to put it in my mama's name.

Wallace's truck had been acting up for the last few days, and the way the news described all the debris around the city, I wasn't about to try to drive. My head started pounding so I went to the den and sat in the recliner where I dozed off. When I woke up about two hours later and checked the phone, it was working, so I called my mama. Everyone but Wallace was accounted for. I told Mama not to worry about Wallace, unless the tornado touched down at Stop Six, a predominately black area in the hood, otherwise he was fine because lately that was his hangout, underneath the tree with the rest of the homeless. Stop Six got its name because it was the sixth stop on the old train line that went from Fort Worth to Dallas. The homes in that area were small and old—1940s with no air and one bathroom. My stepdad grew up on Ramey Street, which was in the Stop Six area. He talked about moving back one day. Supposedly, a few builders and some banks got together and were talking about building new homes with lots of amenities and large square footage. Who knew if any of this was going to ever happen? All I saw when I rode around Stop Six was what I'd seen before I went in—nothing special, nothing that would make me want to move there if I came into some money. I'd rather live in Rolling Hills, that way I could still be around black people and have a nicer home. I wasn't sure why I was thinking about a house, when I couldn't even get a cell phone in my name.

I was standing outside of Martin Lander's garage, circling his BMW 735 and studying it with amazement while he polished it. It had been so long since I'd seen a car that nice. Martin was part of my old crew, and from the looks of things, he was doing fine. I figured he could tell me about Lisa. Maybe, he'd seen her and knew how I could get in touch with her. We got past all the welcome backs and brotherly handshakes and started talking like old times. I was tempted to ask him why he didn't show up that day Quentin, Arturo, Stanley, and I rode to Kansas, but I didn't want him thinking I was holding on to any old grudges because I wasn't. The thought had crossed my mind that he may have set us up because it seemed like those troopers were sitting in the median waiting for us, but when you're a drug dealer, you're just paranoid by nature so I eventually dismissed those thoughts.

"You get caught in any of that shit last night?" he asked.

"The electricity and phone cut off, but that's about it. You?"

He shook his head. "So I heard you went in and got educated on a brother."

"Where you hear that from?"

"London. I was at the shop the other day getting edged up. He said you'd been in the other day. I was wondering when you were coming to see me. So, that's what you did when you went in, huh? You got educated on a brother."

I nodded. "Yep. Can you believe I earned my associate's degree when I couldn't stand school?"

"Fuck a book. You know what I'm sayin'. I'm out here clocking major dollars. Society ain't for black folks, no way, so we have to use it like it uses us. What's a degree gonna get me that hustlin' can't?"

"So you're still hustling drugs?"

Martin stood upright, resting his towel on the hood of his car. "What kind of questions you asking me, man? I said I was hustlin' but I ain't say it was drugs. That sounded like a question phrased for a tape. You wired?"

"Hell no I ain't wired."

"Well, I heard you got forty years, but now you out in ten, so that lead me to think you been talking. What's up?"

"Ain't nothin' up. I came over here to shoot the breeze and see if you knew how I could find Lisa."

"Nope. I know where Quentin is though."

"I saw Quentin the other day driving some funny-looking big-ass truck."

"You talkin' 'bout his Hummer?" I shrugged. "You must be. Shit, it may be funny looking, but you talking a hundred G's right there."

I shrugged again. "Where's Arturo? You seen him?"

"I heard Arturo disappeared right after the trial. Stanley's people had it out for his ass. Shit, I would too. Stanley sitting in the pen serving Arturo's time." He shrugged. "Shit, I guess that's life. Better him than me."

"And you ain't heard nothin' about Lisa?"

"Nope. I don't think I've seen her since '90 or '91." Martin started wiping his car off again, but his hand went into slow motion as he eyed a black Suburban with custom wheels and tinted windows that pulled in front of his house.

"Damn that truck is sweet," I said, watching the Suburban. I thought back on the days when I was rolling in fancy cars with pretty women and lots of cash in my pocket. "You know them?"

"Hell nah," Martin said. "Nigga, I knew you set me up!"

"Me? What you talking about?" My eyes widened when I saw the truck speed on the grass. The back doors opened and an armed task force jumped out. I felt like my life was traveling in slow motion. I dropped when I heard an officer shout, "Everybody down on the ground." I stayed there lying motionless. I felt a heavy sole press against my back. I turned my head slightly and saw a machine gun pointing toward my head as my cheek rested against the cold concrete. I closed my eyes, allowing my mind to travel back to August 1989 when I was pulled over by the highway patrol. I opened my eyes as the task force stormed Martin's house with their guns drawn. My heart was beating rapidly. Before I'd let them cuff me again, they could pull the trigger and end it.

After several minutes, the heaviness disappeared from my back but not my mind.

"You can get up," one of the officers said to me while they were cuffing Martin. "We observed you as you were walking up. You're free to go."

I looked at the man without saying a word. Then I looked at Martin as he nodded and eyed me with contempt. "I ain't have nothing to do with it," I said to Martin. I walked backward down the driveway and across the street toward my mama's house, refusing to turn away from the guns. Several black uniforms with masks covering their faces walked out of Martin's house with three men and two women in handcuffs. All I could think about was if I had come by twenty, even thirty minutes earlier. . .if I had gone inside just to kick it for a few, I would've been like Stanley Holmes who was serving life for hanging with the wrong people at the wrong time.

"Damn!" I shouted after I was out of the sight of the uniforms. I stood paralyzed in my parents' neighbor's yard. "That could've been it right there. I haven't even been home a full thirty days. I don't know if I can make it out here."

Oh, you can make it, my mean voice said. *You gonna make it 'cause I ain't going back in. So do what I said to do with that Mrs. Davis bitch in* heels so you can get some special privileges. Otherwise, maybe we won't make it.

You'll make it, Tower, my nice voice said. *It's okay. Don't start using folks, especially someone like your parole officer. I can see that backfiring. Leave that one alone.*

Don't listen to his weak ass. Nobody promised you a free ride, just freedom. You got fifteen years on parole. Fifteen years and the slightest thing could send you back in. Now, do you understand why you need Mrs. Davis?

It was the first Saturday of a new month. The temperature was well into the eighties. I was over my parents' house fixing their fence, which had been hanging off the hinge. Dad could have fixed it, but he'd been under the weather the last few days. Mama said that the heart medication he was on was starting to wear him down. I went inside to have a glass of sweet iced tea after Constance dropped by to shoot the breeze.

"I settled," Constance said as she sat in the living room and stared at the television screen, which was tuned to *Oprah*. Oprah and some other man who claimed to be a psychiatrist were talking about marital problems. "That's my problem, too, Dr. Phil. I settled, and now I got two kids by some fool I can't stand to look at. What can you tell me about a man who comes home at three o'clock in the morning and the first thing he does is jump in the shower? What does that mean, Dr. Phil?"

"He's stupid," I said, "because when I was out cheating, at least I had enough sense to shower before I went home."

Constance ignored me. She kept watching TV, listening to all of the couple's complaints. "At least I'm not the only person who's miserable."

I looked over at my glass of iced tea resting on a coaster.

Tea? What you drinking that for? I want a beer and a blunt, my mean voice said. *What you know about tea? Who you trying to be, Mr. Rogers? What you gonna do next, break out with your sweater. It's time for this nice-guy game to end. Tell that stepsister of yours that hell yes her common-law husband is cheating, and Oprah and Dr. Phil can't help her ass.*

"Why do you watch that?" I asked.

"I love watching *Oprah*. Didn't you watch her show while you were inside?"

"All I mainly watched on TV was the news." I heard the doorbell ring.

"It's open," Granny Pearl yelled from the kitchen. Granny walked to the front door to answer when no one walked in.

"Do you know Theodore Evans, ma'am?" I heard a male voice ask. I wondered who it was. Who would call me Theodore? Not even Mrs. Davis called me that anymore.

"Who wants to know?" Granny Pearl asked.

"Ma'am, we're with the Fort Worth police department. Is it alright if we step in?"

I stood, but didn't move.

"No, it ain't alright. What do you want with him?"

"Ma'am, we know he's inside. It would be much easier on everyone if you let us come in."

"Tower, do you know these men?" Granny Pearl asked.

I heard the screen door open and watched as two black men in uniforms stood in front of me. "Mr. Evans. Theodore Evans, is that correct?" I nodded. "We need to take you down to the station for some questioning."

"What kind of questioning?" I asked. "I don't know nothing."

"I'm going to have to ask that you come with us, Mr. Evans. We're also going to have to handcuff you."

"You better tell me what I did first! What I do? Huh! What?" One of the officers took his cuffs from his side and opened them. The other officer had his hand on his gun. "Nah, what I do? I ain't do nothin'. Granny, I ain't do nothin'. I swear. I just went over Martin's house to visit. That's all. The cops didn't arrest me then so what y'all want with me now?"

"What y'all want with him?" Granny yelled.

My mama walked into the living room and screamed. "No. You get away from him," she said as she pushed the officer who was trying to cuff me. The other officer held her back, and the next thing I knew my wrists felt steel again.

"What's all this noise about?" Dad asked as he walked downstairs with his robe on. "What's wrong, son? What y'all fellas need?"

"We need to talk to Mr. Evans down at the station."

"What is this about?" I asked. "I don't have no reason to come down to the station with you."

"Mr. Evans, please. You know exactly what this is about."

"No, I don't. All I did was stop by Martin's house. How the hell was I supposed to know he was under surveillance? I didn't know he was into anything."

"Sir, what is today?"

"Saturday."

"The date, sir."

"April first."

"April Fool's," the officer who handcuffed me said as he unlocked the cuffs. I balled my fist and swung at him, but Constance firmly grabbed my wrist.

"Tower, he ain't worth an assault charge," Constance said.

That's when Tommy walked into the house with a big grin covering his face. He came over to the officers and slapped their hands.

"I got you good, didn't I?" Tommy asked me.

"This was a damn joke? You thought that shit was funny?" I asked.

"What's your badge number?" Constance yelled. "I'm gonna make sure you both get fired. You can't come in here harassing people like that."

"It was a joke," one officer said. "Tommy said everyone was going to get a big kick out of it."

"I served my time. Ain't shit funny about thinking I'm going back," I said.

"You were in prison?" one of the officers asked with a shocked look.

"Yes, he was!" Constance yelled. "So why would he get a kick out of it? What's your damn badge number? I'm not playing with you. I'll get this shit on the five o'clock news."

"You did that to Tower, Tommy?" Dad asked. "This was your idea?"

"Damn, it's April Fool's. I've always been a prankster. All y'all know that."

"My son ain't never do nothin' to you!" Mama yelled. "Why do you hate him so? He ain't never bothered you. Why can't you just leave him alone?" she screamed. Then started crying. "I can't go through this again," she said to Dad.

Dad shook his head. "Get out!" he said to Tommy, pointing at the front door. "Get out my damn house and don't ever come back."

"I'm really sorry," one of the officers said. "We had no idea. If we had known—"

My nephew, Curtis, ran in with a small camera and snapped a picture of the officers and ran out the room. "We don't need your damn badge numbers now!" Constance said.

"Man, this is so fucked up," one of the officers said to Tommy as they walked out of the house. "If we get in trouble for this shit—"

"Dad, it was a joke," Tommy said.

Dad stood there, refusing to look at him. "Get out my damn house! You ain't my son no more."

"But Dad, damn! Why's everybody taking this so seriously?"

"Get out, Tommy!" Constance yelled. "You're stupid, and don't nobody in here want to see your sorry ass. Go!"

I didn't notice Granny when she walked out of the living room, but I saw her come back in with Dad's shotgun. "Granny, put the gun down," I said. Curtis was pointing at Tommy and laughing. "Curtis, nothing's funny right now."

I pushed Mama out into the hallway. Dad walked up the stairs without doing or saying anything, almost like he wanted Granny to pull the trigger.

"Go on and pull the trigger, you wrinkled-up bitch," Tommy said.

As soon as I heard Tommy say that about my granny, I punched him, and he fell to the floor. But that punch may have saved his life because in that instant Granny had pulled the trigger and hit the vase sitting on the mantel instead of Tommy's head.

Tommy got up and hurried out the door without saying a word.

I sat on the sofa and took my glass of iced tea from the table and started gulping it.

"Tower, I'm sorry my brother did that stupid shit," Constance said.

I kept gulping the tea as I focused straight ahead at the TV screen.

"He can't come back in this house. If he even tries, I'll shoot him," my granny said. "I will. I'll shoot him, and I won't miss next time."

"April Fool's. He thought that was a joke," I said. Curtis walked back into the living room and sat beside me. I watched him out the corner of my eye just shaking his head. He kept doing it so finally I turned and looked at him. He had a deep frown set into his face.

"What's wrong, little fella?"

"You know what, Uncle Tower? That was just wrong." I smiled because that was the first time he called me Uncle.

"What was, little fella?"

"What Tommy did. That was just wrong. And you know what, Uncle Tower?"

"What?"

"God don't like ugly. Tommy gonna get his because, Uncle Tower, that was just wrong." Curtis was sitting there mad like it happened to him.

"Well, maybe I'm just reaping whatever it is I sowed."

"Nah, Uncle Tower. You spent your time. You've already done that. Nah, you reaped everything. That was just wrong. Wrong. Wrong. Wrong. And he gonna get his. Ooh, he gonna get his good. Might not be today. Might not be tomorrow. Might not even be next month or this year, but sooner or later, he'll get his. And I want to be there to see it. I want to be there so I can laugh in his face like he was laughing in yours." Curtis started laughing so hard he had to put his hand over his stomach. "That's how I'm going to be laughing, Uncle Tower. I'm going to be laughing and pointing like he was doing to you."

"Yeah, little man, that was wrong."

"It was, Uncle Tower."

"But don't wish anything on him."

"Even if I don't wish anything on him, Uncle Tower, he's still gonna get his."

I couldn't help but smile. My nephew was actually talking to me. Usually, he was running away.

CHAPTER 10

Allied said to expect a letter in the mail, pass or fail. I tried not to think about the job, but I needed to work so I could meet the parole requirements. Mrs. Davis had already stopped by three times the week before when I was still tripping off what Tommy did so I didn't feel like looking for nothing. Only good thing—I guess I shouldn't say it was good—was Tommy had already started to get his back. He totaled his car the day after he pulled his little prank, and since he was late on paying his insurance premium they denied coverage. Of course, he wasn't going to tell any of us that. Sheila told my mama. She also told Mama that she was tired of his mess and wasn't even going to wait until she got up enough money to file for a divorce, that she was going to take the kids and leave because they could do better by themselves. So I no longer had to figure out how I was going to get him back since his was already coming 'round quickly.

I couldn't tell Mrs. Davis that I was too depressed to start looking for work so I lied and said I had. Made up places to tell her I'd gone and filled out applications. She'd already come by a few times that week. She was calling all hours of the day and night. I could tell she was going to go straight by the book as if the last ten years of my life weren't hard enough with all the rules. I still had a copy of the forty-five page offender orientation manual detailing all the prison's do's and don'ts:

Shoes may not be placed on the bed in any manner.

You may not remove blankets or sheets from any bed unless an officer tells you to do so.

Your bed must be made and cell cleaned daily. No exceptions. This needs to be done during free time only.

Sleeping nude will not be allowed.

Do not yell through the doors or other quads.

Do not pass notes or letters to other inmates.

Remember all exercise time over five hours a week is a privilege and not a right.

No visiting in another inmate's cell at any time.

Rules were made to be broken, and most of those were, but for once, I wanted to live without any rules or any kind of schedule and just live like a normal person, but in order for me to do that, I was going to have to put my plan for Mrs. Davis into action.

I was sitting in my bed cradling my legs, refusing to let any tears show. I was too hard to cry, or at least that was the lie I told myself. The doorbell rung at exactly 10:00 A.M., and the only person I thought it would be was Mrs. Davis so I screamed out of frustration. "This bitch about to drive me crazy." I shook my head. "No she's not, because I'm not going to let her."

I ran down the stairs to open the front door as I pulled my undershirt over my chest. I saw Mrs. Davis' smug face peering at me through the glass.

"Good morning," I said as I opened the door.

She stepped through without a response. "How come you're not out looking for work?"

"I'm going to start looking, but I'm waiting to hear back from Allied."

"In the meantime, you need to find something so I can update your records."

"Mrs. Davis, why you so mean?"

"Mean? No one's ever asked me that before. I'm not mean. I'm just strict."

"They call you a bitch in heels."

"Oh well, I'm not here to make friends so I really don't care what they call me."

"But you don't need no enemies, Mrs. Davis. Especially ones with records."

"I was reviewing your file," she said, ignoring me.

"Would you like to sit down?"

While she sat on the sofa in the living room, I was standing on the far side with my hands buried deep in my jeans pocket. "As I was saying, I had a chance to thoroughly review your file, and I'm encouraged by your background. You held down several good jobs in the past. You were with UPS for several years. It wasn't like you were just some thug out there."

"You want something to drink?" I asked.

"No, I'm not staying long. I just wanted to make sure you were taking care of business. Have you noticed that I've eased up on you a little?"

"You have?"

"Tower, I'm hard on my cases for their own good. I know how easy it is to slip back into your same old habits. I've seen that happen time and time again. Before long, some of my cases are back behind bars. I hope you'll be different."

"I'm not a case. I'm a person, Mrs. Davis. But don't worry, I'm not going back in. I'll die first."

"That's what they all say."

"But I mean it."

"Well, at least I can boast of having the highest percentage of success stories in my office. It's usually between me and Mr. Wilks, but he's way too lenient and that doesn't help someone who's just getting out." She crossed her legs and rested her right hand on her thigh. "You need structure and routine right now because that's what you're used to. What are you going to do today?"

"Probably work on my truck."

"You were supposed to say look for a job." She ran her eyes freely up and down my body. "So that's your truck in the driveway?" The tone of her voice changed. It was no longer stern and uptight.

"My brother's but I'm sorta borrowing it from him right now."

"Good, at least you have transportation," she said with a smile. "But do you have your license?"

"You should smile more often," I said. "It makes you look like a real person. Yes, I have my license. I got that my first week back."

"I don't want you to take this the wrong way," Mrs. Davis said, "but last night I had a dream about you."

"What kind of dream?"

"Are we alone?"

"Yes. What kind of dream did you have?"

"If I was a man, it would have been a wet one."

"A woman can have wet dreams too," I said.

"Tower, come here," she said, wiggling her finger, signaling for me. "How long will we be alone?"

I walked toward her. "It's gonna be awhile."

She licked her lips. "Good. Maybe I can make my wet dream come true. I want to feel your biggest muscle inside me." I stood in front of her and looked down at her hands as they opened my belt buckle.

Mrs. Davis is a freak. Tell her to take her hair down. Better yet, you take it down.

I put my hands in her bun and started pulling out hairpins. I stopped after I took out a few because I wasn't sure if she had one of those removable buns on her head like Constance wore sometime.

"You want my hair down, baby? Take it down," she said. She finished pulling out the hairpins and shook her thick, black hair loose until it fell past her shoulders. She was between forty-five and fifty, but I bet she used to be hot in her day. She took off her navy blue blazer and removed her gun holster from her waist, placing it on the coffee table, and then she unbuttoned her blouse to expose her pink lacy bra and her large breasts popping out of it. She pulled me down to the floor by my hand, and took that same hand to rub over her chest. "I've never had a relationship with any of my cases before, but I will admit that I've taken on more of an interest in your case than usual, and maybe I stop by more than I should for a reason. Now, do you understand the reason?"

"If we messed around, wouldn't that be a violation of my parole? And I need to know what I would get out of the deal."

"Sex. Don't you miss being with a woman?"

"I shrugged. "What else besides sex? I've gone this long without it. I can go a little longer."

"Tower, let's just take it one day at a time. I'm assigned to your case for another four months, but I know of ways to get that extended," she said as she stroked the right side of my cheek. "It would be a lot easier for both of us if I were always the one you reported to, don't you think?"

"I don't know, Mrs. Davis. Aren't you married?"

"Yes. And?"

"I don't like messing around with another man's stuff."

"My husband and I don't even sleep in the same bed. I want you to eat my pussy."

"Does your husband eat your pussy?"

"My husband doesn't even look at my pussy, let alone eat it. I already told you we don't sleep together. You're still not listening," she said as she tapped her finger on my eardrum. She pulled her skirt up and her panties down. Then she used her hands to bring my face between her legs. "Do it. Eat me," she said, moaning.

Go 'head. Pussy was all you thought about while you were in prison. Go on and do it, my mean voice said.

Tower, don't. This is a bad move. I know you look at Mrs. Davis and think she might be like Mrs. Lang, the prison librarian, but she's not. I got a bad feeling about this one, my nice voice said.

He got a bad feeling about everyone. Do it!

"Oh," Mrs. Davis moaned as I wiggled my tongue inside of her. "Oh, my cat loves you. You may be a bad listener, but ooh baby, you're a real good eater. Baby, if you keep this up, you won't have to worry about anything. Not a curfew. Not another NA meeting. Nothing." She lifted my head. "Do you hear me, Tower?" I nodded as I wiped her juice from around my mouth. "Good. I can be real good to you, baby. As long as you don't fuck up," she said through gritted teeth.

Did you see how she said that, Tower? my nice voice asked. *I told you something was wrong with her.*

"You're mine now, baby. Do you understand me?" she asked. I nodded. "Good. Now you can go back to doing what you were doing." She put my head back down. "I'm going to take care of you, baby," she said as she rubbed her hands over my head. "You'll see. I'm going to be real good to you."

"Get up!" Bernice shouted as she walked into the den and found me asleep on the rundown recliner with the television tuned to *Judge Joe Brown*. "What did you do all day?" Bernice stood over me, flipping through the mail.

"I did a lot," I mumbled.

"Like what?"

"I rested."

"Here's something from Allied Manufacturing. Weren't you expecting to hear from them?" She tossed the letter in my lap. "Maybe it's a job. You need something other than $110 worth of food stamps, which has long run out. Did the DOC give you any more?"

"No." I wiped the sleep from my eyes and focused on the envelope as I tore it open, reading the letter carefully.

"Well what's it say?"

"Well," I said, sighing, "I passed the test, and they have my application on file for up to a year if an opening should ever become available, but I may be contacted before that time." I crumbled up the letter and threw it on the floor.

"Tower, what's wrong with you? What did you do that for? Don't you care about your life? I'm tired of baby-sitting you. All my life I've had to baby-sit you. But what good did it do?"

"What are you talking about? I don't need a baby-sitter. I'm a grown-ass man."

"Then act like one. That was good news. You passed the test."

"But I didn't get the job."

"Did they say that, Tower? No, they didn't. That's your damn problem now. You want everything so quick. Be patient. We'll talk about this later." Bernice walked out of the den. I picked up the letter and started to read it again, nodding in agreement. This was a start in the right direction. At least I didn't flunk. I'd just wait and see. In the meantime, I'd ask Dad about the job he was talking about getting me at the tire shop his friend owned. I thought back on earlier. Mrs. Davis left with a smile on her face. I could tell the rest of her day was going to be a good one, which hopefully would make the rest of mine good, too, and all my days to come.

I picked up the TV's remote control off the floor and turned to the evening news. A lot of crazy shit was happening. A white man in Austin, Texas, went over his mother-in-law's house and killed his mother-in-law, sister-in-law, his two small children, and shot his wife who survived, but was in critical condition. Home invasions were on the rise; the reporter cited three recent cases. A young girl was abducted on her way from school in Grand Prairie, and she'd been missing for eight days. The only ray of hope was a special report on the Dallas Community Youth Development program, formerly known as Project 75217. It was something the Seventy-Fourth Texas Legislature came up with in 1995 to provide funding to assist community projects that were working on alleviating family and community conditions, which lead to juvenile crime through prevention. But right after that, there was some breaking news of arson in Oak Cliff. I turned the television off because I didn't feel like hearing any more.

CHAPTER 11

It was the twenty-third of the month, which was Easter Sunday, and I only had between the twentieth and the twenty-seventh of each month to report to my parole office. You would've thought since I was messing around with Mrs. Davis that she'd give me some slack by not making me show up at all, but instead she got tougher with me. I asked her if I could stop wearing an ankle monitor, and she yelled, "Why? What bitch are you trying to go see? That monitor is for your own good." She meant to say for her own good so she could know my whereabouts. I had to stay focused and remember my goal—to get off paper so I wouldn't have to report to an office or a parole officer again.

———

The family was having Easter dinner over my brother George's house. Granny said, the last time they went over George's for the holiday, Monique called herself frying a turkey and almost burned the house down. "She tries too damn hard," Granny said. "So afraid he's going to leave her. I tell you what, if she don't get her ass back to work soon, he just might. Three years is a hell of a long maternity leave."

For some reason my family didn't really care for Monique. They said she didn't come around them enough and tried to be someone she wasn't. Not to mention she got along with my aunt Cora too well for my dad to understand.

"Hi, Tower, I'm so glad you could come," Monique said, standing to the side of the door to allow me to enter. Something was different about Monique but I didn't know what it was. Maybe she'd lost weight, I thought to myself.

"Whose Mercedes is that in the driveway?" I asked.

"Aunt Cora's."

My eyes enlarged. "She's here."

"She's in the living room talking to your mother."

I took a deep breath and walked inside, following Monique. It dawned on me what had changed about her. Her breasts were gone. She used to have the biggest set I'd ever seen and they were gone. She looked like a completely different person without them. I still remember when she'd complain about her back hurting all the time from carrying those things around. She'd always threaten George she was getting them reduced. I say threaten because he was a chest man for sure. I tried to pass the living room and go straight into the kitchen but Dad called me. "There go my boy now. Tower, we were just in here talking about you. I was telling your aunt and uncle about all the skills you learned that could qualify you to work on any construction site." I closed my eyes because I was embarrassed about where I'd learned them. "Tell 'em, son. Come on in here."

I dragged myself in to the living room and got up enough courage to smile while I looked Aunt Cora and her husband, Gordon, in their eyes. They were both dressed in cream-colored suits. If I didn't know Aunt Cora's age, I'd think she was in her early thirties. But that's what money does for some folks. Her husband smiled back, and so did Aunt Cora, showing her pearly whites, but she quickly broke the stare by looking across the room at my nephew, Curtis.

"Curtis, you're getting a little taller, aren't you? Come over here and give your great-aunt a hug and a kiss."

"Let Tower give you one," Curtis snapped.

"Tower's grown. I don't want one from him. I want it from you."

"Robin?" I interrupted, looking over at the young teenage girl sitting beside my aunt. "Do you remember me?"

"No," she said with her nose turned up as she took her hand and moved her long, straight hair to one side.

She must have got all that hair from her daddy's side because she sure didn't get it from your aunt Cora—baldheaded bitch, my mean voice said.

"Of course she doesn't remember you, Tower. She was only six when you went in," Aunt Cora said.

"Hell, I remember a whole bunch of things from when I was six," Dad said. "And I'm almost seventy now. You don't remember your cousin, Tower?"

"No," Robin said, still turning up her nose.

"What you turning up your nose for? You got them same bad habits like your mama. You better get out of that now or you ain't never gonna have no friends."

"Honey," Aunt Cora said, looking at Robin, "I want you to listen to your uncle because he is teaching you one thing, which is the incorrect way to speak."

Dad looked over at me in disbelief and then refocused on Cora. "What did you just tell that girl?"

"You heard what I said. I hate all that ghetto talk."

"Ghetto talk. If this wasn't Easter, and if I wasn't hungry, I might have to rebut."

"You've learned a new word," Aunt Cora said, clapping. "I'm so proud of you."

Her daughter snickered.

"Ain't nobody thinking about your bourghetto ass," Dad said. "Now that's a new word. Do you want me to spell it? B-o-u-r-g-h-e-t-t-o ass."

"Mama," Aunt Cora said to Granny, "I know you're not going to allow him to use profanity in front of my daughter."

"I'm sure she's heard it before. Used some too. I'm sure she's exposed to a lot more than you know. Sixteen years old and driving a Corvette to school. What's the girl got to look forward to when she's grown? You should've bought her a Honda Civic or something like that. A Corvette? Now, you know that didn't make no sense at all. You need to take it back."

Robin turned up her nose. "I'm not driving a Civic, Mom."

"Baby, no one said you were. That's just your grandmother talking."

"Yes, baby, I'm your grandmother," Granny said as she pointed at her chest. "In case you didn't know. Since you don't never come to see me. But I realize Plano is rather far, especially when you *have* transportation."

"That went over your head, didn't it," Dad said to Robin.

"I'ma help this child in the kitchen, 'cause I know she need some," Granny said, talking about Monique who was banging pans.

"Tell the truth why you leaving," Dad said. " 'Cause the girl getting on your nerves. Both of 'em. Big Cora and Little Cora." Dad turned his nose up at Robin who grabbed her cell phone from her purse and walked out of the room.

"She got a cell phone too?" Dad asked.

"Yes, she does," Cora said.

She got a cell phone? my mean voice asked. *Must be nice, Tower. You had to beg your mama to put one in her name, and your ass is almost forty years old.*

"I don't even have a cell phone," Dad said. "You're spoiling her." Dad looked over at Cora's husband. "Do you have any say in how your house is run?" Dad asked Gordon.

"I just pay the bills and keep my mouth shut," Gordon said.

"Well, she got the right one, then," Dad said.

At the dinner table, Monique announced that she started working at Verizon in Irving. Dad started clapping. "How did you get on there?" Dad asked.

"Cora."

"Cora?" Dad asked in shock.

"Yes. Verizon is one of my key contacts so I made a few calls. It's temporary right now, but after ninety days if they like her, they'll hire her," Cora said.

"So you can actually help folks, still not your blood, but you're getting closer. Tower needs a job."

I looked away from Aunt Cora because I didn't want to see her eyes roll.

Aunt Cora cleared her throat. "Well, it's difficult to get Tower a job considering his background. Most of my clients don't want—"

"This food is really good, Monique," I said, cutting off Aunt Cora. "Real good."

"Thank you, Tower."

"I see you perfected the fried turkey. It's excellent," I said.

She laughed. "I can't lie."

"Yes, you can," George said. "I've caught you in a few."

"Shut up, baby," she said, smacking the side of his arm. "I can't lie. My girlfriend Lanita made it. She made the sweet potato pie and the strawberry cake too."

"Well, hell, what did you make?" Granny asked. "I didn't know I was being invited to a manufactured dinner. We eating in but still eating out. I should've known it tasted a little too good for you to have done it."

Monique frowned. "But Granny, I made the side dishes."

Granny rolled her eyes. "And I can tell."

"What about the construction company?" Dad asked Gordon, getting back to the subject of Aunt Cora getting me a job.

Gordon looked over at Aunt Cora.

"We don't have any positions available at the construction company right now," Aunt Cora said.

"Well, if you ever do, will you let us know?" Dad asked.

"We can do that," Gordon said.

I didn't look away in time because I caught Aunt Cora rolling her eyes.

"Good, because just like blessings are placed on you, they can be taken from you. God don't like ugly."

"Look who's talking about what God doesn't like. Mr. Texas Lotto and Powerball himself. I don't think God cares for gambling either."

"That can't be true because you were a gamble, and he still brought you into the world," Dad said.

"I'm tired of arguing with you."

" 'Cause you can't win, that's why," Dad said.

CHAPTER 12

On Wednesday, I took the T bus service to the parole office because Wallace had sold his truck to the dope man. He came by Bernice's around 3:30 one morning. I looked out the window after I heard the engine start and saw his truck rip out the driveway. First, I thought someone had stolen it, and I felt bad since Wallace had only given me the truck to use. My brother George was the one who told me that Wallace had sold it to Blue, a petty street hustler, for twenty dollars worth of crack. I would have given Wallace at least a hundred dollars for the truck. Now I had to take a bus just to sit up in Mrs. Davis' face and listen to her ask me those same questions: "Have you started working yet? Is your address still the same?" As if she didn't already know the answers when we talked every night. She even gave me a urine analysis. I walked out of her office mad because things weren't going as planned. I was standing at the bus stop smoking a Black & Mild, wondering how I could turn this around. As usual my mind started plotting. How could I take my plan with Mrs. Davis, whom I was calling Mary, up a notch so I could get off paper and never have to deal with her or any other parole officer again?

Tower, you never should have started fooling around with that woman. I tried to tell you. I do believe your whole plan is about to backfire, my nice voice said.

Don't listen to him. He never wants to do shit. What would've happened to your ass in the pen if you would've listened to him? I'll tell you what would've happened—you wouldn't have made it out. I'll figure something out. I always do.

I threw my skinny cigar to the ground and stomped on it. A black woman pulled up to the bus stop in a silver BMW Z3. "You want a ride?" she asked. I recognized her from the parole office.

"That's cool." I didn't waste time opening her door and getting in.

"Where to?"

"Can you drop me on Ryan off East Berry?"

That's where my boy Scottie Fields lived. Before I went in, he was a young kid fresh out of high school with no plans for a future. He used to hang out at the Berry Street Car Wash, and he'd hand wash my car so I wouldn't have to. I liked the way he hustled, and I knew if he had a chance to rise up, like I did, he'd probably make something of himself, so right before my trial started I gave him enough cocaine to help him run the streets for a little while and the number to my contact who could arrange to get him more drugs if he ever needed any. And he did. I heard through the grapevine that he was large. Controlled Dallas and Fort Worth. Back when I was dealing something like that wasn't even possible. Hopefully, he wasn't under surveillance like Martin who was facing hard time in the federal pen. The word on the street is that the Feds had been watching Martin and his crew for seven years and gathering enough evidence to keep them behind bars for life.

I didn't ask the lady her name. What I really wanted to know was what she had done to end up on parole. She wore expensive clothes. Even the weave in her head looked pricey. She looked like a model, too delicate to break the law, but like the old saying goes, looks can be deceiving.

"Who's your PO, Mrs. Davis?" she asked. I nodded. "Mmm. I guess you fucking her, huh?"

"Why you say that?" I asked, twisting my face.

She smirked. " 'Cause she loves 'em coming straight out the pen. Someone she can control. You did just get out, right?" I nodded. "I knew it. You don't have to admit nothing to me, but I already know because when I saw her come up front and call your name, I knew if she wasn't doing you then, she was gonna be. Did she tell you that same lie about not having sex in years?"

"I don't know what you're talking about." For all I knew, this woman could be from the D.O.C. trying to set me up, so I didn't say one word.

"I understand, but just let me tell you this. You don't get any special privileges with Mrs. Davis. She's psycho. For one thing, she's in a bad marriage. Her husband spends all his time and money at the strip clubs."

"How do you know so much?" I asked.

"Because I know two of the men she's been with. All she's gonna give you is a headache, and to prove my point: The two men that I knew for a fact she was messing around with, guess where they are now?" I shrugged. "Back in the pen for parole violations. She's very possessive. So I just thought I'd warn you because somebody needs to. Besides, she got my man locked back up, and I can't stand her ass for that."

I felt sick to my stomach. I didn't feel like going over Scottie's so instead I had her take me home.

"Tower," Mary whispered over the phone, "I want to see you, baby. Where can we meet?"

"I don't feel good tonight, baby. Maybe tomorrow."

"I want to see you tonight!" she said forcefully. "This is my show, and I'm running it. When I say I want to see you, I want to see you. I'll have your ass on an eight o'clock curfew if you fuck with me."

"Why are you doing me like this? I thought you said you cared," I said.

"I do, which is why I want to see you right now so I can show you."

"It's supposed to storm tonight."

"It's supposed to what? Don't give me that bullshit! You have more excuses than a child. What's the problem? You must have that bitch over there."

"Who are you talking about this time, Mary?"

"Wanda Little. The one who dropped you over your sister's house the other day. I ran her plates. That car is registered to a seventy-five-year-old woman. What does a seventy-five-year-old woman need with a BMW Z3? I bet you it's some kind of identity fraud. I'm having the finance company look into it."

"You mean you've been riding around this house running the license plates of cars in my sister's driveway?" I asked.

"Yeah, that's right I have, and I have every right to. You're under my control. Do you understand me?"

"I don't know about you. I don't like the way you're acting."

"Well, get used to it because I don't like you seeing other women, and don't think I didn't find out that she's on parole. I know everything about that bitch. I know where she lives. She has a shoplifting rap sheet a mile long. She's nothing more than a booster so why do you want her when you can have me?"

"All she did was take me home from the parole office. Who said I wanted her?"

"Don't you know the rules? Ex-cons aren't supposed to associate with each other."

"She was just giving me a ride."

"What happened to your brother's truck?"

"I don't have it anymore. I told you that he sold it."

"No, you didn't. If you would've, I would have remembered because I remember everything you say. You need to hurry up and get your own transportation."

"With what money?"

"It doesn't have to be a brand-new car."

"I'm working on it."

"And this living with your sister isn't working either. You need your own place. My friend LaVonne has a house for rent. I'll ask her how much she wants for it and see if she can give you a good deal. You need me, Tower. Can't you see that? What's wrong with you? I could help you so much, if you would just act right."

I heard the cracking of thunder. "It's about to come down."

She took a deep breath. "Alright. We'll see each other tomorrow.

I won't go in to work," she said. "Be here by nine."

"Be where by nine—your house? How am I going to get there?"

"The same way you get to the parole office—the bus. Oh, but that's not how you've been getting to the parole office, is it? I'll see you at nine tomorrow morning. And be on time."

She is a little off, you know, my mean voice said.

I told you, but no, nobody ever wants to listen to me, and I'm the only one who makes some sense around here. That woman is bad news that will only get worse. You have to pull away, my nice voice responded.

Nah, you don't have to pull away. You just have to play it smart. She's possessive, but she's also the type who would do for you. She's already talking about hooking you up with her friend's house. Pretty soon, she'll be buying you shit. That's the kind of woman you need. Just like Slim Earl said, my mean voice said.

No, you don't, Tower. You need to stand on your own two feet. Users don't last long. Don't take from her. It's just like making a deal with the devil—can't nothing good come from that, my nice voice said.

Shut up, you sound like a whining bitch, my mean voice said.

I was at Mary's house when she told me to be. In fact, I was twenty minutes early because I knew how much of a bitch she would be if I was even one minute late. When I walked into her house, the first thing I said was, "I'm starving. Can you make me some pancakes?" She told me that I hadn't done anything to work up an appetite, but what she was talking about would make me lose the one I did have.

She led me to her bedroom and over to her king-size bed. She claimed that her husband slept in another room, but I knew if I opened the closet or looked through the dresser drawers I'd see his clothes inside. Didn't matter. Wasn't like this was a real relationship. I was doing what I felt I had to do. We both came out of our clothes quickly, and I came even quicker so I could get it over with. It would be one thing if I enjoyed the times we spent together and the sex we had, but I never did. Never could enjoy things that I had to sneak around for because I always felt like, eventually I'd get caught.

"You don't feel bad about cheating on your husband?"

"Not at all." She started kissing my bare chest.

"Why not?"

"Because I don't. My husband is sorry. He had a child outside of our marriage with a stripper of all things, and I'm not sure I can forgive him for that." So I guess Wanda with the BMW wasn't lying, at least not about Mary's husband, but hopefully about all the other things.

"Then why don't you leave him?"

"Why should I? I'll have more fun turning his life into hell. Besides, our house is practically paid for, and I have two boys who need to be raised with both parents. I'll just have to sacrifice my happiness for now. Fortunately, it's not that hard since I have you."

"Have I earned my appetite yet? Can you fix me breakfast now?"

"Yes, you have," she said with a smile as she walked out of the bedroom butt naked.

Tell that bitch to put on some clothes, my mean voice said. *Tell her she ain't no* Playboy *centerfold or no* Penthouse *pin-up.*

"Pancakes and bacon—turkey bacon. I don't eat pork," I yelled to her.

"I know, Tower," she yelled back.

I got to be nice to her. *Do what she says, and be where she tells me to be. Just until I get off paper.*

If Mary took me off paper, I'd be able to mail off my fees each month and submit any updates to my file the same way. I wouldn't have to worry about someone dropping by to check on me. That's what I was shooting for. If I could survive in the pen with all those hard heads, I could certainly survive with a female parole officer.

CHAPTER 13

Time was passing so fast. It was already November. I'd been back in the real world for almost eight months, but I still didn't have a job or any transportation.

So! my mean voice said. *What that bitch in heels Mary tell you the last time you fucked her? She was gonna take care of you. "Don't worry about a job." Ain't that what the bitch said? "I can help you out. If you need money, just ask me." Where the money at?*

She ain't pressing me about not having a job. She was at first, but she's slacking up a little now.

Slacking what? She may not be pressing you for a job, but she is pressing you to eat her pussy. I need you to find us some new pussy to eat because between her and that mortgage lady that you met at the casino, I'm starting to think pussy ain't what it used to be.

I can't worry about pussy right now. I'm trying to get my life in order.

With Mary as your parole officer, I don't see how it's possible. Your case is supposed to be turned over to a new PO every six months. It's November now so tell me how come we still staring at her ass? I'll tell you why, because she found a loophole—a way to keep you tied to her probably forever. Send me back to prison. I'd rather be there then with her ass.

I picked up the *Star-Telegram* and while I was looking through the classifieds I saw an ad for a 1980 white Dodge Mirada for only nine hundred dollars so I immediately called the number listed, but no one answered. I kept trying for four days until finally a young man picked up. He told me that he still had the car but a lot of people had been calling about it.

"None of those people need a car as bad as I do. I can guarantee you that, and I can guarantee you cash so you won't have to worry about a check bouncing."

He laughed. "If you can get here in an hour, I'll hold it for you." George and I got to the man's house in thirty-two minutes, and it was in Denton, which was about an hour away from us.

My family was trying to figure out where the money came from. They couldn't believe I still had some S.S.I money left. Then I had to listen to Bernice fuss about if I could afford to buy a car, I could afford to pay her rent.

"The boy needs a car," Dad said, coming to my defense.

I didn't want them to know that Scottie, the one I rose up before I went in, had given me a few thousand dollars on several occasions and that's what I was basically living on. I never did any runs for him, but I could've. And at least I knew if things ever got real tight. . .if I never found a job or just decided to say, "fuck it" and risk it all, I knew whom to call.

When George and I pulled into our parents' driveway, they were standing on the porch, smiling. Dad walked off the porch after I parked. "Ooh, this car is nice," Dad said. "And all they wanted was nine hundred dollars?"

"Yeah, the guy wanted to get rid of it real quick since it was his dad's car and his dad just died."

"Look, when I croak, don't be selling my shit for that cheap."

"It rides so nice, and he just put in a new exhaust system, valves, and did a complete brake job," I said, smiling. It was the first time in a long while that I felt like I got a good deal on something. The first time I felt like things were starting to shape up for me. Having transportation would help me out a lot. A real job with benefits was coming soon. I could feel it. I was working odds and ends: painting, installing ceiling fans, mowing lawns—anything for extra money.

"Now, you gonna be all ready for the holidays, huh?" Dad asked.

"Yeah, especially for the food. I can't wait for that."

It was the day before Thanksgiving, which was always the biggest holiday for my family, and when I was locked up it became the hardest one for me to handle. My parents tried to visit on a couple of the holidays that we were allowed to have food brought in, and Thanksgiving and Christmas were one of them, so at least once, sometimes twice a year, I knew I'd eat good. After my first couple of years being incarcerated, I told my parents not to worry about driving to Oklahoma to see me. Seemed like a waste of their time and gas. Besides, it only made me feel worse when they had to leave.

Granny needed a few things to prepare for the big dinner we were having the next day so she sent me to the grocery store with a short list and her shopping card. When I walked into the store, I was immediately put on guard. I looked around as I pushed my cart down each aisle, waiting for the worst to happen, preparing myself for when and if it did. I knew just what I'd use for a weapon. I knew how to destroy someone with a can good or my house key.

I stood in the ten-items-or-less line that extended back into the soup aisle. I looked at my watch and then at the back of the man's baldhead standing in front of me. The day before Thanksgiving and only three lines were open. These stores needed a better system—a system like the commissary had. I was used to handing my list to the man standing behind the glass and waiting while someone packed my sack. They were quick about it.

"I don't have all damn day," I said louder than I meant to. People started looking my way.

The man in front of me turned and agreed. "It's always like this in here," he said. "Don't make no sense. That's why I hate going to the grocery store."

Tell his ass to go stand in the right fuckin' line then. Ten items or less and he got about fifty, my mean voice said.

I wanted to tell him and the lady in front of him that they were breaking the rules, but instead I left my basket and walked out. When I got back over my mama's, Granny was waiting, and when I told her the lines were too long for me to stay, she started cussing, so my dad offered to go, but that's why they sent me in the first place so he wouldn't have to. I ended up leaving again, but this time I went to Sack-N-Save with still another wait, almost as long. While I was waiting, I started to think about how badly I needed a female friend, maybe a few of 'em. Someone to talk to because I was tired of talking to men. Tired of being around a bunch of 'em. My brother George told me that women were a lot different than they used to be.

"I could get another woman if I wanted," George said. "They don't care if you're married. Shit, some want you to be, especially if they are. Some don't even care if you working. Basically, the women out here are easy or desperate, one."

I finally left the store after waiting in line for almost thirty minutes. I walked in my mama's house carrying two plastic bags with the items Granny was low on.

Mama wanted me to spend the night, so I did. George was over, playing cards, and drinking beer when his wife called and continued calling every twenty to thirty minutes to make sure he was still there.

"It's your PO on the phone," I teased after about the fourth call.

"Nah, you got that all wrong. You only get a PO after you're out of prison. My ass is still in one."

"I sure wish she'd stop calling so damn much. Why don't she just come over?" Granny said as the phone rang again. "I'm answering the phone this time. Hello!...Yeah, he's still here. How about this? How about we call you when he leaves?" Granny slammed the phone down because she never could understand women who tried to track down their man. She never had Granddad under surveillance, but somehow she always seemed to run into him with one of his other women. Now, his health was starting to fail, but Granny didn't feel sorry for him. She'd cuss him out in a minute and tell him that he made her sick, but I knew better. Granny loved him. They were married at eighteen and had four girls. One of my aunts died of cancer while I was in prison. She was closest to my mama in age. My other aunt, Tina, lives in New York with her Jamaican husband and their six kids. Mama says it's been years since she's seen Tina but Tina calls and writes her regularly.

Granny says when Granddad comes around, he acts like he

doesn't want to leave. "I want to be around my family," he says, practically in tears.

"You should have thought about that twenty-six years ago," Granny says. That's about how long they've been separated.

"Is Granddad coming over tomorrow?" I asked.

"I hope not," Granny said. "I sure don't feel like dealing with his mess."

Granddad arrived three hours before Thanksgiving dinner was served because he told George he liked sitting in the house and smelling Granny's good food, so George picked him up, and Granny made sure to cuss George out for that. "I don't mind him coming over for dinner, but don't ever bring his ass over three hours ahead of time, holiday or not. Now, I need to take me a Tums because my stomach is upset."

Even though he walked in the house with the assistance of a cane, Granddad still had his strut on. When he saw me, he lifted his cane, pointed it in my direction, and smiled. I felt sorta bad that I hadn't bothered to visit him or even call in the eight months since I'd been out, but he wasn't really around me that much growing up, even when my grandparents were together. He was always too busy running them streets. I can't help but look at Granddad and see myself. To think that of all the women he had over the years, he still ended up alone and sick in his old age, while Granny's full of life and healthy as a horse. She's never taken anything other than a multivitamin. She wears a hearing aid, but Mama says nothing's wrong with Granny's hearing. "She hears better than a dog."

"There's my twin," Granddad said to me, not because we look alike, but because we are alike. I was a player just like him.

Bernice and her boyfriend, Marshall, walked in with Curtis, who was pretending to be happy, but I could tell from the look on Curtis' face that he was far from that. He was confused. I'm not sure what happened to his father, Edwin. He'd stopped calling me to check on Bernice months before and sorta disappeared like Lisa, only Bernice didn't seem to wonder where he was or if she'd ever see him again. She seemed to have all her eggs in Marshall's basket now.

Constance arrived next with her family. I looked at her fiancé, Tim, and I saw a lost man. Maybe because of all that I'd heard about him from my family. Bernice told me that he had six babies by four different women, all scattered throughout the United States. He met Constance at either Trader's Village or Big T Bazaar on a Saturday afternoon, and by that evening, they were in Constance's queen-size kicking it. Said they had been living together for a year before he left Constance when she was six months pregnant for another woman, one who provided more. He came back five months later, after that "more" the other woman provided disappeared.

It takes Granny to explain Tim. "He can be bought and sold," she says. "But eventually those women who were so eager to give get tired of taking care of his ass. Even if they think they can, most won't for too long because it's not in a woman's nature to carry a man, and we will lose respect for him sooner or later. The man was meant to be the head, not the tail."

I thought about this and about the fact that I was not looking to be the head of anything at the moment. I just wanted to chill. I wouldn't mind having a woman take care of me, helping me just while I was getting on my feet, tear me off a few dollars here and there. But I didn't want someone who was trying to control me like Mary. I wanted someone I could control. Someone I could see when and if I wanted to see her. I came from a place where I didn't have nothin'. Cigarettes were currency. You had to have your hustles on. All prisoners do is scheme and steal so it wasn't gonna be that easy to switch back. I'm not even that sure if I want to because at least this way I was guaranteed not to get hurt, and since life had so few guarantees, I need to grab hold to all the ones I could and run with 'em.

As I watched Constance and Bernice stuffing their faces, I wondered why women let men bring them down. Both of them used to be built so nice. Not skinny or nothing like that. They were a healthy size. Now, they're using their food like a drug. Granny said, "Every time they lose a man, they gain ten pounds." So I look at the two of them and how much weight they've gained, and I realize how many men they've lost.

"Pearl, is there any cranberry sauce in there?" Granddad asked to no reply. "Pearl, did you hear me. I can't yell. I'm not up to all that."

"Pearl," Constance's four-year-old daughter Zora yelled as she walked toward the kitchen, "you know you hear Russell in here calling you." Zora stood near the entrance to the kitchen with her hands on her hips.

Granny walked into the dining room, placed her hands on her hips, and looked down at Zora. "Child, you better learn some respect. Who told you to call me by my first name?"

"I did," Zora said, frowning. "Now, tell the truth, Pearl. Didn't you hear Russell calling your name?"

"No, I didn't."

Zora puckered her lips and rolled her eyes. "Well, he wants to know where the cranberry sauce is and so do I."

"Zora, hush your mouth," Constance said.

Granny shook her head and grinned. "This little girl is something else. You gonna have you a handful."

"Where are you going?" Mama asked me as I stood, holding my plate.

"I'm going to the kitchen to wash my plate and then I'm going upstairs."

"Are you feeling okay?" Mama asked me.

I nodded but really I felt like crap. All of a sudden my funky mood set in. I didn't feel like being bothered with nobody, not even my family. As I was washing my plate, I realized that just last year I was having Thanksgiving dinner in the chow hall. It made me scared. Something could happen and I could end up back in prison, even though I said I'd have court in the street, I might not feel like killing myself that day or the police might arrest me before I had a chance to. I was trying to figure out if I could make it, now that I was out. I was trying to figure out how everything was going to shake out with Mary, and if that didn't work, what was my plan B.

I went upstairs to my old bedroom and sat on the edge of the bed.

All you need right now is a nice young thing with a big ass who can get freaky and take your mind off all the bullshit that's going on in the world. Then you'll be able to deal with Mary's demanding ass, my mean voice said. *Otherwise, you're doomed. Right now, her sex is bad and her attitude is worse. You're not getting any special privileges, unless you think not having to use a condom is a special fuckin' privilege. Shit, she's not worried about you having AIDS. Maybe you're the one who should be worried about her having something. One of these days you're going to choke the shit out that bitch because you can't stand her, and you know it.*

Call Mary at her house right now. You got the number saved in your cell phone from one of those times she called you. One of the many times she was hunting your ass down. Make her shit in them thongs she loves to wear. Go ahead and do it!

I picked up the phone and found Mary's number.

"Hello," Mary said.

"I miss you."

"Who is this?" she asked with panic in her voice.

"It's your man. Who do you think it is?"

"You know you can't call me here."

"Why not? You call me all the time."

"That's different. Don't call over here anymore. I'll talk to you later." I grinned after she hung up because I actually heard fear in her voice, which I didn't think was possible, but now I knew just how to get to her. I made a mental note for the next time I needed to press her buttons.

Eventually, I closed my eyes, even though I wondered what would play back that night. Would it be those two dudes humping each other in the back of the chapel at the prison or would it be E.J. breaking off a shank in some muthafucka's heart while I watched out for guards? I was afraid of the things I'd seen and done so I tried to keep my eyes open because I was in no mood to watch reruns.

CHAPTER 14

Dad gave me my Christmas present two weeks early. It was a job. He didn't lie to Ron Vegas, the owner of Vegas Tires-to-Rent on West Division in Arlington, when he told him I was a hard worker and I needed a job doing anything that paid. He also didn't lie about my record. Dad told Mr. Vegas that I had gotten out of prison almost a year ago, and that I had served ten years for drug trafficking. Dad and Mr. Vegas went way back—grew up in the same neighborhood and went to Dunbar High School.

Mr. Vegas didn't care that I was an ex-con because he used to be a hustler himself when he was younger, just never got caught. Said it was his hustling that allowed him to open so many businesses. In addition to the tire shop, he owned a restaurant and a bar.

"Everybody got some kind of hustle," Mr. Vegas told me. "It's just they love to throw the book at black men."

I hadn't even been working a full week before Mary pulled up in her white state-issued car and came inside to verify my employment. She didn't tell Mr. Vegas where she was from because PO's really aren't supposed to, but I'm sure he knew. She was wearing a navy blue blazer to conceal the pistol she was toting and a long skirt and a pair of spike-heeled boots. I'm sure the guys working with me could take one look at her stern face and tell she was in law enforcement.

She walked into the break room where I was sitting at a table with a few other guys. She didn't stay long, and I was so glad because I was ready to explode on her this time for real.

Ask somebody how you go about meeting bitches, my mean voice said.

This guy named Roderick, who had one leg shorter than the other, said ever since the Internet got so big, he stopped going to clubs. "What you need a club for? All you need is a username and a password. If you put up the right profile, you'll probably get five responses a day. Five a day times thirty days, that's 150 women. Out of 150 women you're bound to find a few you wouldn't mind kicking it with, I'm sure."

"You find any?" I asked.

He shook his head. "Mostly, I found a bunch of booty calls, a lot of lesbians. The fine ones online are selling their bodies. When I hooked up with one of them, all she talked about was her rent and car note and all that she'd be willing to do to me if I helped her out. It's always your desperate ones online too. Do anything to say they got a man."

Make sure you search by income when you go online. The women can be baldheaded and big as an elephant as long as they have a good job and some money they can spend on you, my mean voice said.

I left work late, trying to wait until closer to the time when I was supposed to hook up with tightandjuicy69 from my Internet connection. The day after I set up my online profile, she signed my guest book, even included her picture—damn near naked. I called her and we talked a few times that week and arranged to hook up. She cut right to the chase, telling me she had what I wanted, but she needed to make sure I had what she wanted. "It's no different from taking a woman out four and five times before you get some. If you add it all up, that's about two hundred dollars, and then you still don't know if her stuff is worth it. With me, you getting it all upfront," she promised.

"And if I don't like it, do I get my money back?" I asked. "Does your pussy come with a hundred percent satisfaction guarantee?"

"You gonna like it. They don't call me tight and juicy for nothing."

I was driving north on 360 and had just connected to 121 when the rain started coming down. I saw a small black BMW lose control near the William D. Tate exit. Luckily for the driver, there weren't too many cars on the highway, which was unusual for Texas. It was a good thing whoever was driving was barely going thirty miles per hour, even though I was behind them cussing them out because they were holding me up for my date.

I looked back in my rearview mirror and noticed the BMW had managed to pull along the side of the highway. It looked like at least one of the tires was blown, possibly two. I watched a few cars pass by without stopping. I knew how it felt to be abandoned. I thought about going back to help whoever it was. My conscience wouldn't let me go any farther so I took the William D. Tate exit and looped around to get back on 121. The car was sitting off to the side with the engine running. I pulled up behind it and sat there for a second. I couldn't tell if it was a male or female, if the person was alone or with someone because the windows were fogged.

Ever since I got out of prison, I just go with my gut because I no longer carry a gun. Don't mess with Texas. Some people take that saying literally, and you can't walk up to everyone's car even if you're offering assistance, but my gut said go, so I went.

I ran over to the car with a jacket over my head to shelter me a little from the heavy rain. I knocked on the driver's side window. "Need some help?" I asked. No one said a word. "Do you need some help?" I asked much louder. I stood there for a couple of seconds. Then I walked back to my car and sat inside. I cracked the window and lit up a Black & Mild, smoking while I stared across at the car. I started to pull off, but I figured the person might be unconscious.

That ain't your problem—and you got enough of 'em not to take on no more. Why would they be unconscious anyway? They didn't get in an accident. Just a couple of flat tires is all. You knocked. They ain't answer. So move on. Tightandjuicy is waiting, my mean voice said.

I had a cell phone and could call 911. *You need to be calling tightandjuicy, not 911, and tell her you're running a little late.*

The police weren't going to do anything. They were real good on arresting folks and giving out tickets, but when it's time to change a tire or help a stranded motorist, that's not their job. I'd rather do it myself. I walked back to the car, throwing my cigar to the ground, and started banging on the glass. A lady let down the window, but she didn't move her collapsed head from over the steering wheel. Her straight black hair was covering her face. All I could see were her beige hands grabbing the steering wheel. At first, I thought she was hurt, until she turned toward me and stared with a blank expression. Her mascara was running down her face, and strands of her hair were stuck to her cheek. She'd been crying.

"Do you need some help?" I asked.

"Go away," she said softly.

"You're sitting on two flats and there's a storm coming. You sure you want me to go away? Have you called someone?"

"I left my cell phone at home, and besides, I don't know anyone to call."

"Do you want a ride?" I asked.

"I don't know you."

"Then do you want to use my cell phone?" I asked.

"I said I don't have anyone to call."

"Lady, look, I'm not going to just leave you out here. That'll be on my conscience."

"It's okay. Nothing can happen to me that hasn't already."

"You can die, and you ain't already dead."

"Yes, I am."

"Then I guess I'm crazy, 'cause I didn't think dead people could talk or drive."

She smiled, and I saw her dimples slicing the center of both cheeks. "Can you take me to my house? I don't live that far."

"Where you live?"

"In Keller."

"Where the hell is Keller?"

"Off 114 going west. It's not far from here at all."

She didn't say one word while she rode in my car. She seemed sorta nervous. Then suddenly she burst out with, "Oh my God, my book! You have to go back. Now!"

"Back where? What you talkin' 'bout?"

"Back to my car. I can't leave my manuscript. That's all I have. Please, I've been working on it for almost a year."

"But, it's getting worse out here. Ain't nobody gonna—" I started to lie and say nobody was going to mess with her car, but hell, somebody might fool with it. She might come back, and her manuscript would be sitting off to the side where her car used to be. "It can't be the only copy you have."

"It's my only copy. And it's handwritten. I planned on transferring it to my computer tonight."

I sighed. "Lady, if I crash because of you. . ."

"Please," she said loudly, and then looked over at me with sad eyes.

"You have the clearest eyes I've ever seen. You ain't gone through nothin'. Alright, I'll take you." She smiled and I saw those cuts in her cheek. "So you're a writer? What you write, poetry?"

"No," she said with an attitude. "I write fiction. Do you read?"

"Yeah, I read. What you trying to say because I'm a black man, I can't read?"

"Why would I say that when I'm black too?"

"You'd be surprised how some of us are."

"Well, I'm sorry, but I meant to ask if you read fiction, that's all."

"Yeah, I read fiction, and I used to write fiction a little bit."

"Oh, really?" She smiled. "Everyone has a story to tell, or so they think."

"I know I have one."

"What's your name?"

"Tower Evans."

"Nice to meet you, Tower. I'm Gail. Gail Adams. Are you going to take me back to my car?"

"I'm fixin' to do it right now," I said as I turned to look at her and saw her smile again. "What?"

"You fixin' to?"

"Yep." I nodded. "I'm fixin' to."

It took me almost thirty minutes to make it back to her car because the rain had gotten worse, and I had to pull to the side of the road and wait for it to stop coming down so hard.

When I pulled behind her car, she opened the door before I stopped completely.

"You in a rush or somethin'?" I asked, irritated. I stopped my car so she could get out. She ran in the rain without covering herself, but she made sure to cover those papers of hers. She came back with them stuffed inside of her black denim jacket. Her hair had gone from bone straight and shoulder length to wavy and chin length.

"You got good hair, huh?" I asked as I lifted up some of it. "Or did you buy that at the store?" I asked, messing with her. I knew it was hers. She rolled her eyes and didn't say much for the rest of the ride. "So what you writing about?" I asked as I approached the Southlake Boulevard exit.

"A man who's in prison for selling drugs."

"You serious?" I asked. "What made you come up with that?"

"I've been having a recurring dream about my main character, Mason. Take this exit. Turn left and keep going straight. You're going to be driving for about ten or fifteen more minutes before you get to my house."

After driving for a few minutes, I started noticing large homes.

"You live in a house out here?" I asked as I looked around at all the phat cribs nestled in their fancy subdivisions.

"Yes, but I'm just house sitting for someone."

"Dang, they must be loaded."

"They are, I guess," she said.

"Tell me about that recurring dream of yours."

"Almost every night he'd come to me—"

"Who?"

"Mason, my main character. And every time I saw him, he was in his cell crying. He wanted another chance to do right. He has three strikes, and he's in for life. His appeal is granted and he's freed, but the entire book is a dream except for the end when he wakes up and discovers he's still in prison."

"That's corny."

"What?" she asked, twisting her nose.

"If you write a book about a prisoner who's out, only you don't find out it's a dream until the end, people will get pissed, especially people in the pen. A person's freedom ain't nothin' to play with."

"I'm doing it tastefully."

"I don't care how you doing it, it just ain't cool. Come up with something else."

"You don't think he should be in prison?"

"Nah, I ain't sayin' that. That part is cool, but have it where he gets out, and show him struggling to adjust. Don't you think readers would be interested in that?"

"I guess," she said, dragging her voice. "Really, I'm not sure what readers are interested in. If I knew that, I'd probably be published or at least have a literary agent."

"I think they would. In fact, I know they would. Just have it be powerful."

"What, like *Shawshank*?"

"Who?" I asked.

"*The Shawshank Redemption*. I know you saw that. Everybody saw that," she said, eyeing me skeptically.

"Yeah, I saw it," I lied.

"No, you didn't. How did it open?" she asked.

"I can't remember. It was out a while back, wasn't it?"

"Yes, a little while, but still. Anyone who saw that movie would remember it. Describe one scene from the movie."

"I don't know," I said, dragging out the words as I stopped at a red light.

"Who was in it? Name one actor."

"I can't remember all that."

"You haven't seen it, have you?"

"Nah, I ain't seen it. I work a lot of hours. I don't get time to watch TV or go to the movies."

"Are you sure *you* didn't just get out of prison?" she asked, laughing.

"What if I did?" I asked as I turned to face her. I wanted to be myself with someone. I needed that. So why not with a stranger who I'd probably never see again?

"Well, did you?"

I nodded and then pulled off when the light turned green.

"You just got out of prison? What did you do?"

"It's a little too late to ask that question, don't you think?" I asked, laughing.

"Please don't say you're a murderer," she said as she turned to face me.

"The prosecutor said I was. Said I contributed to the murder of hundreds of people's lives."

"What did you do?"

"Drug trafficking." She closed her eyes and breathed a sigh of relief. "I guess I'm your character who's come to you from your dream or maybe you're still dreaming and you're going to wake up at the end. Don't you see how stupid that premise is?"

"What do you know about a premise?"

"Oh, what, an ex-con can't know things? I took a fiction-writing class in prison." She faced forward and looked straight ahead in a daze. "So I guess you're scared of me now, huh?"

"No. I don't really have many fears."

"Everybody got some fears."

"I don't."

I pulled into her driveway. She lived in a new subdivision where all the houses basically looked the same and were probably worth three or four hundred thousand.

She stuck her hand in her large leather bag and started searching around.

She pulled the garage door opener out of her bag. "The roads are getting bad. Do you want to come in just until it clears up?" she asked.

"I can make it okay."

You a stranger. Why she inviting you in? She must be a fool, my mean voice said.

She turned on my radio, searching for a station. She stopped when she heard a young woman talking about the weather conditions. "An extreme weather advisory is in effect for the entire listening audience. Please do not attempt to drive on the roads. High winds, heavy rains, and flash floods expected throughout the rest of the night, causing hazardous driving conditions. If you are driving, we suggest you get off the roads immediately."

"I don't think you should go anywhere right now." She pushed the button to her garage door opener. "You can pull in the garage if you want."

"Well, I do have to use the bathroom."

"I have three and a half of those."

"I only need to use the half."

She smiled again, and I saw those cuts. Her smile almost made me want to smile back, but I didn't.

I looked around the house. One of the first things I noticed was a liberal arts degree from Howard University on the middle bookshelf in the living room.

"Where's Howard?" I asked.

"Where's Howard? You're joking, right?"

I shook my head. "Is it in Atlanta?"

"No, that's Spelman. You've never heard of Howard?"

"Yeah, I've heard of it, but colleges ain't something I exactly keep up with."

"But it's a well-known historically black university."

"So you went there, huh?" She nodded. "And you majored in liberal arts?"

"How did you know that?"

I pointed at the degree. "What kind of job can you get with a liberal arts degree?"

"Well, I also went to Howard's medical school. I just didn't finish."

"What kind of doctor were you going to be?"

"A psychiatrist."

My eyes bugged out. "You were going to be a psychiatrist?"

"Yep, that was the plan. And I was almost finished, too, but I had to pull out."

Ask her if she can help you, Tower. You need somebody to help you. Ask her, my nice voice encouraged.

She ain't got no degree. Didn't you hear her say she almost finished— keyword, almost, my mean voice said.

"Why'd you have to *pull out*?" I asked, smirking.

"You have a one-track mind."

"You don't even know me or know what I'm thinking about to say that. So why did you have to pull out?"

"Just because of some things that came up, which were out of my control. Are you thirsty? Do you want something to eat?"

I shook my head but kept looking around the place, at the stacks and stacks of papers that were divided into several piles on the dining room floor. The built-in computer center was between the living room and dining room and it was loaded with high-tech equipment. The furniture was a mixture of contemporary and turn of the century. The walls were stark white and there weren't any pictures hanging, but there were several tiny holes in the wall like someone attempted to put some up or maybe take some down. I was starting to get depressed because I felt like I was back in solitary. The house didn't have a lady's touch or a homey feel. It didn't even seem lived in. But Gail did say she was watching the house for a friend so I guess her friend was a man.

"What are all those for?" I asked as I looked at the fifty-plus boxes stacked against the dining room wall. "You moving?"

"No. Those are books."

"You collect 'em or something?"

"No, I told you I write. Remember?"

"All those are books you wrote?"

"It's two thousand of the same book."

"Two thousand of what kind of book?"

"A novel. I have boxes of books all over this house—in the garage, the second guest bedroom upstairs. They're like pieces of furniture, unfortunately."

"Let me see one." She took a book out of one of the boxes and handed it to me. "*Where Is the Love?*" I said, reading the cover. "Is this fiction or non-fiction?"

"It's supposed to be erotic fiction."

"What you mean by it's supposed to be?"

"I'm classifying it erotica because that's what's supposed to be hot now."

"How long did it take you to write this?" I asked, flipping through the pages.

"Eight months."

"It took my writing instructor a couple of years to finish his first novel."

She shrugged. "I think there's no hard, fast rule on it. It just depends."

"So you're just going to keep all these boxes in this person's dining room? Aren't they supposed to be in bookstores?"

"I can't get them in bookstores."

"Why not? Can't your publisher help you with that?"

"I am the publisher."

I scrunched my face. "How are you the publisher?"

"I self-published because I couldn't get a literary agent or publishing house to sign me."

"So you paid to get all these books made to just sit in these boxes in this person's house?" I asked. She nodded and I shook my head.

"What?" she asked.

"Nothing."

Go on and tell her what you thinking—she's dumb as hell, my mean voice said.

I smirked. "Nah."

"Nah, what?" she asked.

I shook my head. "Nothing. Can I keep this copy?"

She put her hand out. "Do you have $14.95?"

"Yeah, I got $14.95," I said, digging in my pocket with no intention of giving her a dime.

"That's okay. You can have it."

"Thank you." I yawned.

"You sleepy? There's a bedroom over here," Gail said, pointing, "straight through that door. Do you need me to wake you at a certain time?"

"I'm not staying over."

"Why are you trying to drive in all of that rain? Is your wife waiting up for you or something?"

"I'm not married."

"Then please stay." I stood in the middle of the living room, holding her book. "I mean, I understand if you're scared," she said.

"Me, scared of you? Come on now. You must not know what it means to have been in prison."

"Believe me, I do," she said as she started to walk up the stairs. "Are you staying?" she asked, looking back at me. I nodded. "Have a good night, and I'll see you in the morning. Oh, if you get hungry, there's plenty of food in the refrigerator."

I went back in the bedroom to call tightandjuicy69, but no one answered. I guess she called up another username. So then I called Mary. "Where are you, and don't lie?" she asked as soon as she answered her cellular. I told her I got stranded over my parents' home. "You're a damn lie! I been by your parents' house. Where are you, Tower? Don't start fucking up."

"I'm not fucking up! Have you checked the weather lately?"

"But don't say you're somewhere that you're not. I get enough of that from my damn husband."

"But I'm not your damn husband. I'm your damn case."

"Don't piss me off. I'm still your parole officer, and don't you ever forget that!"

I hung up the phone, turned off my cellular, and sat up in the bed. My throat was dry. It felt like the thermostat was turned on full blast, so I went to get some water to cool off. I opened the refrigerator because Gail seemed like the bottled water type and that's where I found the tiny bottles of Ozarka. She had more than enough food lining each shelf in her fridge and plenty of meat in the freezer, all organized perfectly. I opened the cabinets and found so many canned goods that I started wondering if she was a branch of Goodwill. I guess the family who lives in the house left her stocked up pretty well 'cause that was too much food for one person.

I drank my water then sat up in bed and started reading her book, but I couldn't get past the first few sentences: *Donny woke me up from my sleep and told me he didn't love me anymore because he was in love with someone else. But that's not what shocked me. What shocked me was who that someone else was—our neighbor, Mr. Meyers. I couldn't* believe it. *After twelve years of marriage, I finally found out why my husband kept begging me for anal sex.*

I shook my head and threw the book across the room. No real man wants to read about two dudes together.

Like you don't know about two dudes fucking, my mean voice said. *Where you been? Huh? Where you just come from?*

It was 1:15 A.M. My body was covered with sweat. *Where am I?* my mind questioned. I turned my head and canvassed the room. This wasn't my four-by-nine cell. *I'm out. I'm really out,* I reminded myself. I blinked, trying to erase my thoughts, but instead my mind captured everything again: two steel bunks, each covered by a thin plastic mattress; a skinny window that was about five inches high and eight inches wide with a partial view of the back of another unit; a sink; a toilet; and a steel door that had a small opening for the guards to look through when they took count or just felt like it. I hated confinement. I closed my eyes. *Those things I did inside will stay there. I did them to survive, and I survived.*

Prison rule number one: trust nobody.

Prison rule number two: don't rat. no matter what you see, you didn't see it.

I could remember lying on my bunk with my hands behind my head, plotting an escape. I used to run around the field of the prison every day to build up my endurance so I could get out of the two-mile perimeter before the guards had time to set up. Even though the dogs had the run of the entire center around the fence, I knew that I could always arrange for someone to throw rocks to distract them like they did for Miles and Jeff, two lifers who broke out. Miles was caught days later, but Jeff never was.

I glanced back at the time. It was 2:37 A.M. and I was now thinking about Stanley Holmes who was riding in the rental car behind mine the evening the troopers pulled us over. He was sentenced to life which was really fucked up because he was just along for the ride. Didn't even have drugs in his car, wasn't even his car. But the troopers found guns in the trunk that weren't registered to anyone so they instantly became Stanley's since he was the driver.

They wanted to tie him to the drugs that were in the trunk of my rental car so bad that those troopers went out and made a duplicate of the key I had on my key ring and said it belonged to Stanley. They had to have done that because there were only two keys, and one was on my ring. The other one was back in Texas. Then if all that wasn't bad enough they traced one of the guns in the trunk of the rental Stanley was driving to a murder that went down in Texas a few months before we were arrested. Two out-of-state drug dealers got jacked of nine thousand dollars, and their bodies were found near Bachman Lake. It never made the news, but I knew all about it because I knew who did it—Quentin was the ringleader. But the state of Texas made a case against Stanley.

It went from bad to worse. One of the machine guns found in the trunk was linked to a shootout that happened at The Glass Key, an after-hours joint where a baller could get his gambling on until four in the morning. That place served some of the best pork chops I'd ever had, even better than my granny. One night masked gunmen came in blazing up the joint, leaving very few survivors. I can't say if Arturo or Quentin had anything to do with that. There was a chance whoever they got the guns from did, but I wouldn't put it passed them, especially Quentin.

Gail walked downstairs around 4:00 A.M. I waited about ten minutes before I cracked the door a little and peeked out. She had on a pair of black jeans and a black turtleneck sweater. She was kneeling on the floor, raising her hands in what looked like a silent prayer. I watched as tears poured down her face like someone had turned on a faucet. I watched her until I got tired of standing behind a tiny crack in a door, and I got back in the bed because I didn't want her to catch me spying. I sat up for more than an hour, thinking about my writing class.

———

I started taking my fiction writing class at the start of 1993. By this time, I'd been in prison for a little more than three years. I always sat in the last row of my writing class, which was held three times a week for eight weeks and lasted two hours. The class was a good way to burn time, and it fit in well with the rest of my schedule.

The instructor was a white man, a college professor by the name of Ingram Pitts who was born and raised in Oklahoma City. He moved away at eighteen to attend college in New York, and after graduation went to Los Angeles where he married and started a family. He wrote his first book at the age of thirty-three when he felt he had matured enough to discover what he called a voice. By the time he turned forty-nine, he'd written twelve novels and was in negotiations to make his latest book, *Summer Stream,* into a movie. Eight of his books became *New York Times* bestsellers. He was divorced with three kids and more money than he'd need in his lifetime. He came to Oklahoma in the summer to give back, and the prison's writing program was his way of doing so.

He talked a lot, mostly about himself, and when he wasn't talking, he was making us talk or read what we had written. It was mandatory that we read at least one excerpt before the eight weeks ended. Every time he called on me, I passed. I figured there were fifteen others in the class, so why not give one of them a turn? They were all so eager to step to the front and try to get deep for a few minutes anyway.

"Mr. Evans, we only have one more session after this. Would you like to read your excerpt today?"

"I'll pass," I said.

"Alright then, who will?"

"I will," Harvey Washington, an inmate, said.

"Washington, you're always reading an excerpt. Let's give someone else a try."

"But I was the first one to raise my hand," Washington said.

"Mr. Evans, I really want to hear from you today." I sat still for a moment and stared that white man down. I wasn't in the mood to walk to the front of the class and read shit, but I figured I might as well get it over with. It was either this class or the next one, so I went ahead.

"Please start by telling us your name and the title of your story."

"Who don't know my name by now?" I asked with an attitude.

"I don't," Harvey said.

I stared at Harvey. He probably didn't know my name. His brain stayed fried on them drugs. "My name is Tower Evans—Theodore actually, but I prefer to be called Tower—and my story is called, 'Hardened Reality.' "

"Tell us how you got your name, Tower," Mr. Pitts said. "I find nicknames to be very interesting."

I shrugged. "I've had it ever since I was a little boy. My granny gave it to me. My older brothers and sister used to push me and I'd never move, never fall down. So my granny started saying, 'That's a tower right there—a tower of strength.' And then my family started calling me that." I stood holding my paper. I cleared my throat and recited my piece from memory.

No need in crying over spilled milk 'cause you can't do nothin now but mop it up. And don't even look at it like it's wasted. It's just gone, forever gone. Like the years I'll be spending on the inside—gone, forever gone. My reality is that I have become something I thought I'd never be, a statistic— a black man serving time for selling dope. And if I had to do it all over again, I can't say I wouldn't have done just that—it all over again. You must understand where I'm from—the hood, where street hustlers rule and young boys worship you like you're God because you flash hundred-dollar bills and new rides. "How can I be down?" *That's the question a nine-year-old posed to me.* "Let me be down."

You want to be down, little fella—look at me now. When you empty my pockets, you won't find a dollar bill, not even some change. "How can I be down?" *This is as far down as a person can get without being dead. How can you be down? Do the stupid shit I did and you'll be down. Doing time like me—forty years asking not how can you be down but when can you get free? When can I get free?*

As I walked back to my seat, a few of my classmates were nodding and saying, "good job." After class, my teacher pulled me to the side. "I really felt that, and I think you should consider expanding your story."

"I ain't no writer. I just signed up for this class so I could burn a couple of hours, that's all."

"Who is a writer, but someone who enjoys writing?" he asked. "Aren't you supposed to go to school for the shit? Take English or something like that?"

"My major was biology."

"Well, you a white man. You can do whatever you want."

He shook his head and looked at me, instead of past me, like most whites do.

"And you're a black man and you can too. Good day, Mr. Evans." He handed me the paper I had turned in the week before, "Out from Trouble." It had a big red A-plus on it, and he had written: *Your vision is remarkable. your insight reminiscent of Richard Wright. You have a gift—please don't waste it.*

―――

Around 7:30, I went into the bathroom that was attached to the guest bedroom and took a shower and then got dressed. When I walked out of the bedroom, Gail was in the kitchen cooking breakfast. I looked around the house again and wondered why she was living there. Whose house was it? Why couldn't she afford her own place?

"When you gonna put your Christmas tree and decorations up?" I asked.

"When I get published."

"Oh, so Christ don't have a birthday until you get published?"

"No, I'm not saying that."

"Well what are you saying?" I walked over to the blinds and opened them. "Plants can't survive without water and light. Did you know that?" I asked as I touched one of the leaves from a plant and caused four more brown leaves to fall on the floor.

"If I could get a major distributor, I wouldn't care about getting hooked up with a big publishing house, but without that, your books stay boxed up. Distributors rarely deal with one-book publishers. They really like dealing with a company that has at least ten titles. Plus, your book needs to get reviews, but *Publisher's Weekly* rarely reviews self-published titles and *Kirkus* doesn't at all. Thank God for *Booklist* and *The Library Journal*."

"Can I watch your television?" I asked, not interested in her book problems.

Tell her that shit you read this morning wasn't no good, my mean voice said. *Tell her she's not only wasting her money, but she's also wasting all of her damn time.*

"I don't have one."

"What?" I asked.

"I don't have a TV."

"Who in America doesn't have a TV?" I asked.

"Me."

"No offense, but I think I'm going to hit the road. Your place is starting to depress me."

"No, don't leave. I'm making you something to eat. I was hoping we could talk."

"What are you gonna do about your car?" I asked as I sat on the sofa.

"I hate that car. It's old."

"What year is it about a '98, '99?"

"It's a '93, and I've had so many problems with it. The minute it was paid off, my transmission went out, and then my air conditioning. I've invested more than four thousand dollars in it this year alone. Now I'm going to have to buy two new tires."

"I work at a tire shop. I can get you a discount on some tires. You heard of Vegas Rent-a-Tire on Division?"

She shook her head. "I don't need to rent tires."

"We sell 'em, too, and I'll make sure you get a good deal. We got all kinds—Goodyear, Pirelli, Michelin."

"Do you want some breakfast? I'm making grits and scrambled eggs."

"I'm not hungry." I looked out the window at the golf ball–sized hail coming down. "It's bad out there."

"Looks like you'll be here for a while."

"You better call somebody about your car. I'm sure it'll get tagged."

"Who should I call?"

"You can try a tow service, but I'm sure they're busy today. Just keep trying," I said with a yawn.

"Are you tired? You can go to my bedroom and lie down."

"I'm always tired. I got sleeping problems."

"I have a waterbed," she said.

"You do?" I asked, excited. "The kind with waves?"

"It's waveless but I guarantee you, if you have a sleeping problem, this bed will cure it."

"Nah, I need to be heading home." I looked out the window again. "Come by the tire shop, and I'll hook you up."

"It's really bad out there. It would be silly for you to try to leave right now."

"I guess I better stay a little while longer. Just until it clears up." I looked over at Gail and saw her smiling as she fixed breakfast.

Chapter 15

"It's a woman at the front to see you," one of my coworkers said as he walked into the garage. I had just finished putting four tires on a Jeep Grand Cherokee.

"A woman?" I asked, wiping my greasy hands off on a cloth. I was afraid it was Mary checking up on me again. I stayed over Gail's two nights in a row and kept my cell phone turned off. When I finally turned it on, I had eleven messages waiting from Mary. "What does she look like?"

"Kinda light-skinned and slim. She's got dimples and curly hair."

"Curly hair," I said to myself. "Must've got wet again." I was so relieved it wasn't Mary.

I walked to the waiting area and saw Gail standing near the vending machines reading *Ebony*.

"Hey," she said as she looked up and tossed the magazine on the table. "I brought in my car like you suggested."

"How'd you get it here?"

"I had it towed, and a coworker dropped me off," she said.

"Where do you work, anyway?"

"Bank of America," she said. I checked my watch. "Did I come at a bad time?"

I walked closer to Gail. "A lot of these folks have been waiting for a while," I said in a low tone. "I can't really take you before them because you know how we black folks pay attention to shit like that."

"Doesn't matter when you take me. I don't mind waiting."

I looked back down at my watch. "I was about to take my lunch."

"This late? It's almost six."

"Yeah, but tonight's my late night. We stay open until nine, and I didn't come in until one. I've been busy all day. You're welcome to come. I'm just going across the street to Whataburger, but I don't ask twice."

I didn't have time for much conversation. Thirty minutes was all I got for lunch and I had three big burgers to down and a large order of fries. "You're not hungry?" I asked when I noticed Gail had only eaten a handful of fries and a couple of small bites from her hamburger.

"I thought I was, but I guess not."

"You're not anorexic, are you?"

"What?"

"You too skinny not to eat. Give it here. I hate to see good food wasted." She put her fries on my tray. "The burger too."

"But I ate off it," she said.

"I don't care. You look clean."

She smiled and put the hamburger on my tray. "You can sure eat a lot," she said.

"Food is good for you. Didn't you know that?" I asked.

"I know that."

"Then you ought to try it sometime."

"How do you know that I don't?"

" 'Cause you skinny. Where you from, city girl?"

"How do you know I'm not from here?"

"I don't hear no accent, and you don't seem like you from here. You seem like you from the city. I can tell by the way you dress."

"What's wrong with my clothes?"

"Why something got to be wrong with 'em? They just say city." She smiled. "I'm from Chicago."

"What I tell you? One of my boys on the inside is from Chi-town. He lived in the Robert Taylor Homes. You ever heard of those?"

"Those are the projects."

I nodded. "You live around there?"

I grew up on Lake Shore Drive. I don't recall seeing any projects near me," she said with a grin.

I looked at my watch. "Damn, I only got fifteen minutes." I finished the rest of my burger quickly and started on hers.

"Why do you eat so fast?"

"Habit." I started sipping lemonade from a large cup with a straw. I lifted the lid and slid the cup in front of her. "We used to pack cocaine in these," I whispered.

"In the cups?" she asked. I nodded. "When you were in prison?"

I shook my head. "Nah, before prison. Before I started trafficking and I was still petty hustling, that's one of the things we used to do. People would put money in one cup. I'd put drugs in the other. Then we'd trade. You want to write a book about something? I'm a book. You could write about me. I'm your Mason."

"I was thinking about that. Would you let me?"

"Let you what?"

"Write a book loosely based on you."

"Depends. I don't want no book about me to stay boxed up. If you write it, I want people to read it. Otherwise, I can hold out for Stephen King."

"You go ahead and do that. I'm sure he'll be contacting you soon."

"I think so too."

"Although, as I'm sure you're well aware, he mainly writes horror."

"That's right, and my life's a horror story."

She stared at me for what seemed like forever, but it was more like a few seconds. "Will you let me? I won't let you down. I promise."

I slumped down in the seat and started slurping more of my drink. "Maybe. Let me think about it first."

"If you decide to let me, we'd have to meet a lot."

"What you call a lot?"

"At least once a week."

"I'll let you know."

"What's to think about? You have a story to tell, and I want to tell it."

"Yeah, I know I do, but that's my life, and I'm not sure I want it on paper."

"Don't worry. I'll mix things up so it can be considered fiction. I want to get started on it as soon as possible. I really do believe that you're my character Mason come to life."

"What am I going to get out of the deal if this book does good? You gonna draw me up a contract?"

"What do you want out of the deal?"

"A Lamborghini or a Porsche. I love fast cars and fast women. Are you fast?" She rolled her eyes. "I'm just messing with you."

"I take my writing very seriously. Are you going to let me do it or not?"

I shrugged. "I guess."

"Good. Let's meet tomorrow afternoon."

"Tomorrow afternoon? So soon? Besides, how do you know I don't work on Saturdays?"

"Do you?"

"Not this Saturday."

"Good. Come over to my house tomorrow around one for our first session. You remember where I live?"

I nodded. "Out in the boondocks."

She smiled. "You're so funny to me."

We walked out of the restaurant, and I saw Mary's state-issued car parked in the lot of the tire shop. "Listen, why don't you go ahead and walk over there without me. I think I left my wallet inside."

"You put it in your pants pocket."

"Well, I got to use the bathroom. I'll be over there in a minute. Go on."

Can you believe that Mary bitch in heels. She acts like you're her only case. Well, one thing's for sure, you helping them other muthafuckas out 'cause she ain't got time to fool with them. She's too busy fuckin' with you! Take a deep breath. It's going to be alright, my mean voice said.

CHAPTER 16

Gail had her blinds open. She even put up a few Christmas decorations. Not much—still no tree, just a wreath on the front door and a few knickknacks in the living room. Her hair was straight this time, but her clothes were wrinkled and black. That's the only color I'd seen her in. She took my coat and invited me to sit on the sofa. She had a fire going in the living room, and I noticed a small tape recorder lying on the coffee table.

"Can I sit in the chair?" I asked. I wanted to feel like I was getting a therapy session.

"You can sit anywhere you like," she said, smiling.

"I might be schizophrenic," I said as I sat down.

"Nice to see you again too."

"Paranoid schizophrenic. I figured you should know since you're writing my story. Now are you scared of me?"

"No. You really want me to be, though. Why do you think you're schizophrenic?"

I shrugged.

"You don't seem like a paranoid schizophrenic."

"Oh, you know many of 'em?" I asked.

"No, but I know the symptoms: delusions, hallucinations, disorganized or no speech, flat emotions, no motivation. And two or more of these behaviors need to exist for at least six months to truly be schizophrenic. Do you have any of those symptoms?"

"Maybe one—flat emotions. I snapped when I was in solitary at this place called Granite. I started hearing voices. But I'm jumping ahead. You gonna tape this?"

"Oh yes, I guess I should," she said as she reached for the tiny recorder and hit play and then stop. "Before we start, I just want to say that you could have simply had a mental breakdown due to the stress. A lot of people have breakdowns due to a traumatic experience, but that doesn't mean you're a paranoid schizophrenic."

"Well, I hear voices. Two main ones that go back and forth. They mix in with my own thoughts so it's hard for me to make decisions because it's like three ideas on how I should do something."

"When did you first start hearing voices? You said in solitary?"

"Okay, well—" I sighed and looked around because there was so much I wanted to tell her. I was breathing heavily through my nose. "Can I get some water?"

"Are you okay?" I shook my head. "Take a deep breath, okay?" I nodded. "I'll get you some water." When she left, I put my hand on my forehead and started rocking.

"Here," she said after she returned quickly with a large glass of water. I downed nearly half of it instantly. "It's okay, Tower."

I was glad to be able to finally talk to someone, but I still said to her, "You don't understand."

"Help me to. You said you went to prison for selling drugs. Tell me what happened."

"What happened when?"

"The day you were arrested. What happened when you first woke up?"

"I'm sure I was probably arguing with my girl the night before, and it carried over into the morning like it usually did."

"Why do you say you were probably arguing with her?"

" 'Cause we always argued. I never did right, but I still wanted her to be my woman and only mine, but I was always staying out late, getting into things I wasn't supposed to be getting into. I like the ladies. I like 'em a lot. I can find something attractive in almost every woman. Like you—I like your dimples."

"Thank you, but tell me about your girlfriend. What was her name?"

"Lisa. I thought you said you wanted to know about the day I got arrested. Do you know what you're doing? Can we stick to one thing?"

"Okay, if that's how you like being interviewed."

"Yeah, it is. I don't like jumping around. My mind does enough of that on its own."

"Take me there as much as you can remember."

"I can remember a lot."

It was late August 1989. Quentin and I were parked outside of J.W. Kream, a burger joint in Fort Worth, in a rented brand-new Ford Tempo, didn't even have a thousand miles on it. We were eating our burgers and fries while we sat in the car waiting for Arturo and Martin to roll through so we could hit the road for Kansas. I couldn't help but notice all the traffic rolling in and out of the Douglas Boys' detail shop.

"What's taking Arturo so long?" Quentin asked. He took out his cell phone. We used pagers and pay phones at first, but that became too inconvenient so we stepped it up to cell phones, and back then the phones were big and bulky and they didn't have package deals so not many people could afford them. If you could, you were making big bank because you were charged by the minute to talk. Our bills were three and four hundred dollars a month easy, but we made enough to afford a thousand-dollar phone bill, and mine had gone that high before. "I'm gonna call him. You noticed lately Martin been acting strange."

"Strange how? What you mean?" I asked.

Quentin shrugged. "I don't know. He just ain't into it." Quentin looked off into space as he held the cell phone to his ear, waiting for an answer. "Maybe he's trying to go off on his own. There they go." Arturo pulled up in a red Mustang, probably a rental, with some other dude who I didn't recognize. "Who the hell is he with?" Quentin asked.

"I don't know, but I'm going to find out," I said as I got out of the car and walked over to Arturo as he was pulling into the empty space three cars down from us. "What's up?" I said, leaning down at the driver's side and staring across at the other dude.

"Nothin', man. You ready to roll out?" Arturo asked.

"Almost, but ah, who is he?"

"Oh, this my boy, Stanley Holmes. Don't you remember Stanley from high school? Marletha's brother."

I nodded. "I thought you looked familiar."

"He's gonna ride with me and help me drive since Martin can't. You know my attention span is a muthafucka on the road."

"How come Martin can't?" I asked.

"I'll explain all that to you later," Arturo said as he looked over at Stanley than back at me. "Ready to head out?"

I took a minute before I nodded because I had a bad feeling. Something just wasn't adding up. I didn't like that Martin had been calling me all morning asking me what time we were leaving, and all of a sudden, he wasn't going. Maybe I was just paranoid. "Let's do this thing," I said.

Stanley sat in the passenger seat grinning like he was excited about something. I guess his square ass felt important since he was rolling with the big dogs.

I walked back to the rental car and started the ignition.

"Who's that fool with Arturo?" Quentin asked.

"You remember Marletha, Arturo's girl in high school? That's her brother."

"I know Arturo ain't still trying to get with Marletha. I thought she was married."

"She might be, but I know he still hits it from time to time," I said as I pulled off.

"You notice that all the fine girls from high school are all fucked-up looking and sprung and the ugly ones looking all good now?" Quentin asked.

"I ain't notice shit. And all I want you to notice is if you see five-O on 35."

We were riding down I-35 heading south toward Kansas. Arturo and Stanley were behind us. We had just pulled to the side of the road so Arturo and Stanley could switch seats. Once we got to Wichita we were going to drop Stanley off somewhere, maybe the mall, so we could handle our business without him getting in the way. I'm sure he knew what we were into, just not to what extent, and he was probably surprised to see me as part of the crew because the last time I ran into him I was wearing a UPS uniform. I may have been the last of my crew to enter the drug game, but I was the first to rise so quickly.

After I started moving a kilo in a matter of days, my Mexican contact committed to doing business with me on a regular basis. I was getting what I needed fronted to me. Finally, the time had come. My road dogs and I could stop peddling weed, crack, and small quantities of cocaine from our homes and get a cut of some real business. This was our way out of the hood. So, if Kite, a petty drug dealer out of Wichita, thought he was going to fuck that up, he was wrong—and he was going to be dead and wrong if he didn't have my money.

We had just entered Oklahoma and were turning off onto the ramp toward I-40/I-35/US-62/Wichita/Fort Smith. I merged onto I-35/I-40 East. Quentin popped in Bobby Brown's tape and started singing along to "My Prerogative," but he was all off key.

"Man, please, don't sing if you can't," I said.

"This is my shit right here." Quentin started singing again. He probably liked the song because the lyrics were true to his own life. Getting girls was the way he lived. He was short but he got more play than a tall dude. Women loved him. I think they liked his straight, black hair; his caramel skin; and hazel eyes. He looked like one of those brothers from an island.

When all the rest of us were trying to keep a low profile with our money, riding around in old cars, keeping everything out of our names, Quentin was out spending his. He had a sweet house built in Meadowbrook that looked like a mansion, and he could afford it because his girl, Misty, had her man, Big Reg, a big-time Dallas drug dealer, knocked off after she got tired of him beating her. Misty had three policies out on Big Reg and was able to collect more than $400,000 in insurance money, but that wasn't nothing compared to what Big Reg already had, like close to a million in the safe of their house. I wouldn't want to mess with no bitch like that, *and* she was ugly too. I'm not going to totally diss her because her body was on point, but that face made me want to throw up. All Quentin wanted was her money. And he got it. They had three, four cars in the driveway at all times, and a wrought-iron fence around the house like they were living on a compound. Misty was always flying back and forth to New York to shop, bringing Quentin something back that you wouldn't see on nobody else because she said she wanted to make sure her man looked good at all times, but she was quick to cuss another woman out for looking at her man too hard.

My cell phone started ringing. I gave it to Quentin and turned the music down. "Who this? Is this Kite?" Quentin asked as he looked over at me. "Where the hell you been?...Nah, we been trying to reach you for over a week now...'Bout what? You got amnesia all of a sudden? About our fuckin' money, fifteen G's that you owe us. What up? You got it?...Don't worry about where we are. Worry about where our money is...What you mean you *gonna* have it? When you *gonna* have it, nigga? I don't want to hear that shit." Quentin put the phone away from his ear when Kite started talking loud.

"Put Tower on the phone," Kite yelled. "I got to explain something to him. I ain't tryin' to pull nothin' on nobody, or why would I call? Put Tower on the phone please!"

"Tower, you want to talk to this punk-ass nigga?" Quentin asked.

"Not if he don't have our money."

Quentin put the phone back to his ear. "Okay, did you hear that? Tower don't want to talk if you don't have our money...*Gonna?* We don't deal in gonnas. Either you do or you don't, so which is it?" Quentin asked. "Another week? You already had two. Are you high, Kite? You must be high. Is that why you can't pay us? I guess it's our fault. We should've known better than to trust our shit to a muthafucka named Kite. You been using our shit, haven't you? That's what the word is on the street. Reason you ain't got our money is because you ain't sold shit, for using it...Nah, you ain't no supplier. You're a fuckin' thief is what you are. Get our fuckin' money."

Quentin shook his head and looked over at me. "We gonna have to kill this muthafucka," he said calmly. "That's what we gonna have to do." Quentin spoke into the phone. "Since you deal in gonnas. We gonna have to kill your ass." Quentin disconnected Kite and tossed my cell phone on the backseat. "That nigga just fucked up my mood," Quentin said, searching through his cassette case. "Where's my tape? We gonna have to kill that nigga tonight." I nodded. "Damn!" Quentin yelled out of nowhere. "I ain't tryin' to kill nobody tonight." He replaced Bobby Brown's tape with N.W.A.'s "Straight Outta Compton."

"Me either. I ain't happy about it. But what else can we do? We can't let him get away with keepin' our money. Word get out in Kansas that we soft…you know what I'm sayin'. Then everybody be doin' it," I said.

"Listen, I will put a bullet in that nigga's ass in a minute, but my girl just bought me these damn shoes, and I pray to God that I don't get no blood on 'em," Quentin said as he turned the volume full blast.

It was almost six o'clock. I didn't notice how fast I was going, just that a lot of cars seemed to be passing me. I checked my rearview mirror and saw Arturo's boy driving so close he was almost on my bumper.

"Damn, if I have to hit the brakes that muthafucka's gonna ram right into me," I said.

I noticed everyone started to slow down and then I saw two highway patrolmen sitting in the middle of the median. It seemed like their eyes were fixed on us as we passed by. "What the fuck?" I said. When I heard sirens and saw the flashing lights coming my way, I changed over to the far right lane and eased my foot from the gas to reduce my speed from eighty. Arturo's boy changed lanes, too, and was still on my ass. Next thing I know, here the state troopers come. One car pulled over Stanley and Arturo, and the other car came after Quentin and me.

"What you think he stopped us for? For speeding, right?" I asked.

Quentin nodded. "It's cool. Just play it cool," Quentin said, turning off the music.

I watched as the officer instructed Stanley to get out of the car and then walked Stanley over to their patrol car.

"Something don't feel right," I said to Quentin.

"It's cool, man. It's cool," Quentin said to me, but I got the feeling he was trying to convince himself.

I opened my door slightly and was just about to get out when the officer said firmly, "Remain in your car, sir."

I sat in the Tempo, studying the clock and each minute as it passed. Five minutes seemed like an eternity, so after twenty-two minutes, I didn't know what to think. Stanley was still sitting in the front passenger seat of the officer's patrol car talking to him.

"I don't like this," I said to Quentin. "It don't take that long to give someone a ticket. And since when do you have to take somebody out their own car to do it?"

"I don't know," Quentin said. "Maybe that's how they do it in Oklahoma, besides, what can Stanley say?"

I had never been so nervous. All that sneaking around I was doing—lying to my family, pretending to still be working at UPS, and basically leading a double life—had come down to this.

"Why is your hand trembling?" Quentin asked.

"My hand ain't trembling."

"Yes, it is. You gonna tell me not to worry, but your hand is trembling. Come on, man. We got to think. How we gonna get out of this?" We weren't getting out of it. One of the officers came over to our car and asked if we had drugs, after I said "no" and refused to sign a consent-to-search form, the dogs were called out.

It took the canine unit almost an hour before they finally pulled up in a gray station wagon. I saw a large shepherd pacing around in the back of it. Two troopers got out of the wagon. One of the officers opened the back, pulled down the gate, and took hold of the dog's large leather leash. The shepherd jumped out of the wagon. His ears were slightly pointed and standing at attention as he stood and surveyed the area. The trooper stooped down and removed the leash from the dog's collar. "Sniff out," he said to the dog. The shepherd started with Arturo's car, walking around it only once very quickly, and returning to the officer. "Sniff out that one," the officer said to the dog, pointing at my rental car. The shepherd walked over to it and circled it twice. He stopped at the trunk and stood, placing both paws on the trunk and then barking loudly. "You got something, boy?" the trooper asked the dog. "Something in there?"

Two more highway patrol cars pulled up and suddenly every trooper had his gun drawn. "Come out of the car, nice and slow," a trooper said.

They put Quentin and me in different patrol cars. I sat and watched as a trooper went into the rental car from the driver's side and popped the trunk. Two troopers walked to the trunk, throwing out clothes we used to hide the contents of what we were transporting, but little good it did. The next thing I saw was the safety deposit box. I shook my head because I knew it was over.

A trooper walked back to the patrol car. "You got the key to that lock?"

"No, sir," I said.

"Is it on your key ring?"

"No, sir. I've never seen that box before."

"I'm sure you haven't."

I stared that shepherd down. I'd always loved dogs, but that one, I couldn't stand.

The phone was ringing. Gail looked at it in shock. "Answer your phone," I said on the fifth ring.

"Hello," she said and held the receiver toward me. "It's for you."

"For me? Who is it?"

Gail shrugged. "Some woman."

"Some woman?" I took the phone from her. "Hello."

"I suggest you leave right now unless you want me to ring her doorbell," Mary said. I hung up on her. I couldn't believe she was following my every move.

"I got to go."

"Who was that, your girlfriend?"

"No, I don't have a girlfriend. I thought I already told you that."

"You said you weren't married. I never asked you about a girlfriend."

"That was my sister. She's having problems with my nephew. I got to go."

"When can we meet again? I want to know what happened after the arrest."

"I'll call you."

I walked out of the house and looked around for signs of Mary, but I didn't see her white car anywhere. I barely made it into my car when she called my cell.

"Do you think I'm playing a game? So that's where you go when you disappear. Who's this one?"

"A friend."

"I'm the only friend you need."

"How you figure that?"

"Because I'm your parole officer, and I'm trying to help you assimilate back into society."

I started laughing. I couldn't control myself. Trying to help me assimilate. "You sure about that?"

"Yes, I am, Tower, but I think you need to take a class in anger management, and I'm going to look for one to sign you in to."

"I'm already going to those damn NA classes. The ones you said I wouldn't have to go to anymore. I don't want to go to anymore classes. They're not helping."

"Well, what will?"

"I need to be left alone."

"Did you tell that bitch that?"

"She's trying to help me."

"Oh, she is, is she? We'll see about that. Does she know that you were in prison?"

"Yes, she does, and she's fine with that."

"Well, she must have a record herself."

"She doesn't have a record."

"Something's wrong with her."

"Bye, Mary.

CHAPTER 17

Before I left Gail's house, I promised her that I would come over the next day, which was a Sunday, to continue with the interview, but before I could get out the bed good, Mary was calling on my cell phone.

"I'm tired of you hanging up on me all the damn time! You must be seeing another woman. Are you?"

"Look, I'm tired of you trying to control me. I had enough of that in prison."

"I'm sorry. I just know how these no-good women are out here. You have more important things to concentrate on, like finding a better job, and moving out of Bernice's house."

"You said you weren't going to bug me about no job!"

"I'm not, but don't you want to work?"

"I have an interview with Allied this week, but even if they like me they don't expect to fill any positions for eight to twelve more weeks."

"Did you tell them about your record?"

"What do you think? Shit, what they don't know won't hurt 'em."

"So you lied on your application?"

"No. I just didn't answer the question."

"Let's just hope they don't find out."

"I'll call you back when I get home from church."

"Are you still going to Potter's House with Bernice?"

"I only went one time. It's too big for me to join, but I've been visiting other churches. I'm going to a Church of God in Christ in Arlington today. If I don't leave now, I'll be late."

"Well, enjoy the service, and call me as soon as you leave out."

After church, the last thing on my mind was calling Mary. For what? I hated that I had to talk to her every day. I hated checking in, letting her know my whereabouts. I decided I wasn't going to talk to her. I was going home to relax my mind, think about my day. What, if anything, it all meant. I had gone to church and stood before the congregation so they could welcome me along with their many other guests, and then I went forward for altar call, nervous as I walked up front knowing all eyes were on me, wondering if the congregation could tell where I'd been because I felt like I was branded. I was taken in the back after service so members could pray over me. Tonya was the lady who read scriptures to me. I forgot exactly what she looked like after I left. Couldn't even remember the style of her hair—whether it was short or long. I remembered her size—queen. She breathed real heavy, almost like she needed to sit down and rest for a while. That's all I really remembered, though. She held my hands while she prayed for me. I got so caught up in the moment that I told her about my past. "I been locked up," was just how I said it. Her brother was locked up for life for killing his baby's mama, so my past didn't bother her. My charges were mild compared to her brother's. She gave me her home number and address because she said that she could be my mentor.

"You're a baby in Christ, and I can help you grow in the word." I felt comfortable with her because I grew up in a devoutly religious household, and I was used to women talking about God all day. My mama and granny used to live in church, attended three and four times a week. Both of them had been hurt by men. They called it their curse that no man would do right by them. The difference between the two of them was that my granny was hurt by only one man—my granddad—who knew how to love, but had no limit to how many, but many men had hurt my mama.

By the age of twenty-four, Mama had four kids by three different men. I was a newborn. George was five. Bernice was seven. And Wallace, the oldest, was nine. Bernice and George had the same father. Even though their dad never married our mama, he stayed with her for three years, the longest of any man, outside of my stepdad. I didn't know too much about Wallace's dad because Wallace was born when Mama was only fifteen, and his father wasn't someone Mama ever talked about. All I knew about my dad was that Mama heard he was dead. I never asked her anything about him, other than his name, which was Horace. I figured if there was anything she wanted me to know, she would have made sure to tell me, especially the bad stuff, because she was certain to tell all of us what God had delivered her from.

She met my stepdad in church when she was thirty-four. Almost six years later, when she was forty, they married. She had almost given up any hopes of being loved and then he came. By that time, though Mom and my stepdad were both getting tired of church. They had a long list of things they felt needed to change. They'd been paying into the building fund for well over ten years, and there was still no new building. My stepdad got tired of that bucket being passed around so many times in the same service. One time was fine, but three and four didn't make any sense. The straw was drawn when the minister refused to preach the Word until more offerings were thrown on the altar. Dad decided to tithe into the lottery and casinos instead. They still love the Lord, but can't stand that church, and my stepdad didn't feel like looking for another one. "Church is all a racket," he'd tell us. "One big scheme to make money. I can keep my little money right in my pocket. I ain't tryin' to help pay no preacher's mortgage and car note."

By the time I made it over Gail's house, it was late. The nightly news had already gone off, and I took my chances with her opening the door. Gail wanted me to spend the night—not in the guest bedroom this time, but in her bed lying next to her. It was there that she said she would interview me. She practically begged me. I couldn't figure her out. Her phone barely rung and whenever it did, she'd look at it like it was a wrong number and when she'd answer, sure enough it would be. I wondered why her family never called, especially when I saw their photos lined up on the middle bookshelf. She told me that everyone lived in Florida but her sister had moved to L.A. and then to New York. I wanted to leave her house but my sexual urge made me stay. I knew how vulnerable she was. She cried when I described being in solitary and how alone I felt. She wept when I told her I could feel my mind slipping away, and at times, I'd reach out and pull at the air, hoping to catch fragments of my brain cells.

"I just want to help you," she said. "Help you feel again."

You can help him alright. Give him some so he can take his mind off his past and concentrate on the present—mainly your pussy, my mean voice said.

She would have let me. I could have had Gail if I wanted her, but I let her lay her head on my chest instead while I answered her interview questions.

"I'm interested in knowing about the trial," Gail said and yawned.

"Are you sleepy?" I asked. I had noticed how glassy her eyes looked when she answered the door, like she had been crying again.

"I'm fine. I want you to tell me about the trial."

"You don't go straight to trial. They have the jury selection, evidentiary hearing, and the preliminary hearing. It's a lot before the actual trial starts."

"So are you out during this time?"

"It all depends on whether or not you can post bond. My parents posted bond, so I was out for a few months, going back and forth to the courthouse."

"What was that like?"

"Like hell. Your fate is in twelve people's hands, thirteen counting the judge, fourteen if you count your attorney, but my attorney was doomed from the start. The district attorney's office was on a mission to send a message. The prosecutor said in the paper, 'If you want to run drugs through our town, you will end up in a four-by-nine cell.' Let's just say I wasn't looking forward to my trial, and the way it all went down at the preliminary hearings didn't put me at ease one bit.

"What happened?"

I was arrested on August 24, 1989. The following week, my parents posted bail. I knew before trial even started that I was going to be found guilty. I had a feeling in my gut, which was exactly why for the next few months while I was out on $100,000 bond, I kicked it. I abandoned my house and let the bank foreclose. I was staying at my parents' house with my girlfriend, Lisa, and I was coming in drunk every night but none of them said anything because they knew what was about to happen to me too. On December 1, 1989, my preliminary hearing started.

"Please state your name and who you represent to the court," the judge said.

"Your Honor, I'm Jonathan Brown, and I represent Theodore Evans."

"Mr. Hutchinson, isn't it?" the judge asked Stanley's attorney.

"Yes, Your Honor. I'm Dan Hutchinson, and I represent Stanley Holmes. Your Honor, if I'm not mistaken I do believe Arturo Watts' case has been dismissed by the prosecution."

"Who do you represent again?" the judge asked.

"I represent Stanley Holmes and Arturo Watts but I believe that Arturo Watts' case has been dismissed."

"Is that correct?" the judge asked the prosecutor.

"If it please the court," the white male prosecutor said. "I have announced to counsel that as to Mr. Arturo Watts and Mr. Quentin Harris, who is here represented by Mr. Thomas Brunson, that I do intend, prior to the start of these proceedings to dismiss the cases against both gentlemen. I apologize to counsel and to the court for not having done this sooner, but I didn't receive the file until six o'clock yesterday, and after review of it as well as conversations with witnesses, in the best interest of justice, I believe that it would save everyone's time to dismiss these cases because quite frankly there's not enough evidence to bind them. These gentlemen were only passengers."

"So you're prepared to move to dismiss the cases against Evans and Harris?" the judge asked.

"Yes, Your Honor," the prosecutor said. My eyes got big. I was excited to hear my name mentioned along with a dismissal. I watched as a man sitting near the prosecutor stood and whispered into his ear. "No, Your Honor, I'm sorry, not Evans. Just Arturo Watts and Quentin Harris."

"Okay, the other two defendants, your case is dismissed," the judge said. "You're free to go."

Arturo and Quentin stood and hugged each other. Big smiles covered their faces and the faces of their families and close friends. They didn't look over at Stanley or me. Didn't even look in our direction. They simply hurried out of the courtroom. "Is the state ready to proceed as to the Defendants Evans and Holmes?"

After going through a few more preliminary questions, the first witness, Peter Owens, who was the trooper who stopped me, was called to the stand. I'll never forget that white man's face. Not as long as I live. When I closed my eyes and went to bed, I saw his face, and when I opened my eyes I still saw it. He looked different in a suit, without his trooper hat and boots.

"Would you please state your name and occupation for the record?" the prosecutor asked.

"My name is Peter Owens, and I'm a trooper with the Oklahoma Highway Patrol."

"And how long have you been employed there?"

"Just about seven years."

"In what capacity are you employed as a trooper?"

"I am a road trooper, sir."

My nose was turned up, and I stared him down with hatred.

The prosecutor asked him what area he worked the night we were pulled over, what hours he worked, the time he stopped Stanley and me, and where and why we were stopped. I hung on to every word the trooper said, waiting for him to trip up. The attorney asked questions that took the court step by step through the night that I'd never forget.

The trooper stated that he and another highway patrol car were parked in the center median when his radar detected our speed, and they proceeded to stop us.

"And at the appropriate time, did you issue a citation for speeding?" the prosecutor asked.

"Yes, sir, at the appropriate time I sure did," the trooper said.

"He's lying. He never gave me a ticket," I whispered to my attorney, but I guess my whisper carried through the hollow walls of the courtroom because the judge banged his gavel and said, "Please instruct your client to refrain from conversation during testimony."

"Yes, Your Honor," my attorney said.

I took a pen from inside my suit pocket and wrote on my note pad, HE'S LYING in large letters and slid it in front of my attorney. He looked down at the pad, nodded, and slid the pad back to me. I wrote down, HE NEVER GAVE ME A TICKET. NEVER GAVE STANLEY ONE EITHER. THAT'S A LIE! And I slid the paper back to my attorney. He looked down at the paper and nodded again. Then he wrote, OKAY! I KNOW! and slid the pad back to me.

"And why did you decide, sir, to ask for a consent-to-search form be signed?" the attorney asked.

"I had reason to believe they were transporting drugs."

"And why did you have reason to believe that?"

"During the interview that I conducted in my patrol car, I found several inconsistencies with both of the defendants' stories."

"Such as?"

"One said they were traveling together going to the horse races, which I knew were closed, and the other said, that he didn't know the occupants of the second vehicle and that he was going to see his girlfriend, but then later admitted to knowing them."

"So they weren't being honest with you, and that began to raise suspicion?"

"Yes, that and other things."

"What other things?" the prosecutor asked.

"Mr. Holmes was very scared. He was trying to distance himself immediately from the others in the car. He told me that he was just going along for the ride, and that he didn't normally hang with them, that there was no telling what they were up to or what was in those cars and he just didn't want to be associated."

"And why would he tell you all of this, sir?" the prosecutor asked.

"I asked him if either he or the person he was riding with had a criminal record, and he said he didn't but he wasn't sure about the other person and then that prompted him to say all that other stuff."

"So once again that raised your suspicion?"

"Well, yes, because, I didn't understand why he would say that there was no telling what they were up to or what was in those cars. It just seemed strange. Up until that point I was only going to issue a speeding ticket, but then I thought maybe I should search the cars so I asked for the consent form to be signed."

I leaned forward so that my arms were resting on the table as I turned to look at Stanley who was sitting two chairs down from me, next to his attorney. I wanted Stanley to turn and face me, but he kept staring straight ahead. I wanted him to turn so he could know how I felt right then. So he could know that it was because of his dumb ass that we were sitting there. I stared at him until my attorney nudged me and shook his head.

I sat back in my chair and refocused on that trooper testifying. I couldn't believe it. Stanley had fucked up, and we were both going to pay for it. He may have been innocent of the charges brought against him, but he was guilty of being stupid. I couldn't listen to that trooper or the prosecutor. I didn't start paying attention again until the cross-examination.

"Mr. Owens, you need to clear some things up for me, sir," my attorney said.

"Okay," Mr. Owens said.

"My client was traveling northbound. You said to the court that your radar picked up my client going eighty miles per hour, but isn't it correct that you would need to be behind the other car and if that car passes you, then it could pick them up on radar? And weren't you in fact, traveling southbound and crossing over to the center median when you spotted them?"

"No, sir, that's not correct. We were already parked in the center median, and the radar can pick up vehicles that are speeding and traveling in the opposite direction."

"But how, sir, would you know which vehicle it picks up, assuming there are three, four, let's say even ten cars on the highway at the same time, which is quite possible. How would you know which car was speeding?"

"The beam would pick up the closest object to it. If there are five vehicles or like you said up to ten or even more, it would pick up the fastest of the bunch."

"So which car did the radar pick up, the Tempo or the Mustang?"

"The Tempo."

"So why then were both cars stopped?"

"I had a feeling that they were traveling together."

"Even if they were, did that mean they both had to be stopped?"

"I began to profile, and I realized that this was probably more than a simple traffic infraction."

"Oh, so in fact, before Mr. Holmes had said anything to raise your suspicion, your mind was already made up that this was more than a traffic violation."

"Sort of. They began to fit a profile."

"Could you explain to those in the courtroom how you are trained to profile?"

"There is information that is provided to us that we use about black males transporting a controlled dangerous substance, what we refer to as CDS from Texas to Kansas. It's just something that we've been trained to watch for. We know that the role of the vehicle that travels behind is that of a chase vehicle. That if an officer attempts to stop the vehicle that is transporting drugs, the chase vehicle speeds off in hopes that the officer will go after it."

"And is there anything else that you know?" my attorney asked.

"Well, we have been informed that in the past, black males traveling from the Dallas/Fort Worth area northbound on the interstate are transporting contraband. By a profile, what a trooper or any law enforcement officer looks for when he makes a traffic contact are different things. For instance, the area they're traveling from and to, if the car is their own or rented."

"Why would that matter?" my attorney asked.

"If the car is rented they know if they're incarcerated they're not going to lose their own vehicle."

"What other things do you look for?"

"If they're traveling light, without clothes. If they have beepers, which often are used to contact drug dealers to make a buy or give messages, cellular phones for the same reason. It's a lot of things an officer looks for. If you're traveling, we expect to see long-distance maps, eating on the run. We saw none of these things with the defendants."

"Thank you for clearing that up because what I'm hearing you say is that you stopped them because they are black."

"No, sir, that's not what I said."

"You said you stopped them because they were black men traveling from Texas to Kansas."

"No, sir, my initial reason for stopping them was for speeding."

"Sir, correct me if I'm wrong, but your response was because you had reason to believe, due to your training, that these two cars of black men coming from Texas heading toward Kansas were carrying drugs. Isn't that basically what you said?"

"Yes, sir, it is."

"Because these men matched a profile. Isn't that also correct?"

"Yes, sir. They did."

"So when you stopped them to issue speeding tickets, was there anything that gave you any indication that either had committed something other than a traffic violation?"

"As I began to profile the men, I was starting to get a feeling that there was a possibility that CDSes were involved."

"What was it that made you think drugs were involved?"

"Well, sir. We had black males traveling. He said he was coming from Fort Worth to go to the horse races, but the races were closed."

"Who said?"

"Mr. Holmes."

"So black males can't travel the highway without drugs being involved? I wonder if you started stopping white males and searching their cars, what you'd find then. You said you didn't tamper with the drugs. Is that correct?"

"Yes, sir, that is correct. I didn't."

"But you took the drugs home with you overnight. This can't be proper procedure."

"I took the drugs home because I couldn't book them into the Oklahoma State Bureau of Investigations and due to the large quantity of the drugs and the nature of the crime, I didn't want to risk something happening at the jail. It's a small jail in a small town, and these people were from a big city. I felt the drugs would be safer at my home. The drugs didn't leave the trunk of my patrol car."

"Are you telling me that you took the drugs home with you where your wife and your kids are because you felt they would be safer there than in a police station? If we had these big-time drug dealers, as you like to imply, then why weren't you afraid that someone was outside watching you and could have easily followed you home? It just doesn't make any sense. None of this makes any sense."

"These men were allowed to make phone calls," the trooper said. "We knew they were telling people where they were, and we figured whoever gave them the drugs would want them back. We're not talking about a small quantity here. This was the most we'd ever confiscated at one time."

"Your Honor, at this time, I make a motion that my client be released and that all charges be dropped on the grounds of unfair due process," my attorney said.

"Motion denied," the judge said, banging his gavel.

"But, Your Honor, you heard what this witness has said as to the reason for the stop and the search—they were black men traveling the highway. Also, how do we know that the evidence wasn't tampered with?"

"Your motion is still denied," the judge said. "Do you have any further questions for this witness?"

"No, Your Honor."

Two weeks later the case was heard before a jury. I was the last person to take the stand to testify in my own defense. It was my idea to go before the jury and tell my side. I wanted to convince them that I didn't know there were drugs in the trunk—shadow of a doubt was what I was trying to cast so I had my story all planned out, but I was so nervous that my testimony didn't make much sense. "We stopped at a gas station and when I went in to pay for the gas, Arturo asked if he could put something in my trunk," I said.

"What are you saying, Mr. Evans, that the safety deposit box was put in your trunk by Mr. Watts at the gas station?" the prosecutor asked.

"It wasn't there before that, unless the last person who rented the car left it in the trunk."

"I think they'd remember to take out $250,000 worth of drugs. And how can you explain the key on your key ring?"

"What key?"

"The key in State's Exhibit A. The one found on your key ring that opened the safety deposit box."

"I guess Arturo or one of them put it on there."

"So this was all a conspiracy against you, Mr. Evans? Is that what you want the jury to believe?"

"Objection," my attorney said. "Argumentative."

"Overruled."

"Is it, Mr. Evans?"

I shrugged. "It don't matter. They gonna believe whatever they gonna believe and nothin' I say or do is gonna matter no way."

I sat in the courtroom with a fresh, short haircut, wearing a black suit and tie. The trial, which lasted a day and a half, had ended an hour earlier and the jury left to deliberate. My attorney was saying things to sound optimistic. Things like, "I think we really proved that you were stopped because of racial profiling. We brought up a lot of key points that should cast doubt in at least some of the jurors' minds," but I knew before the jurors filed back into the courtroom exactly what the verdict was going to be.

Still, I was optimistic about one thing. I had no priors so I didn't think I'd be in prison for more than three years, which was too long to be locked up. Any amount of time would be. The only other time I had gotten in trouble was four years prior for possession of one pound of marijuana, but I received deferred ajudication, which meant it wouldn't go on my record as long as I stayed out of trouble for two years, but the prosecutor found out about it and brought it up during my trial. Even though my attorney objected, and the judge sustained it, the jurors had already heard.

After about an hour of deliberating, Mr. Ross, the jury's foreman, came back into the courtroom and requested a transcript of my testimony.

"You may not have a transcript, however, you may listen to a tape in open court to the entire testimony of Theodore Evans. If you desire to hear said testimony, notify me in writing," the judge said, and they did.

"Mr. Ross, has the jury reached a verdict?" the judge asked.

"Yes, we have, Your Honor."

"Everyone please rise. Would you hand the forms of verdict to the bailiff please?" I watched Mr. Ross hand the forms to the bailiff who took them to the judge. I tried to read the judge's face as he looked them over, but I couldn't tell one way or the other. "The court has reviewed the forms of verdict and finds them proper. The court clerk will read the verdicts please, omitting the style of the case."

"We the jury, drawn, impaneled, and sworn in the above-entitled case do upon our oaths find the defendant guilty of unlawful possession of narcotics with intent to distribute cocaine as charged in the information herein, and set punishment at fifteen years and a fine of $50,000."

I dropped my head and shook it. "Damn, I can't do fifteen years," I whispered.

"They're not finished. There are still two more charges," my attorney said.

"What?" I asked, looking over at him in disbelief. How could I forget about the other two charges? I guess because fifteen years was long enough. Longer than I thought I would get. Then I heard the court clerk repeat everything she had just said changing the last sentence to "guilty of failure to affix a controlled dangerous substance tax stamp as charged in the information herein, and set punishment at five years in the state penitentiary and/or a fine of $10,000." They still weren't finished because there was the third charge, and the jury found me also "guilty of trafficking in illegal drugs, cocaine, as charged in the information herein, and set punishment at twenty years in the state penitentiary and a fine of $100,000."

All I heard was guilty, and I knew my life was gone. My knees began to buckle as I quickly added up the years, realizing that I would be an old man before I'd ever see the world again.

"That's forty years," I said to my attorney.

"Don't worry. I'll ask for the sentences to run concurrently."

"Sentencing will be set for January 12, 1990, at 10:00 A.M. Bail is set at one hundred thousand dollars, correct?" the judge asked the prosecutor.

"Yes, Your Honor," the prosecutor said.

"Is there any objection to the defendant being released on bail?" the judge asked.

"Yes, Your Honor. I would request at this time, due to the seriousness of the charges that bail be revoked. In that the harshest punishment is twenty years, I doubt that this defendant would appear for sentencing if he was let out on bail."

Christmas was just a few days away. I turned to face my attorney. "I want to be home for the holidays one last time."

"Mr. Brown," the judge said to my attorney.

"Your Honor, Mr. Evans has appeared at every hearing and was always aware that the possible range of punishment was up to life imprisonment. He doesn't have a past criminal record. He's a lifelong resident of the state of Texas, and he's living with his parents. The holidays are approaching, and Mr. Evans would like to be home for them. I don't know of any instance where he's demonstrated why he would not show up for sentencing."

"Your Honor, if the court is going to allow bail I'd ask that it be increased to a million dollars," the prosecutor said.

"A million dollars, Your Honor? My client isn't a member of the mafia. Setting a million-dollar bail is just like revoking it."

"He's never been convicted of these crimes before so I'm not going to revoke bail, but I will reset it to five hundred thousand dollars. Until bail is posted, he'll be remanded to the custody of the county sheriff. Deputies, if you'll take charge of Mr. Evans. Give him time with his family. We're adjourned," the judge said, banging his gavel. I knew that there would be no way for my family to come up with ten percent of five hundred thousand dollars to post bail, and I didn't even want them to try.

Two deputies walked over to me and requested that I stand so they could handcuff me, which I did. They took me to a room off to the side of the courtroom and gave me fifteen minutes to spend with my family.

Constance, my stepsister, was the first to burst through the door in tears, followed by my girlfriend, Lisa, who had a zombielike expression on her face. Quickly, the room filled with more of my family members. I looked around for Aunt Cora, but she was nowhere to be found.

"Can't you take off the handcuffs while we're in here?" Mama asked. "My boy isn't going to go anywhere. You're the ones with the guns," she said with tears.

"It's okay, Mama," I said, calmly. "I'm okay."

"We're not supposed to, ma'am, but I will," one of the deputies said as he unlocked my cuffs and removed them.

"You gonna be fine, son," Dad said. "All you have to do is file an appeal because what went on in there was nothing but a bunch of bullshit. A black man still can't get no justice."

"Calm down," Mama said.

"It don't make no sense. Child molesters get less time than that, and so do some murderers," Dad said.

"They haven't sentenced him yet," Mama said. "I'm praying and believing in God for a miracle."

"I don't even think God can help him out of this one," Tommy said.

"Shut up, fool," Dad said to Tommy. "You just showing how ignorant you are. That's alright, we gonna get you out of here," Dad said to me. "A half a million dollar bond." Dad shook his head. "We'll get the fifty thousand dollars up somehow so you can be home for the holidays."

"Damn, they threw the book at your ass!" Tommy said. "Let's see, I guess you gonna be eligible for social security by the time you get out, huh?"

"What the hell you just say?" Dad asked. "With your retarded ass."

"Tower," Lisa said softly. I felt her hand tugging at my arm. "Tower, it's going to be okay, baby. You're going to get out soon enough to see our baby being born." I looked down at her, smirked, and shook my head. Forty years wasn't nowhere near soon, but I had to think positive. The judge could still decide to go easy on me. After all, it was my first offense.

My family members took turns hugging me, and then one of the deputies said, "Sorry, your time is up," and slapped the handcuffs back on me. I watched as my mama collapsed in my dad's arms and the tears fell from her face. It seemed like my whole family was crying, except for my stepbrother, Tommy, who stood back grinning.

"Y'all, don't give up on me yet. It ain't over. I still got my sentencing hearing. Who knows?" I asked with my voice crackling.

I was in the county jail while I awaited my sentencing hearing. I told my parents not to worry about posting bond for me. I wasn't going to make it home for the holidays or many more to come.

I stood before the court in a gray suit with almost my entire family, including my granny Pearl, watching from the front row of the courtroom. Even though the jury had already spoken, I was still waiting for someone to stand and say, "April Fool's" even though it was January. I knew what I had done. I also knew it was wrong, but I still couldn't accept the fact that I was going to do that much time in prison. In seven months, I was going to be a father, but I wouldn't be around for my child's birth, and who knows how many more years after that I would miss.

The judge went back over the jury's verdict and their recommended sentence for each charge. I listened, but my mind couldn't quite comprehend it all because I was still telling myself that I was about to do some hard time. I didn't know what to expect. I had homeboys who had been in, but I guess prison isn't something you really want to talk about once you're out. They never said nothin', and I never asked.

"Do you have anything to say, Mr. Evans?" the judge asked.

"Huh?" I asked, snapping out of my daze.

"Is there anything you wish to tell the court?" the judge asked.

"I'm sorry for everything that happened, you know."

"Mr. Dobson, do you have anything to offer to the court?" the judge asked the prosecutor.

"I would tell the court that the amount of drugs that was found in the back of that car was enough for hundreds of individual doses. Cocaine is a very serious problem in our society, and I believe that the crimes of which this defendant is convicted warrant that those sentences be run consecutively instead of concurrently, and that's all I have to add."

"There being no other legal cause to show in this case why the defendant should not be sentenced in accordance with the recommendation of the jury, the court having previously received, accepted, and filed all of the verdicts in CRF-90-13, 14, and 15, it now becomes my duty to impose sentence pursuant to those verdict forms. In CRF-90-13, unlawful possession of narcotics with intent to distribute cocaine, the court sentences you to a term of imprisonment in the Oklahoma Department of Corrections of fifteen years and a fine of fifty thousand dollars. In CRF-90-14, failure to affix a controlled dangerous substance tax stamp, the court sentences you to five years in the Oklahoma Department of Corrections and a fine of ten thousand dollars. And in CRF-90-15, trafficking in illegal drugs, the court sentences you to a term of twenty years in the Oklahoma Department of Corrections and a fine of one hundred thousand dollars to run consecutively with CRF-90-13 and CRF 90-14."

He then concluded his sentencing with, "The court is of the opinion and belief that you were not truthful in your testimony. You may have been innocent and only a mule carrying drugs for somebody else, but you participated in the chain of distribution of a substantial amount of cocaine, $250,000 worth. Although this appears to be not crimes of violence, I think they are crimes of violence because cocaine causes violence. I'm sorry that you were caught in the net. But the jury of Murray County has spoken, and I'm going to go along with their verdict because I think this is so serious that those sentences have to be imposed. Do you understand what I'm saying, Mr. Evans?"

"Yes, sir."

He then proceeded to tell me that I had ten days to file a Notice of Intent to Appeal. Then he told me about my right to remain in the Murray County Jail for an additional ten days before being transported to the Department of Corrections because the Oklahoma prison system was so clogged up. I had the choice to waive my right and go straight to prison, and that's what I chose to do to get it over with.

"Mr. Evans, the best of luck to you, sir," the judge said. "I hope you are able to get yourself straightened out over the next several years and become a productive citizen after your release. Do you have any questions, sir?"

I shook my head.

The court bailiff rushed over to put my handcuffs on. I heard the faint cries from my family as I was being led away. I didn't look in their direction because I had to hold myself together. Eventually, I knew I would break down, but it would not be publicly.

CHAPTER 18

It was Christmas Day 2000, and I was over my parents' house. I got there around four in the afternoon, and they already had a house full. Mama was playing Christmas music by her favorite male singer, Johnny Mathis. I went upstairs to my old bedroom and called Gail from my mama's phone. She answered on the first ring.

"What you doing?" I asked.

"You don't need to ask me that. You know exactly what I'm doing."

"Writing, I hope. That's all you need to be doing."

"I love to write. It keeps my mind occupied."

"Maybe I should start writing, then. I need something to occupy my mind. Have you added in all the stuff I told you about so far?"

"Not quite. I finished the first chapter and I outlined the next six. I'm trying to figure out the best way to put in everything."

"You haven't put in all the stuff I gave you yet? What you over there doing, playing with yourself?"

"We just started this, remember? You haven't given me that much yet. You still haven't told me anything about when you were dealing."

"I don't want this to be a typical book about a drug dealer. This ain't no *New Jack City*."

"So what's it going to be about, prison?"

"I don't want it to be about prison either. I want it to be about a man's struggle to free his mind. Freedom is a state of mind moreso than a condition. I heard a scholar say that one time."

"I get it. You want the story to be inspirational."

"If that's what you think, then you don't get it at all. I'm not looking to be nobody's inspiration, nobody's role model, and nobody's mentor. Men who are locked up are going to read this book. When you inside, all you think about is being out, but when you out—you just out. You can't even rent an apartment with a record. It's hard as hell to find a job. So it's like you've served your time, but you still have to serve more once you get out for serving any in the first place. I don't want them dudes thinking it's a cakewalk, 'cause it ain't. I'm not the only one who feels this way. Occasionally, I talk to dudes I was locked up with who are out now, and they're having a hard time too. I don't know what I want you to do. I just want you to do something."

"I think you're looking at your experience in a negative way. It's possible to come out of prison and completely turn your life around. Look at Charles Dutton. He was in prison for murder and he turned out to be a television star. There's also Nathan McCall who's a journalist and author. I'm going to get you his book, *Makes Me Wanna Holler*."

"I don't need to read a book to holler. I can holler all on my own. What's your point?"

"You're out. You're free. There are other more positive ways to look at what happened to you."

"Like what?"

"Like, if you hadn't gone in, you probably would've gotten killed on the street."

"Or maybe I wouldn't have. You named two people who turned their lives around. Do you know how many others are out here lost, confused, can't even get a five-dollar-an-hour job?"

"Maybe I should do a whole prison series. Maybe three books on the subject. I'm just fascinated by it."

"What is it to be fascinated by? You go and get yourself locked up and live among nothin' but the worst. All you think about day in and day out is how you're going to survive. The majority of the time, you're not thinking about nobody on the outside—not even your family. You won't be fascinated by it then. You'll be fucked up is what you'll be."

"So what exactly are you looking for this book to do, Tower?"

"I'm not sure. You're the writer. You figure it out. You're the one who was almost a psychiatrist. Hell, it might not do nothin' but tell a story of a man who's fucked up, because that's what I am. Everything don't have to have a happy ending. For all I care, you can have him die at the end, and that can represent my dead spirit." I heard my mama yelling out my name. "I got to go. They want me downstairs. Keep writing, okay? You're my only hope."

"Gee, thanks for the added pressure. Maybe you need to hold out for Stephen King like you said."

"Nah, a white man can't write my story."

"Can a black woman?"

"You can handle it. I'll talk to you later, okay?"

"Alright. Please call me back. You never do when you say you are."

I hung up the phone and then I walked downstairs, I saw Wallace hurry through the front door. I was surprised to see him because the last I had heard, my parents had convinced him to check into another rehab center.

"They're after me," Wallace said as he rushed into the house passed a bunch of us and went in to the den to hide in the corner next to the loveseat. He had the smell of outdoors in his dirty clothes and whiskey on his breath.

"He came over here high!" Dad shouted. "Christmas Day, and this is what we have to deal with."

Bernice and Mama started packing up the gifts, putting them in large black garbage bags, and giving them to whoever they belonged. They knew better than to keep the presents under the tree while Wallace was there. Anybody who would go over their own brother's house and run out with the base to a cordless phone would definitely run off with brand-new gifts. Mama's gold bracelet and diamond earrings were under the tree, and so was Curtis' Nintendo 64.

"Man, get up," George said to Wallace. "Nobody's after you, and if they were, you shouldn't have led them our way."

"If he owes a drug dealer some money, they'll come after him. We'll be on the evening news. Is somebody after you?" I asked Wallace.

"I couldn't stay in that place," Wallace said as he clutched his knees and started rocking. "They not trying to help. All they want to do is take somebody's money."

"Who's after you?" I asked again, much louder.

"I'm going to go," Wallace said as he tried to stand, but George and I kept him hemmed in the corner.

"Let him go!" Dad shouted. "I'm tired of this mess. Let him get back out in the street. Me and your mama have done all we can."

"I'm tired of it, too, Daddy," Wallace said. He was crying like a baby. "I'm trying my best to get myself together." He wiped the tears away with the back of his hand. "Anybody got some money I can borrow?"

"Let him go! I want him out this house!" Dad broke us up so Wallace could walk away. "Don't step foot back in this house until you can come back looking and acting the way you used to—you hear me?" Dad said to Wallace.

"Can I get a plate of food?" Wallace asked as he headed for the door.

"Yes, Wallace, sit down," Mama said.

"No, he can't," Dad said. "Leave. Go to the shelter. I'm not going to make it easy on you no more, 'cause it hasn't helped."

"Can I have a slice of ham before I go and a piece of bread, please? Or just give me five dollars so I can go to Taco Bueno."

"Show him the door," Dad told George and me, "'cause you don't want me to."

"I got this," I said to George. "Come on, Wallace." I pushed his back to get him to start walking.

"Mama, you know I can't help this, right? You know that, don't you? It's that bitch's fault."

"Get out!" Dad yelled. "I don't want to hear that talk in my house. It ain't nobody's fault but your own. The girl left you because you were using that shit. Ain't nobody a fool in here but you,

Wallace. Nobody in here feels sorry for you either."

"You gonna let him treat your firstborn like that, Mama? What kind of mother does that make you? He ain't my daddy. He ain't none of our daddy."

"You better get that fool out of here!" Dad said to me.

"Come on, Wallace," I said, pushing him all the way to the door.

"I'm going. I don't need to stay nowhere I'm not wanted. I got places to go. I guess you think I don't. I still live on Yuma. I'm still cutting hair and cleaning up the church. I can turn my life around. You watch."

"Good, turn it around, but get out of here," Dad said.

I pushed Wallace on to the porch and stood, watching tears run down his face. "Y'all don't give up on me, okay? I'm going to get it together. Especially you, Tower. Don't give up on your big brother. I used to baby-sit you. I still got a picture with you sitting in my lap when you were about six months old." He searched his pants pocket. "I got it somewhere. Damn, I just saw that picture the other day."

"It's in Mama's photo album, Wallace."

"Is that where it is? How did I see it then?"

"You didn't."

"I saw it," Wallace said, pointing to his head. "It's up here."

I shook my head. "Don't waste your life, Wallace. Don't throw it away and wake up one day wondering where it all went."

"Okay. You got five dollars you can loan me? I promise to give it back to you tomorrow. Come on. Don't turn your nose up. You used to make money off people like me. Don't think you better. You were a drug dealer. I'm a drug user. What makes you any better?"

"I *was* a drug dealer. You *are* a drug user." I turned away from him and walked back in the house. He was right. I sure did make money off people like him. People who would sign over their welfare and disability checks so they could get high all night. I used people like him to test my drugs for purity. Nobody could judge good drugs better than a crack head. If their eyes opened up real wide, their chest blew up, and they looked like they were getting ready to have a heart attack, then I knew we had some good shit. But now, all that was coming full circle. I never expected Wallace to get strung out.

He was my hero. I see how my brother's condition is tearing apart my mama, and it's sad but true that nobody can help him. If he doesn't want to change for himself, he won't. He'll die addicted to that shit.

"Lock the door behind you," Dad said when I walked inside. "I don't want him turning around and trying to get back in."

"Why didn't you let me give the boy some food?" Mama asked. "You see how skinny he's getting." She wiped her eyes with a tissue.

"I don't feel sorry for him," Dad said. "We been going through this with him for too many years now, and I'm sick and tired of him blaming that girl. She left him because he was strung out. It's only so much a woman can take—anybody for that matter."

"Calm down," Mama said to Dad.

"I'm going upstairs to lay down," Dad said. "Everybody was ready to leave after Dad hit the steps. I left the house then too. Got in my car and sat for a minute in the driveway waiting for Bernice to move her car because she had me blocked in.

I took out my cell phone and called Gail again. "How's it coming along? You finished yet?"

"Not funny. I'm nowhere near finished. I thought of some questions I needed answered."

"What are they?"

"I can't remember right now. They'll come to me, though."

"Next time, write them down," I snapped. "You not taking this seriously."

"I am so," she said.

"I hope so because I need out." I started up my engine after Bernice pulled off.

"Do you have the transcripts from your case?" she asked.

"Yeah, why? What you need those for? I told you everything that went down. I don't know where you're going with all this."

"I just want to take a look at them. Can you please bring them over tomorrow?"

"What's all this?" Gail asked as she picked up my old plastic Ziploc bag filled with newspaper clippings.

"Articles that can help you."

"Where are your transcripts?"

I pulled the two thick legal files from my backpack and handed them to her. "But make sure you start with the articles first."

She put on a pair of black-rimmed glasses, the fancy kind that made her look like an artist, and in a way, I guess she was one. She sat down at her dining room table and started reading my transcript.

"Read the articles please!" I said.

"Okay." She closed the legal file and took the articles out of the Ziploc bag. "Traffic Stop Ruling Spurs Procedure Review," she said, as she began reading the headline of each article. "Another Suspect Ruling: Police Profiting from Seizures of Drug Dealers' Assets. Gosh, this is from February 24, 1991. Life Term Possible for 'Bootnose,' Brothers Get Stiff Sentences in Drug Case." She looked up at me. "What a name—Bootnose? Do you know him?" she asked.

I shrugged. "Who I know doesn't matter. It doesn't have anything to do with the book you're writing so make sure you don't put his name in it."

"I don't know Tower. What good are any of these articles if you don't want me to use any information from them? It's already a public record so who are you protecting?"

"It's not about protecting anybody. What he was convicted of doesn't have anything to do with my case. Read the one about the traffic stop ruling."

She picked up the article and scanned it. " 'They lacked probable cause to stop and search two cars for drugs.' That sounds just like your case."

"That's what I'm trying to tell you. Keep on reading."

" 'The cars had California license tags and were occupied by four black men. The lawmen seized more than six pounds of crack cocaine and more than four pounds of marijuana with an estimated combined street value of more than a hundred thousand dollars.' You still had that beat."

"Keep on reading."

" 'But because Judge Flowers ruled the search was unconstitutional, prosecutors can't use that evidence although the defendants are still under indictment. Judge Flowers ruled that the purpose of the traffic stop was not for genuine traffic law enforcement, but instead was motivated by the officer's desire to search the car for drugs without presentation of probable cause before the stop.' That's exactly your case."

"It happens all the time," I said.

"I can't believe you still have this article from January 17, 1994. Listen to this. 'In this case, the cars were stopped last October on Interstate 35 in Edmond. The troopers claim the first car was stopped for going sixty-three miles per hour in a fifty-five mile-per-hour zone, and the second car for following too closely.' If that doesn't sound exactly like what happened to you..."

"That's what I'm trying to tell you," I said as I paced her living room.

"Okay, hold on. I'm still reading. 'Judge Flowers said Trooper Bill Warner testified he intended to give the drivers either a warning or a ticket, but neither was given and the team moved right on to the sniff and search.' Woo, this makes me mad. 'The two drivers were plucked out of the stream to be sniffed just because of the way they looked, the judge said.' Too bad you didn't have that judge."

"See, Gail, you have to understand. The cops who arrested us were crooked because first, they took us to Browerton police department to book us. I had nine hundred dollars on me, and Quentin had about fifteen hundred on him, but none of that money was ever booked into evidence. They kept it. And they really wanted that bust. Nothing like that had ever gone down in that small town."

"I feel so sorry for Stanley." Gail's eyes started to water.

"What's wrong with you?"

"I just hate the way this world is. There's no justice. Most of our black men are in prison or on drugs. The black family is dying. I hate this."

"I want you to read all of those articles, especially the one about how much police departments profit from the drug business." I put on my leather jacket.

"Can't you stay?"

"No." I held my arms open for her. She walked over, and I squeezed her tightly. "I need you to be my friend. I think you might be the only person who knows this much about my life, and yet there's still so much more I have to tell you."

"I'm never going to leave you. I'm always going to be your friend." I kissed her on the cheek and walked toward the front door. It seemed like I'd known Gail for a lifetime, but in reality we hadn't even known each other for a full month. "Tower." I turned to face her. "Do you have a woman?" I shook my head. "Someone who you're seeing?"

I shook my head again. "I'm too fucked up to be in a relationship."

"Well, I'm here for you."

I nodded. "Okay." I walked out of her house. I didn't understand Gail or what she saw in me. I couldn't give her anything. Not even the simplest of things.

Mary and I were in the bed at a motel near DFW airport. I was moving my dick in and out of her very quickly when suddenly I saw Gail's smiling face and heard her ask, "Do you have a woman? Someone who you're seeing?" How could I explain this to her? I was planning on telling her everything, except this. She wouldn't understand. I didn't even understand.

"Is this what you want?" I asked as I rammed myself harder inside of Mary. Frustration fucking is what I was doing. "Is it? This is all you care about, isn't it?" I had a handful of her hair as I yanked her head back. "Now, who's in control?"

"You're getting a little carried away. This isn't cute. Let go of me. It hurts."

"Don't you like it like this?"

"Stop it!"

I pulled my dick out of Mary, stood, and looked down at her. "When are you taking me off paper? I'm not trying to report to you for the next fifteen years."

"I don't like what you just did to me. What was that all about anyway?"

"I thought that's what you wanted. You're always talking about my big dick so that's what I gave you."

"You're acting different. Have you been with another woman?"

"No, why? What difference does it make if I have? You got a husband. You mean to tell me I can't get with another woman if I want."

"You don't need a woman, Tower," she said forcefully. "You're not ready for a relationship. How many times do I have to tell you that?"

"It doesn't have to be a relationship," I said as I stepped into my boxers and then my jeans. "Maybe I want to have sex with a woman, someone other than you. Someone who knows how to move and get freaky."

You better watch how you talk to her. Is you crazy? Well, even if you are, is you that crazy? Do you know what she can do to you? my mean voice asked.

"I don't care what she can do to me," I said.

"Who are you talking to, Tower?"

"Myself. I do that occasionally." I headed toward the door.

"I don't like the way you're acting, but I'm going to excuse it for now. I think you'll be much better off once you move out of Bernice's house. She's a very angry woman, and it seems to be rubbing off on you. Call me when you get in so that I know you've made it safely."

"Hopefully, I'll crash."

"What?"

"You heard me."

"What is this all about, Tower?"

"I want to be off paper."

"We'll see."

"We'll do more than see. Get me off paper, Mary, I mean it!"

"Or what, Tower? I've been patient with you, but I'm tired of you making demands when you're in no position to. I said I'll see, and that's what I mean."

I stood at the front door with my hand tightly gripping the knob.

That bitch don't know who she's fuckin' with. She thinks 'cause she carry a gun and work for the Department of Probation and Parole that means something. She don't know you. She don't know that you know niggas who would gladly go over to her house and kill her and her entire family just 'cause you asked them to. See, that's how those kinds of people are. They think they can get away with treating people like shit. Everybody got a fuckin' breaking point. You been too quiet with her ass, but sooner or later, you gonna snap on her. I know you, and I know what you capable of. She don't though. But if she keeps all this shit up, the bitch 'bout to find out.

CHAPTER 19

On Sunday I went to church alone. Bernice had stopped going, but she'd be back, just as soon as her life let her down again. Just as soon as she started adding on more weight, because that's when the family knew there was something wrong with her. She used church like a drug. Used God. Went four Sundays in a row after Marshall told her he needed some time to reevaluate their relationship because he felt he might need a woman who was equal to him, a woman with a college degree, who didn't have kids, and owned a home instead of rented one from her parents, and most importantly, a woman who wasn't still married. That's when she started attending church faithfully. Going to the 8:00 A.M. service, but just as soon as Marshall called back saying he had decided to stay with her after all because he realized no one was perfect, she buried her Bible underneath a stack of old *Ebony* and *Essence* magazines in a wire magazine rack in the living room.

Now I was the one asking Bernice if she wanted to go to church, instead of the other way around. She was the one rolling over in bed with the cover over her head, trying to get more rest like I used to, or else her door was locked because Marshall was over, which usually was the case on the weekends.

When I walked into church, Tonya, the woman who considered herself as my mentor, was standing in the center of the pulpit singing

"The Battle is the Lord's." I guess it was her voice that held me captive. I loved the fact that she could hold a note. She had the best voice I'd ever heard, better than these new singers out now. It made her outside look so beautiful. Never mind she was more than two hundred pounds and short. Never mind she was just a plain-looking woman, who at twenty-eight could easily pass for forty. When I heard her voice, my spirits were lifted.

I thought it was special that Tonya smiled at me whenever she saw me. Even if she didn't have Gail's smile, I still felt important, which is why I sat in the front instead of near the back as usual. As she sang, I kept looking at her, wondering what I could do with her. Everyone had to serve some purpose in my life. And I wondered what hers would be. Slim Earl, the pimp from the pen, used to tell us, when he got out, he wasn't slinging dope 'cause he could easily sling women.

Fuck her fat ass and forget her, my mean voice said.

Don't talk like that in the house of the Lord, my nice one said.

I guarantee you this ain't the Lord's house. That preacher looks like a pimp. Looks just like Slim Earl. You know damn well his ass spent some time in the pen. Preaching ain't nothin' but another hustle for him. This ain't no Church of God in Christ, this is Church of God and a Pimp, my mean voice said.

I bet she's nice, my nice voice said. *I bet she'll treat you good. I bet she'll cook for you.*

You damn right her fat ass will cook. She ain't that big for no reason.

Don't listen to him, Tower. I bet she'll help you. That's all you need right now is help, not a relationship, my nice voice said.

He got that other woman for that, the one writing the story on him. You want somebody to fuck. Fuck her. You seen the lips on that bitch. With those lips I know she can give one hell of a blow job, and besides that, the bitch trying to work on some cash flow for you. You never know, that story could be a bestseller and if it is, tell that bitch you want your damn cut. You better make that shit clear. I still don't see no contract. Go over her house today and demand you get everything in writing. Otherwise, it's your word against hers, and you know who they gonna believe—the one without the record, my mean voice said.

He can't take her to court anyway because the court's going to want its cut from all the restitution he owes them, my nice voice said.

Oh, that's right. Well she can pay your ass under the table then. And while you over there, go on and get you some.

Tower, don't listen to him. Pray. Pray for peace of mind.

Peace of mind? After all we went through, I don't care how hard you pray, nothing's gonna change.

When service ended, I went over to talk to Tonya. I didn't want to say much to her. Didn't know much of what to say. I did know not to ask her how she was doing. Didn't need to because I knew the response would always be, "blessed." And I knew if she asked me, how I was, I had better say, "The Lord is good. I'm truly blessed." She didn't want to hear nothin' like, "Okay." And she really didn't want to hear the truth. Didn't want to hear that I was crazy. Hearing voices. Couldn't make up my mind from one minute to the next and didn't know how to tell the truth for lying. Best thing I could do with Tonya was fake it. I told her some things, but not all. I reserved my truth telling for Gail who seemed to thrive on my problems. I did tell Tonya that Gail was writing a book about me. She got mad and wanted to know why I didn't let her write it. "Is she saved?"

"Not sure."

"Then she must not be. Does she even attend church?"

"I'm not sure about that either."

"Why would you let some worldly woman write your story? Tell her you've changed your mind. God's not going to bless that. I'll write it. I've always wanted to write a book."

"Let me think about it."

After I left church, I sat in the parking lot and waited for the cars to leave so I could too. While I waited, I called Gail on my cell phone. She always answered on the first or second ring. If it went to three, she wasn't home, and that was rare. Every now and then she'd go to TJ Maxx or Ross, but never to a mall. She knew how to do her own hair and did her own manicure and pedicure. I don't think she liked going out. I think if she didn't have a job at the bank, she would stay in her house all day, every day. In fact, I know she would. I don't even think she much liked people. I think all she had patience for was one person at a time and writing.

"What you doing?" I asked her as soon as she said hello.

"What I'm always doing—writing."

"I just came out of church, and I wanted to call to see how you were."

"Are you coming over later?"

"Not today. I have a headache."

"The voices again?"

"What you mean, again? They're not going anywhere."

"Maybe they will. Maybe if you start ignoring them. Try that."

"You always make things sound so easy. When you go through what I've been through then I guess you can give advice. Just because you were almost a psychiatrist doesn't mean you can help me—sorry."

"If you feel like talking later, give me a call. I'll be here."

"Why?"

"Why what, Tower?"

"Why don't you ever go anywhere? Why you always stay in that house? It's Sunday. You need to be in church."

"I just signed off from church."

"What you mean?"

"I went to church online."

"You went online? That's for people who can't get out of the house. Nothing's wrong with you."

"Okay, Tower. I'll talk to you later." She held the phone. I knew I had hurt her feelings because she was so sensitive. Couldn't tell her nothing without her jumping to the defense most of the time or ending the call at a moment's notice.

"Why you got to go? I'm just trying to help you," I said.

"Help me how?"

"By telling you that you need to go to church."

"Why, so I can be like you? You go to church every week, and I don't see you exactly overflowing in optimism and happiness. In fact, most of the time you're telling me about how unhappy and empty you feel. Don't you know that your mouth is a sword? When you speak, you give life to those words."

"That's so easy for you to say. You've never been through nothin'."

"You don't know what I've been through. Just because I choose not to talk about my problems doesn't mean I haven't had any."

"I'll talk to you later, Gail." I heard a dial tone before I could say good-bye. I was used to her hanging up on me. She'd be fine the next day because she didn't hold grudges.

I had planned on calling Gail, but I changed my mind after talking to Tonya for almost two hours on the phone about God and listening to her break some things down about the three different kinds of people: the natural man is dead inwardly and alive outwardly, the spiritual man who has been born again, and the carnal man who is born again and being fed by his flesh.

Tonya said that if a person worries at all, he's carnal. She said, "People have to hear no evil and speak no evil." The way I looked at it, I was a natural man with carnal instincts. I was just like the guy I attacked while I was on the inside—a dead man walking—only I was worse than him because he didn't know he was a dead man, but I knew for sure I was one, which is what made me a natural man. What made me carnal were all the issues I had dealing with my flesh. I had a problem with looking at women. I'd imagine myself having sex with them. If some woman walked into the tire shop, don't let her have on a skirt and a pair of heels. Don't let her have nice legs. I didn't need to ask for her number. Didn't have to try to date her. I could take a permanent picture with my eyes, and my mind could play with her for weeks or months, probably years, which is what I did when I was locked up, and I preferred it that way because you didn't have to listen to a woman complaining all the time. I didn't have to answer questions about my whereabouts, 'cause if it's one thing I can't stand, it's somebody asking me where I am or telling me what I better do or not do.

"Hello," Gail said, answering the phone with a groggy voice. It was 2:15 A.M.

"I'm carnal."

"You have the wrong number," she said and hung up. I called right back.

"Gail, this is Tower," I said when she answered. "What you hang up on me for?"

"Didn't you say you wanted to speak to Carol?"

"Nah, I said I'm carnal."

"Oh, so am I," she said and hung up again.

I dialed her area code but then hung up. I figured it'd be best for me to catch her at work the next morning, since I was off. I could stop by the bank just to say hello.

CHAPTER 20

There was a closed sign in Gail's teller window, but she was still standing there, wearing all black as usual. She was staring at nothing because nothing was in front of her. I supposed her mind had traveled into the fiction world, the one she told me she preferred to live in. I waved, but she didn't even notice me. It wasn't until I walked up to her window that she snapped out of it and smiled. I saw those cuts cave in on both cheeks. Wouldn't be long now. My mean voice was getting impatient. He wanted to feel Gail from the inside. If she kept smiling at me like that, it wouldn't be long at all.

"Are you closed?" I asked.

"Not really. I'm just working the drive-thru. What are you doing here?"

"I came to take you to lunch," I said as I pushed my check under her till.

"Did you come to take me to lunch or to get your check cashed?"

"Well, can you cash my check and then I can take you to lunch."

"Do you want any large bills?" she asked.

"Are you trying to be funny? It's not like my check is that big, Gail."

She smiled and handed me fifteen twenties, four tens, three fives, two ones, and sixty-eight cents in change. "Don't worry about lunch."

"Why, you can't go or you still refuse to eat?"

"I never refuse to eat. I just don't eat that much. Besides, I brought my lunch today."

"When we gonna start back working on the book? I thought of some things the other night."

"What kinds of things?" she asked.

I looked around as a line started to form. "You gonna have to take down that closed sign."

"But I'm closed while I'm helping out the drive-thru."

"When can we see each other again? Can I come over tonight?" *Tell her she looks pretty today.* "You look nice." She smiled. A car pulled up to the drive-thru. "I guess I better let you get back to work."

"You can come over tonight, but please try to make it earlier than one in the morning."

"And can you please try to wear a color other than black?" She smiled. "Anybody ever tell you that you have the prettiest smile in the universe?"

"Maybe," she said, smiling. "I got to go," she said after the car blew its horn.

"I'll see you tonight," I said, shoving my money in my pocket and walking outside.

That's what I'm talking about. We gonna get us some tonight—the prettiest smile in the universe. Mmm-hmm. Whatever she needs to hear, say it. I just got one request: Make it last forever.

I took off my coat and hung it in the entry closet of Gail's house as soon as I came through the door. I'd visited enough times to where she no longer considered me a guest.

Look at her! She ain't got on black today, my mean voice said.

She was wearing a green skintight sweater dress. The front was cut low enough so I could see her cleavage and the tiny heart-shaped mole in the middle of her right breast. Even though Gail was nearly half of Tonya's size, her calves were much larger than Tonya's. My mouth fell open slightly and my tongue was hanging out as I watched her walk up the stairs, swaying her hips. She wasn't as skinny as I thought. I think all that black she wore made her look smaller than she really was. Now she had on something where I could see what I was getting.

You ain't getting shit! I'm getting this, my mean voice said.

I imagined myself moving in and out of Gail. I pictured her using her large lips to satisfy me. Her legs were long enough to straddle my entire body.

"Come here and give me a hug," I said after we made it into her bedroom. When she fell into my arms, I smelled how fresh her skin was, how clean her hair was. I wanted to kiss her lips, but instead I sucked her nipples like I was trying to get milk from them. "I haven't been with a woman in years," I lied. "Will you let me?" I asked. I took out the gold condom package and held it between my two fingers. "Please let me."

She stared at me for almost a minute.

Don't say shit. The first one who opens his mouth loses. She's thinking about it. Let her think.

She nodded.

I pulled off my sweatshirt, undershirt, and dropped my pants and the condom package on the floor.

"Don't forget to put on the condom."

"Why I got to put one on? I still remember how to pull out."

She shook her head. "You just have to. There are diseases out there."

Don't press it! Put it on! It's still gonna feel good.

I sat on the edge of the bed and tore open the condom package. Then I handed the rubber to her so she could slide it on me. I wanted to feel her soft hands touch my rock-hard dick.

I sat on the bed with my legs spread open so she could kneel between me and slip on the rubber. "Will you kiss the head before you put it on?" I asked. She looked up at me hesitantly. "That's okay, forget it. Just put it on." I looked down at her. "Kiss it. Please." I put my hands on her face and tried to guide her toward my dick, but she shook her head. "No, let's just have regular sex."

"You don't like oral sex?" She didn't respond. "Okay, regular sex." *Beggars can't be choosers.* She sat in my lap, wrapping her long legs around me. "You're real limber."

"I was a ballerina and a gymnast."

Damn! She's limber and graceful.

I pushed my body farther back on the bed and laid down. She turned so that her her back was facing me, and she pushed her ass in my face. She was making a lot of exotic movements, and before I even had a chance to slip my dick inside of her, I came.

What the fuck was that? I ain't wait all this time for you to get off by yourself. We ain't in prison no more. This is a real woman we got now. I don't believe this shit.

"Shut up!" I screamed.

Gail's eyes enlarged as she turned to face me. "But I didn't say anything."

"Not you."

"Oh, the voices?"

I nodded. "Ooh!" I shouted. "I wanted you so bad. That shit ain't never happened to me before—ever."

"It's okay."

"It's not okay! And don't tell me it is! Ooh," I said as I started hitting my forehead with the palm of my hand. "You just don't know how bad I wanted to be inside of you."

"It's okay. Stop doing that." She held both of my hands, and then put them up to her lips and started kissing them. She took my middle finger and stuck it in her mouth, and began sucking on it, but stopped a few seconds later. "We have plenty of time to be together. Let's work on the book." Gail opened her nightstand and took out her microcassette recorder. "We ended with your sentencing. By the way, I finished reading those articles."

"You think I'm weird, don't you?"

"No," she said, looking away from me.

"Yes, you do. You think I'm weird because I hear voices and because I wasn't able to do nothin' with you just then. No telling what your mind is thinking, but whatever it's thinking, it's not true."

"So you're not a nice person?"

"That wasn't what you were thinking."

"Yes, it was."

"What you want to know? Ask me some questions. Do you have the tape recorder on?"

"Yes. What happened after the trial? After you were convicted and they led you away?"

"I stayed in a holding cell for a couple of weeks and then they took me to Murray A&R."

"What's A&R stand for?"

"I think admittance and receiving, something like that. Anyway, every prisoner in the State of Oklahoma goes through A&R. That's where they take your dental records, cut off all your hair to see if you have lice, and throw powder all over your body to kill any lice you may have and to make sure you're not carrying any germs in with you."

"How did you feel?"

"How you think I felt? I was freaking out. All I could think about was all of those years the judge gave me. I kept telling myself that I would wake up soon and be home. I knew I couldn't do that much time. I wouldn't have done that much time. I don't know how I did ten years. Some days, I thought about killing myself."

"Like Phillip Ross."

"Who?"

"He sat next to me in my ninth grade English class."

"Why'd he kill himself if he was only in the ninth grade? What a ninth grader got to worry about?"

"They said that he did it because his father remarried this young woman, and she treated Phillip like crap. His dad started ignoring him. Plus, Phillip's mother had just passed and they were real close, and his girlfriend had broken up with him, but mostly because the suicide was a mistake. Phillip didn't want to die. His friend said that Phillip told him he was going to hang himself a few minutes before his father and stepmother came home. He wanted them to find him hanging there. He wanted to get their attention. He figured he could stay like that for a few minutes and since they always entered through the side door every day by 6:07, he hung himself at the bottom of the basement steps so they'd see him as soon as they walked in. Only they didn't get home until 8:30 that night, and Phillip was hanging there with his dog laying under his feet, crying." Gail had tears in her eyes. "If he would have confided in me, I would have told somebody. I would have tried to help, but his friends didn't take him seriously. That was my buddy."

"Death don't mean nothing to me," I said. "I've seen so many people get killed in the pen. I got so many obituaries mailed to me when I was in, that now, death don't mean nothin'. I think maybe some people are better off being dead, 'cause life ain't about shit no way. What's there to look forward to?"

"Plenty."

"Name something. What do you look forward to?"

"Being a best-selling author."

"What if you don't become one? Everybody don't get what they want out of life, so what's your plan B?"

"That is my plan B."

"Well, you better start working on a plan C then. Keep on going down the alphabet 'cause, one thing I learned about life: it's full of twists and turns and a bunch of brick walls you can slam into."

"Why are you so negative?"

"Why am I so negative? Have you been listening? Rewind those tapes of yours and play 'em back! I was in prison trying to survive. Do you understand where I just came from?" She nodded. "I don't think you do. The person I've introduced you to is not the same person I was while I was in prison. And trust me, you don't want to meet him because he doesn't give a fuck about you. I would've done anything in there to survive. I had to be ready at all times just in case some scandalous shit broke out. Some dudes walked around with their shoelaces untied, but I never did. That's not a secure position to be in. 'You have to have your seat belts on.' That's what we used to say in the pen. That meant you had to be ready at all times to defend yourself. If I saw a bunch of Aryans in a group walking toward me, I had to be ready to fuck 'em up."

"Did you have sex with men while you were in there?"

"What kind of shit is that to ask? Hell no I didn't have sex with no man."

"Tower, why are you acting like that doesn't go on when you know it does?"

"I guess it does. It depends what prison you in. I don't want to talk about this right now. Move on to something else."

"Eventually, we'll have to talk about it because I can't write a book about prison and not discuss it."

"Move on!"

"I hope you don't think I have anything against homosexuals. I had another friend in high school who was gay, and he died of AIDS in '90."

"I said, move on!"

"What happened to Stanley?"

I shrugged. "We were in A&R together, but they ended up sending him to the Oklahoma State Penitentiary, a maximum-security prison, where I was almost sent, but a bed opened up at Murray. I saw Stanley from a distance as the guards at the Department of Corrections prepared to bus him. I remember thinking that he wouldn't make it."

"Why didn't you tell them he was innocent? You could have told someone that he switched seats right before they pulled you all over. Why didn't you?"

"Stop the tape," I said. She took the tape recorder off the nightstand and pressed the stop button. "Oh, so you putting all the blame on me now, huh? Who you think was going to listen to me? Besides, I was looking out for myself. We all were."

"Is he still in there?"

"I nodded. "Serving life without parole."

"Why so much time?"

"Play the tape back! I already told you why. They linked his ass to some murders in Texas, and he went to trial for that in Texas and was found guilty. He was also sentenced to forty years in Oklahoma just like I was. So whenever he finishes serving his time in Oklahoma he's going to go to a Texas prison to serve a life sentence without parole."

"You never told me all that."

"Rewind your tape and listen."

"You told me some of those things, but you never told me that he went to court in Texas—"

"Okay, well, I'm telling you now!" She sighed and got real quiet.

"What's wrong with you?"

"I don't understand why you yell at me all the time."

"I yell at you because you ask too many questions."

Too many damn questions. Say it the way I would, my mean voice said. *And because you're frustrated since you couldn't get no damn pussy! Be sure to tell her that.*

"I'm writing a book on you, I have to ask questions."

"The same questions over and over. I don't think so."

"I need to be writing a book about Stanley."

"Why, you don't like my story no more?"

"He's serving life without parole and he's innocent. You need to do something."

"What can I do about that?"

"I don't know, but you need to do something."

"There's nothing I can do, Gail."

"You can't keep an innocent man in prison. That's not right."

"Hell, you think he's the only one?"

"But I'm sure there's something you can do. Someone you can talk to surely."

"It's not like there's DNA evidence that can be used to clear him. It's just me saying he's innocent."

She puckered her lips. "Where are Quentin and Arturo?"

"Nobody's seen Arturo since the trial. And Quentin's around. I see him driving his expensive cars from time to time. He settled down and got married. Supposedly went clean and got into real estate, but I know that's a lie. He's still doing dirt."

"How do you feel about them?"

"Don't matter how I feel because how I feel won't change what happened."

"What did happen?"

"What do you mean what did happen? I went to prison. I lived in a box for eight years and then in a community center for two more. Gail, think about that. I was in a cage like a fuckin' animal. That's too long. I ain't right. Then when you get out and you run into people on the street who knew you were in, they treat you all funny. Don't want to associate with you no more. I've had that happen. That's why I mainly stay to myself and don't have many friends."

"I don't treat you funny."

"That's you. You're an exception. Let's just say we started dating. You couldn't tell your girlfriends that your man is an ex-con because they would dog you out."

"I don't have any girlfriends."

"If you did."

"I don't."

"Hypothetically speaking."

She shrugged. "I don't."

"Well, your parents then. You can't tell them."

"They just want me to be happy."

"They don't want you with an ex-con. Happy or not."

"Believe me, they just want me to be happy." She looked off. Then she looked over at me and stared into my eyes in silence.

"What?" I asked.

"I don't want to feel sorry for you."

"I'm not asking for your pity. If that's what you think, you wrong."

"I just wish it wouldn't have happened to you, but it did, and there's nothing you or I can do about it now. Maybe by telling me everything you went through I can write this book so that a weight will be lifted from you."

"This is one heavy-ass weight, Gail."

She pressed the play button on the recorder. "Let's continue. So you went to Murray A&R, which stands for admittance and receiving," she said as she held the tape recorder close to her mouth for a second, "and then what happened after you found out you were staying there?"

"First thing they did was give each of us one bar of soap, a small comb, a tube of toothpaste, and a toothbrush, and then the guards took us to our unit. I was sent to Unit 4. Each unit had four quads, and there were around forty-eight people to a quad, unless they were overcrowded. Prison is big business in Oklahoma. You do realize that, right?"

"Realize what?"

"That the prison system is a big business, especially in Oklahoma.

Did you know that Oklahoma has more women incarcerated than any other state?"

"Even Texas and California? Are you sure about that?"

"Yeah, look it up. Go on the Internet."

"What would I look under?"

"I don't know. I read it somewhere. Look it up if you don't believe me."

"I'll take your word for it. So when you first walked into the prison, what did you think?"

"There you go with that what did I think and how did I feel. I was scared, but then I looked around and dudes were standing around or walking away from the commissary carrying bags with potato chips sticking out of 'em, so I figured it might not be so bad."

"Just because of that."

"Hell yeah. I didn't think there would be a store in there, and I love junk food. Anyway, the other inmates knew we were the new fish coming in because we had on orange jumpers and everyone else was wearing state-issued blue jeans and shirts. It took the Department of Corrections a few days to issue clothing to new inmates. On arrival day we were issued a plastic mattress, a blanket, one sheet, one pillowcase, and then the guards took us to our cell."

"Explain the quad for me so I can describe it in the book."

I sighed. This was getting difficult. The more Gail made me talk about prison, the more I had to relive it, and the harder it became for me to separate being in from being out. "Each quad shared a common area called the dayroom. There was a TV, a bunch of chairs, and some tables in the dayroom."

"Was there a VCR?"

"Where do you think I was?"

"I just thought—"

"No!"

"Could you have a TV in your room?"

"You mean my box. Yeah, we could have a TV. No larger than thirteen inches and it had to be shipped straight from the manufacturer."

"Why?"

I shrugged. "I guess because if it came from your people, they could hide something in it."

"Could you have a VCR in your box?" she asked. I stared at her in silence. "What? Why are you looking at me like that?"

"What did you just ask me?"

"Could you have a VCR in your box?"

"If we couldn't have a VCR in the dayroom, why would we be able to have one in our box," I said, jabbing my finger at the side of my forehead. "If you use your head, this project will go a lot faster." She smiled. "Like I was saying, each quad had two individual shower stalls and one pay phone. You had to have your timing down because there was always a line of people waiting for both the shower and the phone."

"So wait a minute, you mean you didn't have to shower with a bunch of other men?"

"No. That's what I'm trying to tell you, our prison wasn't like that—none of that don't-drop-the-soap shit."

"So when you got to your cell and saw your roommate, you knew you had to get along with him, huh?"

"You mean my celly? Hell yeah, I knew I had to get along with him. It's not enough space not to."

"What was he in for?"

"He told me he was in for armed robbery, but I found out later he was in for assaulting his ex-wife."

"What was he like?"

"He was cool. He had a serious nature, and he seemed to be living on a short fuse, but we got along. He worked in the cafeteria and snuck out blocks of cheese. We'd buy nachos from this old man who ran a store from his cell, and then we'd sell nachos and cheese from our cell for a dollar. That was one of my hustles."

"Oh, so you had more."

I nodded. "Many more."

"What else can you tell me?"

"What else can I tell you? Let me think."

"Altogether, I had six cellys before I was transferred to the community center. Three were paroled. One was killed on the yard. Another was transferred to a different unit within our same prison because we didn't get along. The other took a catch-out, which is a transfer to another prison. Usually that's done to avoid a beat down. In my celly's case, he took a catch-out because he owed Bill, the old man who ran the store from his cell, a lot of money and he couldn't pay him so he knew if he didn't get out of there, the old man's crew would come after him. Everybody in there was cool with Bill, and you just couldn't take from him, not pay for it, and expect to get away with that. I wouldn't have let him get away with that, and he was my celly.

"I'd say of all my cellys, Melvin and Punisher were the two I considered to be friends. I'll tell you about Punisher later. He was a straight-up character—a white boy who was a hit man for hire by trade and was in for life without parole.

"Melvin was my first celly. When I first went in, I had to get used to the guard coming to our cell at 5:00 A.M. every day to let Melvin out so he could report to work in the kitchen and get breakfast ready by eight. I'd hear the guard's keys jingling from his side as he walked toward our cell. I could never sleep in because of that. At 7:50, the electricity was cut on to everyone's door, but we had a button inside of our cell so we could keep our doors locked, and often that's what I did because sometimes I didn't feel like going out, and I definitely didn't want anybody coming in on me. 'You always have to remember where you are,' an old-timer said once. 'Somebody could've spent the whole week plotting on how they're going to jack you, and your door being unlocked with you laying up there won't help the situation none.' But even if I locked myself in, I knew if someone really wanted to get me, for whatever reason—and in prison the reason didn't have to be much—they could do it. They might know a guard and arrange to have the cell door popped. That's happened before. I remember this one time in particular when some Aryans went in and stabbed a Mexican in the middle of the night. I didn't see it happen. A lot of things you don't see happen, but you hear about 'em, and you hear who did it. You realize the guards are in on it after they do their little investigation and can't come up with one lead.

"First week I was in, a muthafucka in the cell next to me was torched. Some dude walked by his cell, threw some gasoline on him, and then flicked a cigarette in at the same time. By the time the guards got to him, he was burned nearly to death. His skin was peeling off him. That's one of the many times we were put on lockdown for seventy-two hours straight while an investigation was done. The guards came up with something that time. One of the lawn orderlies, which explains where the gasoline came from, was responsible for the take down. Some of my boys from inside thought it was a hit and that someone from another prison got a kite, which is a note with instructions, to the orderly.

" 'Choose your friends wisely in here, boy,' an old-timer told me once. ' 'Cause when you choose your friends, you're also choosing your enemies.' In my mind, it would've been a hell of a lot easier not to deal with nobody, but you can't be a loner in prison. That's one sure way to die or get jacked for shit that you just bought out the commissary. It's a whole lot of trouble on the yard, and you need people who have your back. When I went out on the yard, I went where I needed to and came back because I knew the guards would be watching me from above. When you're new and they don't know nothing about you, you're guilty by association. If you start hanging with a gang-banger—a Blood or a Crip—then you're automatically one in the guards' eyes.

"There were a lot of gang-bangers coming in with life-without-parole sentences, but they acted like it was just another day because a lot of them had friends and family members in the pen, and they were able to see them again. I guess it was cool for them to play basketball and talk shit with their boys. Most of them were young—seventeen, eighteen. Probably didn't have any responsibilities on the outside—no woman who loved them, no kids, no house. But I was waiting for reality to hit their ass, to wake them up and let them know where they really were and that they were going to be there forever.

"A typical afternoon for me in prison would be to go to Slim Earl's cell and watch TV because he had the better one. We'd watch the news to get advance notice of who might be coming in and why.

The other way we usually found out was through the law clerk, Spivey, because he had access to everyone's records. The reason this was important was so you could be prepared for whoever might decide to strike or who you might need to strike against. A child molester won't go around bragging that that's what he's in for. If you know you're about to get into it with some crazy muthafucka, like the one I heard about who chopped off his mother's head and put it into the microwave, then you know you either have to kill him or be killed. Even though the system decided to spare his life, I don't have to. That's just the way it works on the inside. If child molesters aren't transferred into a protective custody unit then they're what we call dead men walking. You have to understand there are too many men on the inside who will never have the opportunity to see their children, and it's eating them up inside. Imagine, along comes a man who's molested someone else's child or his own. Most inmates take that personal."

"Turn off the damn TV!" Slim Earl shouted. He had a high-pitched voice, and if you didn't listen carefully, you might miss half of what he was saying because he spoke so quickly.

"Let me get them clothes for you," Famous said as he stuck his head in Slim Earl's cell. Famous worked in laundry and knew how to make spray starch. He called himself having a pick-up and delivery laundry service, and Slim Earl was one of his VIP customers. Slim Earl looked like the stereotypical pimp, even in a prison uniform. We were only allowed to wear one gold chain and one gold ring, but Slim Earl always wore more, especially on visiting day. He wanted to be as sharp on the inside as he was on the outside, and I never saw anybody in that prison who could hook up state-issued jeans and a shirt the way Slim Earl could. He had plenty of stories to tell, and he'd go back as far as you'd let him, talking about his Cadillac Seville and his many hoes. He felt because he had about ten hoes out on a track, that somehow qualified him to be every male inmate's relationship counselor. But to me, he was nothing more than a comedian, a fast talker who tried to look good.

I liked being around Slim Earl because if he didn't do anything else, he always made me laugh.

"The remote's next to you, fool," his celly Foster said.

"Then I guess I got to turn it off, huh? I must be smoking too much chronic." He was sitting in the chair that he had one of his runners steal from the cafeteria with his legs crossed and the one hand that was covered with diamond rings dangling off his bony knee. His hair was in processed waves. He had as much gold in his mouth as he had around his neck.

"This nigga over here crying over a bitch!" Slim Earl said with his nose turned up, eyeing Malcolm, another inmate who lived in the cell two doors down from me. I looked at Malcolm, trying to figure him out. I thought it was strange that he was so worried about what his girl was doing on the outside when I'd seen him coming out a fag's cell with his head and his fly down.

"Nah, man, it ain't that I'm crying," Malcolm said, fighting back tears. "I ain't crying. You don't see no tears over here."

"Yes, we do," we all said.

"I'm just sayin'. She ain't have to do me like that when I care for her."

"Oh, shit," Slim Earl said, spraying the word. "Man, don't you ever let a hoe run over you. What you think this is? You need to take control of that bitch right now. Shit, you may be locked up, but you ain't locked down. You got to control the situation. I have ten hoes in control, and you can't handle one. You need to get you a bitch up in here who can help you. If she can't help you, what you need her for? Let her ass go. You need you a bitch who's gonna put some money on your books and send you some shit. You need to get you one up here who's pulling you off something. Put you a better TV in your own damn house so you muthafuckas can stop coming by mine. You can do bad by your damn self. You sure as hell don't need a bitch keeping your ass down." I laughed so loud I fell off the bunk onto the floor. "What the hell is wrong with him? Don't let me turn the spotlight on your ass," Slim Earl said.

"Man, you funny as hell," I said.

"This ain't no joke. You think it is? Come to Lubbock when you get out so I can show y'all how I'm really running things. You see how I run things on visiting day, don't you? It's a revolving door—hoe in, hoe out. You, on the other hand, I ain't seen your bitch in what? How long you been in?" Slim Earl asked me.

"I don't know," I said.

"Oh, you know. If you don't know shit, you know how long your ass been in. Well, it don't matter, 'cause I know one thing about your bitch: She ain't been to see you in a long time. What's up with that?"

I had probably been in for a few months. I knew why Lisa stopped coming to see me, because I made sure she wouldn't be able to, but I wasn't going to tell them fools my business. "She's busy with school, but she writes me," I lied.

"Write? What the hell you need a letter for? Tell her to save her stamps, put away the pen and paper, and put some money on your books. I'm quite sure when you were out hustlin', you bought her ass plenty of shit. Now, tell her it's time to reciprocate."

"It's cool. She don't need to do that," I said.

"Cool for who? She must have you pussy whipped all the way from prison. I need to have that hoe working for me."

"Don't talk about my girl like that. She ain't no hoe."

"Every woman's a hoe. Don't ever forget that. She might not be a hoe with you, but she's a hoe with somebody."

"I mean it, man," I said. "Don't talk about the mother of my child like that. She ain't no damn hoe," I said, standing.

"Alright, calm down. If she ain't a hoe, she ain't a hoe. But here I am trying to tell Malcolm to move on, and your ass is stuck in park. Put your shit in drive. You need to have enough control over your hoe—" Slim Earl looked at me—"woman that you don't worry about her straying. If I was sentenced to 999 years like old Bill's ass, I know my hoes would wait, and I can call my hoes hoes." The way old Bill's story circulated, the first sentence he served was for possession of marijuana. He didn't get much time at all. The second time he was in was ten years prior, and he'd spent five years for a minor drug offense before he was paroled. He turned around and got arrested a year after he was released for trafficking cocaine. Since that was his third offense, the judge gave him 999 years. I guess that's why the guards let old Bill do much of whatever he wanted. Hell, with 999 years, why not?

"That's a long-ass wait," Slim Earl's celly, Foster, said. Right around that time, my celly, Melvin, walked in and stood near the doorway.

"It's an eternal wait. And that's how long these hoes I got will wait," Slim Earl said. "Malcolm, on the other hand, has a hoe letting another nigga answer her phone to accept Malcolm's collect call so he can cuss Malcolm out."

"I wish my wife would do some shit like that," Melvin said as he took a hit from his cigarette.

"Tell me about it," Slim Earl said. "See, Melvin got control."

Melvin shook his head. "I wouldn't stand for that. That's your woman—that's yours." He continued shaking his head and squinting as if he could visualize his wife with another man. "Nah, you can't have that. The mother of your children, that's enough to make a nigga snap."

"*Woo*," Slim Earl burst out with loudly. "That's it! That's what I'm talking about. Ain't no hoe gonna make me snap." Slim Earl pressed his index finger against his temple. "That's why you have to have control of your hoes before they get control of you. Do you know how many niggas are in the pen right now for snapping? Not me, not me, not me. A hoe will snap before I will. I know that. Just as long as the hoe don't snap on me."

"You never know. Love is a funny damn thing," Melvin said.

Another way to pass the time in prison was by working. At Murray, it was each inmate's responsibility to see his or her caseworker and ask for a job. Sometimes, this meant having your name placed on a waiting list. I wanted to work. I wanted to do whatever I could to keep my mind occupied and away from the reality that I was facing. I knew the minute my mind became idle long enough to realize where I was, I'd snap. And even still, part of me knew that I was going to snap anyway, but the other part of me was trying to delay it as long as I could. Eventually, I got a job emptying trashcans around the prison. Six dollars a month was what it paid. If you work your hustle right, which I always did, you can survive on six dollars. Besides, in the pen, cigarettes were the real currency, and I always found a way to get 'em. Loaning 'em out was the quickest way. I give you a pack, you give me two back. For somebody hard up, they'd do it. But if they don't pay up, they'd get fucked up.

In 1994, I started working in the visiting room. This was my best gig ever. The hustles that I could do involving the visiting room were limited only to what my mind could conceive. Of course, controlling the influx of drugs was one, but I had a hand in that even before I started working there. There was more beyond drugs. A lot of the inmates were looking for ways to have sex with women. I knew if I could figure out how they could, I would get paid.

One day, while I was sweeping out the snack room, I looked at the four vending machines and a lightbulb immediately went off. All I had to do was pull the machines back about two feet from the wall. From the guard's perspective from his booth, it would look the same. Then I would arrange for a crowd of people to stand around the machines and pretend they were buying something while Slim Earl's women took their customers behind them and got busy. I ran the idea by Slim Earl, and he was down for it. It was the inmate's choice of whether he wanted one of Slim Earl's women or his own woman. Either way, the cost for the "room" was the same. I was the main one watching out for the guards just in case they got up to make their rounds, and if so I'd warn everyone. They'd have about five minutes to sneak out because that's how long it took a guard to go through three other glass doors before they could get back to the vending area. When visitation was over, I'd ease the vending machines back in place. Visitors were allowed to bring in change in a clear bag to purchase items from the vending machines, but they couldn't leave an inmate with any because money was considered contraband and inmates weren't allowed to have it. So Slim Earl and I would arrange for our payment to be received in advance and placed on our books. We charged ten dollars for five minutes. We'd split whatever we made. I'm not sure how Slim Earl worked out the payment for his women. Knowing him, he didn't give them much, if anything. The visiting days were Friday through Monday. On the weekdays the hours were from 5:30 P.M. to 8:00 P.M. and 9:00 A.M. to 4:30 P.M. on the weekends. On a good week, we could make six hundred dollars. I ran that hustle for almost two years. I got caught once, but luckily, the guard agreed to keep it a secret as long as he could get with one of Slim Earl's women every now and then for free.

CHAPTER 21

It was March 2001 when I opened my mail and saw Bill's, the old-timer with the 999 year sentence, obituary. It was sent to me by my boy, E.J., along with a note saying, he only had a few more years before he'd be out for good. Bill died of colon cancer at the age of seventy-one. He'd complained to Medical many times, but all they did was give him two Tylenol like they did for everyone who said they didn't feel well. Tylenol and Thorazine is all Medical must've stocked—Thorazine to keep those out of control spaced out, and Tylenol because they could care less if you were sick, care even less if you died.

I was tired of doing the same old thing. Tired of seeing the same old people. Tired of having sex with Mary. Tired of spilling my guts to Gail. Tired of praying to God with Tonya. Tired of doing all of this with no results. My head was still empty. My mind still cluttered with those voices. It seemed like I was adding a new voice every week. It was a new voice that said, *I hate that Gail bitch. She's trying to get over on you.* I was tired of it all. Tonya was too holy to let me have some, I thought, but after my second Bible study visit she said, "I know you want it bad. I know you haven't had any sex in a long time. I know you must be horny." I was convinced that some women liked being with ex-cons. Maybe it was a sexual fantasy. They think that we'll worship their pussy since we went so long without any, but for me it was almost the reverse. Since I did go so many years without any, it was easier for me not to have sex. Tonya, on the other hand, wanted it all the time, and there was no limit to what she'd do to satisfy me. It's just that it was hard to satisfy me. All in all she was a good woman. I looked at the fact that she always kept a clean house, took good care of her child, knew how to throw down in the kitchen almost as good as my granny, and she could quote scriptures. My biggest problem with Tonya was she was too judgmental of others, especially women, especially those who looked better than her and were thinner than her. I got tired of hearing her talk about pretty women who were in commercials or in music videos. "Her hair is fake. She has breast implants. She's too skinny. She needs to put on some clothes. Those are color contacts." Who cares?

I decided it was time for me to meet a new woman with a new set of problems. Someone whom it might take me a while to figure out. So I called up Scottie, my boy I helped to raise up, and asked if we could hang out at a club in Dallas. He was in the middle of conducting some business, but he told me as soon as he finished up he'd swing by and even let me push his Viper.

My mind was set to go out on a hunt for a new woman. While I was getting dressed, Mary called.

"What are you doing?" she asked.

"Nothing."

"Are you sure?"

"Yes, I'm sure. You asked me what I'm doing. That's what I'm doing—nothing."

"I want to see you," she said.

"I'm busy right now."

"You just said you weren't doing anything, Tower!" she shouted.

"I'm not, but I will be. I'm baby-sitting for Bernice."

"Bernice doesn't have any babies. Your nephew is ten now so don't fuckin' lie to me!"

"I'm not lying."

"Okay, then I'll come over there."

"Nah, not with my nephew here you won't."

"You're up to something. I can hear it in your voice. Where are you about to go, over some woman's house? Is that what you call yourself doing? Don't lie! You know I can find out. I already know that that Gail Adams bitch works at Bank of America. That's right, I know her name, where she lives too. It's amazing what a phone number retrieved from a cellular phone bill—*your* cellular bill—can give you. Don't fuck with me! Don't have me pay her ass another face-to-face visit."

"What do you mean by another face-to-face visit?"

"I have an account at Bank of America. True, Grapevine is a little out of my area, but I had to see the bitch for myself. She's cute, but out of your league, and if you keep fucking with her, she's going to be out of more than your league. Do you hear me?"

"I hear you."

"And I do believe you're fucking somebody that goes to that Church of God in Christ you seem to love to frequent every Sunday, but I do hope I'm wrong. I might have to join just to see."

Damn!

"Now, your excuses have to stop, and I need you to start spending more time with me."

"How much more time do you need? Shit!"

Watch it! Remember who you talking to, my mean voice said.

"How much more time?" I asked, lowering my voice. "I see you three, four times a week, Mary. We talk on the phone every damn day. Two and three times a day. I just need a little space. That's all. Everybody, even your husband, needs that. Your kids need that. Everybody needs some space, Mary."

"I don't give you space? Is that what you're saying? I'm crowding you?"

That's exactly what he's sayin' but he ain't gonna tell you that. He 'bout to clean this up right now 'cause I don't like the way this conversation's going, the mean voice said.

It's going the exact way I told Tower it would go if he messed around with that woman. I knew it was going to backfire. If he'd only listened to me instead of you for a change, my nice voice said.

"Nah, Mary, I'm not saying you're crowding me, baby. I just want time to myself."

"Are you going out? Tell the truth, Tower."

"No, I'm not."

"I hope not. I hope you don't call yourself going out to a club because you know that you're not supposed to be drinking, or do you need to look back over your interstate compact agreement?"

"I know the do's and don'ts."

"Tower, listen to me, I'm only trying to look out for your best interest."

"No, you're not. You're looking out for your best interest."

"Tower, I was just about to take you off paper. Don't mess this up. Isn't that what you want?"

"Yeah, it's what I want. You know that."

"Then play by my rules, baby. I need to see you."

"Take me off paper." My other line clicked. "Hold on."

"No, I'm not going to hold on! The other person can hold on or call you back. I need you to meet me somewhere. I knew I should've kept your ass in that ankle monitor."

"You make me feel like a damn slave. You know that? Maybe we shouldn't see each other again. I don't really see a benefit in it. It was a mistake is how I see it."

"What do you mean, we shouldn't see each other? It's not that easy."

"Why isn't it?"

"Because you're one of my cases, and I have to see you regardless, and if you think you're about to drop me for some other bitch like my husband did, you can think again."

"And if I do, what you gonna do?"

"I didn't let him go, and I won't let you go either so you don't want to see what I can do. Believe me."

"Mary, I don't care what you do no more. If that's how you want to exercise your little power, go right ahead. You're taking, but you're not giving shit."

"What do you mean, I'm taking? You don't like it when we're together? You get some, too, you know."

"Like I said, you're taking, but you're not giving."

"What do you want me to give, Tower?"

"Mary, you don't even have to ask me that question. You know exactly what I want."

"I'm working on it."

"Okay, then, we can see each other after you take me off paper."

I hung up the phone and called Gail just to hear her voice. She was my stash. I never had to worry about her being with another man. The only men she spent time with outside of me were the characters in her book.

"What you doing? I mean, how's it coming? How many chapters you got done?"

"It's coming along good. I got the first chapter ready. And I have the next thirteen chapters outlined."

"The first chapter. You've been had that ready. What are you doing over there?"

"What do you mean, what am I doing? I'm writing. What are you doing?"

"What do you mean, what am I doing? You know I don't like nobody asking me what I'm doing. This is about you right now. The next time I ask you how many chapters you have done, I want you to say all of 'em."

"Tower, I'm just a little depressed right now."

"What's wrong with you?" I asked with an attitude.

"I received two rejection letters in the mail today, one from a publisher and another from a literary agent. This makes nineteen rejection letters this month. I guess I really can't write."

"You ain't even done with the book yet so what are they rejecting?"

"I'm talking about my first one."

"Forget about that one for now and concentrate on mine."

"I'm trying but it's hard. Maybe I can't write."

Maybe you can't. Shit. You getting those many rejections, maybe it's time to move on to something else. Plan C, my mean voice said.

"I read some of your first book, and it was pretty good."

Don't lie to the girl.

"It could have been better but for your first try it was alright."

"Gee thanks."

"What I say?"

"That I can't write."

"I didn't say that." My other line clicked. "Okay. I didn't want nothin'. Just wanted to see how you were doing and how the book was coming."

"When are you coming over again?" Gail asked.

"I'ma try next week, you know I got a new job, and I work Wednesday through Saturday and every other Sunday so my time is limited now. But we'll see each other soon."

"You didn't tell me you had a new job."

"I didn't? I thought for sure I did. Yeah, I got a job at Allied Automotive. It took me forever, but it finally came through. I'll be making fifteen dollars an hour plus full benefits. It ain't what I'm used to, but it's better than nothing."

"That is so good, Tower. I'm very proud of you."

"Thanks. Well, I got to go. I'll talk to you soon. Take it easy."

My other line clicked, and it was Tonya. "Are you ready to read the scriptures?"

"I got a headache."

"Well, just pray and it'll go away."

"I been praying. It's just I'm under a lot of stress."

"Well, God doesn't put on you any more than you can bear. You have to remember that. Don't even claim that headache," Tonya said.

"I got a headache. I can't help but claim it!"

"Why are you yelling? You sound like you're letting the devil take over your mind."

"Oh, brother, I'll talk to you later," I said and hung up.

My cell phone rang and it was Gail, which was unusual. Gail rarely called me and especially not after we had just talked.

"What you doing?" she asked.

"Nothing. Can I call you back?"

"But I want to talk to you. I didn't have a good day. And now that we're getting closer, I want to tell you some things about me."

"Like what?" I asked impatiently.

"Well—"

I heard a car horn blow. "Let me call you back," I said to Gail.

"Why?" Gail yelled. "I want to tell you something that will help you understand me."

"I'll call you back, Gail. All you probably need to do right now is take a break and spend some time by yourself. You had a bad day, that's all."

"I'm always by myself!" Gail shouted. "Go on and be with your friend. This didn't even have anything to do with the book, but just forget it and go! I know I don't matter to you. Even if it did have to do with the book, it still wouldn't matter to you. You know why, because I'm not Terry McMillan so to you, me spending all this time writing doesn't make any sense because I'm not getting paid for it. Nobody takes you serious until you become somebody, but I won't need anyone to take me serious then. I need you now. Right now!"

"Who is Terry McMillan?" I asked.

"Forget it! It doesn't matter!" Gail screamed.

"I'm gonna call you back later, baby. Okay?"

"Don't call me at all! Never again. I'm sick of you."

"You don't want me to call you anymore, Gail? Huh? Tell me."

"What?"

"Do you want me to stop calling you?"

"No. You can call."

"Are you over there crying?"

"It doesn't matter if I am. You still won't talk to me tonight, will you?"

"Gail, I don't feel sorry for you, baby. You're pretty. You live in a big-ass house. It's probably your boyfriend's or for all I know your husband's. Whatever is up with you, you're living better than me. You're the one choosing to cry and be unhappy right now."

"You don't know what I choose to do because you don't know anything about me. You don't want to know anything about me. This is all about you."

"Yeah, it is, because you're writing a book on me. Now, if you were writing a book on you, it could be all about you. You're the one choosing to stay locked up like you're on house arrest. I ain't never met nobody like you. I wouldn't even believe somebody like you existed if I hadn't met you for myself." I walked out of Bernice's house talking on the cell phone as I headed for Scottie's ride. "It don't make no sense. I be damn if I stay inside when I can walk right out and start living."

"Have a nice time with your friend."

"Don't try to make me feel guilty. I said I'll call you later."

"What time?"

"I'm not sure. It'll be late though."

CHAPTER 22

I pulled up to the valet parking section of Club Phenomenon. I was dressed in khakis, a white ribbed shirt, and a pair of Timberlands. Scottie had on some jean overalls, a short-sleeve red shirt, and a pair of hiking boots. His expensive car drew much attention. That, and the ice we had on. Scottie loaned me about fifty thousand dollars worth of jewelry to flash around my neck and wrist. I had just walked into the club and over to the bar when I saw a young white woman who reminded me of the main character on *I Dream of Jeannie*. She had a long blond ponytail sitting on top of her head and a skimpy top tied at the waist, exposing her breasts. Her tan made her look almost as brown as I was. She was outside when I pulled up. I watched as her eyes turned into slots with green dollar signs spinning—*cha-ching*—jackpot, or so she thought.

Kara Dennis was her name. She was a flight attendant with American Airlines. I thought when I first met her that she was going to be a one-night stand, especially after Scottie and I followed her and her girlfriend back to Kara's town home in Addison that night and got busy. Scottie and Kara's girl were downstairs in the living room, and Kara and I were in her bedroom. She made me feel like the king of the world. She screamed so loud as I entered her that at first I thought I was hurting her, but then she started moaning with satisfaction and telling me to give her more. I wasn't stupid. I knew why she liked me—because of what she thought I had—and

I knew she probably wasn't any good for me. A lot of pretty women aren't used to giving because they've taken all their lives. I really wasn't the one to give a whole lot because I needed so much, but it was fun to pretend to be another person. I invented a whole new life for myself. I told her that I was a former professional football player for the Denver Broncos. She really perked up then. I went on to explain that due to an injury I was cut, but I still had lots of money. She said she loved football players, and she claimed that she was a former Dallas Cowboy cheerleader. When I asked what year, she quickly changed the subject. I told her I'd used the money that I earned in the NFL on various investments. I had her thinking I owned a dozen rental homes throughout the Dallas/Fort Worth area and was considering opening up a restaurant.

In April 2001, one month after I met Kara, I moved into Mary's friend's house, which was in a nice section of Irving near Las Colinas. I had it furnished with odds and ends that my mama and granny gave me. Mary financed the bedroom set from Rooms-to-Go through a no-pay-until-2003 option, and she expected me to take over the note. But by then, I'd be off paper and so far out of Mary's life it wouldn't matter.

Kara was pressing to spend time at my house. Up until that point, I hadn't had her over, and I mainly spent the night at her place. She was starting to question if I was married. I didn't want her to pull away from me, especially since her sex was so good and I was actually starting to feel something for her. I couldn't say I was falling in love. Maybe it was almost love like I felt for Lisa. I got along with Kara's little two-year-old daughter, Briana, who was half black. I could see us all becoming a family. The fact that Kara was white didn't bother me. She was used to being with black men—preferred them to white men. That's what she told me. I think though, her favorite color was green. Even still, I could see being with her.

You can? Okay, let me bring your ass back down to reality. What happens when the bitch finds out those cars you've been driving aren't yours? Better yet, that you never were a football player. You don't own a dozen homes. . .not even one. You drive a Mirada. That Benz and Viper don't belong to you. You make fifteen dollars an hour, and how could I forget, you spent ten years in the pen. I'm sorry eight in the pen and two in a community center. She don't strike me as the type of bitch who would accept that, my mean voice said.

Tower, I hate to, but I have to agree with him this time, my nice voice said.

Maybe I'll hit the Lotto, I thought.

In order for you to do that, you're going to have to start playing it first and even if you do start playing, the odds say you won't hit. Look how long your daddy been playing. Need I say more? the mean voice asked. *Fuck that bitch a few more times and then leave her alone. She's out of your league.*

I can't leave her alone. Not yet, I thought.

I don't trust I Dream of Jeannie. Go by her house since the bitch gave you a key. But don't call first.

I almost rung the doorbell because I felt strange just walking in, even though I had Kara's house key and an understanding that I was welcomed to drop by at any time, I still felt funny, 'cause I sure wouldn't want nobody doing that shit to me. Something inside of me said to walk in and be quiet in the process, and I was glad I did because I found out the truth about Miss I Dream of Jeannie. Kara had Brianna by a married football player. Based on the conversation I overheard, the daddy played for the Dallas Cowboys and he lived in the area.

"Girl, can you believe he moved into a five-thousand-square-foot home in Frisco...What do you mean, how do I know? I know because I saw it," Kara said in the phone as she sat outside on the back patio.

I was standing in her living room on the other side of the wall. I couldn't see her, and she couldn't see me, but I could hear her conversation crystal clear because she had the glass patio door open.

"He told me that he was leaving that bitch," she said, "which is why I can't trust his ass. This little money he's giving me ain't shit compared to what he will have to give me if I ever decide to go to the Friend of the Court and file on his ass...Yes...that's what I'm telling you...Yes, he is still with that white bitch." Kara laughed. "I know...Have you seen her? We look just alike...like she could be my twin sister. Her boobs are just a tad bit bigger than mine. I'm trying to get their number so I can call over there. Do you know anybody that works at the phone company?...I sure would. Why not? I wish I knew what tanning salon she went to so I could show up and start talking about my man real loud. Day spa. Anything like that. Hair salon. You know. Anywhere, where I can just show out...He's okay. He's got money and that's all that matters, right? I still have yet to confirm exactly how much. When a man hands over his black American Express card, you know he has money. Until then everything is questionable. I haven't had that happen yet. Well, I take that back, my Italian friend did. The one I met in New York a few months ago. Yeah, I'll probably go see him next month...Who? Oh. He's okay. I hate when we have sex though, but I make him think I love it. You know how you have to do. Oh yes, you do know...What? I don't know. He's just too big and he goes too fast like he's in a race to nut off."

She started laughing. "Did you ever think you'd hear me say that a man is too big when that's one of the main reasons I like black men.....I know, I know, I know. It's a stereotype. I know, Mario is Italian and he's big, too, but hell Italians got some nigga in 'em. Mmm-hmm...I don't know, he's probably about nine or ten inches. Yes, he is. Girl, that's what you like. I don't need all that in me. Actually, I don't need nothin' in my pussy. Sex ain't all that. I'm an actress..... Listen to you. No, I don't need your tongue in it either. Girl, don't talk like that. I let you do that one time just to try it. I am not gay. I didn't even like it. You heard me. I was half drunk...No, I wouldn't do it again. Well, everybody has a price. You want some of this? You gonna have to pay just like the niggas do. What?...Yeah, right. I'm about to cut his ass off, too, until he does. Believe me, he's sprung. I got them toes curling.... Alright, I'll talk to you later, girl. I'm going to call that nigga and see where he is."

I walked into the kitchen as Kara was stepping through her patio door into the kitchen. "Hah," she gasped, putting her hand on her chest. "You scared me. How long have you been here?"

Long enough! my nice voice said.

"I just got here," I said.

"Oh," she said, standing on her toes to kiss me.

"Where's Brianna?"

You know she's going to say over her mama's, my nice voice said.

"With my mother."

"Oh," I said, pulling her short skirt up.

"What are you doing? Not so fast. What's up?"

"What you mean, what's up? My dick. I want you."

"So you're going to come over here and treat me all common now?"

"No, but I want you. I can't have you?"

"I'm on my period, and I'm cramping." I followed her into the living room.

She ain't no more on her period than you are, my mean voice said.

"You're on your period, huh? Well, we can put a towel under you, and I can wear a condom." I hadn't worn a condom with her in the past, but after hearing that conversation, if we ever had sex again, I'd probably put on two.

I started reaching for her skirt. "No, Tower. Let's get something to eat."

"You're cramping, remember?"

"I still have to eat."

"Why don't you cook us something, then?"

"Cook? Me? Please. Let's go out."

"No. I'm going to let you rest. Since you're cramping, I'll see you a little later," I said, turning away from her.

"Wait." I turned to face her. "Don't leave out mad. Just because I'm cramping," she said, looking down at my crotch and licking her lips. "I still know how to satisfy you. You know what I mean?" I walked over to the sofa and sat down. She kneeled down and unbuckled my belt. I let my head fall back and rest on the sofa cushion, closing my eyes.

After she finished she said, "I want to spend time over your house. Otherwise, it'll seem like you're married."

So bitch, evidently that's what you're used to, my mean voice said. *You got a baby by a married man.*

"You can come over this weekend."

"Good, I'll have my mother watch Brianna."

I woke up when I heard Kara scream. I looked over at her, and she was clinging to a bedsheet. I followed Kara's eyes to the foot of the bed and saw Mary standing over it.

"Who is she, Tower?" Kara asked.

"Yes, Tower. Who am I? Tell this little white bitch who I am. She needs to know. Better yet, tell her who you are, 'cause I'm quite sure you haven't told Miss Beauty Queen that yet."

You should've known she had a key. Why didn't you change your locks? my nice voice asked.

"What does she mean?" Kara asked, looking over at me. "Who are you?"

"Yes. What do I mean, Tower? Who are you?"

"I knew you were married," Kara said as she sat on the side of the bed and started getting dressed.

"I'm not married," I said.

"Hurry up, bitch. Get dressed and get out of here!" Mary yelled.

Kara looked over at me. "Let me handle this," I said.

"Look, I don't have to fight over a man. You probably do," Kara said to Mary, "but I don't."

Mary shook her head and clinched her jaw tightly. She was past pissed. "Tell her to leave, Tower. Right now!"

"Don't worry, I'm leaving." Kara got out of the bed and finished dressing quickly. She started walking toward the bedroom door. "Wait a minute." She turned to face me. "You drove me here, Tower. How in the hell am I supposed to get home?"

"Mmm," Mary said to Kara, "sounds like your problem to me."

Kara took off one of her high heel shoes and came charging toward Mary who calmly pulled back her jacket to expose her gun. "This bitch has a gun," Kara screamed, stopping in her tracks.

"That's right, bitch, I do because I'm a parole officer, and we can carry guns."

"A parole officer?" Kara asked.

"Mary, why don't you shut up?" I asked.

"Why should I? You don't want this bitch to know where you been for the last ten years. You didn't tell her, Tower?"

"Please tell me she's lying, Tower," Kara said.

"No, I'm not lying! He's an ex-con."

Kara shook her head and clinched her mouth as she looked at me.

"I can call somebody to come get me. I'm out of here." Kara grabbed her purse from the chair near the bedroom door and ran out.

I heard the front door slam.

"What in the hell do you think you're doing, Tower? You brought a woman in this house. You know damn well you can't see another woman. I know you didn't fuck that bitch without a condom. I know you better not have. Do you hear me?"

"And if I did? You don't own me. You don't control me, either. I can see whoever I want, whenever I want."

"No, you can't!" she screamed, walking up to me and pushing me, but I didn't budge.

"Yes, I can. I'm sick of all this shit you're putting me through. As if being out ain't hard enough, I have to contend with your nagging, bitching ass day in and day out. What you gonna do, huh? Extend my parole? I don't care no more. I'm trying to get myself together but you trying to control me. I could kill your ass! I could kill you! You think I couldn't?" I said as I put both of my hands tightly around her neck. "Don't try me," I said as I removed my grip and punched the wall so hard I left an indention.

She held her neck and cleared her throat. "You need to move out of this house tomorrow, and I'm turning your case over to someone else." She continued clearing her throat.

"Moving out ain't a problem. I didn't ask to be here. You know where I just came from—a dark-ass hole so I can survive any damn where."

"Good, you're on your own. Let's see how long you'll survive."

"Gail, close your mouth," I said after I finished telling her what had happened the night before. We were both sitting on the sofa in her living room.

"I should be mad at you," Gail said.

"Why?"

"Why?" She looked into my eyes and sighed. "No reason. I

know we're just friends, but I really am jealous about you and these other women."

"I knew I shouldn't have told you."

"No, I'm glad you did because it does make a good scene for a book."

"Good. I'm glad I could help," I said sarcastically.

"Why didn't you tell me about the parole officer? I thought you promised to tell me everything."

"I'm telling you now, aren't I?"

"But if that incident wouldn't have happened, you wouldn't have. So are you going to keep seeing Kara, Mary, and Tonya? That's a lot of women."

"I don't really see Tonya. She's just my friend. All we do is talk about God together."

"So you haven't had sex with her?"

"No," I lied.

Gail puckered her lips. "Why not?"

"What kind of man do you think I am? You think I just go around having sex with every woman? Besides, she weighs more than two hundred pounds. Close to three."

"A lot of men like big women."

I shrugged. "She's not even like that."

"Like what? Like me? You tried to have sex with me. So that's what you mean? She's not like me. I guess she's better than me because she goes to church and can quote scripture. She's not carnal," Gail said.

"You're crazy," I said, standing.

"So now I guess you're going to rush over to the cheerleader's house."

"I'm not rushing over anywhere. You know how I get when you start questioning me. I already told you I don't like that. I don't let anybody interrogate me anymore. Not even my mama. I had enough of that, don't you think?"

Gail sighed. "You don't understand what it means for a person to have feelings about another person. Where are your emotions?"

"I don't have them anymore."

"Why don't you?"

"What you need emotions for in prison? When do those come in handy? Before or after you break a shank off in a muthafucka? I didn't need 'em."

"You're not in prison anymore, Tower. Why can't you realize that?"

"I realize that, but I still don't need emotions out here. Most people can't be trusted no way. Everybody running game."

"I'm not most people. I'm writing a book on you, Tower. I'm not running game."

"So. You got your game too," I said, rotating my shoulder. "I worked out too hard today. I benched-pressed more than 450."

"I've never, ever felt like this before," she said, continuing her mushy talk.

"Felt like what?" I asked, turning up my nose and looking her up and down.

"Stop looking at me like that."

"How am I looking at you?"

"Like I'm crazy."

"You are. What did you want to tell me that day?" I asked, remembering when she was begging me to talk to her because she had something she wanted me to know about her. I was becoming curious because she was starting to seem real strange all of a sudden.

"What day?"

"Remember that day I called and you had received a rejection in the mail from a publisher, and you said you wanted to tell me something?"

"You mean like three years ago?"

"I ain't even known you for one year yet."

"Well it was a while ago, like three months ago."

"So, what was it?"

"It's not important now."

"But I'm curious, 'cause you don't really tell me much about yourself. Why is that?"

"I told you it isn't much to say. Besides, you never ask."

"Whose house is this? And when are they coming back?"

"It's a friend's. I already told you that. You don't answer any of my questions. Why should I answer yours?"

"You already know everything about me. I'm about to go." I held out my arms for her. "Get up and give me a hug."

She stood and walked into my arms, resting her cheek against my chest. "I love you, Tower." She looked up at me with those clear eyes. "I love you."

I kissed her on the forehead. "I got to go."

She walked me to the front door and stepped on the porch, which she never did. "Whose car is that?" she asked, looking at Scottie's Mercedes 500 roadster that was parked in her driveway. He had six cars—three Mercedes, a Corvette, a Hummer, and a Viper—and he told me there would always be one available for me when I wanted to floss. Only time I drove my Mirada was to work.

"A friend of mine."

"Who?"

"You don't know him," I said with an attitude.

Damn that bitch is nosy, my mean voice said

She's not nosy. She's a writer so she's inquisitive, my nice voice said.

"Don't speed," she said. "You know how the police are, especially out here."

"I'm grown, thank you."

CHAPTER 23

"So how are you doing?" Leonard Wilks, my new parole officer, asked while he riffled through his desk. He wasn't concentrating on me. Spending ten minutes once a month with my parole officer was required, but I had better things I could be doing with those ten minutes. I guess I should be thankful that I didn't have to deal with Mary anymore, just her emails, which I never responded to. And when she called my cell I never picked up if I saw her number or one I didn't recognize. "How are you doing, Tower?"

How am I doing? I thought that was one hell of a question. I have a job earning fifteen dollars an hour, but I still remember when I used to net ten thousand dollars in one transaction.

I studied the black man's face, noticing no genuine concern. What was in that desk drawer that was of such importance that every time I sat in front of him, he had to open it and start searching? Almost five months I'd been assigned to him and in a little more than a month I'd have a new parole officer.

Leonard was young. Early thirties. Younger than me, but he had a family—a wife and some kids. I knew because I saw them in a framed picture sitting on his desk. I was sure he had close friends. And I was sure he had a house.

"That's your family?" I asked, trying to say something to see where he was coming from.

"Where?" he asked, looking around.

"The picture on your desk."

"Oh," he said, shoving it in his desk drawer. "She left me, and those were her kids."

I smiled inside of myself because Constance had just left her husband, boyfriend, live-in man, common-law—whatever Tim was, he was gone. If I could get Mr. Wilks over to my parents' house for Labor Day for some barbecue, maybe I could hook the two of them up, and Mr. Wilks could cut me some slack, take me off paper before I moved on to another parole officer. He was a lot better than Mary, but still he called to check on me and would drop by Tonya's every now and then. That's who I decided to move in with. Big mistake. I was paying her half on the rent and utilities. "We're just friends," I said often, but she still treated me like I was her man. Even though Tonya wasn't as possessive as Mary, I could see her getting that way. I could go out, even spend the night. But I wasn't stupid. I could tell when a woman was trying to gradually work on you.

"Can you drop by my parents' house for Labor Day? They're cooking. That's if you want."

"I might do that. Thanks. So you never answered me. How are you doing?"

"I'm alright."

"Really?" Mr. Wilks asked, looking at me, but still fumbling in his desk drawer. "The job going well? No changes?"

"It's a job." I slumped farther down in my chair, planting my Timberland boots into the Berber carpeting.

"You still got those issues with your supervisor?"

"I still can't stand her."

Mr. Wilks closed his desk drawer. "Tower, most ex-cons get out and can't find a job. You lucked up on a good one that could turn into a career. Don't blow it. Well, that's all. I just wanted to leave you with that bit of advice."

You call that advice? Tell him he could have saved that. We learned more in prison, my mean voice said.

I used a computer at work to go online and check my email. Gail and I had exchanged email addresses shortly after I started my job at

Allied. It was supposed to be another means of us staying in contact since I had stopped seeing her as much. I had a bunch of junk mail in my inbox, but I didn't have time to delete them. My main reason for logging on was to send Gail an email. I hadn't talked to her in a while. It was hectic now that I was living with Tonya.

Gail,

Sorry I haven't had a chance to call lately. I've been busy working a bunch of overtime so I can afford all these bills I'm starting to accumulate. I'm trying to do right. I hope everything's going good with the book. I'm still counting on you to change my life. Take care! Send me an email back. I'll try to call soon.

–T

A few days later, Gail replied with:

What happened to you? We haven't talked in a while. Well, I'm glad to know you're still hanging in there. I'm finishing up the book or trying to. I've been a little depressed lately. I feel like something bad may happen. Maybe not. Maybe your paranoia is just rubbing off on me. Try to call me if you can. Usually talking to you makes me feel better. Take care!

Love,
Gail

CHAPTER 24

Dad was standing over the barbecue grill in his backyard, flipping steaks, preparing for our Labor Day celebration. He had his portable radio tuned to K-104.

"I just want you to be nice to him," I said to Constance, who was stretched across a lounge chair sipping on a glass of freshly squeezed lemonade while I sat beside her in a lawn chair.

"What's he look like? Is he cute?"

"What you asking me for? I don't look at men."

"Is he short, tall, fat, what? Describe him?"

"He's about my height. I don't know. You'll see him when he gets here—if he shows."

She curled her nose. "Yeah, well, I definitely have to see him first."

"I'm not asking you to marry the man, just be nice to him. Let him take you out a few times. At least you'll get to eat for free."

"That's low down. What are you trying to say? Just because I'm big, you think all I want to do is eat? Am I really that big?"

"Nah, that's not what I'm saying at all. I don't even think you or Bernice is all that big. Y'all are the ones always tripping about your weight. You need to love yourselves, or how else do you expect a man to love you? Besides, a lot of men love big women."

"A lot of men love big women, so in other words, I'm big."

"I didn't say that."

"You did say that. I heard you. And let me ask you something, how come you didn't bring Miss Tonya over here today? Is it because she's big? And she really is big with a capital B. Is that why, Tower? You shamed of her?" I regret the day I told Constance about Tonya. I was just trying to get some advice from a woman, so I told her about Tonya and Gail. The next thing I knew, my whole family starting asking about them. They knew about the book Gail was writing even though I wanted to keep it a secret, just in case it never came out.

"I'm not ashamed of her. She went to visit her family and I came to mine. Besides, I don't want to talk about her. Will you just do it?" I pleaded.

She cut her eyes at me. "Why? So he can help you out?"

"You're single now, and so is he—"

"But you're not playing matchmaker, Tower. I know what you're really doing and why." I smiled. "You're hoping that I'll throw something on him that will make him sign you off parole. I know you, Tower."

"Okay, maybe you're right. So then help me out. I can't stand being under somebody's thumb."

"I'll see. I have to look at him first."

I walked over to Dad.

"Tower, if it were up to me, I would have thrown all of this meat on my George Foreman grill, but it ain't big enough. I'm too old to be out in all this heat. Don't make no sense to be almost a hundred degrees in September," Dad said as I walked over to him.

"You in Texas," I said.

"Let me hit that Lotto and see where I be. Me and your mama won't be in no damn Texas, that's for sure."

"You would move out of Texas, Daddy?" Constance asked. "Leave your kids."

"Would I? You wouldn't even have to watch me because I'd already be gone."

"Where would you go, Daddy?" Constance asked.

"Hawaii. Somewhere with some scenery and some decent weather. Tower, did I tell you that I almost hit Saturday? I had the seventeen and the thirty-two. All I needed was four more numbers."

"You were real close, huh?" I asked with laughter.

"I don't mind if I'm laughed at. Just remember you talked about me when I hit all six."

"I didn't talk about you. I just laughed. I know you're going to hit one day." I walked back over to Constance and took a seat in the lounge chair.

"Tower, there's someone here to see you," Mom said as she walked out of the house through the back door with Mr. Wilks behind her.

I watched Constance's mouth drop open and her right eyebrow raise. "In case you didn't know what fine is for a man, that's it," Constance said to me while she watched Mr. Wilks as he stepped off the porch. He was wearing a pair of jeans, Nikes, and a royal blue pullover T-shirt. "And he's built too. Mmm. I can definitely help you out."

"Good, but close your mouth before one of these grasshoppers jumps in." I stood and walked over to Mr. Wilks, shook his hand, and started introducing him. "Glad you could make it. This is my parole officer, y'all."

"Thank you for inviting me, but I'm not going to stay long," Mr. Wilks said.

"I hope you at least stay long enough for me to fix you a plate," Dad said.

"Thank you, sir. I will. As long as there's enough."

"One thing I'll say about this family, we may run out of money, but we'll never run out of food. Have a seat," Dad said. Mr. Wilks sat down at the patio table. "You want a beer?"

"No. I'll pass. Thank you."

"Okay, well, while you're sitting here, let me ask you a question."

"Oh, Lord," Constance said. "Daddy, don't embarrass us."

"Nobody's going to embarrass you," Dad said to Constance. "I'm just going to ask the man a question, that's all. Do you enjoy your job? I wanted to ask Tower's first parole officer that same question but as many times as she used to pop up here, I could tell she loved what she was doing."

"Who, Mary—I mean, Mrs. Davis?" Mr. Wilks asked. "She used to come by a lot?"

"Oh hell yeah. Two and three times a week. Sometimes four. A couple weeks she went by Bernice's every day."

Mr. Wilks looked shocked. "For one case. No, I don't do that. You can't. You won't have any time for your other cases. But I guess everybody has his own style."

"Don't you feel like an overpaid security guard sometimes?" Dad asked.

"Actually, if we were to speak the truth here—"

"That's what we speaking, the truth," Dad interrupted.

"Okay, I can't stand my job. Not really."

"Constance, get this man a Budweiser," Dad shouted. Constance used that as her opportunity to get closer to Mr. Wilks. She got up from the lounge chair and sashayed into the house. I sat back in my seat. "You can't stand it, huh? Well, I don't blame you."

"Not really, because the majority of my cases are black men who think I can't relate, and the funny thing is I can put myself in their shoes, but they just can't put themselves in mine. They're the ones who can't relate. They see me as the enemy when all I'm truly trying to do is help."

Constance handed Mr. Wilks a beer and smiled. "There you are, Mr. Wilks."

"Thank you, young lady, but please, call me Leonard." He took the bottle from her. "I like that outfit you have on. Very flattering."

"This old thing," Constance said, brushing her hand over her sundress.

"Very nice."

"Thank you," she said, smiling.

"Okay, this ain't the *Love Connection*," Dad said. "I want to get back to our conversation 'cause my boy is having a hard enough time out here and you parole officers just make things more difficult."

Mr. Wilks took a swig of beer and watched Constance sway back to the lounge chair.

"Hello," Dad said, snapping Mr. Wilks out of his stare. "Back to the conversation over here," Dad said, pointing at himself.

"Yeah, well, I only make things difficult for the ones I know need structure, and there are some who definitely need it. The system doesn't always work. Very few things *always* work."

"What about my son? How's he doing?"

"Tower is way ahead of so many other ex-cons. He's got a job—a good job. He's drug-free. He reports when he's supposed to. Tower's no trouble."

"Somebody get me a plate so I can get this gentleman a large T-bone," Dad said.

"The paper plates are right beside you," Mama said.

"Get me some china, please."

"China, for a barbecue?" Mama asked. "Don't be silly."

"No, really, sir, a paper plate will do fine," Mr. Wilks said to Dad and then glanced over at Constance and smiled.

"Looks like you won't need me to be nice to him. Daddy's doing a good job," Constance whispered.

"Yeah, but he likes you."

Constance smiled back at Mr. Wilks.

I watched Dad put the largest steak from the grill on a paper plate and hand it to Mr. Wilks. They continued talking, almost like they'd always known each other.

Things were getting real crazy. On September 10, 2001, one week after Mr. Wilks came over for barbecue, I received a letter in the mail from the Department of Probation and Parole advising that I'd received a change of status and would no longer be supervised by a parole officer. The letter stressed the importance of staying gainfully employed in order to maintain that status. I realized that in order for me to receive this letter that soon after Mr. Wilks' visit, it must've already been in the works. I read the letter over and over. If I was on unsupervised parole that meant I could leave not only the county but also the entire state. I could start concentrating more on finding Lisa and my child, something I'd put out of my mind, but now I was ready to start looking.

I smiled. I was happy and also shocked. Have you ever felt like you were on top of the world only for your world to suddenly come crashing down?

My cell phone was ringing, and because I was caught up in the moment, I answered without checking the Caller ID.

"Congratulations, I heard the good news," Mary said. "Mr. Wilks couldn't wait to come in my office and let me know how one of my cases was doing now that he's no longer under me. What did you tell him, Tower?"

"I didn't tell him nothin'. Why?"

"He said he was on to me. What's that supposed to mean?"

"I don't know. He said it, so ask him."

"I guess you feel like a million dollars right now. You used me, dumped me, and yet you still ended up getting what you wanted. Well let me tell you something. That little piece of paper that you have doesn't mean shit. You are still on parole. You may not have to come into the office, but the slightest little thing can put you right back where you just came from. And don't forget that."

I hung up and started plotting.

Listen up. You need to call one of the craziest muthafuckas you know and have him put a cap in that bitch's ass, my mean voice said.

Don't do that, Tower. You won't get away with that, my nice voice said.

So what you gonna do? Let her call you every other day and fuck with your head?

Don't, Tower. Don't listen to him. Block him out.

He can't block me out!

"Wait a minute!" I shouted. "Let me think because I'm tired of her."

"Tired of who?" Tonya asked as she walked into the living room. I didn't hear her when she came through the front door carrying grocery bags from Albertson's. Are you tired of me?" Tonya set the bags on the coffee table.

"No, not you," I said, dragging out the words.

"Well, who then, Tower?" She put her hands on her large hips. "Who are you tired of?"

"Nobody."

"You said you were tired of her. If you weren't talking about me then who were you talking about?"

"I said nobody." I grabbed the four grocery bags and walked into the kitchen to start putting everything away.

"It was somebody," Tonya said, following me. "And I want to know who because you've been acting funny lately. You didn't even go to church Sunday. The only way this relationship is going to work is if you go to church every Sunday, Bible study on Tuesday, read the Bible every day, and pray. I never see you reading the Bible anymore. I know what's wrong. It's that woman who's writing that book on you, isn't it? Why did you tell some stranger all of your business?"

"You were a stranger when we first met, and I told you a lot of things."

"That's different. I was providing spiritual guidance for you. What's she providing? I hope you're not having sex with her because I know you can with women like that."

"Women like what? I'm having sex with you so what kind of woman are you?"

"I'm different. We live together, Tower. Aren't we trying to work on becoming a family soon?"

"How could you think that when I've told you that I don't want a relationship? I'm here because I need a place to stay, and you know that. It's not like you can tell your church members we're shacking. What would they think?"

"I don't care what they think. What's wrong with me, Tower? How come you don't want a relationship with me?"

"Did I say it was you who I didn't want a relationship with? I don't want a relationship, period."

"But I've lost fifty pounds. I'm practically starving myself so I can fit in that size sixteen dress by next summer and you're telling me that you don't want to be with me."

"Oh, brother," I said, shaking my head. "You already knew that, Tonya. Why are you home this early anyway?"

"I came home to spend some quality time with you."

"Mmm." I put the last few items away and headed for the front door.

"Where are you going?"

"I need to spend some quality time alone."

The next day was September 11. Gail didn't even know anything about what happened in New York at the World Trade Center because she hadn't gone to work that day and she didn't have a TV to turn on to get the news so she had to hear about it from me. "How can you live like that? You got to know what's going on. Buy a TV!" Outside of writing, there was no evidence that Gail did anything else or even wanted to. She'd studied how to write. I remembered seeing at least a dozen Writers' Digest books lining her bookshelf: *Novel Writing; Beginning, Middles & Ends;* and *Revisions* were a few. I felt like she was wasting her time, but never told her. Instead, I let her waste it on me because she made me feel important every time she pressed play on the recorder. I felt like I was Rubin "Hurricane" Carter. I felt like maybe I hadn't wasted ten years if someone was going to write a book about me and make sure that Mason character was likeable.

Maybe Tonya was right when she started discussing the Book of Revelations and it being the end of the world. If it truly was the end then I guess none of what was going on or had been going on really mattered. I guess my prison record didn't matter. The fact that Wallace kept bouncing in and out of rehab and we'd probably never see him clean up didn't matter either. The fact that Edwin had finally filed for divorce from Bernice and was even fighting for custody of Curtis shouldn't have mattered none since it was the end of the world. My granddad's kidneys failing and him refusing to hook up to a dialysis machine should make no never mind. The world was almost over anyway. Gail said I focused too much on the negative. Maybe because there were a lot of negatives to focus on.

Okay, my brother George and his wife, Monique, were doing fine. He'd just gotten a promotion at Nokia, and Monique was pregnant again, which meant another long maternity leave. Granny said that Monique always got pregnant after she ran out of her vacation days. It was ironic that George and Monique's relationship would probably be the one to pass the test of time when Monique had to be one of the most possessive women in the universe. When they were dating, she slashed George's tires three times. She's the only one in the house who's allowed to answer the phone, and George can't even have a cellular. But they trust each other. Monique didn't need to be working at Verizon. Nah, she had the traits to be the perfect parole officer.

The alarm went off at four in the morning, and Tonya hit the off button instead of snooze. I woke up on my own almost an hour later, and even if I had flown down highway 635, I'd still be late for work. I wondered if she did it on purpose. It had gotten to the point I wouldn't put nothing past that girl. I wanted out, but I knew I wouldn't be able to rent an apartment on my own with a record because most places automatically decline you, and the house rentals in the paper were so expensive. Cheapest I found was nine hundred dollars but that was in the Mexican hood.

First thing I did when I got to work was sign on to my computer and check my email. Mary sent me a message. I wasn't sure how she got my email address at work. I might have emailed her one time, but I couldn't remember.

I wonder what they'd do at Allied if they knew one of their employees was an ex-con. You need to think about that and start answering your phone. The court still thinks you're not working. Fifty dollars a month can get increased real fast once they learn the truth. You need to think about all this and call me.

I almost hit the reply button.

Is you crazy? Don't reply to her. If she was going to do it, she would have done it by now. Talk is cheap. She still wants your ass, so you got the upper hand, my mean voice said.

"Tower, you late," my supervisor said with her foreign accent as she walked up to me. "We couldn't start cycle. Now, we behind."

I stood looking down at her with anger swirling inside of my chest like a tornado. "I'm ten minutes late. Ten minutes, and usually I'm never late."

"Still, you late, you call. We pay you to be on time."

"I thought I was going to be on time."

"You late, you call," she snapped and walked away.

Learn to fuckin' speak English, bitch. One day you should kick her ass. Talkin' to you like she's crazy. I don't trust her, Tower, and neither should you. She's the one probably plottin' to get you fired, not Mary, my mean voice said.

You think?

Hell yeah, and if you lose this job, what you gonna do? You got a damn record. Might not be that easy to find another one.

"I can't stand her," Milton, a parts engineer, said. He'd been working at Allied for twenty-three years, and not much bothered him, except for our supervisor, Jan Nguyen.

"She needs to learn how to talk to folks. It's only yes or no with her, no in between," I said. "If she keeps messing around with me, I'll go on night shift. Let us do our job; we know what we're doing. We've been doing it longer than her."

"She's never done it. I wish I didn't have a family and could go back on night shift. I'd do anything to get away from her. I'm about ready to take an early retirement," Milton said.

"Well, I don't have a family, and I'll go on night shift if she keeps messing with me," I said. "She's the only supervisor who comes in our area the minute shift starts. All the other supervisors wait about two or three hours. Not, Mrs. Nguyen. She's all up in our faces, smelling our morning breath."

"I can't stand her," Milton said, shaking his head.

"I'm not a chauvinist, but I can't work for no woman. They got that PMS thing, and then they let their man mess with their head. They're not strong enough to manage nothing. I can't work for no woman," I said.

"I can work for a woman. My wife's a credit manager. That's not the problem. Some female managers know their stuff. I just can't work for foreigners, whether they're male or female."

"If she messes with me one more time, I'm going on night shift," I said.

CHAPTER 25

It was early November. I hadn't talked to Gail since September 11. I decided to call her.

"Why didn't you return any of my calls?" Gail asked.

"What, you mean you actually called me?"

"Yes, I had some questions to ask."

Gail needed more and more time with me. She told me that she wanted to finish the book so she could start mailing the manuscript off to literary agents, but I had less and less time because of my work schedule and Tonya. I basically had to lie to Tonya by saying I was going to the store just so I could call Gail, but this time I went over Gail's after I talked to her on the phone because I needed to see her in person, smell her fresh skin, and watch her cheeks cave in.

"I need to know why Lisa stopped coming to see you," Gail said as we sat in her living room. "That's one of the questions I'd written down to ask you the next time you called. I didn't realize it would be two months later."

"Can we go upstairs and talk in the bed?" I asked as I grabbed her tiny waist and pulled her body toward me.

Gail shook her head and moved my hands away. "No, we better not. I just want to concentrate on the book."

"You just want to concentrate on the book, do you? What, you got a boyfriend now?"

"You already know the answer to that question."

"Do you?"

"No, I don't, Tower."

"Then let's go upstairs so we can talk about this in the bed."

"I'm developing strong feelings for you, Tower, but you haven't been around. I barely see you now. I know you don't want me. You may want to sleep with me, but that's about it."

"Oh, so just because you're writing a book about me, you think you can speak for me?"

"No, but your actions can. I've never even been to your house. For all I know you could be married or living with someone."

"No," I said, shaking my head. "I don't let anyone come to my house. I'm paranoid schizophrenic, remember?"

"Oh, so you're too paranoid to have me visit, but you can come over here whenever you feel like it. Believe it or not, I'm not stupid, Tower. I enjoy your company. You're the first person—male or female—whose company I've appreciated in a very long time."

"I'll spend more time with you, I promise. Can we please go upstairs?"

"No," she said and pressed the play button. "Tell me more about Lisa and why she stopped coming to see you."

I had only been in for a few months, but in that time I got close to this dude named Cooper. I would have done anything for him. We came into Murray A&R together and shared a cell for a brief time while we waited for placement into the prison system, and we developed a bond. Neither of us had been in before, and we didn't know what would go down when we did get released out with the other inmates. Cooper was a drug dealer out of Chicago who was on the highway heading to Dallas with drugs when he was stopped in Oklahoma. It was his idea to start running drugs in prison, not that it wasn't already being done. He just felt he could get a piece of the action. He had his girl call Lisa and tell Lisa to meet up with her at a gas station. After they met, they rode separately to the prison, making sure they arrived at the same time with Lisa walking in first. Lisa was supposed to refuse a search, drawing the suspicion on her and away from Cooper's girl, who was smuggling in crack through the lining of her purse. Drugs were brought into prison by visitors, usually in body cavities, false bottoms of shoes, on the back of stamps, and the adhesive on envelopes, but the main suppliers in the prison system were the guards. Their salary wasn't about nothing, so selling drugs was a quick way to make a lot of extra money. Still, Cooper was going to make sure that he got his cut of the drug trade, even if he had to risk it all. For him, it was the principle. He didn't appreciate correctional officers taking his business away. The reason I allowed Lisa to get tangled up in this web was simple—one paragraph on the back of the visitor's request form:

Everyone entering the perimeter of this facility shall at a minimum be subject to a pat search. Bags, purses, boxes, etc., carried by a person entering a faciility will be subject to search. All vehicles and their contents are subject to search upon entering the grounds. Should a visitor refuse to grant permission for the search, entry to the facility shall be denied and may be grounds for turning the person over to the appropriate law enforcement official. In addition, the person shall be barred from future access to the facility.

I wanted Lisa barred.

I had hurt Lisa so much while we were together that now that I was locked up, she was fucking with my head. Sure, I made her cry a bunch of times over where I was and who I was with, but I always came home, and she was the only woman I cared about, but it's hard for a woman to understand that men can cheat and still care for you. A lot of women think that if a man has sex with another woman, they care about that woman. I never cared about any of the many women I had sex with other than Lisa, and I never really cared about Lisa to the level that some men care about a woman. Like I said, it wasn't love. It was almost love. And I figured that's the closest I was ever going to get. Who knew what my so-called boys were telling her on the outside? They knew how I was and every lie I ever told Lisa. Half the time they were with me when I was doing my dirt. So in the beginning when Lisa started coming up to visit me, and all she could ever talk about was which one of my boys was trying to holla at her, I knew I had to cut her off. There's no room in prison for insecurity. No time to worry because you're too busy planning out your next move—*Just in case some nigga think he gonna try to do that then I'm going to do this.* That's how your mind is constantly plotting.

I thought about the best way to get rid of Lisa. First, I was going to tell her that I slept with her mother because I knew that would hurt her since her mother had slept with one of her boyfriend's way back, but she would know I was lying. I never had an opportunity to, even when Lisa and I went to Reno while I was out on bond awaiting trial. I was never alone with her mother. Lisa made sure of that. Otherwise, I probably would have slept with her. She looked just as good as Lisa did, and I was facing possible life imprisonment so I probably would have done it because I didn't care about anything at the time.

"Did you ever hear from Lisa after that?" Gail asked. I shook my head. "How did that make you feel?"

"You always want to know how something makes me feel. I'm going to make it real easy for you. I don't feel. So don't ask me that no more."

"Why don't you feel?"

I shrugged. "I thought I already told you that I buried my emotions the first day I stepped inside the prison. You don't need them there."

"But even knowing that she was pregnant with your child, you never even considered that?"

"At the time, I threw all that out my head. She wasn't showing yet so I pretended she wasn't pregnant. I wanted her barred before her stomach started poking out. She needed to go on with her life and stop fucking with mine. I couldn't help her, and she couldn't help me."

"That must've been hard," she said. I shrugged. "So your dog, Cooper." I smiled. "What's so funny?"

"You talk so proper, even when you're saying slang. No, I'm sorry, go ahead."

"What kind of person was he?"

"He was cool."

"You'd do anything for him?"

"I'd die for him, E.J., and Spivey. When any of them said, 'come on, let's go,' I went without question. I beat plenty fools down for them 'cause I knew they'd have my back if and when the time came."

"Did the time come?"

I shook my head. "Nobody ever fucked with me."

"Why not?"

"Because I fucked with them."

"Oh, so you were a bad guy. You were one of the ones jacking people for the food they just bought out of the commissary?"

"Nah, I didn't do no shit like that. They just didn't fuck with me is all. Once I got in tight with E.J., and his crew—some of the Muslim brothers—nobody fucked with us. True, we did fuck with people, but you don't need a reason to beat somebody down. Waking up in a four-by-nine surrounded by a bunch of niggas is reason enough. I was mad at the world. How could I go from strapping myself with layers and layers of magazines around my chest and waist to use as protection against a shank and something I heard might break out on the yard, to hearing my woman talk about some no-good drug dealer throwing a few hundred dollars her way that supposedly she never took? How was I supposed to deal with standing in a long line with seven, eight others, allowed ten minutes each for a phone call only to hear my mama say, 'Lisa's not here and I don't know where she is. I haven't seen her in a few days.' After I waited in line an hour, then I stayed on the phone, trying to get my mama to tell me the last time she'd talked to Lisa, and where the hell she thought Lisa was. Then when my time was up, I wanted to call back but I knew if I did, somebody was going to be ready to fight. So I made it real easy—I had her barred.

"Is that why you hate Quentin, because you think he may have slept with Lisa?"

"I don't hate Quentin no more. I was the one behind the wheel so I was the one who had to do the time." I shrugged. "It's that simple. I'm not trying to go over his house to say, 'Hey man, look who's back.'" I paused. "How come your phone never rings?" I asked, changing the subject.

"Are you talking to me?"

"Yeah. How come your phone never rings?"

She turned off the recorder. "It does sometimes."

"I ain't never heard it ring but a few times. Why don't your family ever call you?"

"You act like we're together all the time. There are plenty of days and many hours that we don't see each other, especially the last couple of months."

"Do you have any family or friends?"

"Of course, Tower. What kind of question is that? And why are you asking me questions all of a sudden. When I wanted to talk, you weren't interested."

"I just ain't never met nobody like you."

"What am I like?"

"How can you stand staying in this house all day long working on something that may not even materialize? You work two days a week at the bank, but the rest of the time, you're here. How can you do it?"

"Do you believe that you can turn your life around, Tower?"

I shrugged. "I don't think about that stuff. I just take one day at a time."

"Well, I believe I can turn mine around. All I have to do is change my mind, tell myself that this existence that I have now is not enough, and that it will never be. That's all you have to do, too, Tower, just change your mind."

CHAPTER 26

"Where's everybody?" I asked Mama as I was fixing my plate and looking into my parents' empty dining room. I was over their house for another Thanksgiving dinner. "Bernice is on her way. They're picking up your granddad."

"Oh hell," Granny said, dropping her mixing spoon into the sink and putting her hand on her hip. "Since when he got to come over every holiday? I see him more now then I did when we lived together."

"The rest of them are probably coming over a little later," Mama said to me, ignoring Granny.

"When he called over here and asked if I was cooking, I told him no, that we were going over Cora's, so he must've called back and talked to you or either you called and invited him," Granny said to Mama.

"Mama, Daddy knows Cora didn't invite us over to her house. Since when has she ever? Daddy knows how Cora is just as good as anyone else."

"Whatever," Granny said, throwing her hands in the air.

"How's Aunt Cora doing anyway? I haven't heard anyone mention her in a while," I said.

"Forget Cora," Dad said, walking in with his Texas Lotto numbers in his hand. "I tell y'all I feel lucky. I wish they were drawing these numbers today. I sure don't feel like waiting 'til Saturday to fill out my claim form."

"Ooh, Willie," Mama said, putting her hand on her chest as she looked down at the thick stack of tickets Dad was holding, "how many of 'em did you buy?"

"Two hundred."

"I hope it was a sale on 'em," Mama said with an attitude. "Buy one, get one free."

"Oh, woman," Dad said, scrunching his face, "come on now. We can afford it."

"You may think we can, but you done just about run through my little fifty thousand."

"Wait a minute now. Your fifty thousand?" Dad asked while he looked over at me. "You starting to seem more and more like Cora every day. If I had hit at the casino like you did, it would be *our* fifty thousand, but because you hit, it's *your* fifty thousand. I see how things work around here. I didn't say nothing when you went out and bought a damn Dodge and a bunch of furniture that I didn't like with your fifty thousand."

"What's wrong with my car? It's better than the one we did have, breaking down every twenty minutes."

"*My* car?" Dad shook his head. "Nothing's wrong with your car, but I would've much rather kept our raggedy one with no note and moved out of this ghetto into one of them new homes."

"Ain't nothin' wrong with this neighborhood," Mama said.

The front door opened and Bernice; her boyfriend, Marshall; Curtis; and Granddad walked in.

"Look who's back," Dad said to Granddad. "You must miss your wife. Pretty soon you gonna be telling her to pack her bags and come home."

Granny hit Dad on his arm. "That ain't funny."

"I've been trying to get her to come home. Stubborn woman," Granddad said as he walked in and sat on the loveseat in the living room.

"I'll take your coat, Daddy," Mama said as she walked in to greet them. I followed behind her.

"Bernice, let me holla at you for a second," Dad said.

"At me?" Bernice asked, pointing at herself.

Dad nodded. "Let's go in the kitchen."

"Oh, what now?" Bernice asked.

I walked in behind them, not to spy but because I wanted to finish making my plate.

"What is it?" Bernice said.

"I just want to holla at you for a second," Dad repeated.

Bernice sighed impatiently. "Yes. I'm here. What?"

"You a little late, don't you think? And I'm not talkin' 'bout your period."

"Late for what?" Bernice asked, frowning.

"Late for rent. It's due the first of the month and it's now the twenty-second of the following month. You owe us for October and November. If I was a real landlord, I'd be down at the courthouse filing eviction papers."

"I've worked it out with Mama."

"Oh, you have, have you?"

"It's her house anyway, not yours."

"Betty," Dad said, yelling for Mama. "Betty, come in here for a minute. I want to hear this one."

"And besides, do you have to bring this up today while I have company," Bernice whispered.

"Ain't nobody thinking about him," Dad said. "Maybe, he needs to know so he can help you out with paying it. What do you do with all your money? You're working full time."

"I got bills."

"And what you think, we don't? Betty," Dad yelled.

"I'm in the bathroom," Mama yelled down.

"I will give you the damn money before I leave," Bernice said under her breath.

"What's wrong with right now?"

"Daddy, I see y'all practically every day."

"And you still managed to let quite a few of 'em go by without paying us."

"Hold on," she said as she stormed into the living room and returned with her purse. "How much is it?"

"You mean you ain't paid in so long that you forgot? It's $425."

For a three-bedroom, one-and a-half bathroom house, so you tell me where you can live for that?"

Bernice snatched her checkbook from her wallet, wrote the check, and handed it to Dad. "It's $425 per month, which means $850 is what you owe us," Dad said as he stared at the check.

"My car insurance is due this month."

"So, what you telling me for? Your rent's due every month."

"Christmas is coming up, Daddy. I'll pay you next Friday when I get paid."

"Please do. I don't want to start calling you like I'm a bill collector, but I will if you force me to."

"Ooh," she said, rolling her eyes at Dad. "Is dinner ready or does Tower always get to eat first?" she asked Granny.

"In a minute," Granny said, walking back into the kitchen. "You can help us set out the food."

After the food was set out, we all sat down at the dining room table ready to dig in. I had finished my first helping in the kitchen and was working on my second.

Granny Pearl looked down at Granddad's feet and said, "Them look like those shoes I bought you."

"What shoes, Pearl?"

"Them shoes you got on. They look just like the ones I bought you right after we got married. The ones you had on when you were walking out of Leonard Brothers all hugged up with that woman." My granny shivered in disgust.

"Oh, here we go again," Granddad said. "Back down memory lane, but you can't never remember nothin' positive."

"I remember something positive. I remember when I left your ass. That was real positive."

"Granny," Bernice said, "don't scare my company off with all your foolishness."

"How is Marshall company when he's been coming over here to eat every Sunday for who can remember how long?"

"Well, he's not used to hearing you yell and cuss."

"If Marshall wants to worry about anybody yelling and cussing, he better worry about you."

"He has never heard me yell or cuss," Bernice said.

"What you say? Let me turn my hearing aid up because I couldn't have heard what you just said. You ain't never heard this child yell and cuss?" Granny asked Marshall.

"No, ma'am," Marshall said.

"Mmm, well, get ready," Granny Pearl said to Marshall. "You will one day."

"We have a very good relationship, and that's how it's going to stay. Isn't it, baby?" Bernice gave Marshall a smack on the lips.

"Sure is."

"Yeah, sure is. As long as you keep that job, that is," Granny said to Marshall, "and pay all the bills." Granny never bit her tongue. "And don't ride too slow down Rosedale Street or you might wind up in jail for solicitation." She didn't care whose feelings she may hurt in the process of being so honest.

"Why did you have to go there?" Bernice asked. "Mama, you told her about Edwin, didn't you?"

"I didn't tell her anything."

"Yes, you did, Mama. I told you not to tell nobody. If I had wanted Granny to know, I would have told her myself. Now, I'm going to hear this for the rest of my life."

"No, you not," Granny said, " 'cause I'm not gonna be alive for the rest of your life. You just gonna hear it for the rest of mine."

"This family makes me sick," Bernice said as she stood, threw the napkin that was in her lap on her plate, and stormed out of the dining room.

"Excuse me," Marshall said to us as he got up and went after her.

"You excused," Granny said. "You need to be, for dealing with that girl. Yeah, those are them shoes," Granny said, looking back down at Granddad's feet. "Same color and everything. You got some nerve coming over here wearing those shoes."

"These ain't the same shoes," Granddad said.

"Might as well be. Don't matter. I'm filing for divorce soon."

"You been saying that for more than twenty-five years," Granddad said.

"I've been waiting for you to do it. Least you can do since you ain't never done anything else."

"Ain't never done anything else, huh? I fixed it so you never had to work, but I guess that ain't nothing, huh?"

"Oh, I don't work?"

"Cooking? You call that work?" Granddad asked. I had never heard him talk to Granny like that before, and I was surprised because he was supposed to be so sick.

"Yes it's work. I make money doing it, don't I?"

"Yeah, you make a little money, selling dinner plates, but you've never had to hold down a real job." Granddad started coughing.

"Take your nasty coughing away from my food," Granny said.

"I'm not trying to argue with you today. I'm trying to eat some of your work, so can I please?" Granddad asked as he reached for the plate of corn-bread dressing, took some, and passed it on.

"So, Tower," Dad said as he cut a piece of ham and placed it on his plate, "how's everything going with your job at Allied?"

"Pretty good, I guess. I just can't stand my boss. She gets under my skin."

"Don't let her get to you," Dad said. "We've all had those bosses we couldn't stand. Just ignore her and do your job."

"Oh, I always do that."

Bernice and Marshall returned to the table.

"You over it now?" Granny asked.

"Granny, don't start," Bernice said.

"I just asked if you were over it."

I took my plate into the den when the arguing started back again. I put my plate down on the end table and went searching through Dad's video cabinet. "You got *The Shawshank Redemption* in here?" I asked.

"Sure do. Should be on the second shelf," Dad said.

I put the movie in, sat back, and watched it for a little while, but it didn't take long before my own story began to play.

When I first went to prison, I didn't understand why everyone got so excited for mail call, but eventually as the days, weeks, and months passed, I started to feel the same way. Friendly, one of the guards, brought the mailbag to our quad during shift change every day at 5:00 P.M. He got along with most of the prisoners, especially the black ones, better than he did the guards and that was rare in prison because a lot of the white guards were racist.

If I never saw anyone any other time, I'd see them at mail call. It was something we each clung to as a connection to the outside. For me, the mail was something that kept me sane by providing a small taste of freedom. Along with the letters that my parents wrote, they also sent newspaper clippings of stories they thought I'd want to read.

But at times, others prayed for days when their names weren't called, especially, if their woman had been threatening to file. Divorce papers were the last things you wanted to receive in prison because there was nothing you could do to stop the divorce. I'd seen that happen. I'd seen men break down in front of a large group of us as soon as they opened a letter and read the contents. The more I saw those reactions, the more I started to put things into perspective. You really can't count on another person for your happiness. And you can't trust that someone else has your best interest. I don't care who they are. I don't care if they're your wife or the mother of your kids, inside, you learn not to depend on anyone.

This particular mail call I'll never forget. My celly, Melvin, only had nineteen more days before his early release was granted. I knew, but not too many others did because something like when you're getting out, you have to keep to yourself as much as possible. There are a lot of jealous muthafuckas in the pen who ain't never gettin' out, and if they can't stand you, they'll fix it so you won't either.

Friendly reached into the bag and started calling the names of those who had mail. If you didn't come up when your name was called, your mail went back in the bag.

"Theodore Evans," Friendly said and then handed me two envelopes. I waited to see if I had any more before I walked back to my cell.

I sat on my bunk bed and opened the Christmas card from Mrs. Johnson, the clerk who read my sentence in court. There was a bear on the front with snowflakes and it read, *Let there be peace on earth. Inside, it read: And let it begin with us. Merry Christmas.*

She wrote:

How are things with you? Have you adjusted to the situation there? I have been wondering if you have received an appeal. If so, I pray it goes well. I know this is a hard time for you and your family. Just remember how much they love you. I know this sounds frugal, but have a Merry Christmas! I think of your situation and wonder how you are and if you are adjusting. Take care and I'll try to write again.

I almost threw the second letter in the trash without reading it. It wasn't addressed to anyone. It just said IMPORTANT in small letters in the center of the envelope. I opened it and started reading.

Melvin, the goon squad is coming for you tonight. They're going to plant something. I don't know what, but I overheard a few of them talking. It has something to do with Beard.

Even though it wasn't signed I knew it came from Friendly. Somehow it must have gotten out that Melvin was being released soon. Melvin obviously had some dealings with Beard, an Aryan who was in tight with a few guards.

We'd never been raided before, and I didn't know what to expect so I didn't go to sleep or even close my eyes most of the night. I heard Melvin snoring right after he made love to his wife—or at least that's what he said he was doing when he took out her naked picture and started jacking off. I was lying on my back, staring up into darkness. Just as my eyelids started to close, our cell door slid open and the goon squad came in, dressed in all black with plastic masks over their faces, shining flashlights in ours.

"On your feet and against the wall!" loud voices said. "On your feet now!" I jumped off the top bunk.

Melvin and I stood against the wall while three guards stood over us.

"What's this?" one of the goons asked, holding up a large shank. "Looks like a shank to me. Is this yours, Melvin?"

"Where'd that come from? That ain't mine," Melvin said.

"We got it from underneath your mattress."

"I ain't put it there! What's this about? What you trying to do to me? This is bullshit."

"Shut the fuck up!" the goon said, jabbing Melvin in the stomach. "Is this your shank?"

"No, it ain't mine!" Melvin said while he was doubled over.

"Is it yours?" the goon asked me.

"Yeah, it's mine," I said, putting my hand out for it.

"Is this shank yours?" the goon asked again. "Don't fuckin' lie, bitch, or you'll find yourself in the hole eating your own shit for breakfast, lunch, and dinner."

"Yeah, it's mine."

"This shank right here is yours?"

"I said it was! How many times you gonna ask me that?"

"Don't lie, boy!" A different goon said.

"I don't have to lie, *boy*. It's mine," I said.

One of the goons sprayed Mace in my face, jabbed the middle of my stomach with his club, and when I bent over I felt a stick crack across the center of my back. "You're going to the hole until you decide to tell the truth."

"The truth is a lie. So which do you want, the truth or the lie?" I asked as they led me out in handcuffs. "But you already know both, the truth and the lie."

"Shut the fuck up," one of the goons said. "We'll show your dumb ass what the hole is all about."

They took me to solitary, threw me in the cell, and beat me. "Look at this bitch," one of the goons said, "trying to be his girlfriend's hero. I guess they're fucking in that cell at night. Must be. Why else would he go down for him?"

" 'Cause he's used to going down on him," another goon said. "That's why!" They started laughing and kept beating me. My eyelids were so heavy with fluid that they were swollen shut. As the goons were leaving, I tried to stand, stumbling in the darkness and feeling around with my hands before I collapsed on the hot concrete. Then the door slammed, shutting the darkness in. I felt my mind slipping, but I knew the minute I got tired of fighting, that would be when I'd die. That was my first time in the hole.

Food and water were slid through a tiny opening at the bottom of the steel door. I drunk the water, but I didn't eat that shit that was supposedly food. The guards probably pissed in it. I wouldn't put nothing pass the goons who wanted to break me, but I was too strong to be broken, and all this shit was doing was making me stronger. My imagination was my weapon. As long as I could dream, I could make it.

The jingling keys woke me.

"Your time is up," a guard said as he was unlocking the steel door. I'd been in for five days. I stayed on the floor until the dark room filled with light. Then, I tried to stand, but my knees gave in. "Get up. You get to go back to your cell." I stood and stumbled out the hole. "Tell Friendly just because he hides behind a dark shadow and disguises his voice, it doesn't mean nothing. We know he's the one who went to the news." I stopped in front of the guard and raised my chin so I could see his face through the small opening of my eyes. "You smell like shit," the guard said to me.

"I want to take a shower, and I want some clean clothes."

"Did you ever hear us say, 'Welcome to the Marriott'? You can shower and change when you get back to your quad.

I was in the individual shower stall. The semi-warm water hitting my dirty flesh relaxed me. I put the soap up to my nose to smell the freshness. It was good soap that some other inmate must've left behind. Not the state-issued shit that didn't clean worth a damn— only thing it did do was break me out. This soap reminded me of a woman. And in the pen, just like a woman—good soap was a luxury.

When I came back to the cell, Melvin said, "You went to the hole for me? You basically took a bullet for me, man, and you didn't have to. I owe you. I could have been in this bitch for three more years. As soon as I'm able, I'm going to put some money on your books."

I thought about what he said. He owed me. He was getting out. He was going to be able to move around and make some calls.

Things I couldn't do. "Find my girl, Lisa. Tell her I need to talk to her. That's all I want you to do. Just find my girl and my baby."

"I'll find her, man. I'll find her."

I opened my eyes and stared at the TV screen in my parents' den. *The Shawshank Redemption* was still playing. I woke up at the part when one of the characters, Red, was reading a letter from Andy. "Hope is a good thing. Maybe the best of things and no real hope ever dies." I felt a stinging in my throat when I heard that, and that little feeling gave me hope. Hope, that with time, I could move on.

CHAPTER 27

Tonya started asking me about the book Gail was writing. She wanted to know when it was coming out and if I had a contract. I shrugged and told her that I never got a contract. "I don't trust Gail," Tonya said. "She never gave you a contract and you don't even get to see what she's writing. What if you don't like it?" She handed me a floppy disk. "Next time you see her, make sure you get a copy of the book for yourself. Bring it to me, and I'll start working on it. Remember when I told you about the three types of people? Well, Gail's a natural woman. You don't need to deal with her." I took the disk and nodded.

I met Gail at Bennigan's one Sunday. The weather had changed—it was spring 2002—and Gail said she came out of her hibernation in the spring and summer. We started having lunch, sometimes dinner, about once a week, and she always paid because she knew I didn't have any money, especially not for an overpriced meal at a restaurant. I've always been the type who preferred eating at home.

"You mentioned a lot about the law clerk who helped you get out."

"Spivey, yeah. It was funny because in the beginning I was trying to con him so he'd look at my case, which is why I'd bring him ice cream and cigarettes. He had a lot of cases. Some people were arranging for money to be sent home to his wife so I had to come with something just for him to take a look and tell me what I needed to do."

"So did he file all the paperwork for you?"

"He helped me with it in the beginning, and eventually I took it over."

"Was it a fast process?"

"Getting a case looked at by the court of appeals is anything but fast."

It was in early 1990 when I received a letter from the Oklahoma Appellate Public Defender System in the mail. I walked into the law library with it, searching between the bookshelves for Spivey's baldhead and round glasses, but I didn't see him anywhere so I sat down at a table and waited.

As I grew impatient, I started tapping the letter on the wood table, then before long, I found myself reading it all over again.

Because the legislature has been unable to supply us with enough attorneys for our large and growing caseload, it may be four years before your brief can be filed in the court of appeals, unless your appeal is one that will be automatically placed on accelerated docket. This also means it will be three years or more before an attorney is able to read your transcripts.

I had read that letter at least a half-dozen times. I didn't understand why I continued reading it. Nothing in the letter provided hope. I skipped over the next couple of paragraphs and turned to the second page.

In about ninety percent of the cases, or nine out of ten, the court affirms the conviction. One of the dangers you face if the court reverses your case for a new trial is that you may get a longer sentence on retrial.

I guess they really wanted to get that point across because they made sure to highlight and underline their next sentence.

<u>One of our clients got fifteen years on robbery with firearms at the first trial and forty years at the second trial.</u>

I didn't know where Spivey was but as I sat staring out of the barred windows, remembering where I was and how long I might stay, I told myself that I had to get out, and nobody else was going to give a damn about me getting out as much as I did so I had to work this case like I was fighting for my life, because I was.

The letter stated to send all correspondence or any information I might have concerning my appeal to the attorney handling the case. The night before, I started jotting down some things that immediately came to mind. I didn't bring my notes with me. I'd planned on working on my appeal again that night. I decided to put all that daydreaming to the side while I worked on my freedom because it was my life, and if I kept dreaming, I'd mess around and dream it away.

"Are you looking for Darrell?" Mrs. Lang, the law librarian, asked. Most of the inmates had a crush on her. She was a middle-aged, white woman who liked to wear dresses, high heels, and sweet-smelling perfume. If I had to guess, I'd say she was in her mid- to late forties. She seemed to really enjoy her job, especially being around all those men. Spivey worked with her, and he knew her real well. He said what Mrs. Lang loved most about working in the law library was the privacy. The guards never came in there—we never gave them reason to—and I think after she started working in the law library and realized the freedom she had, and how she could use that freedom to change a man's life, Mrs. Lang did, by having sex with some of them.

"Who? I'm looking for Spivey. You seen him?"

"Darrell Spivey, right?" she asked.

I shrugged. "I guess. I just call him Spivey."

"He had his parole hearing today. Maybe I can help you." Mrs. Lang sat beside me. The smell of her sweet perfume had my head spinning. It was a light smell, like roses. "Do you want to go to my office?" she asked as she rested her hand on top of mine.

I looked around at the others in the library. I knew they'd be watching because they always watched Mrs. Lang, hoping they'd be the one chosen. "I need to wait for Spivey. He knows about my case already."

"I can help you, if you let me. I've been watching you. If you're not careful, you'll let this prison get inside of you so even when you're out, you'll still be in. Let me help you."

"How can you help me?"

She smiled. "Come to my office, and I'll show you."

"I heard you don't like black dudes, just whites and a few Mexicans."

"What are you talking about? I help everyone. Before Spivey started reviewing cases, I did it all. Your color doesn't matter."

"So you're taking me back to your office to review my case?"

"Why else would I be taking you back to my office?" she asked.

"You know."

"No, I don't know, but perhaps you should wait on Spivey's return." She stood and walked away.

"Where's Spivey now?" Gail asked while she used her fork to play in her salad.

"He's back in Oklahoma with his wife now. She really stuck by him. I never had a woman to stick by me like that."

"If I had been your woman back then, I would have waited on you. I would have wrote you every day and been home to accept all of your calls."

"Well, you weren't my woman back then so who knows what you would have done."

"I wish you would trust me," Gail said.

"Why? Why should I?"

"Because I love you."

"Love the book you're writing. Don't love me."

"I want to make love to you, Tower. Tonight. I don't care how late you come over as long as you don't stand me up."

CHAPTER 28

I didn't make it over to Gail's house the night that she wanted to make love to me. It took me almost one week later.

She answered the door wearing an off-white silk pajama outfit, holding a cordless phone.

"Hi," she said, flipping her straight hair away from her face and yawning.

"Were you sleep?"

"Well, it is about 3:30 in the morning."

"So why'd you open the door?"

"I was about to call the police until I looked out my peephole."

"Can I come in?"

She stood back from the door, clearing the path for me to walk through.

"I'm tired," she said, walking up the stairs.

"Gail." She stopped on the staircase and turned to face me. "How come you trust me?"

"I just do," she said, yawning. "Have a good night, and I'll see you in the morning."

"Gail."

"Yes," she said impatiently as she turned to face me once more.

"Have you ever been in prison?"

"I'm serving life in one right now. Good night," she said then walked upstairs. I heard her door close.

I booted up her computer and copied her book file onto Tonya's floppy, then I walked upstairs and started to undress as I stood over Gail who seemed to be sleeping peacefully. I pulled back the covers. She had taken off her pajamas. I examined her naked body and decided to get on top of her and take what my mean voice had wanted.

She opened her eyes wide when I entered her.

"Put on some protection," she said.

"No. I can pull out."

I tried to go slow with Gail, remembering what I overheard Kara say about me to her girlfriend. At least, I guess she was talking about me.

"Am I going too fast?" I asked, looking down at her. She had her eyes closed, and she was shaking her head. "Does it hurt?" She continued to shake her head. "Can I go deeper?" She nodded. "Deeper." She kept nodding. "Can I put it all in?" She nodded some more. "Oh shit," I said and pulled out quickly, spilling my cum all over her chest and stomach.

I walked into the bathroom to wet a hand towel so I could wipe her off. As I sat beside her, cleaning off her naked body, she opened her eyes.

"How come you don't have a man?" I asked.

She shrugged. "I've had men."

"What about right now?"

"No one right now, except for you," she said, stroking the side of my face. "I do have a friend."

"What kind of friend?" I asked.

"Just a friend."

You know what we call our friends. . .women we fucking, my mean voice said.

"You having sex with him?"

She shook her head. "No."

"Is this his house?"

"No. He's just a friend. He has a rap album coming out."

"I don't give a fuck about that muthafucka," I said, frowning.

"You're the one who asked about him."

"I just wanted to know if you had a man, that's all. You said you don't, so I don't need to know about no bogus rap album."

"It's not bogus. He really has one coming out."

"Under whose label...probably his own. He's probably nothin' but a drug dealer. My boy Scottie has a record label, and it's all a front to launder dirty money."

"Not my friend. He's not like that."

Why did you move from Chicago to Dallas?"

"Actually, I moved from Chicago to D.C. to Philadelphia to Detroit to Denver to Dallas. I just wanted a change, that's all. Just a new environment."

"When's your friend coming back?" I asked.

"I don't know."

"You know what I'm starting to think? You're married and killed your husband and buried him in the walls."

"Wasn't there a movie out like that a long time ago...I mean a long time ago?" she asked as she sat up.

"I think so."

"No, I don't have anyone in the walls. Why did you tell me that you'd been in prison the very first day we met? Are you always that open?"

"No, but I didn't think I was going to see you anymore so it didn't matter. Besides, that life is a part of who I am."

"When I make you relive it, does it hurt or help?"

"I think it does a little bit of both, but sometimes when I'm reliving it, I think I'm living it. That's when I get depressed."

"I'm sorry."

"Don't apologize. It's just one of the side effects I suppose."

"I guess we need to continue," she said, sitting up on the bed and reaching over for her microcassette recorder. "I didn't realize there was so much more to add, and I want to finish real soon. Melvin got out. Then what happened?"

I was down at Slim Earl's cell playing solitaire and listening to the radio. I had a new celly coming that day. The Department of Corrections didn't waste no time filling that vacancy. Melvin had barely been gone a week. I didn't know much about this dude. Not even his name, just what they called him—Punisher. I started asking around and found out that he had been transferred from the Oklahoma State Penitentiary, the same prison Stanley was in.

Now, I had to try to get cool with some other muthafucka and find out what he was all about, observe him for a while and decide if I could trust him. One thing I knew, I had to get along with him because we were sharing a four-by-nine, but the things coming off the wire weren't too good. For one, he was a lifer. Some of the muthafuckas in here claimed Punisher arranged his own transfer 'cause it was some other muthafucka in here he had marked. Nobody knew who the other muthafucka was, so for all I knew it could've been my muthafuckin' ass. Supposedly, he staged a fight so he could get transferred. Whether or not he'd be sent to Murray was a gamble that he eventually won after being transferred twice.

"Where's Malcolm?" I asked. "I haven't seen him lately."

Slim Earl chuckled. "You won't see his ass in my cell no more."

"Why? What the fuck happened?" I asked, even though I figured Slim Earl found out what I already knew.

"Did you see when the warden's ass came on TV saying if anyone had sexual contact with Hodge to report to Medical because Hodge has full-blown AIDS?"

"Yeah, and?" I asked.

"Malcolm's ass reported. He didn't think nobody knew, but I found out about that shit, and his ass tested positive too. He's on his own now, fucking buzzard. In my cell crying about a bitch when all the while he's the bitch."

"Did he move out the quad 'cause I ain't seen him?"

"I don't know what his ass did," Slim Earl said. "He probably took a fuckin' catch out or in a damn PC unit or medical one. What you care for? You looking for him? You got something you want to tell me?"

"Nah, you know I don't go down like that."

"I don't know shit. I thought he didn't."

"I was just wondering. I thought maybe he got out."

"His muthafuckin' ass ain't got out. And the way it look, when the bitch does, it's going to be in a body bag. What you need to be curious about is your new fuckin' celly."

"Yeah, what the fuck you know about him?"

"I know that he's in here on a hit."

"Who the fuck he after?" I asked.

Slim Earl shrugged. "All I know is it ain't my ass."

———

I walked back to my cell, but hesitated before I went in after I saw some white boy standing inside. People were usually kept grouped together by race, so I was put a little off guard at first. He didn't speak or look my way when I entered. I knew that couldn't be Punisher, because he looked too straight-laced to be a killer. Looked like your average blond-hair, blue-eyed white boy, close to thirty who probably killed his parents for the inheritance or some shit like that, but nothing hard core. He introduced himself to me as Punisher, and I had to play off how shocked I was.

"Lockdown—everybody go to your unit for lockdown," came across the PA system from the guard tower. Punisher and I stood by the steel door as count was taken. Neither of us was looking at the other. The guard came to our cell, opened our door, and looked around. He looked behind the small corner to make sure there was no one hiding inside, and then he walked out.

The rest of the night was quiet. Almost like my celly wasn't even there.

———

"I was in here a few days ago looking for you," I said to Spivey as soon as I entered the law library. He was sitting at his usual table with an open law book lying on it but his head wasn't buried deep inside it as usual. "Let me show you the letter I received in the mail about my appeal. I want you to tell me what you think." I tossed the envelope on the open page of the law book.

Spivey looked up at me. "You were looking for me, huh? Well sorry I missed you, but I met with the parole board the other day."

"That's right, I heard. How did it go?"

"Same way it always goes. They give your ass a few minutes to tap dance for them, show 'em what you got. 'Impress us, muthafucka.

Hurry up and tell us what you think we want to hear, but you'll never be able to figure out what you're supposed to say, and no matter what you say, we're still going to reject you.' But you still better say you're guilty and you better say you're rehabilitated." He slapped the air. "I'm sorry, man, but today I ain't in the mood to hear about nobody's case because I got my own shit to deal with."

I nodded. I understood that. If I could feel this trapped, and I hadn't even been in a full year, I couldn't even imagine how Spivey must've felt after twelve years, so yeah, he had reason to be pissed. I never really thought about Spivey. I was too busy thinking about myself. Never considered that he wanted the same thing I wanted, the same thing that we all wanted, except for those who were institutionalized. But they didn't count. I never wanted to turn into one of them either. I never wanted to be content with my cell and three fucked-up meals a day. I already told myself if I had to spend forty years inside, I'd get used to one thing—daydreaming. If that's what I had to do then that's what I would do, and that's what I was on my way back to my cell to do.

"Tower, get in here. They talking about Melvin," Foster, Slim Earl's celly, said after he hit my closed cell door. I opened my eyes slowly and saw the steel. Foster had to bring me back to this shit. My celly Melvin was out. Enjoying his freedom. So what the hell was he doing on the news?

"Melvin killed his wife and some other dude and had court in the street."

I jumped off the bunk and ran over to Slim Earl's cell. I heard the reporter's voice before I saw anything. Foster was adjusting the antenna, trying to get the picture to appear and the lines to disappear. He banged on the side of the TV trying to get clear reception. "Come on," he said.

"Some late-breaking news this midday for those just tuning in. I'm at the scene of a homicide involving twenty-nine-year-old Howard Melvin Crutchfield who is believed to be dead along with his ex-wife, twenty-eight-year-old Monique Sanders, and her thirty-one-year-old fiancé, Miles Brown, in what appears to be a murder. What we do know at this hour is that Mr. Crutchfield was recently released from Murray State Prison. He showed up at Monique Sanders' residence. Reports indicate that the couple was stabbed some fifty times each with a butcher knife while they slept. During this time, Monique Sanders' two children, ages seven and nine, ran to a neighbor's house for help. Police were called to the scene and upon arrival Howard Crutchfield walked on to the front porch with a knife in his hand, telling officers that they'd have to kill him because he wasn't going back to prison. Joining me is Monique Sanders' next-door neighbor, Champagne Worthy. What can you tell us about this horrible incident?"

"They should have warned Monique that he was getting out because he was crazy!" the lady said.

"You don't think she was aware?"

"I know she wasn't because had she known he was getting out, she wouldn't have been around to get killed. It's just senseless. Why did he have to kill her and they have two kids together?"

"Did you know Howard Crutchfield well?"

"Well enough to know he was crazy. And had Monique known he was getting out early, I know she would have moved."

The reporter pressed her hand against her earpiece. "Thank you, for your comments," she said to the lady then walked a few steps in front of her, clutching her microphone. "This just in. Howard Melvin Crutchfield was pronounced dead on arrival at Huntsville General Hospital. We are already expecting the governor to receive a great deal of backlash against the early-release program. This is just one case of violence involving inmates out on early release. Coming up on our nightly edition, we will have Neil Newsome, a criminal justice analyst and opponent of the early-release program, to share with us some startling statistics."

"Damn," I said as Foster turned off the TV. I couldn't believe it. Melvin was free. He was where I wanted to be, and he snapped over some woman. Lost his life that fast. I didn't want to ever love someone to the point of insanity. Not Lisa. Not nobody.

"I spent five days in the hole for nothin'," I said.

"What I tell you about a muthafucka snappin'?" Slim Earl asked.

"Yeah, but the last thing a man wants to find when he gets out of prison is his woman with another man. I probably would have done the same thing," Foster said.

I walked back to my cell in a daze.

"What happened to your old celly?" Punisher asked as I walked through the door. He was laying on the bottom bunk looking at me.

"He killed his wife and her fiancé, and now he's dead too."

"Oh," he said and rolled over.

"That's fucked up!" I said.

"You ain't been in prison long, have you?" he asked with his back facing me.

"Not too long, why?"

"I can tell. You'll know when you've been in for a while when don't shit faze you. The more you see on the inside, the less the shit that's happening on the outside matters. When you can walk out on the yard and see a muthafucka die right in front of you, and you don't even blink, that's when you know you've been here too long."

"How long you been in?" I asked.

"Too long."

He was right. As the years passed, and I saw more and more muthafuckas die, death no longer fazed me.

"You in here after somebody?" I asked.

He turned to face me. "If I was, do you think I'd tell you?"

"Everybody in here knows you after somebody."

"Everybody in here knows I'm after somebody except the muthafucka I'm in here after, so don't worry. It's not you. Maybe I'll point the bitch out the next time I see him. That way you get to see what a dead man looks like walking."

"What's his name?"

"Dead Man."

"What's his real name?"

"Don't matter."

"What he do?"

"You sure haven't been in long, 'cause if you had, you'd know not to ask me so many fuckin' questions. What it matter, what he do? Whatever he did, he's dead."

It took a week before I saw Dead Man. He was on the yard lifting. Punisher and I had just walked out on the yard and were heading for the weight pile. Punisher played it so cool, that I never would have thought Dead Man was out there. "That's Dead Man over there," Punisher said as we slowly approached the weight area. "The sloppy white boy lifting. He don't even know he's on death row. Look at him, working out like it matters."

I liked Punisher. Once he started talking I thought he was cool, just a little off.

He had that southern drawl that made him sound kind of like a brother, probably because he was born and raised in New Orleans and listened to a lot of black music. Even had a black girlfriend—well, Creole, so she had some black in her. As far as I was concerned he was one of us. He didn't hang or talk to anybody but me and a few others from my crew. He liked to talk real late at night, around two or three o'clock in the morning.

He'd just start talking—telling his story.

"Look at him. Take a real good look, Tower, 'cause that's a dead man you lookin' at right there."

I stared at Dead Man as he sat on the bench, his face drenched in sweat, his chest and arms covered with satanic tattoos.

"He's dead," Punisher repeated.

We were in our cell and I was sleeping when Punisher said, "I'ma kill that muthafucka. I'ma kill him. Do you understand when I get through with his fuckin' ass no one will be able to recognize him? I'm going to cut his nut sack off and stuff it in his mouth. They're going to find little pieces of him all over the yard."

"What he do?"

"He raped my daughter."

"Your daughter?"

"My girlfriend's daughter. Same thing. His days are so short they're not even numbered."

"When you doing it?" I asked.

"You'll know when I've done it. You'll probably step on one of his fingers or maybe a toe. Well, I'm going to sleep now so I can dream about killing his ass."

"Pleasant dreams."

"Oh, they will be."

"What you in for, man?" I asked.

I closed my eyes because he was quiet for a few minutes after my question so I just figured he wasn't going to tell me, but then he started talking. "I had a business with a buddy of mine who I thought I could trust, but when the business started doing good, he locked me out. Least he could've done was buy me out, but he just locked me out. He went and incorporated behind my back, and I just didn't feel like talking nothin' over with him. We didn't have nothin' to talk about no way. I just blew his fuckin' brains out."

"A buddy of yours, huh?"

"Associate, I guess you could call him. But your friends can fuck you up, too, which is the reason I don't have any."

"You regret killing him?"

"Not really. Nah, actually I don't. I took some time to think about it before I did it, and killing his ass was the only thing I could come up with that made sense."

"See, that ain't what I heard about you."

"What you hear?"

"I heard you was in for murder, but that you did it for hire. I heard that some rich white lady paid you ten thousand dollars to knock off her old man. And the reason they call you Punisher is 'cause that's what you do for a living—punish folks by taking their lives. Any truth to any of that?"

"Maybe. Maybe not. I'm done talkin', unless you want to talk about Dead Man. Otherwise, shut the fuck up."

I woke up and smelled breakfast cooking at Gail's home. I was still tired because she kept me up until almost three in the morning with her questions, and yet I was walking downstairs at only 9:00 A.M. One of these days I was going to sleep in.

"I hope that's turkey bacon I smell," I said, "but I doubt it."

"No, it's pig bacon."

"I don't eat pig."

"Well, I also have eggs, grits, and crescent rolls," she said. I stood in the kitchen and yawned. "So how do you feel this morning?"

"Not too good. I still need help, but I don't know what I'm supposed to do to get it. Should I check myself back in to the prison and say, here 'fix me first'? Maybe I should get psychological help."

"I thought I was helping you."

"You are in a way, but I need more help than just you."

"Are we best friends, Tower?" I shrugged. "Well, I'm your best friend, even if you're not mine and I'm going to help you."

"I wish you could help me. I really do. I got the worse headache. I think I'm going to go back to sleep."

"Pleasant dreams."

I wished I could say they would be, but I knew better. I laid down on the sofa and closed my eyes.

Every night for weeks while we were in our cell, Punisher talked about killing Dead Man. He didn't need to make a shank because somehow he got hold of a knife. And not just any butter knife either. This was a long, sharp knife that could do much damage. He buried it out in the yard because you couldn't keep your weapons in your cell just in case there was a shakedown. I knew Punisher wanted to kill Dead Man, slice him up the way he described so vividly each night. I knew just how bad he wanted to so I never would have done what I did intentionally.

Some of the muthafuckas in prison might have thought I planned it, like I was trying to take away from Punisher's glory, but that's not how it happened. It wasn't my intention to snap. My mind was just fragile after all those hours in the law library. My hopes of an appeal had started to slip away. I was fed up, which is why I nearly killed Dead Man on the yard for using my free weights after I stepped away for a second and walked over to the weight pile to get fifty more pounds to stack on the four hundred I already had. When I saw him lifting with my weights, I snapped. I walked over to him and while he was in the middle of a lift, I used all of my strength to force the bar back down and across his neck. I was going to kill him. I wanted to kill him anyway for raping that little girl. It was just a matter of time before he was dead anyway, but I snapped, so that moment became the time.

Fortunately for Dead Man, Spivey the law clerk and a few Muslims pulled me off him while E.J. stood around egging me on. It took four of them to stop me, but I still could have killed him. All it would have taken was one more second. His white face was completely red. His eyes had started to roll back in his head and the vein in his forehead was so pronounced it didn't seem to have skin covering it. One more second and he would have been gone. And I would have had my sentence increased from forty years, which already seemed like life, to life for real. Was it worth it? Was he worth it? Hell no. I loosened my grip. My friends pulling me and telling me to keep it together didn't save Dead Man—I looked over at Punisher and watched him slowly shake his head. I couldn't be the one to kill Dead Man because that was Punisher's job. I almost killed him. I prolonged his life for only one week, because the day I was walking to the van in shackles preparing for my temporary transfer to Granite Prison, I stepped on a toe and knew Dead Man wasn't walking no more.

One year in Granite was the sentence they gave me for assaulting Dead Man, but if I had waited one more week, his ass would have been dead, and I wouldn't have been going anywhere but back to my cell. Instead, I went to Granite, the place I was warned about only a few days after I first stepped inside of Murray. Warned never to assault a guard or another prisoner, warned not to be caught with drugs on my person or in my cell. There were other things that could put you in Granite, like being caught having sex with another inmate, but I wasn't worried about that one. In fact, most of the warnings went in one ear and out the other. I couldn't promise anyone that I could control myself enough to follow all those rules, especially the one about never assaulting a guard. I had my moments when I wanted to fight back out of frustration and to end my prison time early. Assaulting a guard wouldn't have put me in Granite. It would have put me in a body bag. And at times I didn't care if I was going to live or die. Then other times I felt like I was fighting to mentally survive and stay alive. I wanted to taste freedom. I missed the simple things like the smell of fresh air, seeing a traffic light turn from red to green, and of course, I missed women—whom I always classified as a simple thing because it was always so easy for me to get a piece of them. But it didn't matter. I felt like my life would end while I was in prison.

Driving up to Granite, I could see it for miles coming up the road, sitting out in the middle of nowhere. It's like looking at a mirage. You think you see something but really you don't, only you do, and the closer you get to it, the scarier it seems. There aren't any windows. The walls are probably, I'd say, I don't know, probably fifty, sixty feet high. All I could see were the high walls and guard towers sitting all around it. There's no barbwire around Granite because inmates can't get over the walls. Once inside the prison, you couldn't even see outside of the walls because they were so high.

There were five other male prisoners in the van with me who were being transported to Granite. The guard drove up to the first fence and pulled up to the concrete circular building that was as tall as an electric pole, maybe taller. There were guards at the top of the building with rifles pointing down at us. They had us in leg irons and belly chains to prevent much movement. Two guards came out of the booth and searched the exterior of the van, looking under it with a pole that had a large mirror attached to the end. I don't know exactly what they were looking for under the van. I guess it was just some kind of security precaution they had to take, just like having one of the guards from above lower a bucket with keys inside to a guard below so he could open the first gate. The second gate wasn't opened until the first one was completely closed. Each of us prisoners walked out of the van and stood completely still as the guards took off our shackles while the guards overhead watched everything through the eyepiece affixed to their rifles, prepared to end our life if we took one step out of line.

Once we got through the second gate, we were taken to holding cells, searched again, and then given jumpsuits. I guess different units had different color jumpsuits because those of us in orange jumpers were all taken to the same unit, and the ones with gray jumpers I never saw again.

I went to the hole—a two-by-eight cell with a toilet, sink, and a steel bed. It was like my cell at Murray only smaller with no windows, just a bright light that never went out. I felt like I was locked inside an oven with the temperature turned all the way to broil. Fans weren't allowed in solitary confinement. There was nothing I could do but stay completely still and close my eyes and imagine how the central air would feel. I got out of the hole for only one hour a day at different times each day. In that time, I tried to take a quick shower and if I was lucky, get some pushups and sit-ups in. When it was time to eat, my food was slid under the door.

I was in lockdown for a few months, but I was at Granite for a year. There I learned to accept my fate because what else could I do? Beat the walls? They weren't moving, so why hurt my fists? I just fantasized. I remembered the old days—things from my past. I escaped through my mind. I closed my eyes and thought about what it was going to be like when I got out of prison for good. I thought about what I was going to do once I was free. That's what kept me going, knowing I had unfinished business on the outside. I was consumed with the thought of revenge, with knowing out of the four of us, Stanley and I were the only ones given time, and that my girlfriend, Lisa, who I thought had my back, was probably laying up with Quentin. I felt sorry for any man who crossed me because I was boiling over with anger.

I sat on my bunk and looked at my surroundings. "I'm in prison," I said to myself. It had finally sunk in.

Only occasionally, when I was doing time at Granite did I see a bird fly over. The walls were too high and the rocks held too much heat for them to even try. I survived on letters and phone calls. I called my mama every day and talked for the allotted ten minutes, clinging to my family's life and the things they were doing like a soap opera that I couldn't get enough of. Bernice was pregnant. Wallace was acting strange, like he was on that stuff. Constance met a guy who nobody liked. George was so miserable with his marriage that he said he'd rather get a divorce and pay child support. Tommy—I stopped my mama when she even tried to discuss my stepbrother. I couldn't stand him enough to even hear his name.

Mama started sending me books. Richard Wright's *Native Son* and Ralph Ellison's *Invisible Man*. Books I probably was supposed to read in high school but could never find the time because I was too busy out in them streets. Well, I had nothing but time at Granite, so I soaked up every page.

I ate at chowtime. Seemed like the food tasted a little better at Granite or maybe it was my mind playing tricks on my growling stomach. My final months at Granite eventually passed and I was sent back to Murray, staring at the same faces, with a different celly, one I couldn't stand because we didn't have anything in common. Punisher was sent away to another prison. Not for killing Dead Man because no one saw Punisher kill him. They said that while I was away, Punisher killed one of the head Aryans for calling him a nigger lover.

"You should've seen it, dog," E.J. said. "Right in the yard while everybody was out, Punisher just snapped the muthafucka's neck. It happened so fast that it took that Aryan muthafucka a few minutes to fall over. His ass was still standing up with a broke neck and all. Aryans went wild attacking. We went wild. Guards were shooting. We were on lockdown for a week. Couldn't go out our cell for nothin'."

After four years of serving time, I found out one of my cases, CRF-90-13 was dismissed, which shortened my sentence to twenty-five years with four already served. It also marked the first year I became eligible for parole.

CHAPTER 29

Gail and I found a booth in the back of Bennigan's, and Gail pressed the play button on her microcassette recorder and started asking me questions.

"I did a search on prison-related topics on the Internet and I found an article about drugs in prison."

"I already told you about the drugs in prison. What, you don't trust my word?"

"I trust you. It's better to have more information than not enough."

"No it ain't. That's being redundant, and you repeat yourself a lot."

"How would you know? I've never let you read anything."

I knew because I had the disk and I took it home and started reading some of it, but I couldn't tell Gail that. "Because if you write the way you talk, I can only imagine."

"Well, if you'd tell me more instead of having me fill in all of these blanks, I wouldn't have to rely so much on the Internet. Look how long it took you to tell me about the parole officer."

"Don't mention her."

"Well, do you talk to her at all?"

"See, redundant."

"That's not being redundant."

"You want to know some more about drugs in prison, right?"

She nodded. "Well, we only earned fifteen dollars a month for working and that was at the high end of the pay scale. So if somebody was going to take their little money and buy drugs that shit better be good or the person selling the shit could get killed. Drugs meant a lot in prison."

"Did you use them?"

"Sometimes. Remember when I said that I had a lot of hustles?" Gail nodded. "Well, smuggling drugs was one of 'em. If someone wanted to bring in drugs, they needed to let me know so I could arrange it. I had to make sure not too much shit was coming in because my mule couldn't put that much up his ass."

"Who was the mule?"

"This one muthafucka I knew. He was the best, and the only one I trusted to keester. He could put plastic bags filled with drugs in his ass while he was sitting with a visitor. He had that shit down, but the key was for the people who brought the drugs in to make sure it was wrapped as tight and thin as possible."

Gail's face was scrunched up. "That's nasty. How could he stick some stuff up his butt like that?"

"Hell, people's turds come out bigger than that."

"But they're coming out, not going in."

"He had some greasy shit with him and he'd stick the drugs up his ass after he greased them up. He had a hole cut in his front pocket, and then he'd reach down in his pocket, move his nut sack back and stick the drugs up as far as he could get them. When he got back to his cell, he'd shit them out."

"What kinds of drugs would he sneak in?"

"Mainly weed, but he also brought in cocaine and heroin. He took a risk because if that shit wasn't wrapped right and got into his system, it could kill him. All he wanted was a cap of weed for smuggling it in."

"What?"

"A cap of weed. That was worth five packs of cigarettes."

"What is a cap of weed?"

"We called it a cap of weed because we'd take the little Blistex cap off, and put the weed in it to measure."

"I get it. Okay, let's move to a different subject and talk about the homosexuality."

"I told you there's nothing to talk about."

"According to my statistics, ninety percent of inmates will be raped while in prison. Does that sound factual to you?"

"I don't know. All I know was I wasn't. Those statistics are probably for large maximum-security prisons in big cities. I was in a medium-security prison in a small Oklahoma town."

"But you told me there were death-row inmates at your prison. So it had to be maximum."

"Not in my unit. We had four units. My unit was medium security. I didn't have contact with anybody on death row, except this one mutherfucka who got off and got sent to my unit. He walked around smiling every damn day. That shit used to piss all the prisoners off. We'd say, 'Is this muthafucka crazy or what? Don't he know where he is.' But later it came out that he was on death row, and he got his sentence changed to life without parole. He was happy with a life-without sentence."

"Tower, if you were with a man, it's okay. I know your environment—"

"I wasn't with no damn man! Why does everyone think that every man in prison been with a man?"

"Because we remember *Scared Straight*. Some of those masculine, hard-looking men looked at those young boys and said, 'Yeah, if you come in here, I'ma make you my bitch.' I was ten when I watched that and I still remember."

"Let's get this shit straight: I wasn't no man's bitch. Make sure you put that in your damn book!"

"Well, was any man yours?"

"What!" I said, standing.

Gail began looking around nervously. "I'm just asking things my readers are going to want to know. Please sit down. People are looking."

"I don't want to talk about that shit no more."

"Okay, just sit down. I'm sorry."

I sat down slowly. "You think I'm a fuckin' buzzard? That's what you think? Why, just 'cause I'm not trying to get between your legs anymore? Maybe I don't want you like that. Maybe you're not my type. Ever thought about that? Don't worry. I get mine. I have women to be with. When I was in prison, I mostly jacked off. After I got tired of doing that, I shut that part down and didn't think about it no more until I got out. If you were in prison, would you be with a woman?"

"I don't know. I can't say what would happen. I know people often become what they're exposed to. If I'm with a bunch of women and we're getting high year after year, I would think the odds of me going ten years without either getting raped or trying it, would be slim. And I'm not gay, I'm just a realist."

"Well that's sad. Most men inside had more pride than to have sex with other men. You got to understand a lot of those guys are married, and it wasn't cool to be a buzzard."

"What do you mean by a buzzard?"

"A man who fucks other men is a buzzard. That wasn't cool. And the warden did crooked shit. He'd put them sissy men out on the yard with their long hair and eyeliner on knowing they had AIDS and leave them in general population for weeks then later get on the TV and announce if you had contact with such and such report to Medical. Shouldn't even have put them muthafuckas with us."

"Okay, wait a minute. You've just contradicted yourself."

"What you mean?" I asked.

"What difference would it make what the warden did with the homosexuals if most of the men in there didn't mess with them?"

"I ain't saying they didn't mess with 'em. I didn't, and mostly none of the mutahfuckas I hung with did. But hell yeah, it was muthafuckas who did. Old-timers. Lifers. Muthafuckas who didn't care and been in there for years, and then it was muthafuckas who came in who had already been with men. Shit ain't gonna change once they inside. But if you go in a man, that's how you coming out."

"How did you come out?"

I stared her down for a few seconds before I said, "I came out a man. The same way I went in."

"I don't understand why you're being so defensive if it never happened to you. That's more characteristic of a person who did have the experience and is quite possibly ashamed of it."

"You trying to use your medical degree—the one you never earned? Don't come psychoanalyzing me with your bootleg credentials."

Gail brushed her tongue over her teeth. "I'll change the subject."

"Yeah, you go ahead and do that. When the spotlight's on your ass, you can, huh?"

"No, I just see how much it upsets you. I'll just have to make up something to put in there."

"I'm telling you now you better not have me being with no man in that book. You hear me? You don't know me. You think you do, but really you don't, so don't piss me off, unless you want to really get to know who I am and where I been. You know what I'm starting to believe? Maybe I'm just not the right subject for your book."

"No, Tower, you are the right subject. Why do you say you're not?"

"Because you're looking for more than what I got to tell. You have a fascination with fags or something. You even put that shit in your first book. Why it got to be about all that? No real man is gonna want to read a book about no fag no way. Only reason you women want to read shit like that is so you can convince yourselves that that's why the man left you, because he was gay. That'll make you feel a whole lot better. Why can't you just write the book about a man trying to adjust in society? Why everything got to be about sex and homosexuality and all that shit?"

"I guess I can do that. You know what it is?" she asked.

"No, but I'm sure you're 'bout to tell me."

She smiled. "Tower, I guess I don't like the fact that you were in prison for all of those years and you act like you were never exposed to homosexuality in any way. That's just not realistic."

"I don't know how you were brought up, but I was brought up not to tell all my business or pry into other people's."

"I'm a writer. I can't help it. If you could just tell me something."

The waiter walked over with the bill and placed it beside me. I slid it over to Gail, who quickly removed her credit card from her wallet and handed it to the waiter before he had a chance to walk away. I started massaging my eyes, wondering if the homosexual activity in prison was relevant. What did it have to do with my problems with life? I could see if I took part in it, then maybe it would explain some things. I told Gail that I masturbated on a regular basis. I thought I explained to her that masturbation and my imagination provided me with some of the best sex I'd ever had, to the point that sometimes it was hard for me to cum when I was really having sex. Even if I didn't get that specific, that would be more relevant than what some of the other inmates did with each other.

"Please," she pleaded with her clear eyes, "I just want to know, and once you tell me, I won't bring it up again."

The waiter returned with Gail's credit card and a receipt for her to sign. Gail added a ten-dollar tip, which I thought was crazy for a twenty-six-dollar bill. "Ain't it still fifteen percent?"

"What?"

"Gratuity."

She laughed. "It's whatever you think the service was worth."

"Then move the period over and take off one zero, 'cause it sure wasn't worth more than that."

"A dollar? I'm not tipping a dollar. They already think blacks don't tip at all."

"So, that's even more reason not to tip their ass."

"He was a good waiter."

"He was doing his fuckin' job, but I forgot, you ballin'."

"I wish."

I stood and stretched. "You gonna stay here or what?"

"I'm just thinking." She paused. I looked around impatiently and put my hands in my pockets. "Don't you want to know what about?" I shook my head. "Why not? It might be important." I shrugged. "Alright. Well, I hope you change your mind and open up to me more."

"I've told you everything I'm going to tell you so take what you have and do whatever it is people like you do to make a book."

"Do you care about me at all, Tower?"

"I do, but not enough to bring into your life all of what dealing with me would bring. I'm complicated, and after you got through dealing with me, your eyes definitely wouldn't be clear no more. They'd be bloodshot and worn out."

"But do you think we could ever be a couple?"

I shrugged and scrunched up my face. What did she want me for? "Just give me some time to try to get myself together, then I'll come back at you."

Don't lie. You ain't coming back at that girl. Tell her the truth. No, the two of y'all can't never be a couple. Tell her. Tell her you ain't never met a woman like her and that shit ain't a compliment either. Tell her! my mean voice said.

"No. I'm not telling her that."

Gail looked but didn't ask. She knew I was having a conversation with my voice and not with her.

CHAPTER 30

January 14, 1994, was the first time I went before the parole board. I had been in for four years, and because mine was a nonviolent crime, I was eligible to go beg for my freedom. Had I been in for something like murder, it probably would have taken at least nine years before I became eligible, like with E.J. When E.J. finally got the chance to go before the parole board, they turned him down the first year and every year after that. Now, he just has a few more years before he's served out his entire sentence and is free like me, but hopefully his freedom will feel better, but after serving his full twenty years, I doubt it.

Spivey was one of the first to tell me about the parole hearings and how full of shit they were. E.J. agreed. Weeks before I was getting ready to go before the board, I mailed each member a package with all of my letters from friends and relatives and my transcripts. It would've been better if I had a letter from someone important like a congressman, but I didn't know anyone important, and I didn't know anyone who knew anyone important—street hustlers only mattered on the street—so I didn't get my hopes up.

I walked into the room and looked at the board members seated behind the long table. There were six of them—five white men and one white woman, and not one of them looked up. Most of the men were old, seventy or eighty. I'm sure they were not only racist but also set in their ways.

"Theodore Evans, you were convicted on drug-related charges and sentenced to forty years," the white woman said as she wrote without looking up. "I see here that one of your charges has been dropped, which reduced your sentence."

"Yes, ma'am."

"So what have you done to rehabilitate yourself?"

"Well, ma'am, I've completed my Narcotics Anonymous course, and I took an industrial building maintenance class."

"And do you think those courses are enough for you to become a productive member of society?"

"Ma'am, it's not the courses. I've been in prison for four years. I've never been in prison before, and I never want to be here again. I want to go home and see my family and friends and my girlfriend and our child. I made a mistake, and being locked up has made me realize it."

She looked at me then, and said, "What do you think about the people who lost their lives because of the drugs you sold? They can't go home to their family and friends. How do you feel about the destruction you've caused, all for financial gain?"

"Ma'am, well, I feel sorry about that. I never really looked at what I was doing as taking a person's life, I guess."

"You didn't. How could you not?"

"Well, I guess I did and I didn't. I was just caught up in making money."

"And how do you know that once you get back out in the world you won't still get caught up?"

"Because I know I don't want to come back here or anyplace like here, that's why."

"Okay, thank you. We have no further questions."

"Is that it?" I asked.

"That's it. Thank you."

A few days later I had my mama call to find out what the ruling was. It was 0/6 in favor of my release. I couldn't even convince one person that I had enough. Not one person. Even though one person wouldn't have set me free, I wanted to at least know that someone believed in me. I went before the parole board every year after that, but it took four more years before they agreed to release me into the community service work program. Some of the inmates said I was lucky. Said they'd tried three and four times for parole. Said I should be glad to be free. I didn't consider myself to be either lucky or free. I had to spend two years at that center where I'd work during the day and be transported back to the center to sleep in a room with fifty or sixty inmates at night, and then after two years, I'd be out, but still not free. I'd be on parole until the year 2015 and under the watchful eye of some power-tripping state employee.

Free? Not quite.

When the community center director came to me and said that my interstate compact was approved and that I was free to call my family to have them pick me up and take me home, I didn't move. I stood in front of him with my mouth hanging open. "You for real?"

"Yes, this is really happening, Tower. You're free to go. You can leave right now if you want, but I assumed you needed transportation to get from here back to Texas. If you can't get any, we'll buy you a bus ticket."

"Oh, I can get somebody to come get me. It's over?" I asked, looking for final confirmation.

"It's over," he said. I thought I was going to cry so I put my hand over my face and waited for the tears to come, but they never did. "God will bless you, son, just believe it and it will happen. I've worked for the prison system for twenty-seven years, but I didn't always agree with some of their practices, which is why today is my last day too," the director said. "I'm free. Just like you. Free to do something that will really help people, 'cause locking them up don't. Not if you ever intend on letting them out. I'm going to seminary school, and when I'm blessed to have my own church, I will put a program in place to help ex-offenders."

I took my hand from over my face and looked at him. I didn't say anything because I didn't know what to say. I was still in shock that I was free.

"Go on and use the phone to call your folks," he said.

"Alright," I said with a smile. "I'm free. Don't forget that."

"Don't you forget it."

CHAPTER 31

"I still need help," I said to Gail on the cell phone. I was parked in front of Tonya's apartment with the windows down. "But what am I supposed to do?"

"I guess you can keep calling me. I'll try to help you as much as I can. And it would help if we saw each other more."

"No offense, but I need someone to help me who's been through what I've been through. Now, I think I need to talk to a black man who's been to prison and who's trained to counsel me. That's probably going to be hard to find, huh?" Tonya pulled up. "I got to go, okay? I'll call you later."

"Wait, I want to talk about this," Gail said. I held on because I couldn't hang up on her, not until she said, "Okay." I had to go, but not so bad that I would disrespect someone who was trying to help me.

"I'll call you tomorrow, okay?" I asked.

"Okay, Tower," she said, lowering her voice.

"I'll call you tomorrow," I repeated because she sounded so sad all of a sudden.

"Why can't you call me back tonight?"

"I'll try, okay?"

I watched Tonya walk into the house with her daughter, Tyra.

"Five more minutes, please?" Gail begged. "I just need to talk to somebody tonight."

"I'll call you back. I promise."

"Bye, Tower." She hung up the phone.

I got out of the car and started walking to the apartment, but I stopped before I reached the building's steps and turned around to go to my car.

"What you doing?" I asked Gail when I called her back. I was driving on 114 near her exit.

"Writing."

"Do you want some company?"

"Who?"

"Who you think?"

"I'm in my writing mode right now, and when I get like this I want to be alone."

"But I just finished talking to you and you said you needed to talk. I won't stay too long. Besides, you're supposed to be writing about me, remember?

"Supposed to is right, but you haven't been supplying me with much information lately. And I thought I was finished with the book, but I'm stuck on the turning point, and I can't decide whether or not Mason should die at the end. I'm waiting for his voice to take over, but he won't. This is much harder to write than my first one."

"Can I come over or not? I got plenty more to tell. I thought of some really good scenes, a lot of things that I haven't told you. Will you let me?"

"Come on."

"Tower, I don't mean to be antisocial but I'm tired. I've been writing since 5:00 A.M. and my mind is fried," Gail said as she stood in the foyer wearing my XXXL white-ribbed cotton shirt that I left at her house months ago, and it was so big on her that it fit like a mini-dress.

"I've been looking for that shirt."

"What, this undershirt?"

"That's not an undershirt."

"Well, you left it, and it was all I had to remember you by."

"Oh, come on now. Don't make it sound like it's been that long since we've seen each other."

"It has." She hugged me real tight, like she was trying to squeeze the love out of me. She was so fragile. Her hand could fit inside of mine, and I'd still have plenty of room left over. My body was so much larger than hers. "I missed you."

"It ain't been that long, has it?" I asked as I closed the front door.

"Yes. Now, what new do you have to tell me?"

"I thought you said your brain was fried."

"Yeah, but I'm curious."

"Can we talk in the bed?" I asked.

"Do you really have stuff to tell me?"

"Yeah. I got a lot to tell you."

She took my hand and led me upstairs to her bedroom.

"Put your hands up," I said.

She raised her hands, and I pulled my shirt off her.

"What do you have to tell me?"

"I missed you," I said as I put her right breast in my mouth and fondled her left one with my hand.

"You did not," she said, pushing me away from her.

"I did. I missed you," I said as I unbuckled the belt to my jeans.

"Tower, I need scenes not sex." She picked up my shirt from the floor and put it back on.

"What about sex scenes?"

She didn't laugh or even crack a smile.

"Okay, what you want to know?" I took off my jeans and lay on her bed in my boxers with my hands resting behind my head.

"Tell me some more about prison." She walked over to the nightstand, pressed play on the recorder, and then crawled in the bed beside me. "I need you to tell me something about the other prisoners. What were they like?"

"Some of them were cool, probably better than a lot of the people I'd meet on the outside. Others you had to stay the hell away from."

"What about the ones who were in for life without parole or those who were on death row? How were they?"

"Imagine if you were in prison for life. How would you feel?"

She shrugged. "I can't imagine doing anything that would put me in prison for life. Not in a real prison, anyway."

"Lifers don't have nothing to live for. They're going to die in prison unless they escape. Some of them found a way to accept their fate, but even the ones who found a way to deal with it had their days when you knew just to leave 'em alone. Death row inmates were another breed, but the general population never came in contact with them. They didn't get out on the yard. Had to stay in their cell for twenty-three hours a day, and for one hour they could go out in the dayroom. Portable showers were rolled to their cell. It's just like my granny used to tell me when I was a young boy, 'every time you think you got it bad, it's somebody got it worse.' Me, I think I'd rather get the shit over with quick. Life in prison or the death penalty? Give me the death penalty. I never would've made it through forty years. I guess that's why God let me out in ten, but now I have to figure out what I'm supposed to do with my second chance."

"What else can you tell me?"

"I don't know. What else you want to know? You're the writer."

"I'm not sure what I want to know. Do you think E.J. would make a good character?"

"Leave him out of it, okay?"

"Why? He might like being a character in the book."

"He don't want to be in your stupid book!"

She was quiet. And she looked away from me.

Oh, you did it now. Stupid book? my nice voice said.

"I'm just telling her the truth."

"Say you're telling me the truth. Not her the truth. Stop talking to those voices, Tower. I'm right here."

"I'm just telling you the truth. He don't want to be in your book."

"Do you? Since it's so stupid."

"It don't really matter. It was fun at first, I guess, but now, it don't really matter."

"Do you want me to still write the stupid book?"

"You can write it."

"Are you sure?"

"Yeah. In fact, I'll try to work on something at home for you. Sometimes things come to me, so the next time they do, I'll write it down and when we see each other again, I'll give it to you."

"Can you think of any positive things about your prison experience?"

"Hell no. There's nothing positive about prison. Your worst thoughts are all true. You're trapped in a place with murderers, rapists, and gang-bangers, and you got to learn how to survive."

CHAPTER 32

"I don't think I want this," I said to Tonya. We were both in the bed. We'd just finished having sex, and she walked into the living room and came back with a bridal magazine.

"I want my bridesmaid's dresses to be violet."

"Did you hear me?"

"I'm sorry, baby. What did you say?"

"I don't want this no more. Us. This relationship. I really need to get my own place and try to get it together up here," I said, pointing at my forehead.

"Nothing's wrong with you. You're a good man. All you need is a good woman, and that's exactly what I am—a help meet. I'd do anything for you, Tower. Anything. I just want to be married."

"Why?"

"I don't know. I guess 'cause I never have been and I'm getting older. I've always wanted to be Mrs. Somebody. If I got married, it would give hope to the ladies in my singles ministry."

I buried my head in my hands. "But I don't love you."

"That's okay. I love you, and you'll grow into loving me. I'm sure you will. I've lost a total of eighty-seven pounds."

"Why is it that every time I tell you that I don't want a relationship you start telling me how much weight you've lost? I don't care if you get a body like Janet Jackson, I still don't want you."

"It takes time, Tower. It could take years for two people to grow together like a real husband and wife."

Tell her you ain't got time. Shit! You already wasted enough of that. I don't think these women out here understand. It ain't even worth having sex with 'em if you got to deal with all this nonsense—marriage. That's the furthest thing from your mind. Tell her! my mean voice said.

"I ain't ready for marriage."

"Why do you say that, Tower?"

" 'Cause I ain't."

"How do you know?"

"Don't you think I should know something like that?"

Her eyes narrowed in disgust. "Does this have anything to do with that woman who's writing that book on you?"

"Gail? No," I said with an attitude. "She's just my friend. That's all."

"Have you slept with her?"

"No."

"Where were you last night? Don't lie."

"Don't ask me questions. How many times do I have to tell you that? I just don't want this."

"What don't you want?"

"Us—me and you. I don't want it. I don't like you. You had me get a disk and copy the book that Gail's been working on so you could start writing it, and you haven't even started."

"I opened the file and read some of it. She's practically finished. I don't have that much to do to it."

"You can't use her stuff!"

"It's your stuff not hers. It's about your life."

I shook my head. "Nah, that ain't right. That ain't even right."

"It's your story." I got out of bed and dressed. "Where are you going?"

"Stop asking me shit!"

"I just want to know where you're going. Let's pray."

"I don't want to pray. Pray about what? I been going to church and nothing's changed. I'm tired of being fake with you. Only reason I'm staying here is because I don't have anywhere else to go, but I'm starting to feel like I'd rather move back with my sister than be here with you. And I hate living with my sister."

Tonya started to cry. "Why are you being so mean to me?"

"Ain't nobody being mean to you. I just don't want you." I walked out on her balcony and started smoking a Black & Mild cigar. Tonya slid back the door and put one foot out. "Don't come out here. Please, don't come out here." She slid the glass door closed.

I took out my phone and called Gail.

"You must be on your period," Gail said nonchalantly after I said a few words.

"Yes, I am," I said.

"Okay, well, I'll let you go."

"I called you so how you gonna let me go?"

"Well, why call with an attitude?"

"You're right," I said and hung up on her. She knew I couldn't help my mood swings. She knew because I told her I couldn't and not that she believed everything I said because she didn't, which explained her tactic of asking me the same question ten different ways.

"I guess I'll work on the book myself," I said.

I called Gail but there was no answer, and it stayed that way the whole day, and the next, and the next, for the whole week and the week after, and the week after that. I didn't understand why she wasn't answering the phone. Even though I didn't see her much, only when I could—if I could, I never expected to call Gail's house and hear, "Hello," in a man's voice. I hung up the phone because I knew it had to be the wrong number, but when I redialed I heard him again. He didn't sound like a corporate executive either. He sounded like some muthafucka from the south side, probably that damn wanna-be rapper.

"Is Gail there?" I asked.

"She's in the shower."

I looked at the phone like it was lying before I slammed it back down and began pacing the floor. Now, I understood how Melvin, my celly, felt after he got out and found his woman with some other man. And Gail wasn't even my woman, didn't have a baby by me, or nothing, but I still wanted to go over there and blast off her head, and that fool's who answered the phone too.

What should I do? I asked myself, waiting for one of my voices to answer but none did. They were probably confused. Gail belonged to me. Even if I didn't want her, I be damn if some other muthafucka was going to take my place. *What should I do? Answer me, please?*

You know that muthafucka's over there having a good time, don't you? my mean voice said. *You know he's sitting over there kicking his feet up on the coffee table, eating all the food, driving her car, hitting it from the back, sideways, she's probably riding him too. Oh, and you best believe that she's going down on him. And I'm sure he's eating her out. It's no telling what they're over there doing. I don't know what to tell you, other than it's your own fault. Too busy dealing with Tonya—some bitch who wants marriage so bad she'd buy her own wedding ring, the dress, walk down the aisle, stand at the altar and say, "I do," without a man if she could. She's already having her child call you Daddy when you have one of your own you've never seen.*

What did you expect, Tower? my nice voice asked. *Gail's a young woman who's lonely, and nothing's wrong with her. Of course, some other man would want to spend time with her. Too bad it wasn't you because I always liked her.*

I always liked her too, my mean voice said.

No you didn't. You just wanted her for sex, my nice voice said.

I just want them all for sex, and? Nothing's wrong with that.

"Life's a letdown," I said to my voices.

It sure is. You won't get no argument from me there, my mean voice said.

I knew Gail was using me.

Using you for what? Let's get real for a minute, my mean voice said.

"For the book."

The book? If anything, you were using her. It takes a certain type of person to sit up day after day, week after week, month after month, listening to all that woe-is-me shit, my mean voice said.

"What if something becomes of it?"

Ain't nothing gonna become of that shit. It's a book. Can't too much become of a damn book no way, can it? It's not like it's an Eminem CD.

"Gail said books are hot now."

Erotica. That's what she said. That shit she's writing ain't no damn erotica. What black person you know want to deal with some serious shit? We got enough issues of our own to worry about. If somebody gonna read, they gonna do it to escape, not to get deep, otherwise it ain't fiction. But if you think she's trying to get over on you, go over there and confront her ass, my mean voice said.

"Did you sleep with him?" I asked Gail as I stood in her foyer the next afternoon.

"With who?" she asked, then turned and walked into the living room.

"That muthafucka who answered the phone last night," I said, walking behind her. "Was he the rapper?"

"You called?"

"Did you sleep with him? Was he the rapper? Answer my damn questions!" She didn't respond. "You slept with him." I stared at her in disgust, giving her an opportunity to change my mind—lie or something.

She nodded.

I let out a loud grunt and started hitting my forehead. "I can't believe it! What for? Ooh." I started pacing and hitting my head. "Ooh. You're such a fuckin' liar."

"What did I lie about?"

"All that shit about you love me. I knew you were lying. I don't trust you no more. Why did you do it? Huh? Why did you have to fuck him?"

She shrugged. "It doesn't matter. He's just my friend."

"So you just lay around with guys who are your friend? Where did you meet him? Off the Internet? What did your profile say, single black woman with an almost medical degree seeking ex-con with mental problem for research, possible book deal, and unconditional love? I'm tired of being lied to by women! Where the fuck did you meet him?"

"He's not an ex-con and I didn't meet him off the Internet. It doesn't matter where I met him, Tower."

"Do you love him?" I asked, following her into the living room.

She shrugged. "I don't know if I do or not. He's nice. And we both want more from our lives. It was also nice to be held."

"But he did more than just hold you, didn't he?"

"It's not like I'm the only person you've had sex with. I'm sick of waiting for you to show up whenever you feel like it. What am I supposed to do, Tower? Tell me."

"Tell you what? I guess do whatever you want to do. That's what people do anyway. I don't have no claim to you. You're single so I don't know why I'm tripping."

"But if you wanted to be with me, Tower, all you'd have to do is tell me. I love you."

I shook my head. "What's so special about a relationship that every woman got to be in one?"

"Every woman doesn't have to be in one, Tower. I'm sure there's some women who don't want a relationship."

"Well, why you got to have one then? Why can't you be alone?"

"I'm tired of being alone," she shouted. "That's why. I've been alone long enough. If you don't want me, that's all you have to say. Say it. Say you don't want me."

"It's like this, Gail: Gail has to look out for Gail. She can't expect Tower to look out for her."

"Well, that really sums it all up."

I shrugged. "I'm just telling the truth. Nobody's going to care about you more than you. Nobody's going to care about that book you're writing more than you. Nobody's going to care about anything you do more than you. Don't you know that?"

She shook her head. "No, I didn't. Say something, Tower. Say something that will hurt me so I won't have to love you like this anymore."

"Something like what?"

"I think the truth might do it."

"I've told you the truth. I don't know what more I can tell you. You know my whole life story and yet you're still asking me questions. All I've ever wanted you to do was concentrate on the book."

"But I'm going crazy sitting in this house alone with no one to talk to. I feel like I'm in prison."

I spit out laughter. "You're livin' large in this big house. Lock yourself in your half bath for ten years and then we can talk about how it feels to be in prison."

"I love you, Tower."

"I'm tired of you saying that. You don't know me, Gail. If you knew the real me, you wouldn't love me."

"I'm tired," Gail said. I followed her up the stairs and into her bedroom. Half of her bed was covered with writing pads, a large red dictionary, a thick green thesaurus, several ink pens, a tape recorder, and a few Writer's Digest books.

"You write while you're in the bed?"

"I write anywhere I can."

"What's with you, Gail? I don't understand you? I don't understand why your phone never rings or when it does, why you look at it like it shouldn't. I don't understand why you rarely leave the house. Whose house is this anyway? Who are you? Tell me something."

"I'm going to be a best-selling author."

"Is that all you want out of life—to sell books?"

"Yes. And I want you. But since I can't have you, I'll settle for the next best thing—selling books."

"You got so much game. You know that? So much game."

"I'm tired. Maybe, you should leave now."

Leave? my mind questioned. Gail never wanted me to leave. It was then that I realized what was really happening. She was changing toward me. Most likely she had finished with the book and she didn't need me. I almost called her a bitch, but I stopped myself.

I saw this coming, didn't you? All those times she smiled in your face, showing her pretty dimples, all an act. Mmm-hmm. Oh well, life may be a letdown, but it sure as hell goes on, my mean voice said.

CHAPTER 33

I signed on to my computer at work and went into my email. I had several unread messages. I scanned the list, picking and choosing. I saw one from Gail. I smiled as I opened it up. I hadn't spoken to her in a few days because I thought she was mad at me, but I guess not if she was writing again. But my smile dropped after I read on.

I saw from the date of the message, January 6, 2003, that she'd left it on a Monday, my off day.

The subject was Fact or Fiction.

It's become my reality that you really want to be with someone else. Someone who's probably more attractive than me, and I know for men that's what it usually starts with. We met on a whim, and I got the sense immediately that you weren't attracted to me, which is why you rarely looked directly in my face, and you never introduced me to your family, or invited me to your house, even though I was writing a book on you. You never took me for a ride in your car. We never went to the movies. All I ever did was hit play on my recorder and listen to you talk about your prison experience, and at times I felt sorry for you, but not anymore. You sold drugs, and you got caught. So what? I feel like I was used to help you either get over some woman or deal with your insecurities about being an ex-con.

I guess it's nice to have someone who's all into you, even if you aren't into them, which is where I came in. Who was I trying to kid? It's rare people find true love, but I won't settle for less. When people start lying for no reason, it's best to move on before you fall too deep in love and while you still have your heart and mind intact, which is what I'm doing now. No hard feelings. None at all. I'm done with the book. I mailed your contract to your mother's address, which I found in your transcripts. Take care! You still make me laugh, and the time we shared together I needed so I would know that I could still feel. I will miss hearing your voice but I guess it wasn't meant to be and Gail has to worry about Gail now.

"Why haven't you been answering your phone?" I said through the phone line. Gail sighed, but didn't respond. "What, you don't want to talk to me anymore? We still have work to do on the book." I called her a week after receiving the email because the more I thought about everything, the angrier I became. I was alone. I moved out of Tonya's and into a small motel room with a little kitchenette down the street from my job. So now was not the time for somebody to be leaving me, especially not Gail. In a weird way I grew to depend on her. I'd never had someone there whenever I called, almost like her sole purpose for living was to be available to me.

"The book is done. Didn't you get my email?"

"Yeah, I got it, but it didn't make any sense. The book can't be done. I still need to read it."

"It's done. All I need to do is a final read and in a couple of weeks I should be ready to print it and start sending it out to literary agents."

"Before I give my okay? And what about the part I was going to give you on dealing?"

"I took that out. A dealer is a dealer, remember? I focused more on prison. I had to do what I had to do because you were always so busy."

"Well, I'm not busy now. I told you it has to be real. It has to feel a certain way."

"I listened to the taped interviews. Besides, it's fiction anyway so I used my creative license and changed a lot of things around. It's better that way for all involved."

"See, this is why I wanted a contract. Now that you're finished writing you gonna forget all about me, and if anything becomes of the book I'm just shit out of luck, I guess—"

"I mailed your contract to your parents' house on Morningside. They do still live there, right?"

"Yeah, they still live there."

"So see, no one's leaving anyone out. I'm glad you feel the book will do well."

"It's more than the book. I got used to spending time with you. I still want to see you."

"I'm finished writing the book. We don't ever have to meet again. And that's probably best because the more we see each other, the more I hold on to the hope that we'll be together, but now I've finally come to the realization that we won't, so I'm moving on."

"I had a dream last night, and you were in it. It was so real. Have you ever had a dream that played like a movie?"

"I have to go," she said nonchalantly.

"Wait." I needed to think of something to say that would keep her around for a little longer. What did she want to hear? "I love you."

"You what?"

"I love you."

"Oh, now you can say you love me, on the day I decide to move on? I guess you're so used to running game that you do it on everybody, even those who care for you. I really thought you were my friend. I really thought we were becoming best friends, but now I realize that you aren't capable of developing a friendship with anyone. All you ever did was pretend to be my friend." She sighed. "Well, thank you for sharing your story. The book is finished, and I'm free. When you finally figure out that you are, too, you'll be a lot happier. Good-bye, Tower. Please don't call me anymore."

When she hung up, I felt little pins sticking me in my chest near my heart. I tried to push back my feelings but I couldn't. When I had Gail, I didn't want her, and now that she might be gone, I did. I called her back, thinking she wouldn't answer but she did.

"Tower, don't do this to me."

"What am I doing?"

"Playing with my emotions. I've told you that I'm moving on."

"Where you moving to?"

"On—away from you."

"On, how many people live in On?"

"I don't know, but I'm sure I'm not the only one."

"Can I move On with you?"

"On is for the hurt people."

"I'm hurt."

"Well, it's for the people who believe in love but just can't find it."

"Can On also be for the people who never believed in love but finally found it when they weren't even looking?"

"I'm not sure. But On isn't for the street hustlers running game."

"What about the used-to-be hustlers?"

"Maybe."

"I'm ready to move on."

"Let me move on alone please," she said.

"I can't."

"You're too fucked up to be in a relationship, remember?"

"I remember, but I still want to move on. What, a fucked-up person can't move on?"

"Eventually, but what about Lisa, Arturo, Quentin, and all the other people who have control of your mind?"

"All in the past. I'm moving on."

"Tower, you need time to be by yourself—you never really had that."

"What you call ten years in the pen?"

"The past—that's what I call it."

"I tell you what. You remember the time and place we first met, right?"

"Yes."

"If you gonna let me move on with you be there tomorrow at the same time. If you're not, I guess we'll just move on separately."

"Good-bye, Tower."

"Not good-bye. I'll see you later."

I was pulled alongside of the freeway waiting in my car. I checked my rearview and saw plenty of cars but none like Gail's. Still, I figured she was just running late so I waited until a quarter after then half past. Waited until I couldn't wait anymore because I knew she wasn't coming so I started my car and left. I guess she decided to move on without me, and I guess I needed to let her, but I couldn't.

I felt it was an occasion just not a special one when I went over Gail's house without calling because I wanted to catch her with that man or convince myself that she wasn't my savior, my friend, and would never be my true lover. I wanted to feel disappointment like I had felt my entire life, and I wanted to feel it as a result of her. I wanted to ask her what she meant by moving on. Why she thought she could write a book on my life and then leave. I knew she couldn't be as good of a friend as she claimed—a so-called best friend. All lies. I knew she was like all the rest. Who was this woman I'd known for almost two years who I knew very little about, nothing more than her first and last name, her phone number at home and at work, her address, the make and model of her car, but not even her age or her birthday? I didn't trust her because I didn't understand why she was so good at listening about my life, but unable to talk about her own. So I picked a Wednesday, late evening to ring her doorbell and demand, "Tell me about yourself, Gail."

"I don't have anything to tell. I just write, and that's all I do. Why did you come over here? I told you I'm moving on."

"I don't feel good about this whole thing anymore."

"What whole thing?"

"The book. You. Just everything. I trusted you, but I don't know who you are. You better tell me something."

She shook her head. "I don't have anything to tell."

I stuck out my hand. "Give me my transcripts. You're done with them, aren't you?"

"Yes, I'm done."

"Then give them to me."

"Can I keep them?"

"Keep them for what? You said you were done with them, right?"

"Yes, I just want to keep them. You don't need them."

"That's a part of my life. I want them. So give them here!"

She walked into her guestroom and returned quickly with the two legal files and handed them to me. "Here."

I took them from her. "I don't want you doing the book either."

"What? What do you mean? I've spent almost two years writing this book."

"I don't care. I don't want you doing it. Erase it from your hard drive."

"What? Why, Tower? You can't do this. Why are you doing this? All I ever did was love you, so why are you trying to hurt me like this? You know this is all I have in the world."

"How do I know that when I know nothing about you? You came into my life pretending to be my friend. You're not my friend—I don't know who you are."

"I'm your friend, Tower. I promise. I'm your friend."

"You don't tell me nothing other than you're moving on, and I see that now, you're moving on—without me. Well, you can move on, but you can't use me and then move on. Erase it!"

"Please," she cried. "Is it money? I'll write you a check right now. Please don't do this to me."

"I don't care about money. I want my life back and off your computer."

"Please," she said, falling to her knees with both hands clasped together in prayer. "I'm begging you."

I shook my head. "Erase it, right now!"

She shook her head. "I can't. I worked too hard on this."

"I tell you what, you don't have to erase it—it's on the hard drive, right?" I asked as I threw my transcripts on the ground and moved toward her computer.

"No, Tower. What are you going to do?" She grabbed hold of my ankle, but that didn't stop me.

"You used me!" I shouted as I picked up the hard drive from her computer station and yanked at it so hard that all the plugs attached snapped free. "You want to see what I think about you and your fucking book? I told you there was another side and you about to see it." I threw her hard drive against the wall. A big piece of metal hit her dining room table and caused a large section of glass to crack. "See what you made me do!" I looked down at Gail. Her eyes were in a fixed position staring straight ahead, and then her eyelids dropped. "I guess you're going to call the police on me now, huh? I know that's what you're going to do, call the cops and have me arrested. Is that what you're going to do? If so, tell me now 'cause I ain't going back to prison. You hear me! Say something!"

She slowly got up from the floor, walked into her guest bedroom and collapsed on the bed.

I looked at her through the opening in the door, listening to her as she started to cry. I almost walked in. I almost told her that I was sorry, but instead, I picked up my transcripts, shoved them into my backpack and left.

I hadn't even started my car before the voices came at me strong.

Why you go and do that to that girl, huh? my nice voice said.

Shut up. He did right. You did right, Tower, my mean voice said

Nah, I ain't shutting up. You didn't do right. You know why? Because that was a good woman who cared about you and you did that to her. It wasn't right, Tower.

I'm glad he did it. I didn't like her. You did right, man. She was weak. You don't need no weak woman. You need a strong woman. She's mixed up is what she is. Been 'round white folks too much. You need you a woman who been through some things like you been through some things. At least one thing's for sure, you don't have to worry about her getting rich off your ass.

Shut up, man! Tower, he wants you to stay sick because once you get well, he dies. I don't want you to hear all these voices for the rest of your life. I don't want you to be so twisted you can't decide which pair of socks to put on when you only have three pair and they all look the same. I want you to get better. Gail could've helped you because she knew about your problems, and she was trained to help you.

Trained! The bitch failed medical school, so how was she trained?

She took psychiatry classes, didn't she?

She took 'em 'cause she needed them for herself because the bitch crazy.

I pressed my head in on both sides with my hands, trying to make the voices go away.

Chapter 34

I waited almost two weeks before I went back to see Gail. I tried calling first, but the number was disconnected. When I pulled up to the house there was a for-sale sign stuck in the grass. I knew I had some nerve going back there after what I'd done, but I went with the disk that I had copied from her computer.

Gail seemed hesitant when she opened the door, but she still let me in. I walked inside holding my backpack.

"Why don't you tell me who you are? You never told me anything about yourself, nothing at all. For all I know, you could be wanted."

"I wish I were wanted," she said and smirked. "Why are you back? You don't think you did enough damage? What, you want to throw my printer against the wall and break that too? Or how about my fax machine?"

"Who are you?"

"Tower, what difference does that make now?"

"I want to know who you are and why you act so strange."

"I didn't grow up in the ghetto or the hood. I never ran the streets. Never had to hustle, so I guess that means you can't relate to me. You can't relate to me because I'm a black woman who grew up around a lot of white people, who had friends of all races, but never forgot I was black."

"I don't care about that. Whose house is this?"

"It's my house."

"Your house? How can you afford something like this working part time at the bank?"

"I don't work at the bank for money. I started working there because one of my characters was a bank teller and I wanted to accurately describe a bank scene. I stayed on because it gave me a reason to leave the house. Sometimes I get tired of shutting myself in."

"So you telling me you don't need to work? What, you hit the lottery?"

"Not hardly."

"Well, what then? What black person don't need to work?"

"All their money came to me. I don't need to work."

"All whose money? What are you talking about?"

"Well, if you'd stop cutting me off, I'll tell you."

"Tell me then. Who are you?"

"Gail Adams."

"And who is that?"

She shrugged. "I'm not sure who I am anymore."

"I don't even know how old you are?"

"That's because you never asked."

"So how old are you?"

"Thirty-four." She sat on the chair in the living room in my usual seat, and I took her spot on the sofa.

"Okay, now it's my turn," I said as I reached for her microcassette recorder and pressed play. "Start talking."

"What do you want to know?"

"Where's your family? Are your parents still together?"

She nodded. "I'm sure they are," she said as her gaze wandered off into space.

"Tell me about 'em. Are they retired or what?"

"My father was a child psychiatrist and author. He wrote a few nonfiction books."

"That's where you get it from," I said. She smiled. "What about your mother?"

"My mother was a housewife. She was so beautiful. I always wanted to look like her."

"Ain't nothin' wrong with the way you look."

"I'm not saying there is, but my mother was beautiful. People used to stare at her when she was out. They'd come up to her and tell her that she was beautiful, but she was never arrogant. She loved being a wife and mother. My dad used to tell us that Mom was smarter than him. They met while they were attending Howard's medical school. But Mom chose her family over her career and decided not to become a pediatrician. We had a good life. I loved my childhood."

"How often do you get to see them?"

"Oh—never. Not anymore."

"How come?"

"Um." She paused. "They're dead."

"What do you mean they're dead? Who's dead?"

"My family."

"All of them?"

"Except for my sister," she said as her throat crackled, "but we lost touch after the funeral and the legal—money—stuff was divided. She went her way and I went mine."

"But you told me your parents lived in Florida. Did they just die?"

"No, they've been dead for eight years." She walked over to her bookshelf and removed the portrait of her family. "A hit-and-run driver took their life away just like that," she said, snapping her fingers. "Killed my family while they were driving my brother to his college orientation. See, I didn't flunk out of medical school. I was in my last year and I had a 3.75 G.P.A. I flunked out of life because you don't call a person up at 1:13 in the afternoon on a Wednesday with that kind of news and expect them to be okay. You can't call them at anytime with that. I wasn't okay then, and I'm not really okay now. I had a nervous breakdown after that. When my husband came home he found me with my head shaved, and I was talking to a blank TV screen."

"Oh, now, I understand why you don't like watching television," I said, trying to make her laugh, but it didn't work.

"I hated him for putting me in a mental hospital."

"Why didn't you ever tell me you were married?"

"Tower, what did I ever tell you? Besides, I'm divorced now."

"Why didn't you write a book about yourself? My life seems mild compared to yours."

She shook her head. "I like your story better. I'm fine as long as I'm writing somebody's story, even if it's a fictitious one. I actually prefer it to be that way so I don't have to deal with real life."

"Did they catch the person who hit your family?"

"He turned himself in three days later because the news reports were hitting closer to home and the police were starting to narrow down the leads. Still, it was too late to determine if he was drunk at the time of the accident. I remember the judge saying to him at his sentencing hearing, 'Since you have been nothing short of an exemplary citizen, it would sadden me to take away your life and the further contributions you can provide our country by putting you behind bars for a simple mistake. Nonetheless, we have the victims and the victims' family to consider here. Therefore, I will sentence you to serve six months on house arrest, twenty-four months on parole, and write an apology to the family as well as provide 160 hours of community service.' I was the family. My sister didn't go to court. All she cared about was the money. My parents and my brother were all I had because I found out quickly my husband wasn't the man I needed him to be. I didn't need a damn apology letter. I needed my family back."

"That's all he got?"

"He was the mayor's son."

I shook my head. "White boy?" I asked. She nodded. "I knew that. Let it had been me who hit a white family. They would have had given me the fuckin' death penalty. That's how the legal system is."

I unzipped my backpack, removed the floppy disk, and walked over to her. "Here."

"What's this?" she asked.

"It's your book. I'm sure you made a lot of changes since that version, but it should help. I don't want to take your life away because I'm afraid somebody might figure out who I am when who I am is fucked up anyway. I wish you the best."

She covered her mouth with her trembling hands and stared at the disk as if she was afraid to take it from me. "Take it. It's yours."

She took the disk from my hand. "Tower, I'm not going to let you down."

I shrugged. "I don't know. I don't have no contract."

"You never got the one I mailed?"

"I tore it up."

"You have something better than a contract. You have my word."

"Yeah, but Judge Larry Joe on *Texas Justice* says, 'Don't take a person's word. Get it in writing.'"

"Tower, I don't need money. I have money. My parents were wealthy. I'm not doing this for the money."

Since she's so rich, ask her for some money.

"No," I told my voice.

What, you love her or something?

"Yes," I said. "I'm not talking to you," I told Gail.

"I know. Tower, you have my word. I'm going to do something big. Just watch."

"Handle your business."

CHAPTER 35

Gail called me once a week, usually on Sundays. But then her calls stopped and I didn't hear from her again until four months later in May. She told me that she had been living in hotels—on the road, promoting her first book, *Where Is the Love?* while trying to get a literary agent to represent her and shop our book, *Shattered Minds,* to major publishers. I heard something in her voice—something that didn't sound certain. "I'm afraid," she admitted.

"Afraid of what?"

"Afraid of all those faces staring back at me like they're waiting for something and I'm supposed to figure out what. Afraid that they won't like what I've written and I'll sign on to Amazon.com and see a bunch of one-star ratings with people saying the only reason I gave her one star is because you had to give something. Afraid of failing because if I do, there's nothing left for me."

"Why are you talking about failing? You know you're not going to fail."

"How do I know that? I'm so comfortable with not going out, not speaking to people. It's hard to break from that."

"You're out now."

"And I'm terrified. I hate book signings most of all. I went to one at The Shrine of the Black Madonna in Detroit, and there were only six people, but I can't count them because they all worked there."

"It'll get better. Nobody knows who you are yet."

"Well, it was better in Chicago. I guess because I made the paper and it's my hometown. Fifteen people showed up, not including the employees. Fifteen people and I was in my hometown!" she shouted. "They were sitting there looking at me like they wanted me to say something spectacular. I felt like a stand-up comedian who couldn't get my routine down. I only sold three books."

"Okay, well, pack up and forget about it. It's not like you need the money, and if it's making you feel that bad then I guess it's not worth it," I said, using reverse psychology.

"No, I can't pack up. Then I'm a quitter, and I'll have nothing but money and an unfulfilled life. I'm a writer and I know I am. I just need the readers to know that. Maybe it'll be better in Atlanta. There's a lady there named Shunda Blocker and she owns *Booking Matters Magazine*. I think I'm going to start placing an ad in there to see how it goes. She said that she'll host a sign and dine for me. That should be less intimidating than a signing at a bookstore."

"Sign and dine? You don't eat."

"I do now. I've gained more than ten pounds."

"That ain't nothing on you."

"I'm afraid, Tower. Maybe I'm not really a writer. If I were really a writer, I wouldn't have to publish my own book. If I were really a writer, I wouldn't have received so many rejection letters from literary agents. I should have abandoned my first book and concentrated more on the one I did about your life. I don't know. Sometimes I feel like I'm trying too hard. If people want to buy my book they will, because when I do those signings I feel like I'm begging. I don't like pressure, and I don't like pressuring people. I've always been that way, even before my nervous breakdown."

"You wanna know what I think?" I asked.

"What do you think?"

"I don't think you're trying hard enough. You don't know what it's like to really hustle. You grew up with everything. If I would've stopped trying to get out of prison, I would still be there. It may have taken me ten years, but ten years is a lot better than forty. If you want something bad enough, you'll do whatever it takes. Those people don't know you. They don't know you're afraid of them. They don't know what you've been through, and most wouldn't care even if they did. I want you to be tough. And I want you to believe that you're just as good as any writer out: black, white, self-published, or otherwise."

"That's being cocky."

"It's being confident. You're gonna do it. You're gonna make it. You better. I'm counting on you." I knew Gail. If she had to make it only for herself, she probably wouldn't, but for someone else, she'd give it her best shot. "I want to tell people I know someone famous. Don't let me down. I'm counting on you. I need to ride on your coattails."

"Okay, okay." Her voice was charged with enthusiasm. "I won't disappoint you. No one knows I'm an antisocial introvert but you and me."

"Yeah, all you got to do is fake it. Most women are good at that. Do what I did when I was in prison—become someone else."

"I don't want to make it by being phony. I just have to learn to be less afraid of people."

"Just always remember one thing: You're not in prison. Always remember that and you should do fine."

"Okay, thanks for listening to me, but enough of me. How's everything there?"

"Everything seems different now."

"Different is good, or at least it can be."

"Not this kind of different. I feel like the bottom's about to fall from under me any day now. Keep in touch, okay? Try to call me when you can. I know you're gonna be busy, but don't forget about me," I said. "We sorta been through a lot together."

"I know we have."

"When are you coming back here?"

"I'm not sure. I'm trying to do a signing at Black Images next month. I'm just waiting to hear back from the owner of the bookstore and Lisa Cross with The Sistah Circle Book Club to see if they'll sponsor me. If so, you'll see me next month. If not next month, definitely by the month after that."

"Okay, well, just remember all the things I said."

"I love you, Tower."

I held the phone for a second before I hung up without saying good-bye.

She said she loves you, my nice voice said. *And you didn't say anything. You just hung up.*

He did right. Love? What's love got to do with this? All we trying to do is make it, my mean voice said.

Gail only let one week go by before she called me the next time.

"What are you doing?" she asked.

"I'm just sitting on the bed, staring at the paint on the ceiling. What are you doing?"

"Praying. I kinda want to give up."

"Give up what?"

"Everything. I'm so tired. This isn't easy."

"What isn't?"

"I keep getting rejections."

"From who? Who's rejecting you?"

"From literary agents." She sighed.

"Look, forget about them. If you'd spend less time trying to get some other company to do something your own company can do, you might sell more books. Oprah is wealthy, not because she's a talk show host, but because she owns the company that produces her show. Stop trying to work for somebody else, just become that somebody. How else can I say it? Don't believe the hype. So much in life is just hype. I went to prison because of a bunch of hype, thinking I was all that because I was dealing drugs and packing nines with hollow-point bullets and AK47s. Even though I made money, I could barely enjoy it because I was paranoid all the damn time, wondering when I was gonna get caught. I knew that day was coming, and damn did it come. I wasn't prepared for that shit. I told you to go out there and handle your business, and that's what I expect for you to do."

"You're telling me to self-publish our book?"

"I'm telling you to finish everything that you start."

"But I'm not sure if I can get distribution and without that—"

"Let me tell you something, you can do anything you put your mind to. My mama told me that when I was little, but my bad ass put my mind toward selling drugs. If I can get out of prison, you can get distribution. You've got the resources to do whatever you want. And you have more than a lot of people—you have money. You can run this thing like a real business. Do you understand that?"

"Tower, I've been living off that money for eight years now. I mean, I still have a lot, more than most, but I'm not a millionaire or even close to one. I split money with my sister. What I have, I have to ration out so I won't have to work. I'm living like someone would who earns close to thirty thousand a year."

"Do you have a lot of bills?"

"I really don't have any bills. I paid cash for my house and that recently sold. I'll probably pay cash for my next one."

"Don't pay cash for the next one. Finance it. Put thirty or forty percent down and use the rest on the business, or hell rent an apartment. It's just you."

"But what if—"

"What if what? I know you ain't about to say what I think you about to say. I know you ain't about to talk about failure. Are you?"

She laughed. "I guess not. It's just that I'm under a lot of pressure."

"The key with pressure is pacing. If you feel like you're under too much pressure and you're not sure how you're going to make it, stop. Take a break. Not too long though. Maybe a few weeks don't do nothing with the book. Just relax and think it out."

"I'm not going to give up."

"Please don't. I don't know how many times I got to tell you—you're my only hope."

"Alright, well, I'll talk to you later," she said.

Tell her that you love her, my nice voice said.

You bet' not.

"Gail?"

"Yes."

"I-I'm here if you need to talk. You can call me on my cell day or night. I—care about you."

"I know you do."

When the call ended, I not only felt like I helped Gail, but in the process, I felt like I'd helped myself. In talking to Gail, I realized that life is a journey. Gail knew where she wanted to go, but she didn't have any directions on how to get there, so she was lost.

CHAPTER 36

I was on my break, and I needed to go outside because the factory was starting to feel more and more like Murray State Prison. It was closing in on me, and I wanted out. I knew I could do more than assemble seat belts. More than live in a tiny motel room. I wanted more out of my life, the same as Gail.

My supervisor walked passed me. I was prepared to give her the dry, "Hey," but she didn't even look my way, just headed straight for the warden's—I mean the foreman's—office. She was in there for a few minutes with the door closed, and then she walked out and passed me again without saying a word. I figured I'd better get back to work. Every manager's door was made of glass and surrounded the main assembly floor. The breakroom was off to the side, but still out in the open, so if you were a little late from getting back, it was obvious.

I had to walk passed the foreman's office, and when I did he waved for me to come in. I gave him a strange look because I had never been in his office. Hell, I had never even spoken to him before.

I walked in cautiously.

"Theodore, isn't it?" he asked. I didn't go by Theodore at the job or anywhere really. "Your full name is Theodore Anthony Evans, correct? Not Tower Evans like you put on your application."

I sighed. "Yes," I said, nodding.

"Have a seat please."

I sat down in front of his desk and looked around. There were two security guards standing in the room with him. They had their hands behind their back. I looked over at the silver pistols that were in their side holster, and then up at their stern faces.

"Something wrong?" I asked the foreman.

"We have to let you go."

I sat staring at his mouth. "What did you say?"

"We have to let you go?"

"What did I do? I'm always at work on time. I'm early. I work plenty of overtime. I do the job. I have the highest production of anyone on my shift, so why you letting me go?"

He pulled out a piece of paper and handed it to me. "You lied on your application. In addition to lying about your name, you also checked no to never being incarcerated, but yesterday we received this fax. He held it up. "This is you—correct?" he asked as he handed me a printout.

"What is this?" I asked as I looked down at the paper that had a picture of me, along with my Department of Corrections number, F.B.I. number, the date I went to prison, and the charges I was convicted of along with the years I served.

"I'm sorry but we have to let you go. You're an excellent worker but we have policies."

I looked at the fax number printed along the top of the page. I knew it was from Mary, and she had faxed it from her office. I could tell because the area code and first three numbers were the exact same as her office number. "Look, Mr. Munson, I need my job. Can't you make an exception? Even you said I'm a good worker. I may have gone to prison but I served my time."

"I'm sorry but we can't. The problem isn't necessarily that you were in prison. It's that you lied about it. That makes us question your integrity. Coupled with the fact that you and your supervisor don't get along, we feel this really is the best solution."

"The best solution for who?" I asked as I stood. "And I didn't lie. I just didn't answer the question."

"You checked no."

"No, I didn't. I didn't check anything but it doesn't matter. That's my word against yours."

The guards came toward me, ready to escort me out, but I held out my hands. "Don't come near me. I didn't take nothin' out of here. I know how to walk out the door. I don't need to be escorted out like some criminal. I may have been in prison, but I ain't no criminal."

"We will send your last check to the address on our file," Mr. Munson said. "Is the address correct?"

"Yeah, it's my sister's but you can still send it there." I started to get on my knees and beg. I started to apologize for lying. I started to tell Mr. Munson how badly I needed my job, but instead, I just walked out.

You better do something to get even. I don't care what it is but it better be something good.

I showed up to the parole office intent on seeing Mary. I had a knife in my pocket, and I was going to do exactly what my mean voice said I would do eventually—fuck up. At least that way, I could go back to the one place where I knew there were people worse off than me—back to prison.

"I need to see Mrs. Davis," I said with force. The receptionist put one finger up because she was busy talking on the phone. "I don't have time to wait for you to finish your personal call. I need to see Mrs. Davis now." I pounded my fist on the counter.

"Girl, let me call you back." She hung up the phone and said, "Mrs. Davis has someone in her office right now. Are you one of her cases?"

"Nah, I ain't nobody's case."

"Tower," Mr. Wilks said as he walked up to me, "what's wrong, man?" I didn't look at him because he'd be able to tell from the madness of my eyes that I'd turned into one of those ex-cons he'd talked to Dad about. "Come on, let's go out in the hallway and talk."

Before we walked out of the office, he went over to a young man who was slumped down in the chair, waiting. "I'm giving you a reprise today. You can go."

"Thank you for the prize."

"A reprise not a prize."

"It's a prize to me. Thank you," the young man said, jumping out of his chair.

We walked out to the hallway.

"Now tell me what's wrong? Talk to me. Why are you here to see Mrs. Davis?"

I shook my head. "I don't want to talk. I want to do something bad to that woman," I said, pacing.

"To what woman—Mrs. Davis? he asked. I nodded. "You had an affair with her, didn't you?"

"An affair—nah. We fucked more than a few times but I didn't ask for all this other stuff. I didn't ask to lose my job just because I refused to see her."

"Calm down. Are you telling me that you were basically manipulated into an affair with Mrs. Davis and because you refused to continue she was responsible for you losing your job?"

"Yeah, she was responsible. She faxed some shit to my employer with my prison record and picture on it. How am I supposed to get a job now? I won't even be able to work at Burger King. The Mexicans got all the fast food jobs 'round here. What am I supposed to do now? Huh?"

"Hold tight. I'm not going to let her get away with it this time," Mr. Wilks said. "I hope you realize that this could get serious. Would you be willing to do a deposition if one is called for."

"Hell yeah."

CHAPTER 37

Mr. Wilks didn't waste much time. Hadn't even been a full month before some attorney for the state called asking me to come down to his office to take my deposition. I told the attorney I'd feel more comfortable if it was taken at my parents' house, so we arranged for a meeting on a Saturday afternoon.

"Tower," Dad said, peeping out the living room window, "it's a bunch of people getting out of a black sedan wearing dark suits. You expecting someone?"

"Yeah, they're here to take my deposition."

"Your who? On what?" Dad asked as the doorbell rang.

I ignored his question and answered the front door.

"Theodore Evans?" the white man asked. I nodded. "I'm District Attorney John Franks. This is my assistant district attorney, Howard Miltner. We also brought along our paralegal Susie Harris and our lead counsel David Helstatter."

They walked in carrying large briefcases that looked more like luggage.

"You need me to go?" Dad asked me.

"Can he stay in here?" I asked them.

"It would be better if we were alone with you."

"Well, how about this, can y'all take it in the dining room and just close those glass doors? I'll make sure nobody swings in from the kitchen. At least that way I can stay here and watch TV," Dad said.

I took them into the dining room and closed the double glass doors leading to the living room.

The attorneys put their briefcases on the floor and started pulling out pads of paper, a tape recorder, and a video camera.

"I'm going to be on video?" I asked.

"Yes," an attorney said.

I took a deep breath.

Remember, none of it was your idea. Not the beginning of the affair, just the end of it. It's not a lie either. Not really. And don't be nervous like you were at your own trial. Don't fuck this one up.

"Is it your testimony on this fourteenth day of June, 2003 that you unwillingly entered into a sexual relationship with Mary Scott Davis, a parole officer for the state of Texas?" The district attorney asked the questions while the paralegal wrote down my response and one of the other men held the video camera to tape me.

"Yes," I said.

"Please share with us in detail how this relationship started."

"I don't really know where I should begin with this. Me and Mrs. Davis started seeing each other not too long after she was assigned my case. She even made sure she got my case back after it went to another parole officer. She said, 'I pulled my strings and got you back.' She was looking for a relationship, someone she could control, and I was looking to get my life back in order."

"How did it start?"

I looked them straight in their eyes and said, "She came over to my sister's house one afternoon and told me she had dreams about me. She told me that she could make things much easier for me if I had a relationship with her."

"And did you understand that to mean sex?" the district attorney asked.

"Yes, I did. We had sex that day."

"So you had sex with Mary Scott Davis that day?"

"I performed oral sex on her that day and when I tried to stop performing it, she told me to keep doing it and if I did I wouldn't have to worry about reporting to the parole office or being on a curfew or anything."

Were those her exact words?"

"Pretty much. I mean, I didn't tape the conversation and it happened a while ago so I can't tell you her exact words but the meaning would be the same. If I had sex with her, she'd help me with parole by giving me special privileges."

Each of the attorneys looked at the other and raised their eyebrows.

"Continue. We need you to be as graphic as you possibly can when it comes to the sex. We need to know how often. Where? The things she said to you that let you know if you didn't cooperate what kinds of problems that would mean for you."

"Oh, that will be easy. I have more than enough examples of those."

CHAPTER 38

It was September. My mind had flipped into survival mode. What to do? I was still living in a motel and I'd spent my last check. I was denied unemployment since I was fired for lying on my application. It was getting so tight that I couldn't even pay my fifty-dollar restitution to the court. And I couldn't get any more money from Scottie because he was dead. His body was found stuffed inside the trunk of his Mercedes out toward Houston.

I hadn't heard from my voices for a while but as soon as I said that to myself, my mean voice said, *Jack up Quentin's ass. You know the ins and outs of that house. Get some other hard-ups to go in with you and jack him up. He probably keeps at least three hundred thousand dollars in his house. Worst thing that may happen is you have to kill him and his girl, but look how many people he's killed. What goes around comes around. But I doubt if you'll have to kill 'em. They'll open the safe. And who they gonna call? The police? And say what, when they asses been under FBI surveillance for years? You tried the job thing, and you see how that turned out. All you need is one big hit, and robbing a drug dealer ain't really a crime.*

I could always go back to the tire shop. I was so confused I didn't know what I wanted to do. I thought about selling my car for some extra cash, but then I wouldn't have any transportation. Besides it was starting to act up, and I didn't want to sell somebody a car that didn't run half the time. *Maybe you should do one quick run,* my mean voice said.

No, Tower, remember what happened to that inmate Oliver? He wasn't out twenty-four hours, went back to his old neighborhood, his boys put a sack in his hand, called themselves helping him, and just like that he was back in. Remember that? You can't risk it. Mary messed up your life, my nice voice said. Even he was getting tired. It wasn't Mary. It wasn't Kara. Not Tonya or Gail. The situation I was in had nothing to do with not knowing my real father. I fucked up my own life all the way around.

No, Mary fucked up your life, and she's about to get hers fucked up. There are rules against having sex with a parolee. She was the authority figure and should've known better but she'll get hers, my nice voice said.

I leaned back on my sofa, staring at a blank TV screen for a while, praying I wouldn't start talking to it like Gail did. I reached for the remote and flipped through the channels to get to the news. I couldn't take my eyes off the screen. Mary was walking to the courthouse with her head down, hand in hand with a man, most likely her husband beside a female who was probably her attorney.

"What do you think about the allegations brought against you?" a female reporter asked, sticking a microphone in Mary's face. Mary moved her face away from the camera and the microphone.

"Is it true that more charges have been brought against your client?" another reporter asked Mary's attorney. "Some being lodged by men currently serving time in prison who allege that your client falsified parole reports and indicated violations so the ex-cons would be sent back in."

"We have no comment at this time," the attorney said.

The doorbell rang so I leaned to look out the window, and I saw a white car parked in the space right in front of my door. For a minute, I actually thought it was Mary, and I wasn't going to answer the door but the ringing kept on, and it was so constant and loud that I felt my blood boil. I stormed to the door and yanked it open.

"You got some nerve coming here," I said before I saw Gail's face and those deep cuts in each cheek. *You just watched the news.*

You should know you're the farthest thing from Mary's mind. "Gail?"

"Hi, Tower."

"Is that your car?" I asked, looking at the white compact.

"It's a rental."

"Oh, I expected you to be driving a Ferrari by now."

"Tower, I have something important to tell you," she said as she held both of my hands with hers.

"You're pregnant with my baby?"

"No, that's impossible, and even if I was I would have already had the baby by now."

"What you got to tell me?"

"I met Lisa at a book signing in California."

"Lisa who?"

"Your Lisa. The one who had your baby."

"How did you know it was her?"

"Well, I didn't. She knew it was you after she read the preview chapter to my second book on my website. That's why she came to my signing to ask about you and how you were doing."

"What are you talking about?"

"Lisa waited for me to finish signing books and when I was rushing out the door to go to my next signing, she gently grabbed my arm and said, 'I know your main character in your book because I'm your other character, Rosa.'"

"You're lying."

"I swear to God. And when I said, 'Lisa,' she nodded."

"I don't think that was her."

"Lisa Alvarado. Isn't that her name? That's what she wrote down on this piece of paper with her address. I promised her that I would give it to you, and I always keep my promises. She wants you to write her but I think you should drive out there."

"Did she have my son or daughter with her? Did she mention any kids?"

Gail shook her head. "I was in such a state of shock that I didn't ask. Besides, my escort was rushing me out to take me to my next appearance. All Lisa said was that she'd been thinking about you a lot lately and needed to talk to you. Go see her, Tower."

"Where? To California? I don't think so. That's a long drive."

"Tower, go on and go. Don't you think you need closure? Besides, you've got a child you'll finally be able to see."

"You going with me?"

She shook her head. "I can't."

"Why not? Oh, I guess you're busy promoting your book."

She nodded. "It's a full-time job, and I have to take it seriously. Besides, this is something you need to do alone. I just came back to tell you that."

CHAPTER 39

I rented a van and drove all the way to California. This was my first time out of Texas since my parole, and because I was unrestricted, it was fine for me to leave the state. I made up my mind that Gail was right. I needed to meet my child and become a part of his or her life, teach him what I've learned from life and my experiences.

Lisa lived in a nice neighborhood with larges homes—almost large enough to be considered mansions.

She must be married, if she lives in one of these. Maybe I should call her, I thought. *I don't even have her number. Maybe I should just go to the door.*

As I walked to Lisa's front door, I couldn't believe it had come down to this day—thirteen years later. When all hopes of ever seeing Lisa or my child were lost, Gail, the woman who I decided to stop for that day on the highway, was the one person who made this reunion possible. Gail, the woman who my only regret of meeting was that it hadn't happened sooner so that I could come to her whole instead of cracked in a million tiny pieces. I didn't care if I looked into Lisa's eyes again. I only wanted to see my child, if not for that reason then I wouldn't have rung the doorbell at all.

I stood in my usual position, with my hands behind my back. The front door opened and the woman standing on the other end stood stiff for a moment. "Tower?" she asked.

"Lisa?"

She nodded. "You don't recognize me?"

"You look different." Time hadn't done her any justice. She didn't look better. She looked older and wealthy and nothing like I remembered.

We stood staring at each other without saying a word until a yellow school bus pulled in front of the house and two kids got out. One was about six, but the other one, the oldest boy, was about twelve, and he was the one I watched.

"Is that my son?" I asked as I walked toward them.

"Your who?" she asked my back. "Tower," Lisa said as I walked up to the boy and hugged him.

"Hello. You're my son."

"Get away from me, freak!" he said. "I'm not your son. Mom, who is this crazy man?" he shouted.

I turned and looked at Lisa. She was standing beside me. "I'm sorry," I said to Lisa. "You probably didn't tell him."

"Go in the house, boys."

"You sure?" my son asked her.

"Yes, I'm sure. I made cookies, so go get some," Lisa said and watched to make sure they went inside. "Tower."

"What's his name?" I asked.

"Brent. I named him after his father. He's not your son. He'll be ten in October. He's tall for his age."

"So where's my child? What, you gave him up for adoption?"

She shook her head. "Tower," she said as she held both of my hands, "I had an abortion."

I snatched my hands away from hers. "You hated me that much?"

"I just didn't want…I didn't think…I thought it would be better."

"You thought?"

"I'm happy now. My life is completely different. I'm married to a wonderful man. You saw our children. We have a good life. I don't have to work. It's the life I dreamed of."

"So you wanted to make sure that I didn't mess that up, right?

"You know that's not true or I wouldn't have given Gail my address. I thought about you over the years."

"My mama's phone number never changed, but you wouldn't know that because you never called."

"I lost your mother's number, besides, I didn't think you wanted to talk to me."

"So what was your point, Lisa? It was listed. If you really wanted to find me you could've. So why did you want to see me now?"

"I didn't want to see you, just hear from you. I never expected you to drive all the way out here. I wanted to know how you were doing. I didn't know what you were going to do or say when the book comes out. My husband doesn't know about my past."

"I get it now. You have to protect this nice lifestyle. This nice house. The nice car," I said as I looked at the Mercedes in her driveway. "You won't have to worry about me saying anything." I turned and walked back to the van.

CHAPTER 40

It was good to be back home from California, back with my family and my own reality. I wasn't worried about getting a job because I decided to do what Gail did and have faith. It was working for her. In six months, she'd sold fifteen thousand copies of her first book, and our book had just been released. Gail's publishing company was gaining a lot of recognition. She was ready to start bringing on new authors to expand her company and offer others the opportunity they may not get on their own.

"Oh no, to what do we owe this honor?" Dad asked as he walked off the porch toward me. I was pulling weeds from my parents' front yard when a pearl-white Rolls Royce pulled into the driveway.

"Who's that?" I asked Dad.

"That, Tower, is Mrs. Bourghetto herself."

"Aunt Cora? She's driving a Rolls now?"

He nodded. "Trying to be Oprah. But somebody needs to tell her that Oprah's a billionaire and she can't compete. But I know Cora and she'll die trying."

"Willie, where's my sister? I've been calling all week," Aunt Cora said as she pranced out of her car, clutching her purse.

"Caller ID, baby," Dad whispered.

"What did you say, Willie?"

"Can't say. I'm not sure where she's been, but she's at the store right now."

Aunt Cora walked toward me, gave me a hug, and kissed me on the cheek.

Dad placed his hand over his heart and started walking around like Fred Sanford, pretending he was about to have a stroke.

"This is it, Lord. I'm about to have the big one."

"Oh, shut up," Cora said, hitting Dad on the shoulder with her purse. "I've been calling all week about you, Tower. I have a job for you."

"A job for me?"

"Yes. Gordon's construction company just received a large contract from the city. He'll be increasing his staff and he needs another superintendent."

"A *superintendent*?" I asked.

"Yes. A superintendent," Aunt Cora said. "I told him the next time the Lord blesses us, we have to bless someone else, and I'm getting tired of blessing a bunch of strangers when I have a big family who needs help."

Dad's eyes grew large like he was in total shock. "What's the catch, Cora?" Dad asked.

"No catch."

"You ain't never been interested in helping out your own. What's the punchline?"

"Yeah, is it April Fool's or something?" I asked.

"Oh, that's a good one," Dad said.

"Stop it! There's no catch. The salary will start off at fifty thousand dollars because you don't have experience, but it should increase in time. Give it a few years and you should start making some decent money."

"Did she say fifty thousand?" I asked Dad.

"Fifty thousand. That's what she said. That's decent to start," Dad said.

"Decent. Yeah, you right it is," I said.

"Okay, well, here's my husband's card. We need you to report to the worksite on Monday, but call him later today for the directions because I'm terrible with those."

Dad snatched the card out of her hand. "Wait a minute, Cora.

The boy's transportation is down. Now, I know a lot of these big-time construction companies give their superintendent's company vehicles like a Dodge Ram quad cab."

"Our company uses Ford F250s," Cora said.

"We're a Dodge family," Dad said.

Cora stood with her hand on her hips rolling her eyes. "We only supply company vehicles to our project managers anyway."

"The project managers aren't your family, are they? I read the paper and watch the news, too, you know. I heard all about the contracts Strickland Construction received in the last six months. Y'all worth more than the Powerball now—"

"I get your point," Aunt Cora said, interrupting. "I'll see what we can do."

"And you know you must be doing good when you can give up your own business to work with your husband's full time. I heard you moved into another new house—a bigger one, much bigger. This one has a six-car garage—four on one side and two on the other. Must be nice to be blessed like that."

"What color Ram would you like?" Aunt Cora asked.

"Black," Dad said.

"I'm talking to Tower."

"Oh, sorry. Tower, what color Ram would you like?" Dad asked.

"Black sounds good to me too."

"I'll have your Ram Monday afternoon," she said as she walked back to her car.

"Don't bring back the basic model either," Dad yelled to her. "Just like you can't sleep on no sheets less than 350 threads, Tower can't drive nothing under a V-12."

"Do they even make a Ram with a V-12 engine?" I asked.

"Who knows? Let her figure it out."

"And what you talking about fifty thousand is decent. You know that's more than decent," I said.

"Life lesson, son. When you're talking to someone who's bourghetto, you've got to be bourghetto too."

We watched Aunt Cora back out of the driveway.

"What you think that was all about?" I asked.

"I tell you what it was all about. What's your friend's name that wrote the book on you?"

"Gail."

"Right. She was on BET with Ed Gordon the other night. Well, your mama told your aunt Cora and your other aunt about the book, so when we saw Gail come on BET we called them both up. Well, Cora was so impressed with Gail and the whole book idea that now I guess you can be her nephew again."

"Didn't I ask y'all not to tell nobody yet?"

"Cora ain't nobody."

"Okay, well, why didn't you tell me Gail was on BET?"

"How was I gonna tell you? We called but your cell phone was cut off. Now that I know you're gonna be working, I'll tell your mama she can go on and pay that bill for you."

"Gail was on BET?" I asked and smiled.

"We taped it."

"You did?"

"Yeah, you think I didn't? Go on inside and watch it."

"I think I'll do that."

I walked in my parents' house and sat down to watch the video of Gail discussing the book and the prison system. She didn't even seem like the same person. *I know her,* I thought and smiled. I knew who Gail was and who she had become. I put the tape on pause to think about life for a moment. Funny how life is and how all things seem to work together for good and also how what goes around does come around. Mary was found guilty of intent to defraud, sexual assault, and a couple of other charges involving not just myself, but three other inmates. She was sentenced to fifteen years, and all of her cases where ex-cons were sent back to prison were being reviewed, to possibly release them. Mary would probably only serve five to seven years, but for her, that would feel like a lifetime, and she'd see what I went through and understand why it wasn't nice to threaten to throw me back inside. The rapper Gail is involved with is on tour with Jay-Z, Method Man, 50 Cent, and a few others. I bought his CD after I watched an interview with him on BET. I have nothing against the brother. I'd be happy if him and Gail ended up together. He said on the interview that he had someone in his life that was special, but that they were both private people and he didn't want the media messing up their relationship because it meant too much to him. I had a gut feeling that he was talking about Gail, especially since Gail was wearing a big diamond ring on her wedding finger during her BET interview.

As crazy as Tonya is, that might be the one I end up with, and not because she got herself down to a size twelve, but she honestly start living the life she was preaching, and I'm starting to see her beauty from the inside. She's not rushing the marriage thing, and we're not having sex. She understands what I mean when I say it could take me awhile to get right in my mind. My brother Wallace is still on drugs. One day, I hope he'll be clean, but it's not one of those things I'm expecting. Honestly, I'm preparing myself to attend his funeral. I hope that day never comes, but my family has done all they can; the rest is up to him.

"She's going to be on *Politically Incorrect* next week," Dad said, interrupting my thoughts.

"She ain't gonna be on *Politically Incorrect*."

"How much you want to bet? Yes, she is, next week. Speaking of betting, I better hit that Lotto today or that book better turn into a movie. I'm tired of being poor, Tower."

"I hear you. I am too."

"You ain't gonna be poor for long," Dad said.

Dad left me alone for a while. I sat and watched the TV screen while it was on pause the way my life had been and thought about how it was time for me to move on the same way Gail had. I may not be fully over my ten-year prison experience, but I truly believe that everything happens for a reason. God had given me a second chance, and with that He'd blessed me with my family who had been there for me, and a friend like Gail who uplifted me.

I pressed play and watched Gail.

"What I learned from my friend, Anonymous, is to never take life for granted because you never know how good you have it until years of your life have gone and then you end up spending more years thinking about how your life could've been, should've been, would've been. So many of us who are free live like we're in prison. I was one of those people. Writing this book has helped me escape my self-imprisonment, and I have Anonymous to thank for that." A closeup was done of Gail's face as she looked into the camera like she was looking directly at me. "Thank you, Anonymous. I love you. Now move on."

"Thank you," I replied. "I will."

ABOUT THE AUTHOR

Cheryl Robinson is a native Detroiter currently residing in the Dallas/Fort Worth area. She is a supervisor with Daimler Chrysler Corporation's Mercedes-Benz Credit division.

Cheryl is in the process of completing her third novel.

For more information, visit www.cherylrobinson.com.

DISCUSSION QUESTIONS

1. Why does it seem there are a disproportionate number of black males serving prison time for drug-related crimes or crimes in general?

2. How do you feel about racial profiling? Do you have any personal stories you can share where you or people you know may have been stopped because of your race?"

3. How do you feel about the sentence the judge imposed on Tower?

4. Tower was a free man whose mind never left prison. Do you feel ex-cons can be rehabilitated? Explain your answer.

5. If you met someone who had been in prison, how would you feel? How would it bias your opinion of him or her?

6. What are your feelings about Mrs. Davis, the parole officer?

7. Between Tower and Gail, who do you feel has a better chance of being freed from his or her self-imprisonment? Why?

8. Do you think Tower was capable of loving? If so, do you think he loved Gail? Why or why not?

9. What are you feelings about the U.S. prison system? What improvements, if any, need to be made?

Memories of Yesterday

by Cheryl Robinson

Meet Porter Washington, a handsome Detroit firefighter trying to live on twenty-seven thousand dollars a year while struggling to provide the materialistic lifestyle required of his long-time, gorgeous girlfriend, Reesey. In high school, he just had to have her, so much so, he dumped Pam, his sweetheart. But after putting up with Reesey and her ego as well as all of her lies and manipulation for ten long years, Porter has finally had enough. Things have gotten so bad that when he and Reesey are making love, he fantasizes about Pam, who's now married to his boy, Damion, a womanizer with plenty of cash to support his habit. When one final lie ends Porter's current relationship, he becomes confused, questioning not only himself, but also his sexuality, and mainly the secrets that he buried with his brother.

Winona Fairchild was never anything special to look at. She never had a real boyfriend in high school, and only one friend, Gina, whom Winona swore was her girlfriend only because she felt sorry for her. Still, somehow Winona managed to trap Derwin, the most popular boy in high school while they were attending Michigan State University, getting him to ask those glorious four words that so many women want to hear—"Will you marry me?" They made it to the church, even as far as the altar, but that's where he left her. After being dumped, Winona packed her bags and fled Detroit for

(continued)

Fort Worth, Texas, with a man she barely knew. Now seventeen years and two kids later, single Winona is embarking on a new career as an automotive designer for a major corporation. Excited with her recent promotion, Winona heads back to her hometown of Detroit with a new look and an even newer attitude. This time she has a chance to hunt down a part of her past that she refused to let go—that's if another part doesn't catch up with her first.

Memories of Yesterday is a novel for every man and woman who has hung on to pain and regret too long, postponing an opportunity for a better today and tomorrow.

For more information, or to order a copy of *Memories of Yesterday* by Cheryl Robinson, please visit the author's website at www.cherylrobinson.com.

WHAT READERS ARE SAYING

Memories of Yesterday is a realistic, hard-hitting, urban contemporary novel that covers everything: Family, friends, male/female relationships, spirituality, old demons, sensuality, secret sins, and more, and does so in a style that is engaging, thought-provoking, and entertaining. It's the type of book that may remind you of *Friends and Lovers*, offering you page after page of characters filled with passions that become their snare; characters that go through so much you can't help but wonder what's going to happen next.

Cheryl Robinson is a superb writer. Everything in this book clicks and flows: from narrative and dialogue, to characters and story development, it is a reader's delight, one that makes you instantly yearn for another book from this fabulous new author.

Memories of Yesterday was one of the top favorite novels of 2002 and is highly recommended.

I LOVE this novel—Cydney Rax, author of *My Daughter's Boyfriend*
(coming 2004)

Cheryl is a powerful dual-gender writer. Her characters are fun, and climb right off the page and into your life, leaving you wanting to know what is going to happen to them after the read ends.

Enjoyed every drop!—San Antonio Black

Memories of Yesterday is a novel that I highly recommend because it is told with an uncanny realism and non-pretentious character development. This is a story about love and pain, the consequences of the choices we make and finally, a concept that promotes healing.

Rebuking My Past—Dawn R. Reeves, The Rawsistaz Reviewers

Porter and Winona individually had riveting stories and the story of them coming together in a relationship is just as interesting. There are several surprising twists and turns in the plot, which makes the reading intriguing. I would recommend it to others.

Good Interesting Reading—Jeanette Frommi, Detroit, MI, APOOO Book Club

Order yours TODAY!

$14.95

Texas residents, please add 8% sales tax.

+ Shipping/handling............$3.50
   (U.S. Priority Mail)

Make check or money order payable to: Sterling Books
(please do not send cash)

Sterling Books
P.O. Box 855
Roanoke, TX 76262

Purchaser information: *(please print)*

Name_____

Address_____

City_____

State & Zip_____

*Number of books requested*_____

Total for this order $_____

STERLING BOOKS